FROST GOD
RISING

FROST GOD RISING

BOOK 2 OF THE PHANTOM FROST SERIES

Alfred Wurr

A Wurreal Games Book

Published by Wurreal Games (https://www.wurrealgames.com).

Book cover by Damonza.com

ISBN 978-1-7780220-3-6 (paperback)

ISBN 978-1-7780220-2-9 (eBook)

ISBN 978-1-7780220-4-3 (audiobook)

First Edition (v1.0.0)

For my sister, Elke.

Contents

Where We Are

While *Frost God Rising* is book two of the *Phantom Frost* series—all told from Shivurr's perspective—it is actually the fourth book related to the series. The novella *Fire Demon Dawn* and novelette *The Shepherd* are both shorter tales that tell side stories related to the main one, which began with *Phantom Frost* and continues in this novel.

For the benefit of those starting the series with this book (a viable option) or who haven't read *Phantom Frost* in a while, I thought it worthwhile to include a quick summary of where we left off. Please note, before reading further, there are spoilers for previous novels in the series, below. With that said, here's where we are . . .

Having recovered vials of his essence and rescued his friends from the Bodhi Institute, Shivurr has returned to the Pacific Ocean archipelago of New Olympus, where many of the gods of ancient Greece now live.

Life is good. Shivurr's enemies lie defeated in his wake: several monsters out of myth, even Bodhi Institute Security Director Harland Dixon—last seen injured and trapped in a crashed helicopter.

Most of his Californian friends have gone home, except for Caleb. Now, along with Caleb and the goddess Olivia (Orithyia) Schmidt, he waits in his god friends' seaside villa on New Olympus for Olivia's husband, Wilhelm (Boreas) Schmidt, to return with their wounded friend, Scott.

FROST GOD RISING

Chapter 1

Remember Me

Olivia Schmidt tossed her hair back, smiled, and ran a warm hand across my icy forehead. "What do you remember, Shivurr?"

"You." I rubbed my hands over my eyes. "Not just from a week ago but from way before that."

Reaching down, I snatched an empty sample vial from the floor of the Schmidts' New Olympus cottage.

The glass bottle glimmered in the Pacific Ocean sunlight as if it had been scrubbed and polished. The substance that it had recently contained tended to coalesce and cohere, ensuring that when I had drunk it, all of it had poured into my mouth, leaving no residue behind.

A good thing, too, I thought.

I'd have swallowed the bottle whole if necessary to ensure I got it all. There was too much at stake, too much risked to leave a single precious molecule unconsumed.

About a week ago, I'd escaped from a secret research facility belonging to an organization called the Bodhi Group. In the months before doing so, I'd been unable to sleep, suffering from nightmares as vague as they were frightening. The world, my dreams told me, lay poised on the precipice of a disaster that I had to avert, even if its nature was still a mystery.

Despite suffering from amnesia—the result of experiments conducted upon me—I guess a part of my mind still recalled enough to know that it had forgotten something that must be remembered. Subconsciously, it had stitched together bits of data still resident in my psyche, trying to reconstruct what had been lost. The desire for answers eventually manifested into a suggestion, an imperative, that had to be satisfied. That or the Allfrost itself had called me, somehow. What else could drive me—a life form of snow, crystals, and ice—to venture out into the sun and heat of the Nevada desert?

The journey should have been suicide, but I'd survived anyway and learned much about my former life and purpose in the process. It turned out that I'd come to the Bodhi Group to seek their help in stopping the disaster—the one that I could no longer remember—and they'd betrayed me.

Instead of helping me, they'd lobotomized and experimented on me, taking tissue samples of me that messed up my mind and memories. All in an attempt to understand my nature and capabilities. Anything to help the Bodhi Group in their development of advanced technology to defend the West against its enemies.

I scowled. *Some people suck.* I shook my head a moment later. *Well, not all of them.*

Not even everyone at the Bodhi Institute, the facility where I'd been held and studied. Some of the residents were kind, and I'd even made a few friends there—like Scott Green and Emmett Feldman—without whom I might never have escaped captivity. And I'd survived my exodus only with the help of new pals like Brad, Lucy, Alan, Lilith, and Caleb, young tourists from California. Without them, I might still have been lost in the desert.

I'd made other recent friends, too, like the Schmidts: Wilhelm and Olivia. As it turned out, they were actually old friends whom—because of my amnesia—I'd forgotten. I'd known them as Boreas and Orithyia in the days before my incarceration, the two being part of a community of life forms once worshipped as gods. Since our reunion, I'd witnessed enough of Wilhelm's abilities to understand why ancient people would have regarded him that way. I hadn't seen Olivia in action during my journey, but I knew that the same could be said of her now that old memories, restored by the potion I'd just swallowed, bubbled to the surface.

"Good." Olivia rubbed her hands together as if to warm them. "Welcome back, old friend."

"It's good to be back, Orithyia . . . Olivia." My forehead creased. "At least part of the way." My eyes met hers. "I remember you from before the past week now, but there are still huge gaps."

I lowered the empty sample vial and let the reintegration of my memories continue. Other empties and many full ones remained stowed in my cap for safekeeping. It had been only a few days since I'd snagged them from the Institute while rescuing my kidnapped friends, and I'd drunk only a handful since then. Partly because they tended to hit me hard, and I'd get dizzy or pass out after consuming them. Like I'd just done. But also because I wasn't sure that I wanted to remember everything that they might contain.

"More should come back, in time." She took a seat next to me on the sofa. "Memory is funny that way. No one holds their entire body of memories at the forefront of their thoughts. They're triggered by association with other stimuli. You're probably remembering me first because I'm right here. I'm a trigger. In the same way, some things may not return without the right situation to bring them out or a conscious effort on your part to remember them." She knelt on the floor before me. "Faces will help. Do you recall when we first met?"

I narrowed my eyes, studying the contours of her face. I leaned forward to smell her hair before staring into the green pools of her eyes. "Constantinople, by the wharf, when the Byzantines still ruled the eastern half of the Roman Empire. Over a thousand years ago." I paused, thinking. "Well over a thousand years ago, but you don't look a day older. If anything, you appear younger now than then."

Olivia laughed. "That was the coldest July the Byzantines had seen in a while. Thanks to you." She stared past my shoulder. "If not for you, our alliance with Justinian may not have come to be." The corners of her mouth rose as her gaze returned to me. "Given the choice between winter as an ally or an enemy . . ."

I chuckled as memories bloomed. "That was awesome."

Olivia smirked. "You certainly cemented Wilhelm's reputation as God of Winter."

I bent toward her. "What was Justinian like? I never met him, did I?"

"Not to my knowledge." She glanced upward. "He was a great man. Quite progressive for his time. Made greater by our influence, I hope. I like to think that our discussions helped shape the *corpus juris civilis*."

"Wait," Caleb said. The teen surfer wore bright-coloured board shorts, a T-shirt, and sneakers. His longish dirty-blond hair already looked lighter than it had when we'd arrived here on New Olympus a few days ago, and his tanned face showed undertones of red. Both signs that he'd spent too much time in the sun in the days since then. I'd only known him about a week now, having first encountered him in the Nevada desert, but he'd already become a close friend. "Shivurr was your muscle?"

Olivia bobbed her head. "He's helped us in that way more than once."

The teen raised a brow. "He's a badass but not all that scary. I mean, he's like a snowman brought to life."

I frowned. "No, I'm not."

"Come on, dude," he said. "Have you looked in a mirror?"

I looked down at myself. "Sure." I'd seen pictures of the snowmen made by people in colder climes. Like many of those crude sculptures, a stack of three large balls, composed of snow and ice, formed my head and body. A couple smaller ovals of snow, flat on the bottom side, were my feet, attached to bones of ice buried beneath snow.

"Well," he said, "you've got to admit ... there's quite a resemblance."

I spread my hands. "So what?" I tapped a finger next to an eye. "My eyes are blue and made of crystals." I tapped my nose. "And this here's snow and ice like the rest of me. Those things are made with buttons and carrots and stuff." I slapped a snowy forearm through the fabric of my jacket. They were long enough that my dagger-like fingertips could almost touch the ground even when I stood erect. "And my arms aren't twigs."

"Okay, sure," he said, raising his hands to his shoulders. "My point is, you've got a friendly face, dude."

I snorted but said nothing, thinking of our first encounter. *He totally freaked*, I thought with a grin.

"See?" Caleb lowered his hands. "Who's going to be scared of a smile that big?"

Olivia looked at me. "Oh, Shivurr can be threatening when he wants to be. He doesn't always look as friendly and lovable as he does now."

"What, he makes a scary face?"

She wagged her chin. "More than that."

"Really?" I asked, intrigued. "What do you mean?"

"You know you can change form, don't you?"

"Uh, no . . . I . . . really?"

"I guess your memory of that is still lost." Olivia waved a hand in my direction. "Well, look, you're made of snow and ice that's constantly flowing. You're shape-shifting every time you move. Growing a bit taller to reach the top shelf or shorter to fit somewhere or reshaping yourself to sit in a chair. Unlike most organisms, your form isn't fixed."

"Sure," I said, "but it's not like I can turn into a bird or a bear . . . or a human being."

She grunted. "There are limitations to how small or large you can become. Doing so requires a change in your body density, and there seem to be practical limits to that. But I've seen you alter your form in the past. You've never been able to master it perfectly, and you're still snow white, but you've managed to at least resemble a human being in the old days."

"Really?" Caleb said. "He grows legs and everything?"

"Of course," she said. "His waist narrows and his face changes too."

"That's so cool." Caleb slapped my shoulder. "If you can do that, then you won't need to hide anymore."

Olivia held up a hand. "He can look more like a human being, but in the bright light of day he wouldn't pass for one for long."

My face fell. "Nuts."

"What if he pulls his hat low and wears clothes?" Caleb flicked the hood of my winter jacket. "He could pull this forward too."

"Sure," Olivia said. "That'll help . . ."

"But?" I asked.

Her shoulders bounced. "You always had trouble maintaining it. You could walk around and maybe carry on a simple conversation, but anything more distracting and you'd shift back to normal."

Caleb looked at me. "Sounds like trying to pat your head and rub your stomach at the same time."

Olivia smiled. "Something like that." She stood and walked toward the kitchen, still talking. "Hair was always the toughest part. You'd make more of a general shape than actual strands."

I slumped in my seat. "Not that it matters. I don't remember how to do it."

"Maybe you should take another vial," Caleb said. "Being able to sort of look human would be awesome. Even if it's not perfect, it'll help when you come visit us back home."

I smiled. Seeing my other new friends, who were now safe back in California after our parting at Dublin Gulch, would indeed have been awesome.

It had been only a few days since we three, along with Wilhelm and Scott, had come here to the Pacific Ocean paradise of New Olympus—a new home for many of the old gods of ancient Greece. We had made the journey in moments, transporting to the tropical islands from the Schmidts' Las Vegas home by means of the gods' spatial transposition technology—but I missed them already. Judging by how often he had spoken of them over the past few days, Caleb, too, was anxious to see them again.

Not that Caleb and I hadn't enjoyed our time here. The teen had spent a lot of time surfing with Hanale—another of my old, forgotten god friends—down at the beach that the Schmidts' cottage overlooked. With a shared love of the water, the two surfer dudes had really hit it off. Today, I'd even joined them, spinning up a frost disc—something I'd recently remembered how to do—to ride the waves. According to both Olivia and Hanale, it was something I'd often done before my memory loss.

"Uh, maybe later." My head still spun from the few vials I'd already taken. "I'm still feeling woozy."

"I think that's best," Olivia said. "Your body is still adjusting. It'll take time for the recovered essence to be fully absorbed and find its place." She tugged open the door to the fridge and rummaged around inside. "Okay, so you remember me. What about Wilhelm? Do you remember him from before the Institute?"

I paused, studying the rafters two floors overhead. "More than I did. Constantinople, of course. You were both there, after all." Flashes of other events sprang to mind as I spoke: a montage of conversations and scenery scattered across ages. "Years . . . centuries earlier, too, I think. Somewhere in Greece, judging by the architecture. Other places too, but I can't remember where or when exactly. Europe, maybe." I met Olivia's eyes as she returned from the kitchen. "Here, too, on New Olympus. We've been friends a long time, just like he said."

"That's good." Olivia handed me a cold can of clear soda pop. "Very good."

"It's hard to believe I'd forgotten it, now." I cracked the can and took a sip.

"Do you remember anything more about why you went to Nevada? About the threat you went to stop?"

I stroked my chin.

The Allfrost—a machine capable of influencing Earth's climate—came immediately to mind. Its hidden chambers and nodes covered the earth, channelling power from a dimension of endless cold known—to those aware of its existence—as the Underfrost. Though the Allfrost's decline was partly due to global warming, in recent days, and perhaps longer, its chambers had also been the target of incursions by fire elementals: humanoid creatures of lava and flame.

When I'd last seen them, they'd been led by a muscular, demonic man—a fire demon—in an attack upon the Bodhi Institute that had left it in flames. The vials I'd drunk hadn't told me anything specific about what they wanted, but I felt a growing certainty that the Allfrost lay at the heart of the danger.

At last, I shrugged. "It's something to do with the Allfrost and those fire elementals. Well, their leader. He's mixed up in it, somehow."

She nodded. "Anything about how the Faction are involved?"

"The other gods?" I paused a moment, thinking. The Faction—Olivia had told me—were the enemy: a group of gods that sought to subjugate or, failing that, destroy humanity. "I don't think so. If they are involved, I'm not sure I ever knew how."

"Oh, well." She pointed a finger above my head. "The answers are in there somewhere. Either in the vials in your hat or percolating in your head."

I poured the rest of the soda down my throat and crushed the can. "Maybe Wilhelm will trigger something." I got to my feet. "Any idea what's taking him so long?"

It had been almost three days since Olivia's husband, Wilhelm, had left the three of us. We had parted ways at the mouth of a nearby lava tube, shortly after arriving on the island. He'd had my friend Scott Green, bleeding out from a gunshot wound, in his arms. Carrying the tall Bodhi Group computer programmer as if he had weighed no more than a puppy, he'd raced ahead, to take him to Aceso—a god and healer—in the hopes of saving his life.

Since then, I'd seen Wilhelm only once, as a hologram projected from the necklace worn about Olivia's neck. He'd kept in regular contact with Olivia since then, though. According to his last update, he should have returned here to the Schmidts' seaside home this time last night, which made him twenty-four hours overdue.

Olivia made a face. "We haven't talked since yesterday." Her eyes flicked to the ceiling. "His work with Aceso must be taking longer than anticipated."

My brow wrinkled. "Scott's definitely okay, though, right?"

"Of course," she said. "He's recuperating at Aceso's domus. I'm sure he's quite comfortable there."

"What's a domus?" Caleb asked.

"A very nice, very large house," Olivia replied. "A mansion of Roman antiquity, I suppose you might say."

"Cool." Caleb glanced around the villa. "She didn't want a house like this one?"

She shrugged. "We take the best of every age rather than

discarding it merely because it's old. Often what's new is not an improvement, or maybe some of us just get set in our ways. We might have built a domus here ourselves, but on the edges of our domain, we try to limit ourselves to structures that won't raise questions in the event that passersby ever make landfall."

"Does that happen?" I asked, thinking of Hanale, New Olympus's hulking protector. I still didn't know what god or gods he might have pretended to be in the past, but judging by his complexion, Hawaiian shirts, tattoos, and manner of speaking, I'd have put my money on one of them being Maui, the Polynesian trickster god.

Olivia waggled her head. "Not often. Hanale and his helpers see to that, but keeping the shoreline looking normal gives us time and options when it does. A layered approach to defense is best."

"Domus," Caleb said. "Is that Greek?"

"Latin," Olivia replied.

His head tilted back. "They spoke Latin in ancient Greece?"

"No," she said, "we spoke Greek. Well, an older version of today's Greek. I speak them both, and many others besides. However, you'll find we tend to use Latin more, among ourselves, these days. Being the more recent, it has largely supplanted the older languages. And, of course, English is most used when we're out in the larger world."

"Is it hard, learning so many languages?" I asked.

"Actually," she said, "the more you know, the easier it gets."

Caleb's head bobbed. "That's awesome. I just speak English."

"It's the most important one these days . . . among mortals." She looked at me. "I'm glad you're able to speak it again."

"What do you mean, again?" I asked.

"You used to speak it," she replied. "Years before the Institute, but you—"

A deep, throaty roar shook the villa's windows, audible above the wind and slosh of the surf down at the beach. The sound seemed familiar, but I couldn't quite place it.

Caleb's eyebrows rose. "Whoa, someone sounds pissed."

"Don't worry, Caleb," Olivia said. "It's just a guardian on patrol. They won't approach the building without good reason."

The teen's eyes flicked to me, then to our host. "What is that, though?"

"One of the ookmir, if I'm not mistaken." Olivia strolled toward the patio doors leading to the broad deck that over-looked the azure waters of the Pacific Ocean. "It could be some-thing else, I suppose. We've got an array of defenders on patrol."

"What are ookmir?" Caleb asked.

"Big green humanoids," she said. "Exceptionally strong."

I made a face. "Are you talking about trolls?"

"Yes." She turned back to face us. "I suppose that's another name for them. Though they call themselves the ookmir and, being real rather than fictional, they're somewhat different from how they've been represented in mythology."

I sniffed. "Ookmir or not, they've got serious attitude problems."

Olivia grimaced. "Now that you mention it, I should get you authorization tokens, just in case."

I cocked an eye. "Tokens?"

She nodded. "So the ookmir and other guardians know not to bother you if I'm not around."

"Oh, man," Caleb said. "What if you're not?"

Her eyes widened. "They may perceive you as a threat."

"That explains the one that attacked me on Allfrost Island," I said, recalling my encounter with a troll—or ookmir—a few days before while I was making my way to the Allfrost chamber that I now called home.

She smiled. "Is that what you're calling your island these days?"

"Sure, what else?" I asked.

"You used to call it Smaragnisos."

"Cool," I said, repeating the name. "Emerald Island. It fits."

"Yeah, sure," Caleb said. "That's great. Can we get back to the guys that might kill us?"

Olivia made a downward motion with a hand. "Settle down. I'm not going anywhere. But, if I do, just keep to the cottage and the beach, and you'll be fine. No running off into the jungle."

"No duh," Caleb said. "After hearing that, I'd have to be totally mental to go anywhere else."

"Yeah, well, even so, I should probably get home." The negative effects of the vials I had drunk had abated, and I felt ready to make the trip back to the cold sanctuary of the Smaragnisos Allfrost chamber. "Maybe I'll remember even more after a night's sleep."

"You must love it there," Caleb said. "If it's as cold as you say."

"It's cool, but . . . a bit boring."

He frowned. "What do you mean?"

"I miss my stuff. I haven't played a video game in days. Not since the arcade in Las Vegas."

"Well," Olivia said, "at least you've got the Allfrost Controller to keep you company."

"Hue?" I shook my head. The Allfrost Controller hologram, Hue, seemed nice enough, but being an artificial intelligence or AI, he operated only within programmed limits. Ask him about the Allfrost, and he'd happily tell you all he could, but beyond advising me on how to fix the Allfrost or helping me use its functions, he had little to say without prompting. "He's more interested in talking about the Allfrost's problems than anything else. He's obsessed."

She shrugged. "Caring for it is his primary function."

"And there's no soda pop to drink."

"Well," she said, "now that you're back, you can renovate a bit. Get some arcade games put in, and stock the chamber with all the soda pop you want."

"That'll be sweet," I said with a nod. "I mean, don't get me wrong. It's mega-comfortable there, but I like hanging out with you guys more."

Olivia touched my shoulder. "And we love having you here."

"Thanks," I said, getting to my feet. "I'll be back before sunrise. I'm going to try talking to Hue again too. Maybe my new memories will help me ask him the right questions."

"About what?" Caleb asked.

"About the threat that brought me to the Bodhi Group."

"That's a good idea," Olivia said. "But for tonight, just get some rest and try not to fret about it."

"All right. I'll try." I slapped Caleb on the shoulder. "I'll see you guys soon."

Olivia accompanied me to the door that led to the villa's front deck. "Be sure to travel in more or less a straight line from here to Smaragnisos."

"Right, I will." A flash of tentacles rising from frothing water appeared in my mind. "Believe me, I don't feel like tangling with a sea monster or whatever you've got patrolling the waters."

"Don't wander too far afield and you'll be fine. They patrol farther out, at the perimeter."

"That's good to know." Smiling, I stepped out onto the deck and into the sun, which, sitting low in the sky, had lost much of its power.

Perfect, I thought. I liked sunlight, but my body didn't, preferring the shade of trees or the dimness of the night sky. I wasn't quite a vampire, but I could sympathize.

"Safe—" The air reverberated with a shriek like torn metal, cutting Olivia off.

Chapter 2

Rover

For a long moment, we stared at each other, listening. We'd heard similar noises over the last few days, but those had been far off, deeper inland in the jungle. This one had come from much closer.

"What's that?" Caleb said at last. His wide eyes darted from mine to Olivia's.

"It's got to be a guardian, right?" I said, looking at Olivia. "It sounds like it's right out back. I thought they weren't supposed to come this close."

"It's not a guardian," Olivia said. "Wait here. I'll go see what it wants."

"Should I come with you?" I asked.

"No need," she said, waving me back. "Keep Caleb company. I shouldn't be long."

Sometime later, Olivia returned, mouth pinched and eyebrows bunched together above her aquiline nose.

"Everything cool?" I asked.

Caleb squinted. "Who or what was that?"

"A herald," she said.

"A herald? Like a messenger?"

"Exactly."

"A messenger from where?" I asked.

"Caelumtor." Apparently noticing my expression, she added, "A mountain on the island at the centre of New Olympus. The tallest of all to be found here. Do you remember it? You've been there before."

I flicked my eyes skyward a moment, then shrugged. "I don't think so."

"No matter," Olivia replied. "You'll see it soon enough."

"What do you mean?" I asked.

"I need to get to Caelumtor," she replied. "There's trouble there."

"What kind of trouble?"

Olivia grimaced. "I don't know. The herald didn't say."

"Why not?"

She scowled. "It succumbed to its injuries before it could."

"Injuries?"

"It appears to have been attacked."

I grimaced. "Dead?"

"Nearly," she said with a nod. "I've stabilized it and moved it where it will be safe until it recovers."

"But how?" I asked. "Who or what would have attacked it here on New Olympus?"

She tossed her shoulders. "I wish I knew. That's why I need to get to Caelumtor."

I nodded. "And you want my help?"

She shook her head. "Whatever it is, I'll handle it. You just need to work on getting your memories back. You need time to do that. However, I would still like you and Caleb to accompany me there."

My brow wrinkled. "But why, if not to help?"

"Scott's there, remember? I know you're eager to see him, and since I'm going anyway . . ."

"That'd be excellent."

"And Wilhelm will return there when he's done helping Aceso." Her eyes flicked to Caleb. "When he does, we can get you home."

"When will that be?" Caleb asked.

"I don't know," she replied, fondling her necklace. "He should have returned last night. I tried contacting him after finding the herald, but I couldn't reach him. He'll be coming through Caelumtor to get here, though, which means we might as well meet him halfway."

"What do you think is keeping him?" I asked. "Do you still think it's his work with Aceso?"

"I'm not sure anymore," she replied. "Perhaps it's the trouble on Caelumtor. The sooner we leave, the sooner we'll know."

I nodded. "Okay. When do we leave?"

"Give me a few minutes to secure things here, and we can be on our way."

Caleb and I drifted outside to watch the sunset, while Olivia disappeared deeper into the cottage. The sun's edge had just touched the horizon when she returned. She'd changed her clothing—beach cover-up over a bikini—and now wore form-fitting brown pants and a dark brown tank top. A watch and fine silver bracelets adorned her wrists, and her matching necklace traced her collarbone, disappearing beneath the neckline of her shirt. She had also bundled her hair into a ponytail, over which she'd tied a red paisley head scarf, the tail of which draped down the side of her neck.

"Nice outfit," Caleb said. "Shouldn't you be wearing togas and stuff, though?"

Olivia smiled. "Not for a few thousand years now, and we wore himation, not togas."

"What's the difference?" he asked.

"Togas are a Roman thing." Tucking a pair of sunglasses into the neck of her shirt, she led us down the north-side stairs to the back of the building. Within the shadow of the cottage and trees, night had already fallen, and little could be seen. Seemingly untroubled by the gloom, Olivia began tugging the tarp from atop a vehicle standing within the carport that huddled next to the house. "Give me a hand, guys."

"I can't see," Caleb said. "Can you do that flashlight thing, Shivurr?"

"Sure," I said, lighting up my palm.

Until recently, I'd have luminesced my entire body, but over the past few days, I'd realized, or maybe remembered, that I could control it more finely than I'd thought possible. By doing so, I could turn my palm into a flashlight. *A true hand torch*, I thought, smiling to myself.

"You're like a huge firefly, dude."

I chuckled. "Kind of. Yeah."

A short while later, a large, boxy four-by-four vehicle stood revealed; letters on the front identified it as a Land Rover.

"Sweet ride," I said, making my way around the front end.

Olivia jabbed a finger. "Other side, Shivurr. Driver's seat is on the right side on this one."

I backpedalled. "Really?"

"Really," she said. "This beauty's from England."

"Uh, okay." Getting into the passenger seat, I added, "I'm not sure how that makes any difference . . ."

"They drive on the other side of the road over there," Caleb said from the back seat. "So the steering wheel's on the other side. I saw it in a *James Bond* movie."

The dashboard lit up as Olivia turned the key.

"Whoa, super quiet," Caleb said. "Isn't this diesel?"

The vehicle rocked as Olivia steered it out the carport's open front. "Not anymore."

Caleb leaned between the seats. "Gas?"

Olivia smiled. "Nope." She waved a hand at the windshield. Twin tracks, lit by the Land Rover's headlights, extended into the distance. To either side, a wall of tropical plants and trees rushed past in a blur. "Not a lot of gas stations around here."

"Then what?" I asked.

"You know that Walkman I gave you?"

I touched the peak of my cap. "Of course." She'd altered it somehow—turning it into a sort of telephone—so we could keep in touch, even thousands of miles apart.

"Well, I upgraded this too." She looked at the rear-view mirror. "I made all sorts of improvements. Switched out the internal combustion engine, for one. Put in better windows, and doors . . . cushier seats . . . better suspension and tires. You won't find another like it in all the world. Which means fuel isn't ever going to be a problem. Not in Rover."

I laughed. "You call it Rover? Like a dog?"

"Sure, that's what it is . . . was . . . originally. A Land Rover."

"Yeah, I know, but I thought you'd named it, like Brad calls his Volkswagen bus Otto."

"I did." Olivia snorted. "Cute. Otto the Autobus." Her fist

made short circles against her door. The window above it lowered, letting in a gust of moist air. "Open your windows, guys. It's a gorgeous night. We might as well enjoy the drive." She glanced at me. "Oh, I forgot. You're probably too warm already."

"Nah." I zipped up my winter coat. "It's fine. I'm pretty much used to it now. At least the sun isn't shining."

"You must hate it," Caleb said. "The sun, I mean."

"Actually . . . no, I think it's great. I love it here, even if it's too hot for comfort. There's so much variety . . . so much life."

"Kind of like enjoying a campfire," Caleb said. "It'll burn you, but it's still beautiful."

"Nicely put, Caleb," Olivia said. "You've got the heart of a poet in you."

He cleared his throat. "Thanks."

"Just telling it like it is," she said.

"So, where are we headed?" Caleb's voice quavered as the Rover stuttered over a rough patch of gravel and the dashboard vibrated.

"Sorry about that." Olivia sighed. "I'll have to get that section of road fixed. With all the rain, it's always eroding in spots." She patted the steering wheel. "That's why I love this baby. It can handle the worst terrain." I rolled toward her as she cranked the wheel to the left. "Anyway, I told you where we're going at the cottage. A mountain called Caelumtor."

"Sure," Caleb said, "but I mean before that. You said it was on a different island. We can't drive there, can we? Is this thing amphibious? Like James Bond's car? What was it called? A Lotus something. The white one."

"I've no idea, Caleb," Olivia replied. "I'm not as up on movies as you two."

I turned in my seat. "The one that turns into a submarine? That was so cool."

"Yeah, that's it," Caleb said. "I knew you must have seen them, too . . . when you were . . . you know, at the Institute."

"I just saw the one. Most of what I know about movies comes from Scott. I guess he's not a huge James Bond guy."

"What made you watch it, then?"

I snorted. "It's kind of weird, but Harland Dixon—the Institute's head of security—showed it to me. He said he wanted me to see a 'good' movie for once, instead of all the science fiction crap . . . his words."

"Not a fan, clearly," Olivia said. "Anyway, no, Rover doesn't change into a submarine."

"Then what? Are we getting on a boat? A plane?"

"Patience, Caleb," she said. "You'll see soon enough."

"Hang on," he said. "Isn't that Dixon dude a bad guy? He's the one that kidnapped Alan and everyone, right? Why would he be giving you movies to watch?"

"I don't know," I replied. "That's the weird part. I mean, he was holding me prisoner. Not the best foundation for a friendship, but, well, I think maybe he felt kind of bad about it. I don't know. I guess he figured he was doing his duty or something, keeping me locked up. Like it was for the greater good. For America and freedom and all that. He sees himself as a real patriot."

"I know the type," Olivia said with a frown. "It's kind of hypocritical of him, isn't it? Kidnapping people in the name of liberty."

I thought of our conversation in Death Valley near Dublin Gulch, as Harland wheezed in pain. "Yeah, that's what I told him. I'm not sure he was paying much attention, though. He was just trying to keep me there long enough for his agents to arrive."

"Wait," Caleb said. "Is Dixon also the dude in the helicopter? The one that crashed 'cause of that Drogre monster?"

I nodded. "Yeah, same guy."

"Do you think he made it?" Caleb asked.

"Probably," I said.

His brow wrinkled. "But he was hurt pretty bad, wasn't he?"

"Sure," I said, "but he'd radioed for help, and trucks were coming when I left him."

"Well," Caleb said, "I guess it doesn't matter. He sounds like a bit of a dick if you ask me."

"He could . . . can be . . . but I still hope he made it." I gave him a lopsided grin. "Crazy, right?"

"Sounds like you've got a bit of Stocking Syndrome, dude."

"Stockholm, Caleb," Olivia said with a smile. "It's called Stockholm Syndrome."

"Sure. That's what I said." His eyes darted to me, then back to Olivia. "Didn't I?"

I lurched in my seat as the Rover decelerated. My nose brushed the dash before my outstretched hands halted my forward momentum.

"What the hell?" Olivia said, craning her neck forward.

A tree stood between the twin ruts of the road thirty feet ahead, lit by the Rover's headlights.

"What kind of tree is that?" Caleb asked, sending a gust of warm air across my cheek.

"Looks like an oak," I said, still staring out the front.

Olivia leaned out her window. "Hello?"

The tree's limbs swayed, and a moan rent the air, silencing the insects in the forest to either side of the road. *Sounds like a cow in labour.*

"Yes, you," Olivia said. "You're in the way." She stuck a hand out the window and made a shooing gesture toward the woods to our right. "Move, please."

My hands flew to the sides of my head as another groan shook the windows.

"Oh, for Pete's sake." Olivia shot me a look. "I'll be right back."

The driver's-side door swung open, and she hopped out. I glanced at Caleb with wide eyes before returning my gaze to the road. Doffing her ball cap, Olivia strode toward the oak, her back lit by the Rover's headlights. Walking right up to it, she touched the tree's trunk. Thick branches descended as the tree leaned toward her, and my fingers grasped the passenger door's handle.

"Holy shit," Caleb said. "It's going to crush her."

I tugged the door open as the oak's forward motion creaked to a halt. Its trunk rested against Olivia's forehead, and she laid a hand against its rough bark.

"Wait, Shivurr," Caleb said. "I think it's okay."

I froze, holding the door ajar, and watched and waited, ready to move to her defense at a moment's notice. After a few tense minutes, the tree straightened, and I exhaled.

Olivia turned on her heel and approached. As she did so, a rumble of earth and stone filled the air. The tree uprooted itself and began to creep to the right. A moment later, Olivia jumped in through the still-open door and pulled it shut behind herself.

"Well," she said, "that's just great."

"Were you talking to it?" Caleb asked.

"Of course." She laughed. "I wasn't giving it kisses."

"Huh," he said, "are all the trees here like that?"

"No," she replied, "most are pretty normal."

My eyes rolled to the side, watching the tree enter the woods. "What did it say?"

"Basically, that we're going to have to drive a bit farther than I thought. The transporter we were heading to is off-line."

"Transporter?" I said, pulling my door closed.

"A Spatial Transposer. Like the one that brought us here. Well . . . not exactly like that one. That one isn't meant for regular use."

Right, just for emergencies, like gun-wielding thugs trying to kidnap or kill you.

My forehead wrinkled. "Is that going to be a problem?"

"No," Olivia replied, "it's fine." She put the Rover into gear. "It's a bit more of a drive to the next one, and we might get wet, but we'll be there before you know it."

We bounced in our seats as the vehicle banged over the potholes left by the departing oak tree.

She gave me a look and grimaced. "I wish he'd chosen to wait at the side of the road rather than in the middle of it." She sighed. "If it's not the rain messing up the road, it's the trees."

"Do they do that often? Move around, I mean."

"No," she said, shifting to a higher gear, "not really, but sometimes they move where the sun's better, like the middle of the road, when they think no one's around. I think he was waiting for us this time, though."

"That was wicked," Caleb said. "Was that the one from your backyard? The one Shivurr told us about?"

Olivia glanced at the rear-view mirror and shook her head. "No. Everyth is still in Nevada. She's probably taken up residence in a nearby yard."

Caleb chortled.

"What's so funny?" Twisting in my seat, I rested an arm on the backrest and leaned against the passenger-side door.

"Imagine being the dude that finds a huge oak tree in his backyard. I mean, you go to sleep, you wake up, and you're having your morning coffee or whatever, when out the window . . ." He threw his hands up and outward. "Boom!" He made short chopping motions in the air. "There's a fifty-foot oak tree that wasn't there the day before. That's going to be one confused dude."

I chuckled. "No doubt."

Giving me a smile, Olivia glanced over her shoulder at Caleb. "Oh, I wouldn't worry about it. Everyth is quite adept at blending in." Her feet danced, and she tugged the gearshift. I braced an elbow against the dashboard and rocked in my seat as we turned left. "No doubt she'll be nestled in among other foliage for camouflage."

"Well," I said, taking off my hat, "I think a drink's in order."

Chapter 3

Low Tide

Resembling a baseball cap, the military-issue headgear had originally belonged to someone at the Bodhi Institute, but I'd taken it with me during my escape. I'd grown quite attached to it, especially since Wilhelm had modified it. Among other things, it actively cooled my head using some sort of god tech. How it worked exactly, I didn't know.

My arm disappeared inside up to my elbow, passing through the crown into the space beyond. I couldn't remember what Wilhelm had called it, but basically it was a spot where I could store things without taking up any room in my hat or adding anything to its weight. I felt around a moment, pushing aside memory vials, enjoying the interior's chill, and pulled out a can of soda. The cylinder hissed as I pulled the tab.

"Got one for me, dude?" Caleb asked.

"Uh . . . s-sure." I inched the can toward him.

He cackled and waved a hand. "Just kidding, dude. You need them more than me."

Olivia looked over her shoulder and jabbed her thumb by her ear. "Check behind you, Caleb. There's a cooler in the back."

"Awesome." Caleb's seat belt clicked, retracting with a thunk, and his butt waggled left and right as he leaned into the cargo area. "Nice, they're cold." The thump of a lid being closed followed. Facing front, he held a silver soda can—half the size of the one in my hand—aloft. He ran a finger over the logo and stylized lettering on its side. "Ambrola . . . what's that?"

Olivia's eyes rolled left. "Soda pop of the gods."

"No way." Caleb cracked the seal, and a puff of mist rose from the opening, illuminated by a rainbow of light that projected from within. "Excellent."

"Let me know what you think," Olivia said.

He pursed his lips. "Pretty small can."

Her eyes widened. "Oh, that's plenty. Believe me."

The can stopped an inch from Caleb's mouth. "What's this going to do to me?"

"Nothing bad," she said. "You'll feel reinvigorated, and your aches and pains will be washed away, for a time."

He held the can near his nose and sniffed. "But if gods drink this . . ."

"Don't worry, Caleb," she said. "It adapts to the drinker's needs and physiology."

His brow wrinkled. "Translation?"

"It won't hurt you."

"Good enough for me." He took a sip from the can, and his eyes darted side to side. "Nice."

Olivia smiled. "Wonderful, isn't it?"

"Epic." Caleb downed the rest in a gulp. "I think it's working already."

"How're you feeling, Slim?" I asked, using the nickname I'd given him when we'd first met.

"Amped, dude. Totally freakin' amped."

"You want one, Shivurr?" Olivia asked.

"Uh." I held up the red-and-white can that I'd already taken from my hat. "Can I save it for later?"

"Of course," she said. "Caleb, grab him one, will you?"

"Sure." He turned and rummaged around in the cooler again.

As he turned back to me, I doffed my hat, and the teen dropped a fresh Ambrola inside. Snugging my cap back into place, I took a sip of my already-opened drink and watched the foliage rush by.

We passed through rolling hills, green grasses, and shrubs before the road dipped, rose, and curved, becoming barren fields of long-cooled lava. The road steepened soon after, the engine changed pitch, and the Rover's tires crunched over loose rock and gravel that pinged against the wheel wells.

My eyelids drooped low, and I soon fell asleep.

Sometime later, my seat fell away beneath me, and I twitched awake. "What the . . ." My hands splayed against the passenger door and dash.

"Hey, sleepyhead." Olivia spun the wheel, taking us around a sharp curve in the road, which dropped away ahead of us. "Good timing. We're nearly at the other side."

True to her words, the ground soon levelled, and we drove out onto a beach of black sand. A hundred feet off, a froth of white washed up the shore before rushing back into the sea. Some miles offshore, lightning danced across a wall of clouds that drifted above the water.

"Here we are." Olivia steered us along the beach a short way, then spun the wheel, taking us toward the water. The Rover pulled to a stop by the water's edge, just beyond the high point of the ocean's wash. She popped open her door and jumped out. "Stretch your legs. I'll get things ready."

Hopping out, I glanced toward the volcanic mountains through which we'd just passed with their summits lost in darkness and cloud. "Nice place."

"I've got to take a walk." Caleb extended his arms above his head and groaned. He looked toward the uprising of lava rock that bordered the sand where low bushes grew from cracks in the earth. "Be back in a sec."

As he walked up the beach, I turned on a heel and looked about. Olivia stood by the shoreline, fifty feet away, facing the water with her back to me. Her shoulders wriggled, and waves of frothing white crashed against the black sand and washed up and around her dancing feet.

As I rambled toward her, a faint melody seemed to mingle with the susurration of wind and waves, and I stopped just beyond the sloshing salt water's high point and listened. *She's singing.* I didn't recognize the song, and the language was unknown to me, but the melody seemed pitch perfect to my ears. The last time I'd heard singing was in the basement of the Schmidts' Las Vegas home, when Wilhelm had transported us and a good portion of their basement here across a distance of many hundreds of miles.

I followed the receding water to stand at her side. "What are you doing?" Her fingers danced in the air before her, and she continued her tune. "Olivia?"

Her head twitched, and she held up an index finger. *All right, I'll shut up.*

With nothing else to do, I looked out at the ocean. Moonlight peeked through a break in the overcast sky and glimmered off the water's surface. The next crash of waves rushed over my feet and the bottom half of my lower sphere. My snowy flesh tinkled as it hardened to a layer of protective ice.

A short while later, she stopped singing, stared out at the water a moment, then nodded. "Well, that ought to do it," she said, smacking her palms against each other as if knocking away dust.

"Do what? Is there a ferry coming?"

She grinned, moving her head side to side. "Nope . . . no ferry." She laid a hand on my shoulder, drawing me into step next to her. Up ahead, Caleb whirled to face us, tugging at the waistband of his shorts. "Come on. Let's have a seat while we wait."

"What's up?" Caleb said as we met him by the Rover's side.

I shrugged and pointed a thumb toward Olivia. "Not sure."

Olivia sat and patted the sand at her side. "Wait and see."

I sat and leaned back on my hands. Raising my nose to the night sky a moment, I glanced at Olivia. "So, how long do we wait?"

She pursed her lips. "Fifteen minutes should be enough."

"Enough for what?"

"For the tide to go out."

"And then?" I asked.

"Then, we take a drive," she said.

Caleb's head slid into view from behind Olivia's, mouth agape. His wide eyes met mine, then flicked right to regard Olivia. "Say what?"

"Uh, yeah," I added. "What he said."

"Patience, you guys." She gestured toward the water. "Enjoy the view awhile. Just be in the moment."

"Okay." I turned my gaze to the sea.

We sat in silence awhile, and with each minute that passed, the froth of water that endlessly clawed its way up the sand seemed to diminish.

Caleb pointed a finger. "What's that?"

"What's what?" Olivia asked.

"Those lights." He leaned across me and pointed again. "Do you see?"

She squinted. "Oh, yeah."

"Where?" My head swivelled until I spotted an array of lights near the horizon. "Oh, yeah. I see them."

"It must be a cruise ship," Olivia said. "They pass by now and again."

"Won't they see the islands?" I asked.

She pursed her lips, giving her head a slight shake. "I'm sure Hanale's got it under control."

The lights began to wink out from left to right as if a curtain were being drawn over the vessel.

I sat forward. "Where'd they go?"

"Probably behind a fog bank," Olivia said. "I told you. Hanale's got it covered."

My chin dipped. "They still might have seen something, though. Before the fog rolled in."

"No," she said. "Fog's just one tool. There are other illusions that also shroud the islands. The ship would have to get much closer to penetrate them all." She smirked. "A permanent fog bank, large enough to enclose all the islands, would be pretty suspicious after a while, don't you think?" She spread her arms wide. "The key is making the rest of the world think there's just empty ocean here."

I nodded. "I suppose that makes sense." Leaning on a hand, I twisted to face her. "So, this herald—if no outsiders can get here, what do you think attacked it? I mean, it's just you guys here, right?"

Olivia grimaced. "I'm not sure. Whatever it was had to be powerful. The heralds aren't guardians, but they're not push-overs either."

"You think it's the renegade gods that you told us about? The Faction, I mean."

"Maybe." She stared a moment. "I don't see how they could have gotten in, though . . . not without us knowing at least."

I closed my eyes and felt the wind on my face and the texture of the sand against my body until the sounds of the surf had grown noticeably fainter. I opened my eyes and squinted at the shoreline that now frothed fifty feet or more away.

"All right." Olivia pushed a hand against the ground and sprang to her feet. "It's almost time. Let's get ready."

Chapter 4

Landfall

We hopped into the Rover, and Olivia turned the key. Against the noise of the surf, the preternaturally quiet engine could not be heard. Only the illuminated headlights and dashboard showed that the vehicle now ran.

Olivia leaned toward the windshield and narrowed her eyes. "Okay, that should do it." She put the truck in gear and glanced at me. "Now . . ." She pressed the accelerator, and the Rover surged forward, heading straight for the water. "We go surfing."

I braced a hand against the dash and my other against the door. "Are you sure about this?"

"It's fine. Trust me." She glanced my way. "Roll up the windows. Tightly . . . and keep them closed until we're across. No sense getting the seats wet."

My hand traced a circle against the passenger-side door, raising the glass within, sealing out the wind and sound of the frothing ocean. Shooting a look into the back, I saw that Caleb had done the same. The Rover rocked and bounced, and salt water crashed against the front window before windshield wipers swept it aside, revealing the ocean stretching into the distance. To our left, water rushed past the lower half of the doors, while in the side mirror, the black beach grew quickly smaller as we made our way deeper out to sea.

We should be underwater, I thought. *Why aren't we underwater?*

"It's a boat," Caleb said. "One of those amphibious deals, right?"

Olivia shook her head. "Nope."

An upsurge to the right sent a splash through the air to land atop the Land Rover's hood.

"Then what?" I asked.

She shot me a look. "Guess."

I thought a moment before shrugging. "Beats me."

"It's an underwater land bridge," she said. "Notice how we're not rising and falling with the waves."

"Land bridge?" I glanced out my side window. The vehicle still dipped and rose, but its movements didn't match the surges of water. The swells all came from the side, and most broke before reaching the road. "Oh, yeah. I see what you mean. It's super shallow. Seems like a crazy place for a road."

"It's built atop the rim of an underwater volcano." Olivia thrust her chin to the right. "There's a huge crater that way. I just needed to lower the water first or we really would need a submarine car." She pointed out the front. "When activated, the road is exposed."

I peered ahead. Twenty feet to either side, a five-foot-high wall of water ran parallel to our direction of travel. Waves broke against thin air and splashed upward before sloshing down and away.

My right shoulder pressed against Olivia's before my left struck the passenger door as the Rover swerved.

"Bitchin'," Caleb said as we all bounced in our seats.

Olivia spun the steering wheel to the left, then the right, before holding it steady. "Sorry, guys. We hydroplaned a bit there. The water's not quite reached its lowest point, but it'll get better as we go. I'd have waited for it to sink fully, but we're in a bit of a rush."

I glanced at Caleb, then Olivia. "So, that singing you were doing on the beach . . . that was to lower the water?"

"Uh-huh," she replied, keeping her eyes on the swatches of slick black rock that intermittently peeked from beneath the retreating water.

"How does singing a song do that? It sounds like magic, but magic's not real, right?"

"Also correct." She swiped a hand next to the steering wheel and the windshield wipers stopped. "I merely invoked an existing technological mechanism using a sung command."

I wrinkled my brow. "Sung command?"

She nodded without looking at me. "We interface with many of our systems through song. It's a security measure."

"How is a song more secure?" I asked.

She shrugged. "Making it a song makes it far harder to fake. The system recognizes the unique characteristics of my voice. It also requires that I know and can replicate the words and tune. There are some things that we don't want just anyone activating."

"That's why Wilhelm had to start over, right?" My mind roamed back to the Schmidts' basement, when Wilhelm had sung the song that had brought us here to New Olympus, along with their entire basement. "When he activated the transposer in your basement, he wasn't using magic . . ."

"Of course not," she said. "He was just singing the notes required to activate it."

"Couldn't someone just record your voice and play it back?" I asked.

She pursed her lips. "It'd be unlikely to work. The system would detect a recording."

"How?"

She glanced at me, then back at the road, which now sat just above the waterline. Only the occasional thin coat of water sloshed across the stones of its surface. "Well, for one, a recording would precisely match a previously sung command. There would also be background noise present in the recording that would give it away."

I shrugged. "It still seems like—if you could get it perfect—you could fool it."

"Maybe," she replied. "But, for our more secure systems, the expected tune varies by authorized person based on the moment it is actually sung."

I squinted at her. "How can you possibly know what it is, then?"

"Math."

"Then the song is different each time?" My eyebrows rose. "You must get some pretty crazy lyrics, in whatever language that was."

"Oh, back on the beach?" She shook her head. "That wasn't a language. I wasn't singing actual words—just different notes for varying lengths of time in various orders."

"Like that scat stuff?" Caleb said. "Skippitybob, bah, boh, beh, bah, bah, bah."

"Careful, Slim." I snickered and waved a hand at the wind-shield. "You're going to start a tidal wave or something."

Olivia gave me a crooked smile. "You laugh, but it happens."

"Really?" Caleb and I said in unison.

"Well, maybe not a tidal wave. My point is our older tech didn't have such safeguards. It still doesn't in some cases. In those days, we did sing the songs in the spoken languages of the day. Greek, Latin, and so on."

"Oh, boy," Caleb said.

Olivia nodded. "You can guess what happened. Human beings started using our tech for themselves, when they could get their hands on it. We were less security-conscious then, obviously. In those days, we didn't even restrict the song to authorized individuals. If you knew the song, the system or device would often obey. You might have to try it several times before you got it right, but sometimes people succeeded."

"Holy shit," Caleb said. "That'd be like magic. Like using a word of power."

"Yes, and we regularly had to deal with some sorcerer casting what they thought of as a spell or using a magic item or some cleric performing miracles. They caused all sorts of trouble."

"You mean," I said, "people figured out how your technology works?"

Olivia pursed her lips. "Not exactly. Artifacts like rings and wands are just tools that interface with and authorize access to our technology."

"What do you mean?"

"Well," she said, "you play arcade games, right?"

"Sure."

"Do you know how to build one?"

"No," I said. "No clue."

"Any idea how to write the software for the game?"

I shook my head. "Uh-uh." *Scott might, though.*

"Yet you put a quarter into the slot, and you can play the game."

"Yeah," I said with a nod. "I see what you mean. You don't need to know how it works. Just how to use it."

"Holy," Caleb said by my ear. "Why didn't you have that shit locked down?"

Olivia shrugged. "In their ... in our arrogance, we didn't think mortals—regular people—smart or daring enough to try."

I cocked an eye. "But, even among yourselves, there must be things you don't want just anyone to use."

"Sure," she said, "but we mainly used the honour system among ourselves. We were far more trusting and open long ago." She grimaced. "We were once one big happy family, mostly."

I turned to regard her. "And now?"

She shot me a look. "Now, we've added security measures to the most important things—whatever isn't already safe here on New Olympus or at other secure locations."

"That must have sucked," I said. "Having your tech stolen, I mean."

Her head bobbed. "We're still tracking down lost artifacts, even today. That or dealing with misuse of our as-yet-unsecured technology." She glanced at the rear-view mirror. "Don't worry, though, Caleb. We've got most of our ... shit ... locked down these days. And we're retrofitting older artifacts when we can. It's still a potential problem with the stuff we haven't gotten to yet, but these things take time."

Caleb smacked my shoulder with the back of his hand. "I guess that's why you don't hear a lot about wizards in the news these days," he said with a grin.

"You've heard of Greek fire?" Olivia asked, and I nodded. "That came from us. There's no command required for it, though. It's just an obscure chemical reaction, not a higher-level system."

"System?" I said, recalling past conversations with Scott. "You mean like a computer system?"

She shrugged. "Sure—that's as good a word as any—and the

physical systems with which it is integrated. But not like the computers you'd have seen at the Institute. Ours are more embedded." She smirked. "And you won't often issue a command to our systems using a keyboard and monitor. Well, sometimes you might, but usually not."

My brow furrowed. "Then how?"

"It depends on the system," she said. "Some have a fixed function. For those, you often speak certain words and make specific gestures."

"Can what the commands do be changed?" I asked.

Olivia bobbed her head. "By those with expertise in our technology. Not all of us have bothered to study and acquire that knowledge, though."

"Have you?"

"I have indeed. It's important to know how things work and how to fix them and also to be capable of doing without them."

"Why's that?"

"If you rely too much on technology, you become helpless without it. Besides, like not exercising atrophies the body, not using your mind makes you a dullard."

"And Wilhelm knows this stuff, too?"

"Of course," she said. "He's been one of my primary instructors. He's among the most knowledgeable and skilled of us except perhaps for Hephaestus himself."

I nodded. "So, you're both like Scott . . . or he's like you."

She cocked an eye. "How's that?"

I tossed my shoulders. "You're like computer programmers or systems specialists or whatever."

"Ah," she said. "Yes, I suppose we are. Among other things." Her eyes flicked to me, then back to the windshield. "We're pretty skilled with the computers that Scott works with ourselves, of course. It's especially useful when operating in the mortal world. But what we do with our own tech is both simpler and more complex. It has to be for some of the things we do with it."

"Like what?"

She shrugged. "Like manipulating space-time or working with energies and forces as yet unknown to humanity. Mistakes with those sorts of things can have dire consequences, so much of our technology works by specifying what you want, not how it should be accomplished. When Scotty writes a program, he specifies everything to be done, step by step, instruction by instruction. With our technology, we simply express our desires. It's like asking a waiter to bring you a glass of water. You don't care how they do it, you just want them to bring you one."

"Huh," I said. "That sounds a lot easier than what Scott does."

"It is, usually." She raised a hand, teetering her palm side to side. "Communicating what you truly want can be tricky sometimes, though."

"How so?"

"It's like the genie in the bottle stories." She glanced at me. "You know, the ones where you get three wishes."

Caleb chuckled. "Oh, yeah. I get it." He nudged my shoulder. "It's like when the wishes all backfire. You know, you ask to live forever but forget to say you want to be young too. Then you just keep getting older and older"—his eyes flared wide—"but you can never die."

"Fortunately," Olivia said, "our systems aren't trying to get things wrong. It's just that you need to—"

"Be careful what you wish for," I said.

She smiled. "Exactly."

I smiled back, then looked outside.

The foaming water ahead gleamed in the Rover's headlights. To either side, the ocean looked calm, blue-black, except where it reflected moon and starlight. To our front, the thick clouds I'd seen from shore still stood in our path, obscuring everything beyond them. As far as I could tell, we were heading out into an endless sea with no sign of land except what lay behind us.

"So," I said, "where's this other island?"

Olivia pointed at the windshield. "It's on the other side of those clouds."

I raised a brow. "Didn't you say a permanent fog bank would be suspicious?"

"It's only there when Caelumtor's power levels drop too low, in case our protective illusions should fail as a result."

"A layered approach to defense is best," I said, echoing Olivia's words from earlier in the day.

"Now you're getting it," she said, giving me a wink.

"How much longer?" Caleb asked.

She shot a look over her shoulder. "About an hour, at our current velocity."

"Is this the route the herald took?" I asked. "The one that gave you the message?"

"No, it flew over."

"Heralds can fly?"

"Some can, yes."

I thrust my chin at Olivia's chest. "Why not call you on your amulet, like Wilhelm did?"

She shook her head. "That's just for Wilhelm and me."

"How about the phone?" Caleb asked.

"Oh," she said, "there are no telephone lines here."

"What if you need to reach someone, though?" I asked.

"For that," she said, "we have the birds and trees. For more sensitive communications, the heralds are used."

Caleb snorted. "The trees?"

"Okay," I said, "but if this is urgent, why didn't you fly back, too?"

"Do I look like I can fly?" She looked at the glowing numerals of her wristwatch. "Even if I could, I couldn't carry you both."

Our conversation soon lapsed into amiable silence. Caleb lay sideways in the Rover's spacious back seat and closed his eyes. I leaned back in my seat and rested my head against the side window. My eyelids drooped as the vehicle rocked gently back and forth, but I remained awake, thinking of what we might be driving into.

After a while, clouds closed in around us, blocking out the moon and stars and all but the nearest ocean to us. The water to each side seemed closer and higher now, its top well above the Rover's roof.

"We're past the halfway point now," Olivia said. "We'll make landfall soon."

The clouds opened up sometime later, and the moon and stars once again shone overhead in the abruptly clear sky. In the distance lay another black sand beach, bordered by a wall of tropical trees and plants. Beyond it, the ground, a deep, dark emerald under the light of the stars, angled upward to a mountain summit encircled by blobs of white cloud. Veins of lightning danced across and between them, occasionally forking down to strike the mountain's peak.

I leaned forward, tilting my chin upward. "Whoa. That's got to be Caelumtor." The stirring of a memory confirmed it even as I said the words.

"You've got it," Olivia said, giving me a glance.

"That's frickin' awesome," Caleb said, puffing warm air across my right cheek.

Leaning to the left, I grinned at him. "You are correct-amundo."

The Rover rocked as we reached the forest's edge and took a right onto a dirt road. We followed the coast for a while until, rounding the far edge of an inlet, we came to a bay. At its deepest point, a dark rectangle stood by the shore, taller than the trees flanking it, yet dwarfed by the mountain behind it.

As we neared the spire, flashes of lightning striking its apex, revealed it to be a square tower of rugged black lava rock. About ten storeys tall, it rested on a thirty-foot-high circular stone base that extended a hundred feet beyond the edges of the tower itself.

It looks like a wheel fallen on its side with half an axle sticking in the air, I thought.

Before long, the dark monolith loomed to our left as the Rover descended to the edge of another beach. Out on the water, towering waves, frothing white in the moon and starlight, rose and curled, then crashed back into the surf. Atop the waves, two figures—a man and woman, by their silhouettes—could be seen riding surfboards toward shore.

"Who's that?" Caleb asked.

Chapter 5

Old Friends

Olivia steered the vehicle toward the water. "Not sure." I braced a hand against the dash as the Rover decelerated and came to a halt. Her hand fiddled by the steering wheel, the dash lights went out, and the engine's hum faded to nothing. "Let's take a look."

As we followed her down onto the sand, the two strangers—each with a surfboard under an arm—splashed out of the surf. With a wave to us, they made their way toward a nearby campfire where flames rose waist-high from a stone-lined depression in the sand. Even at a distance, lit by the flames, their wet, naked bodies gleamed like statues of Degas or Rodin. Wedging their surfboards into the sand, the thirty-something couple stood, hands on hips, awaiting us.

The woman slicked water from her hips as we neared. "Good evening, Orithyia."

"Hi, Cleo." Olivia nodded to the man. "Leonidas. It's been a while. Still taking good care of yourself, I see."

The man's pecs danced a moment. "The body is a temple."

I hung back, eyeing the fire, contained only by a calf-high wall of lava rocks. Its dancing flames coloured the Underfrost in shades of black around and above it. Visions of the fire elementals I'd fought in recent days came to mind, and my throwing-hand fingers stiffened and wrist curled.

Settle down, Shivurr. I took a deep breath and flexed and waggled my icy digits. *It's just a campfire.*

"Holy shit," Caleb whispered, grasping my right elbow.

Cleo fluffed her hair with her hands. "Have you come to join us?"

Olivia shook her head. "We're headed to Caelumtor."

Leonidas stroked his beard and looked toward the dark tower. "You'll have a wait ahead of you."

"Oh?"

"Capacitor levels," Cleo said. "There have been numerous transports tonight. As far as Antara, apparently."

Olivia whistled. "That would do it."

Leonidas grunted. "Short-range transpositions have been limited to preserve power for the Veil."

"Any idea how long it will be down?" Olivia asked.

"I am not sure," Cleo said. "If not tonight, once the sun rises, it'll soon resolve itself."

"We can't wait that long." Olivia glanced at me. "I suppose we'll have to drive up."

Leonidas's brow wrinkled. "What is the urgency?"

Olivia told them of the near-dead herald.

"We have seen no signs of trouble here," Cleo said with a glance at Leonidas.

He turned toward the dark tower. "There has been more lightning than usual, of course, but that is to be expected given the increased power demands."

"When last did you stand atop Caelumtor?" Olivia asked.

Cleo pursed her lips. "We came down a few hours before dusk. All was well then." Her eyes swung to regard me. "Is that Shivurr hiding back there? We had heard you had resurfaced at last. It gladdens my heart to see you well."

"And mine." Leonidas stepped forward and extended a hand. I moved closer, feeling the campfire's heat. "Well met, friend Shivurr."

"Pleased to meet you," I said, clasping his hand.

"Oh, how wonderful," Cleo said with a smile. "Your English is excellent." Her eyes darted to Leonidas. "Hanale mentioned that you had learned to speak it again during your . . . absence."

Leonidas snorted. "Far better than my Borealan. At least something good came from your imprisonment." He glanced to the side. "And who is the lad?"

I looked at my young friend. He stood a few feet away, arms

crossed, clasping a forearm with a hand. His eyes were wide, and his mouth gaped. "This is Caleb."

"Hey, dudes," the teen said with a thrust of his chin. "What's up?"

Cleo studied him a moment before turning back to Olivia. "The mortal child?"

Olivia cocked an eyebrow. "How do you . . . ?" She waved a hand as if shooing a fly. "Don't tell me—Hanale."

Cleo inclined her head. "You are correct."

"Yes," Olivia said, "the mortal and trusted friend."

Cleo bent her knees, moving her arms as if spreading an invisible gown. "In that case, welcome."

Leonidas inclined his head. "Well met."

Caleb swallowed. "Hi," he said, still holding his arms, awkwardly. His eyes darted up, down, and away toward the sea.

Cleo's lips twitched, and she turned her gaze to me. "Do you remember us?"

My forehead wrinkled a moment before I shook my head. "No, I don't think so." I shrugged. "Sorry."

"He may yet, Cleo," Olivia said. "Given time."

"I certainly hope so." Cleo glanced up toward the summit of the mountain, where lightning still flashed. "We must sup together soon, then. Leonidas and I will regale you with stories that may aid your recovery."

"That'd be wicked," I said.

Cleo's chin dropped. "Wicked?" Her brow creased. "If you'd rather not—"

"No, no." I held up my hands, palms toward her. "I mean, that'd be cool. You know, great."

"Oh, yes," she replied. "Of course. I had heard you have become quite versed in colourful colloquialisms."

Leonidas cleared his throat and looked at Olivia. "Orithyia. A word, if you will be so kind." His eyes drifted to me, then to Caleb. The teen—his gaze riveted upon Cleo—appeared unaware of the scrutiny. "Privately."

Olivia touched my shoulder. "Why don't you take Caleb for a walk before he overheats?"

"Uh, sure." I looked at her with narrowed eyes. "But what about me? If anyone's going to—"

"I'll tell you later," she said with a grin.

"Okay," I said, drawing out the O. "Let's go, Slim."

I slapped a hand against Caleb's shoulder, drawing him toward the water. The teen fell into step beside me but kept glancing over his shoulder in the direction of the campfire.

"Oh, dude," he said, grasping my elbow.

"What's up with you, Slim?"

"Didn't you see?" His chest heaved, and he let out a breath. "She was totally naked."

"Yeah." I looked back. "So what? So's Leonidas." I tugged at the fabric of my coat. "Without this and my hat and scarf, I am too."

"Jeez, dude," he said, curling his lip. "Don't tell me that."

"Wait." I thrust a finger at him. "I see what's going on here."

Caleb's face shone red in the light of the campfire behind me, and he looked aside. "You do?"

"Sure," I said. "It's pretty obvious."

He tugged the hem of his T-shirt downward. "Come on, dude."

"Don't worry about it," I said. "It's no problem."

"It isn't?"

"No." I rubbed my chest. "I can fix it."

He stepped back. "Excuse me?"

"I can keep it contained now, mostly." I glanced over my shoulder. "Besides, I wasn't even near her, and she's right next to the fire."

Caleb raised an eyebrow. "What are you talking about?"

I looked down at myself. "You're worried I'll make her cold, if I get too close. Aren't you?"

"Uh." His eyes darted side to side. "No, not really."

My brow wrinkled. "Then what?"

He cleared his throat. "No reason."

I looked him up and down, thinking. Finally, it clicked. "Oh, I get it." I shot another look at the trio. "You're attracted to her."

I should have known, really. I'd grown so accustomed to

human beings that I often forgot how different from me they were, how unusual. I'd read more than just fiction at the Institute. Curious about humanity, I'd also perused a few textbooks, along with the science fiction and fantasy books that I usually read.

Incredibly, they're atoms arranged into molecules that are then arranged to form cells of different types. Cells that cooperate to form an organism larger and far more complex than themselves. Not just human beings, either, but all the flora and fauna of the earth. And these organisms reproduce and consume other organisms to survive, and the entire system is powered by the sun. Amazingly, all this blankets the world in a plethora of unlikely, seemingly impossible life.

I glanced down. Maybe I was cells too—I didn't know—but I made a lot more sense at least. My atoms, elements, and molecules, if I have them, connect me to the Underfrost. Its limitless energy powers my life, not a ball of hot plasma floating in space. Sure, I share the need to consume matter, too, but it doesn't have to be organic. The Underfrost allows me to transform and extract what I need—what the Underfrost doesn't already provide—from pretty much anything. And according to my god friends, my lifespan was effectively limitless. Maybe that's why thoughts of reproducing didn't drive me as they did my human friends.

"Not so loud, dude," he whispered.

I turned back to face him and nodded. "I suppose that makes sense. Aesthetically, she's quite well-formed."

"Aesthetic . . ." He threw up his hands. "I think I'm in love, dude."

I snorted. "Don't get your hopes up, Slim. I get the impression she's with Leonidas, and he's a pretty buff guy." I grinned. "Check out those glutes. I don't think you could take him in a fight."

Caleb sighed and his shoulders drooped. "Yeah, I know." He swelled taller. "It's cool to dream, though."

The crashing of the ocean grew louder as we neared the water's edge. We turned left and walked along the shoreline, taking in our surroundings. The once-towering waves had abated since Cleo and Leonidas had come ashore. No longer twice my height, they were now what Caleb had referred to as ankle busters, a foot or so high. Instead of breaking and crashing into the surf, the waves now rose in wide swells.

I inhaled the sea air, soaking in the ethereal beauty of the tropical night. As I toed the edge of the surf, something moved out on the water, a few hundred yards from shore.

I extended an arm. "Do you see that?"

"Sure do." Caleb glanced my way. "How about some light, dude?"

With a thought, my palm glowed.

"Can you make it brighter?"

I squinted, and the beam of light glared off the water's surface. The light spread to my wrist, eventually engulfing my entire body, and Caleb hugged himself as the air cooled.

The spotlight moved left and right with a twist of my hand. "Do you see it?"

"There." He stabbed a finger at a dark shape cutting through the water in our direction.

We backpedalled, both shouting, as a shadowy form raced toward us like a torpedo. I pushed Caleb behind me with one hand and kept the other aimed at the writhing sea.

As the shape reached the shore, fleshy vines, thick as trees, erupted from the water. Rising twenty feet into the air in seconds, the appendages came down, sending plumes of water flying.

Moments later, a bulbous, conical head rose from the depths, as big as Olivia's Land Rover. From within the mass of flesh, an eye the size of my head regarded me.

Before I could react, the monstrous sea creature gripped me in a circle of suckered arms.

Tugging at the spongy muscle failed to loosen its grip, and my hand drew back and glowed as I plucked frost from thin air. I held off throwing it as a memory stirred.

"Don't, Shivurr," said Olivia's raised voice from somewhere behind me. "He's friendly."

I leaned forward, narrowing my eyes. "Ken?"

My ears and chest thrummed as the creature rumbled, and the tentacle holding me relaxed and withdrew.

I lowered my arm, releasing the frost in my hand back to its source.

Olivia came to a stop by my elbow. "He just wants to say hello, I'm sure."

I nodded, reaching out to touch one of the tentacles that now hovered near my face. "I know. I mean, I remember now." I turned and beckoned Caleb forward. "Come on. Meet Ken."

He didn't move. "Ken?"

Olivia chuckled. "That's what Shivurr calls him. His real name is Agnar."

Caleb tilted his torso away from a waving appendage. "What is it?"

"A kraken," Cleo said, joining us by the shore. "One of our guardians of the sea."

"Gnarly." Caleb took a step back. "I'm good here, dudes."

Olivia touched one of the tentacles. "He recognized your glow, Shivurr. He's missed you."

I walked up to the eye, no longer afraid, and reached out a hand to stroke Ken's skin. "Hey, buddy."

A presence, a consciousness, brushed against my mind. *Race?*

Memories of racing the sea creature across the water—me riding a disc of frost—appeared in my head.

"Later, Ken," I said aloud. "We've got somewhere to be right now."

Feelings of regret and understanding radiated from the kraken. *Promise?*

"Sure," I replied. "Next time."

Understand. He retreated to deeper water. His skin shimmered through a variety of colours, consolidating into patterns and hues that matched the night sky and water, in near-perfect camouflage. As large as he was, I could barely see him now.

"See ya," I said, giving him a wave.

With a splash, Ken slipped beneath the surface and was gone.

"Where's it going?" Caleb asked.

"Back to patrol." Olivia glanced over her shoulder. "Come on, guys. We'd better go. With transports down, we're going to have to drive up and walk in. It's going to take longer."

"Oh, yeah," I said. "Good point."

We said our goodbyes to Cleo and Leonidas before piling back into the Rover. As we drove away, the nude couple grabbed their surfboards from the sand and strode for the sea, where the waves were growing higher once again.

"Nice couple." I bounced in my seat as Olivia's foot pressed the Rover's accelerator harder. "They're together, right?"

"Oh, yes," Olivia replied. "For some time now."

"Are they like you?" Caleb asked. "Gods, I mean."

She nodded. "Yes, they're more like me than most."

"Like you?" I turned in my seat to regard her. "What does that mean?"

"They're ascended," she replied.

"Ascended?" My brow creased. "From what?"

The corner of her mouth lifted. "Humanity."

"Oh." I faced front, considering her words, and a memory surfaced, unbidden. "You don't like to talk about it, do you?"

"Not really," she said. "We try not to think about our lives . . . before."

I held up a hand. "Forget I asked."

"Thanks, Shivurr."

Driving in silence, we followed the road higher toward the summit of Caelumtor. Steep drops down the mountainside and thin waterfalls periodically flashed into view as we climbed. In time, switchbacks in the road became more frequent, slowing the Rover to a crawl, and the trees and tropical plants thinned soon after, changing to slopes of green grass and shrubbery. A short time later, the vegetation diminished and the air grew misty.

The rest of the world, even New Olympus itself, seemed far away until the fog retreated again and Caelumtor's summit stood before us.

"Here we go," Olivia said, taking us down a dip in the road and into an opening in the mountainside.

Chapter 6

Caelumtor

Within the mountain's peak, wisps of light shone overhead, revealing a winding tunnel, which continued to drop ahead of us. Marks in the stone furrowed the walls to either side as if chiselled into the rock or cut by the claws of a massive creature.

Sometime later, the tunnel walls slid away, and we entered a vast hall of stone. High overhead, globes of light, larger than those in the entry tunnel, illuminated a floor that looked big enough to host a game of football. Wide columns of stone dotted the interior, rising to the ceiling high above, and automobiles of varying types sat parked in organized rows throughout.

Olivia tucked the Rover into an empty space next to one of the pillars and killed the engine. "All right," she said, cracking her door. "Time to walk."

Caleb and I did the same, joining her at the Rover's rear.

I smacked Caleb's shoulder with the back of my hand. "We walk from here."

"Classic *Raiders* quote, dude." He looked around. "I hope there are no guys with spears and blow darts, though."

Olivia jerked her head to the side before striding for the exit at the chamber's far edge, and we fell into step beside her.

Caleb nudged my arm. "Is that a chariot?"

He thrust a finger toward a two-wheeled gold-coloured cart parked next to a truck, twenty feet away.

"Looks like it." I pointed to the two bars, resting against the ground, that extended from the cart's front. "I think those bars are where the horses go."

"You've got it," Olivia said.

"You still drive chariots?" Caleb asked.

"We race them, mostly," Olivia said. "Around the Circus Caelumtor."

"Like Barnum and Bailey?"

Olivia smiled. "Not that kind of circus, Caleb." She whirled her finger in the air. "This one's a racetrack that runs around the summit."

"Cool," I said. "That sounds fun."

"Oh, it is," she said. "Come on. This way."

We followed her to a staircase at the far side of the cavern. Atop the broad stairs, strobes of light flickered and flashed from an opening in the wall.

Halfway to the top, Caleb sprinted ahead. "Last one to the top's a rotten egg." He took the steps two at a time toward marble statues of robed men and women in heroic poses that looked down on us from the landing above.

"Wait," Olivia said, giving chase.

Not wanting to be left behind, I bounded after them.

"Whoa." Caleb stood bent over with his hands resting on his knees as we joined him at the top. A wide statue-lined arcade lay before us, extending for a few hundred feet before spilling out into open air. "Nice."

Olivia clasped Caleb's shoulder and spun him to face her. "Stay near me, all right? It's important."

His brow creased, and he looked around. "What's the big deal, Olivia? I was just playing."

"I know," she said, holding up a hand, "but you're not authorized yet. If I'm not around, Caelumtor's defense systems may see you as an intruder. You do not want that."

"Okay. Sorry, Olivia."

She sucked in a breath and exhaled it in a rush. "It's okay, Caleb. Just don't run off again." She held out a hand to each of us. "Come on, guys."

Hand in hand, the three of us walked the length of the arcade with statues watching us from either side.

Ducking under the cover of a massive arch at the far end, we looked out over a green valley that formed a bowl several miles across within the mountain's summit. Near the basin's centre, peaked and domed roofs rose just above the forest canopy, and heavy rain fell upon them from the clouds overhead.

Nearer to us, chain lightning crackled across the sky, lighting a broad staircase that descended to the valley floor. At the bottom of the steps, a wide stone boulevard disappeared into the dense forest and fog.

"We're going to get soaked," Caleb said. "This storm's wicked."

Olivia stepped out from beneath the arch, raising her nose to the sky. Fat droplets of water cascaded against her face and shoulders, drenching her in moments. She pulled the scarf from her head, spread her arms wide and twirled, laughing all the while. Facing us again, she beckoned us near. "Come on, you guys. It's rain. From water comes life."

With a glance at me, Caleb entered the deluge, eyeing the clouds. "Are you sure this is a good idea, dude . . . uh . . . Olivia?"

Her mouth gaped, baring perfect white teeth, and she laughed. "Of course." She thrust her arms above her head. "I love storms."

The air flared blinding white, and I slammed my eyes shut and turned away. My hands flew to the sides of my head as my chest vibrated with the reverberation of thunder. The glare faded as quickly as it had arrived, leaving only a jagged afterimage to linger on the insides of my eyelids.

Cracking my eyes a sliver, I turned back to face her, my stomach in knots over what I might see. Olivia's teeth shone white as she lowered her upraised hands. Electricity crackled across her palms, arcing across her skin to her ever-present wristwatch and silver bracelets.

"Besides," she said, "as long as you walk with me, the lightning will not harm you."

She brought her hands to her shoulders and pushed upward like a weightlifter hoisting a barbell, sending arcs of lightning from her fingertips back into the clouds. Moments later, the rain thinned, then abated altogether, leaving only puddles and streams behind. The latter ran over and between the stones, toward the steps, before cascading over the edge.

"You're awesome," Caleb said, wide-eyed. "You are a god."

Olivia's chin, still dripping water, moved side to side. "Not entirely. Not yet." She beckoned to me. "Come on. We should go."

Glancing skyward, I stepped out. "Did you just stop the rain?"

"Just in this area," she replied as we descended the stairs. "Long enough for us to get to Aceso's." The wind gusted, snapping the scarf in her hand. She trembled and rubbed her arms. "Brr. It's chilly."

I cocked an eyebrow and gave her a crooked smile. "That'd be one of the downsides of dancing in the rain."

She shrugged. "It was worth it." She fanned her face with her hands as if to dry it. "Anyway, it's fixed easily enough." She lowered her hands to her sides with her cheeks still wet. "You might want to brace yourself."

"For what?" I leaned forward and winced as a blast of air blew up the stairs toward us.

Unlike the cool, damp gust that had chilled her moments ago, this one felt warm and dry. I snugged the zipper of my winter coat higher and turned my head. My exposed outer layer of crystals and snow thickened and hardened, shielding me from the wind's bite. My flesh roiled, restoring the integrity of my icy outer shell, moving too-warm crystals and water into the depths of my body, where they would be cooled once again.

Shielding my face with my hands, I peered at my surroundings through splayed fingers. In contrast to me, my two friends seemed unbothered by the sudden gust of wind. Olivia spread her arms and whirled in a slow circle, motioning to Caleb to do the same. The teen nodded, pulling his damp T-shirt from his body, allowing the air inside, also doing a slow-motion pirouette. By the time the gale faded to a slight breeze a short while later, they both appeared considerably drier.

Olivia smoothed her windblown hair and donned her head scarf once again. "Much better," she said, giving me a wink. "Come on, guys. Let's get moving."

Descending the steps, we soon reached the valley floor, greeted by a light fog that drifted above the road. To either side of our path, a mix of plants of numerous varieties crowded the spaces between towering trees. The trees were larger here than those I'd seen in Las Vegas and even most other places in my returning memory. The thickest of the moss-covered trunks looked large enough that the outstretched arms of four full-grown men would not quite encompass them.

I sucked in a breath of air, marvelling at the beauty of our surroundings. Drifting to the forest's edge, I directed light from my palm at the trees. The leaves of one were round-lobed and deep green, the grey-brown bark of the tree furrowed and scaly. While no arborist, I thought it looked different from most of the other trees I'd seen on the islands of New Olympus—definitely not tropical. I panned the beam of light left, spotlighting the conical form of a balsam fir standing sentry among a cluster of trees of even more varieties that I could not identify.

"Hey, Olivia?"

"Yes, Shivurr." Olivia stopped walking and looked back from ten feet ahead.

"This tree . . ." I pointed a hand. "It's not from around here, is it?"

"If you mean 'is it a species native to the area?', then no." She smirked. "Though these individuals have grown where they stand from seedlings. They were born and raised locally."

My eyes rolled side to side. "How do they survive here, though? We're like, what, ten thousand feet above sea level?" The squawks and trills of distant birds filled the woods to either side of the road. "There should be snow at this elevation, shouldn't there be?"

Olivia began to walk again. "Among other things, Caelumtor is an outdoor conservatory, a sanctuary for and fount of life. As such, the area is divided into zones in which the climate is made suitable for those species living within it."

I hustled to catch up with her and Caleb. "But why?"

"For our enjoyment of their beauty and to protect and preserve them." She glanced over her shoulder at me. "Important reasons, don't you agree?"

"Sure." I looked around. "I can see that. They're awesome."

"Listen to those insects." Caleb's head swivelled left and right. "There must be thousands of them." He rubbed a bicep. "I can't believe I haven't been bitten yet. Not even once. Aren't rainforests supposed to be swarming with mosquitoes?"

Olivia shook her head. "There are a variety of insects here, for sure, but there are no mosquitoes."

"Really?" he replied. "That's cool. I heard even Hawaii has them."

"Yes, I know," Olivia said. "They were brought in by ships, but you won't find any around here. They've made it here before, several times, usually via a spatial transposition. But we have protocols in place to prevent that now."

"How'd you do that?" Caleb asked. "Crates of insect repellent?"

Olivia smiled. "Something a bit more sophisticated than that."

"Do mosquitoes bite you guys?" I asked.

Her head bobbed. "Some of us, yes."

I thought about that a moment. "Like you, right?"

"Uh-huh."

"What about Wilhelm?" I asked.

"No," she said. "Not Wilhelm."

I looked at her. "Because you're still human?"

She inclined her head. "For now."

"How long until you're not?" I asked, though I thought I knew.

"It varies," she said. "A few millennia for me, so far." I whistled, and she shrugged. "It's just a drop in the ocean of time."

"You were born thousands of years ago?" Caleb asked.

She nodded. "Mm-hmm."

He frowned. "So, everyone you grew up with . . ."

"Is long gone," she said. "Presumably."

Caleb eyelids fluttered. "Dude . . . that's got to be rough."

A long moment passed before Olivia replied. "Not as much as you might think. Unlike now, it wasn't a particularly good time to be alive."

Another memory stirred. "Weren't you royalty back then?"

She fired a look my way. "It wasn't a great time for princesses either."

"Oh, sorry. I didn't mean—"

She waved a hand. "Don't worry about it. It's hazy now anyway, and I try not to think about it anymore." She swiped a hand at her eyes. "Speaking of insects . . ." She strode ahead. "Come on, you two. Let's pick up the pace."

I looked all around as we walked, absorbing the scenery. I remembered enough of my past now to know that you'd never find the same variety of life on the freezing landscapes of ice and snow that had spawned me. Cold landscapes had an impressive and stark beauty of their own, but the volume and diversity of life here still touched me, deeply. Whatever soul I might have filled with gratitude to be here to witness it. A gratitude simply to be alive.

Sometime later, as we rounded a curve in the road, a forty-foot-high obelisk slid into view from behind the trees. As we drew closer, the obelisk began to glow purple. By its light, paved boulevards and pathways led off in several directions, through the encircling trees.

"Anyone need to use the restroom?" Olivia asked, heading toward a squat stone building with several doors that huddled by the roadside. "Now's your chance."

"Sweet," Caleb said.

I snorted. "I'm good, but you guys go ahead."

"I know," she replied, "but it seemed impolite not to ask anyway."

Left alone, I plopped onto a nearby stone bench and leaned back on my hands. Overhead, glimmers of starlight peeked between breaks in the churning clouds. Closer to the earth, fog drifted lazily among the trees and above the roads in every direction.

Standing, I wandered the area, humming to myself. I stopped as a numinous green glow lit the woods on the far side of the obelisk. Faint and diffuse, the light flickered, changing angles at random as if blocked and deflected by something as it passed through the trees.

Craning my neck, I squinted into the mist. I didn't see much until a dark shape moved into view from behind a tree.

Before I could make out what it was, a creak came from my rear, spinning me on a heel.

"Hey." Caleb strode toward me, wiping his hands on his shirt. "The facilities are righteous, dude. You should check them out."

"Maybe later." I extended a finger toward the trees, where the light source no longer moved. "What do you make of that?"

Caleb flipped his hair from his face, scrunching his eyes. "Only one way to find out." He cupped his hands to his mouth. "Hey, you in the woods. Get over here."

My eyes popped. "What the hell, Slim? Are you trying to get us in trouble? What if it's hostile?"

He shrugged. "Ah, it's cool." He gestured to the glowing obelisk. "It's just one of these fancy lampposts."

I shook my head. "I don't think so."

His eyebrows bunched. "Why not?"

"Because the colour's wrong, and it was moving." I dashed over to the stone building. "Hey, Olivia." I rapped on the door through which she'd vanished. "Something's in the woods."

After a moment, a muffled, unintelligible reply came from the other side.

"Pardon?" I knocked again, casting a glance over my shoulder at Caleb.

Chapter 7

They're Here

The wood thumped as if struck, and a flicker of light pulled my eyes downward. The thin gap between door and threshold flashed blue and an electric crackle came from within.

Huh? I reached for the doorknob. "Everything okay in—"

"Shivurr," Caleb hissed. "It's coming this way."

"Damn it," I muttered, turning and rushing back to his side. "Where?"

"See?" he whispered, pointing a finger. "It's getting brighter."

He was right, but before I could say so, a crack like thunder came from behind us, and I whirled to face the sound.

Olivia's restroom door rattled and shook, and the blue light that had seeped from the crack beneath it now shone from every gap and seam between the door and its frame.

What the hell? Shielding my face with a hand, I eased toward the glare.

"Olivia?" The light died and footsteps approached from the far side. "Hello?"

The portal swung inward, and she rushed out, hair mussed, holding her headscarf in her hand. With drooping shoulders, she turned and pulled the door shut on the now-dark interior.

"What happened?" I asked.

She brushed strands of hair from her eyes. "I was . . ." Her eyes slid to my shoulder. "What's that?"

"Uh, yeah," I said, following her gaze. The radiance continued to brighten, now a gossamer cloud with a ball of green light at its centre that seemed to buzz with energy. "That's what I was trying to tell you about."

Holding her hands to her mouth, Olivia shouted into the woods in a harsh, guttural language that I recognized but didn't understand.

Ookmir, I thought.

A moment later, two bulky silhouettes, twelve feet tall, separated from the tree trunks, occluding the globe of light. Eyeing us with yellow catlike eyes that seemed to glow with a light of their own, they emerged from the woods into the obelisk's purple light. Humanoid, they wore sleeveless vests and knee-length shorts that showed off muscular arms and legs, covered in horny protrusions.

I took a step back. "Why did it have to be trolls?"

Just days ago, I'd fought one of them. If not for a well-placed boulder, I'm not sure I'd have survived the encounter. Now there were two, plus whatever danger the ball of light presented.

Caleb chuckled. "At least it's not snakes. They look just like you said, Shivurr. I can't believe you knocked one out, dude." One of the trolls bared its teeth, grumbling something unintelligible. "Man, this is so wicked."

The new arrivals pounded massive fists against the earth. I stuck out an arm and gave the teen a gentle push back toward the stone building behind us but kept my gaze fixed on the newcomers. "I'm not sure these guys are friendly, Slim."

Like me, he'd been told that the trolls were guardians, but the harsh looks these two were giving us didn't seem right. It might just have been their default resting troll faces, but I wasn't taking any chances.

I raised a hand, and frost formed on the damp stones beneath me, expanding outward in a circle.

Olivia put a hand on my shoulder. "Easy, Shivurr."

I glanced her way with a creased brow. "Are you sure?"

She nodded, almost imperceptibly. "Let me handle this."

"What's going on?"

"I don't know. Something's not right." Her eyes flicked to Caleb. "Just watch the kid."

She stepped forward and shouted again in the language of the ookmir.

A deep, throaty voice gargled a reply in the same tongue, and the light source behind the two trolls swirled and coalesced, transforming into an amorphous many-tendrilled blob.

A moment later, the sky rumbled as dark clouds rolled in overhead.

Olivia's voice grew harsher as the conversation continued.

I fired a look at Caleb. "Get behind me. If anything happens, run."

He swallowed and nodded, eyes wide.

As I looked back to the woods, Olivia stepped forward and her bracelets glimmered. Shouting, she made a shooing gesture, and with a roar, the two trolls hunched over and charged us on all fours. Before they'd made it more than a few feet, forks of lightning arced from the clouds overhead into the shallow water-filled ditch that bordered the clearing. Seeing the danger, the trolls pulled up short, falling and sliding over the grass and mud, coming to a stop ten feet from the electricity's flashing edge.

As they picked themselves off the ground, the lightning spread left and right, creating an impassable line fifty feet long. Behind them, the green sphere of light had become recognizable as something almost humanoid, and its ghost-like arms began to flail.

Olivia shot me a look. "Get Caleb and run for Aceso's. I'll hold them off."

I shook my head. "Not without you."

She grimaced. "They're too fast for Caleb. One of us has to stay and stall them."

I clenched my fists, knowing she was right.

The troll that had attacked me days earlier had moved amazingly fast, especially given his size. Fast enough that I'd have trouble staying ahead of one, even at top speed, and I felt sure I could—propelled by the Underfrost—move a lot faster than a normal human being. Carrying Caleb wasn't an option either; his weight would slow me down too much.

Yet I couldn't bring myself to leave Olivia behind.

"We'll both stay," I said grimly. "He can run for it."

She frowned. "We don't know what's going on." Sweat

beaded her forehead. "There may be more down the road. If there are, he's going to need protection."

Frantically, I looked around for another option. *If only we still had the Rover.*

"I can't keep this up forever, Shivurr," she said. The lightning intensified, and the trolls retreated several steps. "Go!"

I nodded and turned away. Taking Caleb's arm, I drew him toward the middle of the road, thinking back to my race from Dublin Gulch. "Wait."

"What's up?" Caleb asked.

"I've got an idea." I bent over and swirled my hands, spinning snow and ice into a ball that soon flattened into a disc of ice and frost that hovered a few inches above the stones. I leaped onto the three-foot-wide saucer and turned to Caleb. "Come on. Take my hand."

Clasping it, he stepped aboard. The disc wobbled slightly but soon calmed as he settled into position with the balance and skill of a practised surfer.

"Great thinking," Olivia shouted over her shoulder. "Now go."

I held a hand out toward her. "Come on."

Movement to the side drew my eyes toward the trolls. *What the hell?* Fallen branches, rocks and soil now floated among the trees behind the goons.

I looked back to Olivia. "It'll support us all." *I think.*

She pulled in a breath, nodded, and came toward us.

Visible beyond her shoulder, the arms of the green-light-turned-ghostly-humanoid drew back, then snapped forward. Clouds of forest rubble sailed toward us, passing through the wall of lightning unhindered.

Ducking low, I swung a forearm before my face and closed my eyes. With a thought, a glowing bubble of frost energy swelled outward from my middle, knocking Caleb back as it enveloped me.

"Whoa!" He fell from the frost disc and hit the ground with a grunt, and an instant later, the air hummed, and the shield flared brighter, a few feet from my face and torso.

Unharmed, I stood taller and watched rocks, branches and twigs tumble to the road. "Are you all right?"

"Y-yeah," Caleb said, regaining his feet. "What happened?"

"My—" I broke off, spotting Olivia lying face down and unmoving, surrounded by debris. Fifty feet beyond her fallen form, the wall of lightning still crackled, but its intensity seemed to have lessened, and roars of triumph came from its far side.

With the wave of a hand, the nimbus of frost enclosing me vanished, and I leaped down to the road. Caleb rubbed his hands on his shirt, staring with wide eyes and trembling lips at our fallen friend.

I gripped his elbow. "Are you sure you're okay?"

"Huh?" he said, giving me a blank stare.

Grasping his shoulders, I looked into his eyes. "Snap out of it, Slim."

He looked down at Olivia again. "Is she okay?"

"I've got her," I said, avoiding the question. I nudged him toward the frost disc. "Get back on board."

Without waiting to see if he obeyed, I dashed over to Olivia.

As I leaned over her, she put a hand to the back of her head and groaned. *Thank the Underfrost.* "I've got you." I scooped her into my arms, straightened with a grunt, and moved toward Caleb.

"Hurry." Standing aboard the floating disc, he flapped a hand toward his face. "The lightning's almost gone."

My eyes darted to the platform beneath his feet, and he thrust his arms wide as it sank to the ground.

I sidled aboard with my back to him, so that Olivia's dangling limbs didn't knock him off. At my wordless command, the disc rose from the paving stones again, raising the three of us without hesitation.

"It's happening again, dude," Caleb said in my ear.

I glanced to the side. Beyond the fading lightning strikes, more rock and debris hovered above the ground, deadly projectiles waiting to be unleashed.

"Hug me," I said to him over my shoulder. "Grab my jacket. As hard as you can."

He nodded, slipped his arms about my waist, and bunched fistfuls of fabric in his hands.

"Hang on!" Toeing the front edge of the ice saucer, I urged it forward, feeling Caleb's arms squeeze tighter.

As we surged ahead, I inflated another frost sphere out from my middle, slowly this time. My returning memories told me that the frost shield blocked high-velocity impacts but not slow-moving ones. The shield I'd created earlier had been pushed into place too quickly, knocking Caleb back, but I hoped that expanding it slowly now would allow it to pass through my friends unhindered. A moment later, I smiled grimly as the sphere engulfed us all.

"Holy shit, it's freezing," Caleb huffed, shuddering against me.

He was right. The air around me felt thicker and gelid. Pleasant to me, but too cold for my warm-blooded friends to endure for long.

Olivia, her face lit blue-and-white by the enclosing bubble, moaned and sat taller in my arms. "You can let me down." She blinked as if to clear something from her eyes. "I'm okay."

"I will, but just hang on to me a bit longer. There's nowhere to put you down right now."

"All right." She closed her eyes. "That's probably not a bad idea. My head hurts. I think I got my bell rung by a flying rock or—"

The shield hummed as multiple projectiles drove against it, and its sparkling blue-white surface flickered and flashed. Sucking in a gulp of air, I willed the shield to be stronger, and it brightened.

"What's going on back there?" I asked, too focused on carrying Olivia, maintaining the shield, and guiding the frost disc to look myself.

The pressure around my middle loosened a moment before tightening again. "The lightning's gone, dude. They're coming after us."

My eyes narrowed. "Damn it."

"Wait." Caleb's arms relaxed, then cinched tight again. His

sigh sent hot air across my cheek. "They turned around. It looks like they're giving up."

"Keep going for a while anyway," Olivia said, "just in case."

After a while longer with no signs of pursuit, I urged the frost disc to slow, and the blurred terrain resolved back into recognizable trees and plants. Finally, the frost disc came to a halt, and the shield around us vanished.

Drooping, I took a deep breath, let Olivia's feet drop to the ice, and looked around.

A haze of orange-yellow light coloured the gloom a few hundred feet ahead, beyond which—by the light of the stars and moon—the tops of the buildings at Caelumtor's centre loomed large, not more than a mile away.

My two friends stepped down to the road. Dismissing the frost disc, I dropped to the pavement as well, and my shoulders sagged further.

I swept my hat from my head, reached inside of it, and drew forth a red-and-white cylinder. The crack of its seal and hiss of escaping carbonation drew a smile from my lips. I downed half of the dark liquid inside it in a few gulps, then looked to my companions.

Caleb, hugging himself and shivering, hovered by Olivia's elbow, watching as she put a hand to the back of her head and winced.

"How is it?" I asked.

"Sore," she said, grimacing and dropping her hand. "But I'll live."

"Here." I stepped closer, raising a hand. My frosty digits swept over her lustrous hair, brushing across a lump of flesh, warmer than the surrounding skin. Pressing my fingertips against it, I held them steady, cooling the bruise.

She sighed, closing her eyes. "Ah, that's better. Thanks, Shivurr."

"You're welcome," I said, withdrawing my hand. Drops of scarlet stained my fingertips but faded moments later as adjacent snow and ice swelled and spread over the stain like moss, burying the blood beneath its icy surface.

"Do you have an Ambrola?" she asked, opening her eyes.

"Sure." I dug around inside my hat, pushing the larger cans aside until my fingers wrapped around a smaller cylinder. I pulled it out and handed it to her. "Here you go."

She cracked the can and sipped with her eyes closed.

"So, uh, what happened back there?" I asked, flicking my eyes back the way we'd come.

Olivia rubbed her thumb and index finger against her eyes, then pinched the bridge of her nose. "I'm not sure exactly."

"Those trolls looked pissed," Caleb said. "Aren't they supposed to be on your side?"

"Yeah," she said with a frown, "they're supposed to be."

"What about that green ball of light?" My eyes widened. "It looked like some sort of poltergeist."

"Totally, like . . . they're . . . here," Caleb said, drawing out the last word as he smacked my shoulder.

I chuckled. "Don't go into the light, Slim."

"Is that a movie reference?" Olivia said with a smirk.

Caleb and I glanced at each other before shrugging in unison.

She snorted. "I don't know how you remember them all." She waved a hand. "Anyway, to answer your question, I think they may be escapees."

I squinted an eye. "Escapees?"

She bobbed her head. "Even among us, imprisonment is necessary sometimes."

"Are there many of them?"

"More than usual these days." She upended the can of Ambrola and swallowed before handing it to me. "Anyway, I think those ookmir and the poltergeist—as you call it—got loose, somehow." Her eyes slid left and narrowed, looking over my shoulder. "Look, let's talk about this later. Those four may change their minds and come after us, and there may be others on the loose."

"Four?" My brow creased. "I thought there were just three. If you count the poltergeist."

She grimaced. "There was one in the restroom, lying in wait."

"But why?" I asked.

"Hoping to capture somebody, anybody, no doubt."

"Oh," I said, stuffing the empty can into my hat. "That's what that light was."

"Uh-huh, it almost had me too." She fumbled her hands behind her head, and her mahogany hair spilled loose a moment later. "He'd miscalculated, though."

"A troll?"

"No, it was incorporeal." She jabbed her chin toward me. "You must have a lot of empties in your hat now. When we get to Acceo's, I'll show you where you can drop them."

"When's garbage day around here?" Caleb asked with a grin.

"We don't have one," she said, starting to walk. "The cans will be broken down and the material reclaimed and reused. Nothing's wasted here."

"That's awesome," Caleb said, falling into step beside her.

I strode to catch up, my mind returning to our attackers. "How do you suppose they escaped?"

"I don't know," she said.

"They must be what the herald came to tell you about, right?"

"Yes, I think so." She looked thoughtful. "I'm sure we'll find out more when we get to town. For now we should keep conversation to a minimum. For all we know, those ookmir may be trying to sneak up on us."

"Right," I said, "we don't want that." I mimed locking my lips together. "Shutting up now."

I stared forward, catching a ghost of a grin on Olivia's face as I did so.

Giving me a nudge, she winked. "We're almost at Septimius's Arch. It should be safe to talk more then."

Chapter 8

Caelumburg

Gusts of warm air—moist with the recent rainfall—rustled the leaves, burying the whine of insects and the trills and shrieks of nocturnal birds in a wash of white noise before abating a moment later. Overhead, clouds swirled, endlessly coming together and breaking apart, lighting our way toward Caelumtor's centre in an ever-changing twilight of starshine and shadow.

A half mile on, a monolithic block of stone slid into view around a bend in the road.

That's got to be Septimius's Arch, I thought, eyeing the grand sculptures of fantastical creatures perched atop it, ten storeys above, that watched our approach with lifeless eyes.

As wide as it was tall, the massive structure filled the roadway, brushing up against the woods to either side. The only way forward lay through either the six-storey-high arched opening running through its middle, the two smaller passageways flanking it, or, by going around it, thick forest.

At our approach, fires roared to life in broad stone vases set atop three-foot-high platforms, lighting the pillars and bas-reliefs decorating the monument's side with flickering yellow-orange light.

Huddling my shoulders, I rushed past the flames, following Olivia up a short flight of steps and into the centre tunnel. Torches set high on the walls blazed brightly as we entered, revealing more bas-reliefs and colourful frescoes.

I tilted my head back and smiled. "Nice. This is really—"

A rumbling to my left interrupted me. A rock pile set against the wall, ten feet ahead, shifted and clattered, then rose into the air, and I reeled back, wide-eyed as boulders and stones chased each other in a circle.

A moment later, two green spheres as large as my fist broke away from the swarm and took up position a foot apart from each other, ten feet above the tunnel floor. A large boulder rose up behind them, and the two spheres floated back, roosting in depressions in the boulder's surface. As they did, a pair of oblong rocks descended from the main body to land upon the ground. A stream of stones of varying sizes followed after.

Olivia put a hand to my chest as boulders and stones continued to align themselves in mid-air, drawing near to each other but not quite touching. Within moments, a twelve-foot-tall humanoid loomed before us, regarding us with emerald eyes that glowed with their own inner light.

"*Subsistite*," it said with a booming voice. It stepped toward us, limbs moving as if attached by ball joints instead of mere flows of air. "*Quis vos estis?*"

Oh, shit, I thought, rearing back.

"Stand down, Septimius." Olivia took Caleb's hand in hers and put her other on my shoulder. "It's just me and my friends."

"Well met, Orithyia." Septimius nodded and stepped aside. "Fare thee well."

"Has anyone passed this way this evening?" Olivia asked, tilting her head back. "Ookmir, perhaps?"

Septimius's great head swung side to side. "None have entered this night."

She looked around. "Have you heard or seen anything of note this evening?"

He pointed through the arch. "There's been turmoil within. A clash of some kind, hours ago."

"What happened?" Olivia asked.

"I know not," Septimius replied. "None have brought news this way."

"Very well," Olivia said. "Carry on."

Taking her hand from my shoulder, she walked ahead. Caleb and I followed, our steps dogged by green light.

A rumble came from our rear as we exited, and I whirled.

Behind us, Septimius collapsed back into a pile of boulders, ready for whoever else might next travel this way.

"None shall pass," I mumbled in a deep voice.

Caleb squinted. "Huh?"

I shook my head. "Never mind."

"Come on, guys," Olivia said, looking back at us from twenty feet ahead. "Stay close."

I slapped the teen on the shoulder, and we rushed to catch up. The road widened on this side of the arch, and torches flickered at its sides, creating islands of light among a sea of darkness. Built to last, they were thin poles of burnished metal, topped by thicker elongated cylinders of gold—mini vases holding flowers of fire.

"That rock dude was radical," Caleb said to the back of Olivia's head. "What was that?"

"Septimius?" she asked, still walking. "I suppose you'd call him a golem."

"What's he doing there?" I asked.

"Guarding the way in," she said. "He's a guardian after all."

"He's one, too?"

She nodded. "We've guardians of many types. Ookmir, krakens, golems, and more."

"Huh . . . ," I said, trailing off.

She glanced my way. "What?"

"Well . . . couldn't you just go around him?" I glanced back. "You know, avoid the arch. Without a wall, what's the point?"

"Oh, there's a wall, of sorts," she replied. "Any sentient life forms passing through it are detected and tracked. If they are deemed to be intruders, guardians are dispatched to intercept them."

"Then," Caleb said, "how'd those trolls and that ghost get out?"

"They were already inside." She shrugged. "You have to enter through an arch, but you don't have to leave through one. At least, under normal circumstances."

"Was that guy . . . like me?" I asked.

Olivia fired me a look. "What?"

I stared into her eyes. "You know, like me, except made of stones."

She snorted. "No, not even close. Septimius is just a construct. He's not alive in the same sense that we are."

"I don't know," I said. "He seemed pretty alive to me."

"Well," she began, "he's supposed to, but really he's just a machine. You, on the other hand, are a living being."

"What's the difference?" I asked.

"You evolved over eons," she said, "emerging from the dust of the universe. Your final form wasn't specified in advance, nor is it permanently set."

"I get it," I said, "but he could evolve too, right? Evolution doesn't have to start from dust, does it?"

"Okay, maybe he's not yet like you—nor likely to ever be— but the possibility exists." She grinned. "Satisfied?"

I nodded. "Yeah."

"Good." She slapped me on the back. "Now, let's have some quiet time for a while, okay? I need to focus."

On what? I thought as the road took us past a moonlit lake— visible through the trees and boulders to our right—and over an arched stone bridge before entering into a bank of thick fog and scattered torchlight.

Before long, the hazy outlines of shadowy buildings drifted into and out of view. Squat buildings of wood and plaster huddled among stone towers and parapeted walls, connected by broad tree-lined streets. These gave way to square buildings of marble and stone with peaked and domed roofs.

"What is this place?" I stopped walking and turned to admire the largest nearby building. Wide steps ran up to a stone landing. High above this, a massive stone overhang rested on fluted columns, each as thick as an old tree. Within their shadows, statues the height of giants gazed out at me. "The town, I mean."

"Caelumburg," she said, looking around.

I jogged to catch up. "You live here?"

"Uh-huh," she replied. "When we're not on our island or elsewhere in the world."

Caleb's chin bobbed. "It's pretty cool."

"Thanks," Olivia said. "It's home."

"Is it just gods living here?" he asked.

"No," she said. "There are others."

Turning right, she took us along a path through green hedges. A park lay on the far side, filled with flowers and statuary and bordered by trees. At its centre, we passed a burbling fountain lit with a rainbow of ever-changing colours. She passed it by without a glance and took us to the park's far side, where we spilled out onto another broad thoroughfare. Black lampposts, spaced a hundred feet apart, lined the roadside in both directions, casting a soft yellow light to guide our way.

"Almost there, guys," Olivia said, taking a left onto the boulevard.

"Cool." Caleb smacked his lips together. "Any chance we can get something to eat when we get there?"

Olivia nodded. "Of course." She looked back. "You can . . ." She trailed off, looking past us.

I turned, following her gaze. "What is it?" In the distance, muscles of rippling green shone in the street light a moment before submerging into shadow.

"Ookmir," she said. "Trolls."

"Is it them?" I reached for frost. "The ones—"

"No," she said.

I blew out a breath. "How do you know?"

"I know them." Her lips quirked. "Not all ookmir look the same, you know."

I shrugged. "If you say so."

"Where are they going?" Caleb asked.

"I don't know," she said. "After the fugitives, most likely." She jabbed a thumb over her shoulder. "Come on. We should hurry."

The road took us to a broad square hundreds of feet across, bordered by grandiose buildings of white stone nestled among towering trees and forty-foot-tall statues of robed men and women. At the square's middle, water soared from a wide low-walled fountain peopled with stone nymphs frozen in a variety of dance poses. At the water's epicentre stood a grassy island with a single tree growing upon it. Its long limbs extended out over the water, shading the dancers from the moon and stars.

"This way," Olivia said, striding to the fountain's right.

Doing as she asked, I gripped her shoulders as she stopped short. "Sorry."

To our front, piles of crumbled and scattered rocks, some large, some small, littered the ground next to fallen and twisted lampposts. Prone and bent though they were, the latter continued to cast light.

To their right, lay the headless corpse of a marble statue, broken arm resting across shattered torso. Its marble head, minus a nose, sat against the wall of the nearby fountain.

"Shit." Caleb sank onto a marble bench. "What happened?"

Olivia's lip curled. "A fight, by the looks of it."

"The one the herald was in?" I asked, surveying the scene.

"Perhaps." She stalked the area in a half-crouch, studying the pavement, toppled lampposts, and neighbouring benches. "I'm not sure about the herald, but guardians were certainly involved in whatever took place here."

Aiming a beam of light from my palm, I swept it over the rubble, and a glint from beneath a bench drew me closer. The marble seat had been split down the middle, and the two halves had fallen downward, forming a V.

Stooping, I reached beneath it, touching a finger to a dark puddle.

"Who won, do you think?" Caleb asked.

Holding my fingertip beneath the lit palm of my other hand, I studied the red liquid.

"Well," Olivia said, "since those—"

"Uh." I held my fingertip toward her. "You might want to take a look at this."

"What is it?" Rushing over, she grasped my hand, brought it to her nose, and sniffed. "Blood. Ookmir blood."

I glanced over my shoulder. "It was under the bench."

She swept by me, crouched, and dabbed a finger to the pool. "It's still wet." Touching her palms to the pavement, she thrust her legs back, lay flat and sniffed again. "It's definitely ookmir blood, but mostly rainwater now." She sprang to her feet. "The bench must have kept it from being washed away by rain."

"Good troll or bad troll?" Caleb asked.

"I can't tell." She pulled in a breath and let it out slowly. "I just hope none of our more fragile residents were hurt during the melee."

One of the nearby stones jiggled. *What the hell?*

"Are you sure it wasn't more recent?" I said, eyeing her through a veil of fine dust drifting in the glow of the fallen light stands.

She gave me a sidelong glance. "Why do you say that?"

I thrust a finger. "That rock's still moving."

Her eyes slid from mine to the trembling stone. "Oh, don't let that fool you." She took a few strides, crouched, and picked up the baseball-sized rock. "What a mess."

"What is it?"

"Part of a golem." She tossed it to me. "Put that in your hat, would you?"

I snatched it from the air. "Sure."

"Come on." She stood. "The sooner we get where we're going, the sooner things can be set right."

She led us down a street to the right, past more trees and squat buildings.

After a few more turns down empty streets, we walked along a tree-lined lane to a manor house that sat by itself at the centre of a forested clearing. Its walls rose about twenty feet to a terra-cotta roof. Toward the back, the building rose higher still.

"Is this Aceso's domus?" I asked, eyeing the row of stone supports fronting the porch.

"Uh-huh," Olivia replied, "this is it."

Caleb brushed his hair from his eyes. "Pretty big place."

"Do you think she's home yet?" I asked.

She cracked a grin. "There's only one way to find out."

We strode across to the portico and up the short staircase to stand before tall double doors of verdigrised bronze. Ornate figures and symbols decorated every inch of the surface. Olivia whacked the bronze door knocker, shaped like a woman's hand, against a worn metal strike plate three times, and the hollow boom of its impact echoed within.

After several seconds with no answer, she knocked again, and we waited until footsteps grew louder from the other side.

At last, the thick doors swung open, and a thin thirty-some-thing brown-haired man a few inches taller than me yawned and regarded us with half-closed eyes. He wore blue jeans and an ill-fitting black T-shirt. Since we hadn't had time to pack before leaving Nevada, I had to guess that Wilhelm or Aceso had supplied them to replace the clothes he'd been wearing when he'd been shot by a Faction agent.

"Hello?" Scott said, rubbing an eye before slipping on a pair of black-rimmed eyeglasses. My tall, thin friend looked slimmer than ever, but otherwise healthy.

"Hey, buddy," I said, throwing out my arms.

"Shivurr!" Scott's eyes lit, and his jaw dropped. "Hey, man." He lunged forward, wrapping me in an embrace. Pulling away, he rubbed his hands on his chest. "You're still cold as ever."

I laughed. "Well, it is kind of my deal."

Scott chuckled. "Yeah, it is." He smacked my shoulder and turned to my companions. "Hey, Olivia. Hi, Caleb."

"How's it going, dude?" Caleb asked with a grin.

"Hey, Scotty," Olivia said. "I'm glad to see that you're on your feet again."

"Me too." Scott stepped to his left and held an arm out to the side. "Come on in, you guys."

He led us down an entrance hallway to a large room lit by wall sconces and standing lamps. A rectangular pool of mirror-calm water sat at the centre of the room's marble floor, beneath an opening in the ceiling through which starlight shone and the night air blew. Stone benches ringed the pool, with large sofas set farther back. Beyond this inner square, fluted pillars, thick as telephone poles, held up the ceiling. Between them, vases and statues could be seen, resting on pedestals by frescoed outer walls next to doorways leading to other rooms.

"Are they back yet?" Olivia asked.

"Huh?" Scott flopped onto one of the sofas. "Wilhelm and Aceso? No, not yet." He grabbed a pillow. "They've been gone for days." He placed the red cushion against an armrest and laid his head upon it. "Sorry, I'm still waking up. I was in bed when you knocked. I can't seem to get enough sleep lately."

Olivia sat beside him. "That'll be the effects of the healing process." She reached out and placed a hand on his forehead. "Your temperature is good. How're your wounds?"

"Good," he said. "It hardly even hurts anymore."

"Let's see."

Scott sat straight and pulled up his shirt. Three round circles of deep pink trailed across his abdomen, the last of which lay just above his left hip. Aside from the difference in colour, the skin where bullets had torn into his body looked undamaged, as if he'd never been shot.

"I don't think they'll even leave a scar," Scott said, poking one of the circles with a fingertip. "If you can believe it."

Olivia chuckled. "Oh, I think I can." She made a downward motion with her hand, and he dropped his shirt. "You should still rest a few more days, though, before doing anything too strenuous, until your strength fully returns. Despite appearances, your wounds are still healing. Internal organs take longer than skin."

He nodded. "Aceso said the same thing before she left." Scott pointed a thumb over his shoulder. "I've spent most of the past few days drinking Ambrola or asleep in my room or sitting in the courtyard out back."

"It's called a peristylium." She shrugged. "I suppose court-yard works too."

"Whatever you call it, it's nice out there, when it's not raining. Cool plants and birds. I'm getting a bit stir-crazy now that I can keep my eyes open for more than an hour, though." He looked at me. "No computers. Not even a TV. I guess you'd need some pretty big rabbit ears to get a signal out here, but not even a VCR?"

I lay on a nearby sofa and put my hands behind my head. "I hear you, dude," I said, thinking of my ice cave home. "My place is cozy too, but . . ."

"Your place?"

I smiled and told him about my island, Smaragnisos, the Allfrost chamber, and its guardian AI, Hue.

He shook his head slowly. "O brave new world that has such people in it."

"'Tis new to thee," Olivia said with a smile.

Scott's eyebrows rose. "You know Shakespeare?"

"Of course," she replied. "*The Tempest* is one of my favour-ites." She glanced toward the front of the house. "Sorry, guys. I've got to cut this short."

Scott squinted. "Something up?"

"I'll let Shivurr fill you in," Olivia said, getting to her feet.

Caleb stood as well. "Is your head okay?"

She smiled and turned her back to us. "All better." She ran a hand through her reddish-brown tresses from the nape of her neck to the top of her head. "See?"

I touched fingers to where the bump should be but found only smooth, even skin. I leaned in, pushing her hair aside. *No sign of blood, either.*

"Looks good," I said. "You're a fast healer." *Almost as fast as me.*

"I'm glad you're okay," Caleb added, watching her as she made for the front hall. "Do you want me to come with you?"

"No." Olivia waved him down. "Stay." She took a few steps, stopped, and turned. "In fact, don't leave the house until I get back." Her hair whipped the air as she spun away. "You three catch up. I'll be back as soon as I can."

Chapter 9

Catching Up

The front door clicked shut, and I looked at Scott, popping an eye. "She calls you Scotty?" I'd never known anyone at the Institute to call him by anything other than his proper name.

He nodded. "Yeah, I kind of like it. It makes me think of *Star Trek*."

"That makes sense," I said. "You're sort of an engineer."

"Nah, the only things I engineer are computer software and hardware . . . and networks." Scott held up a finger. "But I do have the accent." He cleared his throat. "We cannae do it, Cap'n. We haven't got the power."

Caleb and I glanced at each other, lips quivering.

Finally, Caleb chuckled. "Is that supposed to be Scottish, dude?"

"Wasn't it Irish?" I said, straight-faced.

Scott's face reddened, and he fixed me with a stare. "Laugh it up, snowball."

I chortled. "How long have you been waiting to use that one?"

"Too long, man," Scott said with a smile. "Too long."

Caleb slapped my shoulder. "Nice burn."

Scott sighed. "Yeah, Emmett wasn't crazy about my German accent either." His eyes slid right for a moment, then he sat taller and flapped a hand at us. "Ah, what do you guys know?" He grinned a moment later and leaned toward me, reaching up to adjust his eyeglasses as they slid down his nose. "Anyway, what else has been going on? Why did Olivia have to leave?"

For the next half hour, we blew Scott's mind, bringing him up to speed on everything that had occurred since we'd last seen him, concluding with our journey here to Caelumburg from the Schmidts' seaside villa.

"Far out, man." Scott touched his fingertips to his temples, then threw his hands outward, making a *phoom* sound.

"Really?" I asked. "You must have seen some crazy stuff while you've been here. I didn't see much of the town on the way through, but what I saw looked pretty cool."

Scott pursed his lips, shaking his head slowly. "Nah, not really." He looked around. "I've been here, stuck in the house, mostly. Like I said, I've been too tired to do much else, until today."

My brow creased. "So, what, you've just been sleeping all this time?"

Scott shrugged. "Reading a bit when I've been awake long enough." He looked to his right. "There's a decent library. Lots of big old tomes, but I found a couple of things from this century."

"What about your wounds?" I looked down at Scott's midsection. "I still can't believe how fast you've healed."

"You could've died, dude," Caleb said. "You looked brutal last time we saw you. White as a ghost."

Scott smirked. "I'll have to take your word for it, Caleb. I don't remember much since Wilhelm's place. After that, it's all pretty vague. At least until I woke up floating in a pool of water, cradled in Aceso's arms."

"I'm really glad you're okay," I said. "If you'd died because of me . . ."

"Don't sweat it, man," he said, waving a hand. "It's over."

I shook my head. "You should've stayed in the basement."

"Yeah, maybe." Scott studied the ceiling. "When I recovered after the flash-bang, you were gone. I heard those soldiers, though . . . or whatever they were . . . I went up to look—to see if I could help—but you weren't there either. Next thing I know, I'm lying on the ground." He looked at me. "Look, I know it was stupid, but I don't have a lot of friends, Shivurr. I like it that

way, but the friends I have . . . well, they were kidnapping you
. . . I wasn't going to let them take you. Not without a fight."

"Even if they killed you?"

"I'd do it again." He chuckled. "Well, hopefully I'd do it
smarter next time—if there's a next time—but you know what
I mean. You'd do the same, right?"

I nodded and met his eyes. "You know it."

"Thanks, Cool Hand." Scott smacked my shoulder. "Friends
watch each other's backs."

Caleb's eyes widened. "Cool Hand?"

"My BBS handle," I replied. "You know, on Wilhelm's computer bulletin board system."

"Oh, yeah," Caleb said. "I forgot about that. It sounds kind
of dull, though." The teen turned to Scott. "Why don't you have
a lot of friends? You're a good dude."

"Thanks," Scott said with a smile. "I've got some. Wilhelm,
Olivia, one or two others, but not like I used to. When you grow
older, people grow apart. They get busy with careers, family,
worrying about shit. Others move away. Before you know it, almost everyone's gone, or you are. Sure, you see them now and
again, and you think well of them—when you do—but it's not
the same as when you're young. After a while, you start to wonder if you were ever really friends at all. I guess some people
look at friends like clothes or the car they drive. Something you
need, you might even like a lot, but ultimately replaceable."

The corners of Caleb's mouth drooped. "Bummer."

"Sorry, kid. I'm not trying to bum you out. I'm just explain-
ing why I ran up the stairs and ended up here. Don't worry. If
you're lucky, you'll have a few true friends in your life."

"Like Alan," I said.

Caleb tilted his head to study the floor. "Yeah, for sure."

"So, what's Aceso like?" I asked. "You said you woke up in
her arms."

Caleb sat straighter. "Is she hot?"

I laughed. "Caleb's thinking about Cleo again."

"Never stopped." The teen's eyes widened. "She was
awesome."

"Aceso's a striking woman," Scott said. "She looks to be in her early sixties, I think."

"Sixties? Wow, that's old," Caleb said. "That's weird. For gods, I mean. They're supposed to be immortal, right?"

Scott shrugged. "I don't know. The few others I've seen seem to vary in age. Beats me why." He clapped me on the shoulder. "They're aliens, Shivurr. I always knew they were real. It's pretty cool, you know? To have it confirmed. I mean, they're not quite little green men, but still . . ."

"You were right, dude," I said with a smile, knowing of his interest in aliens from outer space. An interest that had motivated him to apply for employment at the Bodhi Institute and to risk seeking me out in a restricted lower level of the covert facility.

He gave me a look and held out a hand. "Hey, you're not chilly. At least not as much as usual. You all right?"

I wrinkled my lips, lifting my shoulders. "Yeah, I feel great."

"Hmm . . . normally sitting this close to you, I'd be looking for a sweater by now."

I looked down at myself, peering into the Underfrost. Usually, the cold of my body radiated outward, visible—to my eyes—as a deep glow of vibrant blue hues. This nimbus of cold tapered off the farther it got from me, eventually blending with the ambient colours of the Underfrost as a whole. Now it ended abruptly, just inches from my outer layer of ice and snow, as if encased in a barrier of some sort.

Items of clothing like the winter jacket that I wore had a similar effect, preventing the cold within me from radiating quite as far, but no fabric stopped it this well or as abruptly. I opened my jacket, and the cold stayed contained, even to the open front. With a thought, the border of the nimbus expanded, then gave way, sending a wave of cold outward.

Scott reared back. "Shit, man." He hugged his arms to his chest. "There's the Shivurr I know."

"Close your jacket, dude," Caleb said with chattering teeth.

I kept my jacket open and imagined the barrier reappearing. A moment later, it did. "Neat, huh? I can control it." Even better, doing so seemed to insulate me from the surrounding warmth. I still felt it, but less so than usual.

Scott bobbed his head. "Cool. It looks like you're remembering more than just Olivia. Do you want to take another vial?"

"Nah," I said. "I should wait for Olivia to get back. I don't want to get messed up. She might need me."

Scott yawned. "It didn't sound like it hit you all that hard at the beach house."

"Yeah," I replied, "but I seem to react differently each time."

"Fair point." He glanced to his right. "You guys must be hungry. Do you want something to eat?"

"I'm starving," Caleb said. "I don't suppose there's pizza, is there?"

"Uh, there might be." Scott stood. "Come on. I'll show you the kitchen. You're not going to believe it."

We followed him deeper into the house, passing through a doorway at the right side of the atrium and entering a long hallway.

"Uh, lights, please," Scott said, flicking his eyes to the ceiling. Bronze braziers flared to life in answer, guiding our way. At the far side, we passed through an open doorway and stepped out into a columned passage that encircled an expansive courtyard.

The peristylium, I thought, remembering Olivia's name for it.

Lit by the stars overhead and the light spilling out from the hallway behind us, and torches set along the encircling wall, it looked like something out of a painting. A rectangular pond sat at the centre, surrounded by a garden of flowers, shrubs, and trees, dotted with benches, fountains, and sculptures.

Scott led us to the right, along the passageway ringing the garden, past wall art depicting fantastical landscapes and creatures.

We soon entered another room, the walls of which were painted stone. A thirty-foot-long rectangular wooden table sat near the middle, surrounded by ornate wooden chairs with plush padded seats.

He took us toward a collection of appliances at the far end. Two fridges and a stove with range hood, oven, and microwave sat next to each other, nestled among cupboards and drawers that presumably contained kitchen utensils.

A few vending machines stood against the wall to the left. One looked like a drink machine you'd find at any gas station stateside, but the logos and names on the buttons were different. *Huh . . . different flavours of Ambrola.*

I tugged a fridge door wide, enjoying the feel of escaping coolness on my face. Milk, bottles of Coke, jugs of juice, fruits, vegetables, various condiments, and a variety of other food lay within.

"Grab what you want," Scott said. "Aceso told me to help myself."

Caleb ran a hand over the stove. "Is there a chef around here? I don't cook."

"Me neither," Scott said. "Well, except for mac and cheese, maybe an egg or something. Don't worry, though. We shouldn't have to." He motioned us toward a stainless-steel fridge with three doors, each two feet high. He pulled open the middle door, revealing an empty compartment. "Check this out."

"Uh, it's empty, dude." Caleb held out a hand. "It's not even cold. What kind of fridge is this?"

"Ah," Scott said, eyes popping wide, "but it's not a fridge."

"Then what is it?" I asked.

He held up a finger and shot a look at a nearby table. Grabbing the paper pad and pen that rested on it, he looked at us. "What kind of pizza do you guys want? Is pepperoni cool?"

"How about Hawaiian?" Caleb asked.

Scott winced and stuck out his tongue. "Pineapple on pizza?" The teen nodded.

Scott sighed. "All right. We can get that too." He touched pen to paper and began to write. "You're a sick man, Caleb." Straightening, he strode to the still-open cabinet door. Placing the paper within, he shut the door, then banged on it three times. "Now we wait." Turning to face us, he gestured to the long table that sat nearby. "Take a load off."

"How long will it take?" I asked.

"I'm not sure," Scott replied. "Thirty minutes ought to do it."

"Oh, in that case"—Caleb stood—"mind if I grab a snack to tide me over?"

"Sure," Scott said. "As Aceso put it, take as much as you want, but eat whatever you take."

The teen pulled open the fridge door. "That's generous."

A memory sprang to mind. "It's the law of xenia."

"What's that?" Caleb asked.

I lifted my shoulders. "An ancient Greek custom of hospitality. The idea being that guests might be gods in disguise, so you should always treat them well."

"She's definitely done that," Scott said. "It's pretty far out, man. The fridges and cupboards are always stocked. Whatever you take out, the next day it's all back."

I squinted. "There must be somebody coming in and restocking it."

"Maybe." He looked around, then spoke in hushed tones. "It's good that we're up now. I've been thinking about staying awake to see what happens during the night."

"Why?"

"I don't know. Just curious, I guess." He leaned closer. "Besides, I could've sworn I heard movement outside my door during the night."

"Are you sure it's not Aceso?"

"Nah," he said. "She's away. If she'd come back, she'd have said hello."

I glanced at the cabinet where Scott had placed the note. "Well, maybe we can ask about it when the pizza gets here. It beats me how you can order one by putting a note in there, though."

Caleb bit into a deep red apple and took a seat. "Maybe it's tubes. You know, that send messages."

Scott blinked. "You mean pneumatic tubes?"

Caleb nodded, still chewing.

"That's a good thought," Scott replied, bobbing his head, "but I've seen those before. You place those messages into a bottle that goes into a tube, which gets sucked away. This is nothing like that."

Caleb swallowed. "Yeah, but it could be the same principle."

"Yeah, maybe," Scott said. "That could work for a piece of paper." He held up a finger. "But how does the food get here in one piece?"

I raised a snowy eyebrow. "Uh, a pizza guy shows up at the door, right? Just like in the movies."

Scott wagged his head. "No, man. The pizza shows up inside the box. Like magic."

"Are you serious?"

"Wait and see," Scott said with a shrug.

For the next while, we sat, watching for any sign, listening for any sound, that would signal the arrival of the two pizzas Scott had ordered. Finally, a thump came from within the stainless-steel container.

Scott sprang to his feet and crossed to the door. Tugging on the handle, he pulled it ajar and stepped to the side, revealing the interior. Two white cardboard pizza boxes sat within, stacked one atop the other. He slid them out, elbowed the door shut, and walked them over, preceded by the scent of melted cheese, pepperoni, garlic and other pleasant aromas.

With a wide smile, he placed them on the table. "Wait until you—" Three booming thuds sounded from the far side of the kitchen. "Now what?"

"It must be Olivia," I said.

He sighed. "I'll get it."

Chapter 10

Ring Bearer

As Scott made for the door, I tugged the topmost pizza box across the table and scanned the red lettering across the top. "Bleecker Street, Manhattan?"

"It's in New York City," Caleb said.

"Yeah, but how's that possible?" Something like Caleb's suggestion of pneumatic tubes had seemed plausible. I'd figured the pizzas might be made somewhere nearby, in some communal kitchen for the gods, then put on a conveyor belt and deposited through a door at the back of the cabinet, but Manhattan pizza boxes made no sense. *Maybe they've got a supply on hand*, I thought, not really believing it.

"Yeah, pretty weird, right?" He lifted the top and pulled out a slice. Puffing air across the cheese, he took a careful bite.

"How is it?" I asked.

"Still hot," he said, flashing bits of masticated crust and pineapple with each word. "It's good, though."

"I think I'll let it cool a bit first." I got up, wandered over to the fridge, and grabbed a cold drink from inside. "Save some for the rest of us, Slim," I said as I retook my seat.

He laughed. "I don't think Scott's going to want any of this one."

The sound of footfalls drew my eyes to the door.

"Hey," I said as Olivia entered with Scott in tow.

"Hey, guys." Olivia sat across from me and snatched a slice from the table. "Mm, pepperoni." She took a small bite, chewed, and swallowed. "Oh, that's good. I'm starving." Taking a larger bite, she moaned.

"So, how'd it go?" I asked.

She held up a finger as her cheeks bulged and writhed.

I grinned. "Take your time."

Scott reached into the box of pepperoni. "We should've ordered two of these. That pineapple's going to go to waste."

Caleb wagged his head. "No worries, dude. I can finish it."

Scott glanced at me. "He's not going to be Slim much longer. The kid eats pizza like Pac-Man eats pellets."

"I can't stay long," Olivia said.

"Why not?" I asked.

She looked at me. "I'm joining the hunt for the fugitives."

"The trolls?"

She nodded. "Before doing so, I wanted to be sure you three were all set here. I may be gone awhile."

"Is there somewhere we can sleep?" Caleb asked.

She jabbed a thumb at the door. "There are guest rooms off the atrium. Take whichever one you want."

Scott nudged me. "I'll show you."

My eyebrows rose. "Any of them?"

"Uh-huh," she said. "As long as they're unlocked, it'll be fine."

I cocked an eye. "Aceso isn't using one?"

She shook her head. "Her bedroom is on the other side of the house."

I frowned. "Sure you don't want me to come with you?"

"Thanks, but we've got it covered." Her eyes flicked to Caleb and Scott. "Besides, I'm sure Aceso will appreciate you three house-sitting for her, especially with fugitives on the loose."

"Do you think we're in danger here?" I asked.

"I can't say for sure, but I doubt it. They'll be trying to get as far away from here as they can." She lifted another slice to her mouth but lowered it without taking a bite. "Oh, I almost forgot." She pointed a finger at a waist-high stone cylinder near the wall. "You can toss the empties in your hat in there." Her eyes flitted to the pizza boxes. "Actually, put all the garbage in there."

"For recycling?"

Olivia nodded. "They'll be broken down to base elements and the raw material reused."

"For what?" I asked.

She tossed her shoulders. "For whatever we need." Her hands dropped beneath the table, and she looked down.

I craned my neck. "What are you looking for?"

"These." Extending an arm, she opened her hand. Two circles, one gold, the other silver, tinkled against the tabletop, spun a moment, and fell onto their sides.

"Rings?" I snatched up the silver one and examined it.

"Uh-huh," Olivia said. "That one's yours. The other's for Caleb."

"Wow." I ran a finger over the gleaming silver band to its flat circular head, which held a large golden centre stone orbited by smaller gems of blue, red, and green, positioned along circles of black separated by silver. "It's beautiful."

"Cool." Caleb studied the golden ring with a dark centre stone a moment before putting it on.

"What about Scott?" I asked.

"No sweat, man." Scott held out a fist, flashing a ring like Caleb's. "I've got one already."

Olivia jabbed her chin toward me. "Try it on."

"Okay." Slipping it on, I studied the back side of my hand. "Wicked."

She smiled. "It looks good on you."

"It fits well," I said. "How did you know my ring size?"

"I'm a good guesser," she said, "and it'll resize itself as needed."

"How does that work?" Caleb asked.

"The material is adaptive, within reason."

"You're kidding?" I straightened my arm and rotated my wrist. "Thank you. You're the best." Gleams of light sparkled off the ring's stones. "It looks super valuable, though. Maybe I should just keep it in my hat."

"Oh, don't do that," she said. "It won't be detectable in there. When something's in your hat, it's no longer present."

I dipped my chin. "Where is it, then?"

"Didn't Wilhelm tell you this already?"

"Yeah," I said, "but I'm not sure I followed it all. He said something about an inter . . . something . . . non-space."

She snorted. "Close, but I think he probably said interdimensional null space."

I swept a thumb against my middle finger with a clack and pointed at her. "That's it. Thank you. It's been driving me nuts. So, what's that, exactly?"

"Just think of it as a space between dimensions that isn't being used." She pointed a finger above my head. "The inside of your hat is a doorway to it, but the other side isn't here. It's infinitely not here, in fact. Just the entrance to it is here; that being your hat."

"I think I get it."

"Say, Olivia?"

"Yes, Caleb."

"I've been wondering," he said. "How come Shivurr's drinks don't spray all over the place after being in his hat?" He shook the open pop can in his hand up and down. "If you shake up an unopened can of soda, then open it, it sprays all over the place. We used to do it to each other as kids. It was hilarious."

"Good question," she said. "Just like the other side isn't here, it also doesn't move with the hat. It's stationary—only the door moves. Get it?"

"That sounds like a bag of holding," Scott said. "You know, from Dungeons and Dragons."

"Yeah?" She gazed down her nose at him, nodding. "Maybe that's where Wilhelm got the idea. He does love playing that game. However, our use of interdimensional null spaces has been around far longer. Well before even I was born."

Scott snorted. "Yeah, D&D's great, but why would a god be interested in playing games?"

"Why not?" she said with a shrug. "When you've got an eternity ahead of you, you look for amusement wherever you can." She looked back to me. "Anyway, getting back to your hat, what all that means is that when something is in your hat, it can't be detected. And that ring needs to be detectable or it serves no purpose since it identifies you to the people and systems of New Olympus. Without it, our guardians and other systems may perceive you as an intruder, and you don't want that."

"Oh," I said, "so, it's like an identity badge and key card all in one, like they use at the Institute."

"Exactly," Olivia said. "It'll give you access to most systems and allow you to move around Caelumburg freely."

Scott sat straighter. "Does that include computer systems?"

"Yes," she replied. "Though you don't often need a keyboard to tell ours what to do."

"Then," he said, "how do we issue commands?"

"Oh, that's easy," she said. "Just ask for what you want. Our systems are mostly declarative."

I furrowed my brow. "Meaning what?"

"I think she means," Scott said, "you state your desires, but you don't need to know, or care, how the system makes it happen." He looked at Olivia. "And all we need is one of these rings?" She nodded. "That seems kind of insecure."

"Shivurr asked the same thing on the way here," she replied with a grin. "Just because you're authenticated doesn't mean you're authorized, and some things require additional authentication factors to verify identity. Our systems are quite secure."

Except for those that haven't been upgraded, I thought, recalling Olivia's words on the drive to Caelumtor.

"Okay," Scott said with a nod. "Then everything requires a ring?"

"Not always." Olivia pursed her lips. "In other cases, biometrics are sufficient to establish identity. Unfortunately, sometimes authentication is built into the command, which means knowing the command is enough, but that's mostly the case with leftover older tech." She waved a hand toward Caleb and me. "Like I told the guys, that's not as secure, so we've been retrofitting our systems to close those gaps. Anyway, keep it on your hand. It's important, and don't worry, the rings are designed to stay put."

Yikes. I gripped the band between thumb and forefinger. "You mean I won't be able to get it off?"

"No, no," she said, raising a hand, "it'll come off if you pull hard enough. It just won't fall off without a deliberate and sustained effort on your part. It's a good thing. It means you're not likely to lose it."

"Radical," Caleb said. "So we can walk around town, and nothing will bother us?"

"You got it." She held up a finger. "Now, I was rushed and didn't know what you might need, so I gave you full access, but don't go wandering around town until I get back, okay? Shivurr doesn't remember being here before and you've never been here, Caleb. Even with these rings, you could still get into trouble." She stood, grabbing a third slice of pizza, which she stacked atop her as-yet-uneaten second slice. "All right. Now I've really got to go. I'll be back as soon as I can."

"What about Aceso and Wilhelm?" I asked as she walked away.

She turned and looked back. "They're still off, somewhere."

I squinted. "What do we tell them if they come back before you do?"

She put a hand against the door frame and turned back to us. "Just tell them what you know. With any luck, I'll return before they do anyway." With the wave of a hand, she left.

Left to our own devices, we continued to hang out, eating and drinking, chatting and laughing until Scott's head and eyelids drooped.

He twitched, banging his hands against the table's edge. "Whoa." His chair rumbled back across the floor as he regained his feet. "Sorry, guys." He rubbed his eyes. "I'm wiped. Come on. I'll show you the spare rooms."

Chapter 11

Nightmare Scenario

Wall sconces flared to life as I entered the bedroom next to Scott's, revealing high ceilings, a comfortable and spacious bed, a standing wardrobe, and a dresser. An intricately woven carpet covered most of the floor. It didn't quite reach the blue-and-white-painted walls, leaving a two-foot-wide border of marble floor showing along the edges.

Shutting the door, I lay on the bed and stared at the torchlight and shadows flickering across the ceiling. Rolling to my side, I scanned the walls for a switch or other mechanism to douse the lights. Unable to see anything like that, I shrugged and shut my eyes and tried to ignore the glare. To my relief, they went out on their own a short while later. I lay in darkness awhile, feeling dozy, listening to the surging wind and distant thunder, faint but audible even through the domus's walls and ceiling.

It had been quite a day.

A good one, I thought. The troll attack aside, I'd spent it surfing and sightseeing, had restored more of my memory, and had re-united with Scott, who appeared nearly recovered from his wounds. With more vials in my hat, I had reason to hope that I'd continue to recover more memories and abilities, in time. *Things are looking up.*

A metallic squeak, muffled by my closed door, came from the atrium.

I raised myself to an elbow as footsteps drew nearer.

"Too much pop, Caleb?" I asked with a raised voice.

A grumbling reply came from the far side.

"Scott? Hey, man." The footsteps receded. "I thought you were Caleb." I held still, waiting for a reply. "Hello?"

None came.

He must be half asleep. My eyes fluttered and closed. *I know the feeling.* I folded my pillow in two, tucked it beneath a cheek, and let sleep take me.

I woke in near darkness. Groggy, I looked around, scrunching my eyes at the thin ribbon of light blazing from the room's far side. As my eyes adjusted, I realized that it came from the atrium, entering through the thin gap between the door and threshold.

I rubbed my eyes and sat up. Propping pillows under my back, I looked around. A layer of frost covered the bed, floor and walls around me. I held out a hand, palm upward, catching a snowflake drifting down from the ceiling. A dozen others glittered in the twilight as they too fell.

I'd been dreaming again, I realized. If you could call it that. Technically, it was more of a nightmare, and one that I'd had before, at the Institute. Before I'd left in search of answers. As always, the details were vague. All I knew was that it involved a coming apocalypse of some kind. One that involved the Allfrost and that threatened the world.

Though I'd recovered many of the tissue samples taken from me by the Bodhi Group and had reintegrated a number of them, I still didn't have the answers I most needed. I clenched my hand, crushing the snowflake into my flesh. Whatever it was, I couldn't stop it without knowing more about the threat.

I didn't even have a timeline for when it might occur, just a vague notion.

I pulled my hat from my head and looked within. More than half of the vials remained safe in my hat. They tended to be overwhelming, and at the urging of my friends and, truth be told, my own inclination, I'd avoided downing them all at once. I had no way to know what taking too many at once might do; they might knock me out for a while or drive me insane or even kill me.

As if that wasn't enough, Harland had said the removal of my memories had started because I'd asked the Group to help me forget something. Ever since then, I'd been worried that it was something awful. If I'd been willing to let them operate on me to forget it, it must have been pretty terrible, so I wasn't sure restoring that particular memory would be a good thing. That is, unless it was related to the apocalypse itself, which seemed unlikely.

Nonetheless, I took the return of the nightmares as a sign that I needed to accelerate my memory restoration. Countless lives depended on it, I felt sure. I'd meant to wait for Olivia to return, wanting her reassuring presence and support, but I felt that I could wait no longer. Safe in Aceso's domus in the middle of the night, with nothing pressing to do, it seemed as good a time as any to resume my recovery.

Pulling in a breath, I reached inside. My hand passed through the fabric of the crown unhindered, entering the void beyond. I smiled as a chill enveloped my arm, massaging my flesh with its icy touch. I rummaged inside, grasping and releasing several inch-high flat discs of soft metal. *Crushed soda cans.* Then my fingers wrapped around a bottle that had the smooth surface, shape and size of a sample vial. *Yes!* Pulling it out, I grimaced. *Empty.* I placed the used vial onto the bed, next to me. The next two I pulled free were also drained. *Olivia's right*, I thought. *I've got to get rid of some of this garbage.*

Aha. I pulled free another bottle, this one full.

I held aloft the vial of thick glass, swirling and iridescent in the gloom, and studied the contents. As with the others, a white sticker with black writing labelled the contents according to whatever classification scheme or schemes the Bodhi Group scientists had developed in their study of me.

I didn't bother to read this one, and I hadn't read the others. It wasn't like the Group knew what memories were contained in them any more than I did. Still, knowing that didn't stop me from wishing for a label that read, "Pending Catastrophes."

I shrugged, pulled the stopper, and gave the mouth of the bottle a sniff. Without anything to guide me, drinking them in random order was as good an option as any.

Here goes. Tilting my head back, I upended the vial and poured it all in.

The substance inside tended to stick to itself—Institute scientists referred to it as having high cohesion—so not a drop remained in the vial.

I chewed a bit, swallowed, and smacked my lips together. It didn't taste like much—maybe because it was a part of me. Plugging the stopper back into the mouth of the bottle, I returned the vial and other empties to my hat and snugged it back into place. Then I lay back and waited.

A coolness washed through my body, and my outer layer of ice and snow crackled as it hardened, tinkling faintly, the sound like distant bells. A surge of nausea sent my hand to my mouth, and my cheeks bulged.

Not on Aceso's bed, I thought, clapping another hand over the first. I hadn't even met Aceso yet—that I could remember at least—and I didn't want to introduce myself by doing the liquid laugh all over her bedsheets. I blew out a breath as the wave of nausea passed. *Hold on. We have met.* I knew it in an instant as a memory surfaced, no doubt triggered by thinking about her. It was decades ago, here in Caelumburg.

Scott had said she was in her sixties, but I remembered a much younger woman. What we were doing at the time, I didn't know, however. Like so many other memories, especially those that had survived the Group's experiments, it lacked context. All I knew was that we stood at the foot of an immense pyramidal building, located, if it still existed, fairly close to where I now sat.

The Miraculeum, I realized. I knew it to be one of the most important buildings in all of Caelumburg, but I couldn't yet remember why. Rubbing circles against my temples with icy fingertips, I tried to remember more about it, and other names for it surfaced. *Crucible of Life. The Maker.* Details beyond that refused to come.

When Olivia returned, I'd ask her for the tour she had promised me when I'd sat in the Dublin Gulch cave in Death Valley. Once she started to explain it, it would probably all come back. Until then, it would be like having someone's name on the tip of your tongue: frustrating and seemingly locked deeper away the more you tried to force it.

I shook my head. *It doesn't matter right now.* The danger for which I'd sought the Bodhi Group's help was my immediate concern. I thought about the Allfrost, the Bodhi Institute and its leadership, Security Director Harland Dixon and Executive Director Jeffrey Wallace, but nothing sprang to mind.

I leaped from the bed and began to pace. *Wait.*

When I'd encountered Harland in the desert, he'd said something. Something about global warming. "If you could, you'd compel us to help you with your global warming catastrophe," Harland had said. "We certainly aren't going to help you bring about a new ice age."

It made sense that the danger might be global warming. For a snow-based life form like me, nothing could be more catastrophic than a warming planet, and bringing about an ice age made sense too. *That would sure stop global warming.* It also explained the Allfrost's involvement.

According to Hue, one of the artificially intelligent holograms responsible for maintaining and managing the Allfrost, the creation of periodic ice ages was central to the machine's purpose. By Hue's reckoning, the industries of humankind either had weakened the machine or were overwhelming its ability to do what it had been designed to do.

In which case, perhaps the Faction lay behind it all. Just days ago, Olivia had told me of the Faction's habit of tracking down Allfrost chambers and leaving creatures behind. It wasn't a big leap to think that they had also been taking out Allfrost Sentinels, maybe even all Borealans. They had to know that without Allfrost Sentinels like me around to defend and repair it, the Allfrost's decline would go unchecked. They'd done a good job, too. According to Hue, he had not seen another like me in a few hundred years.

But why bother?

I thought I knew. According to Olivia, the Faction were renegade gods that longed for the old days. Days when they had lorded over humanity; days when they had been worshipped; days long past. Humanity didn't need gods anymore. They had advanced far and in a short time. Someday, they might even have technology to rival that of the beings they'd once worshipped. Given that, knocking humanity back to the Stone Age through global warming would be a good first step in restoring the old ways for which they longed. It might take a while by mortal standards, but immortals had all the time in the world. To the latter, fifty to a hundred years would mean little to nothing.

There's got to be more to it, though. The catastrophe that plagued my dreams felt more imminent, promising an abrupt and massive death toll. So while global warming played a part in the Faction's plans, it wasn't the end goal, I felt sure.

The room spun, and I sat on the bed, closing my eyes. Slapping a hand to my lips, I willed away resurgent nausea as my body continued to metabolize the potion and reintegrate memories. I lay flat, tilting my cap over my face, and the sensation slowly passed.

As I continued to lie there, my mind wandered back to the attack on the Bodhi Institute from which my friends and I had barely escaped alive. How did the fire elementals factor in, and what did their fire demon leader want? Were they there just to destroy a Bodhi Group stronghold or to get something?

Wait, was it to get me? I sat up, pushing my hat from my eyes. No. I lay back. *They were heading there before I arrived.*

I had seen that much through the Oculus in the Allfrost chamber on Smaragnisos.

I sighed.

Without more information, I could only speculate. I knew from the vials that I'd previously taken that more memories should resurface gradually over the next few days. Reintegrating them simply took time, and I had to be patient.

I closed my eyes and tried to sleep again. I'd remember eventually. *I just hope it's not too late when I finally do.*

Chapter 12

Thief in the Night

I woke with a twitch sometime later. A figure loomed over me, jostling my shoulder with a hand that felt warm even through my winter jacket. I blinked, struggling to recognize the bespectacled face before me and where I was. As the last vestiges of the dream I'd been having faded, it all came back in a rush.

"Shivurr," Scott whispered. "It's me." He held a finger to his lips.

"What's up?" I sat up, holding my head with a hand.

Blurry images of my friend overlapped in my vision. *It must be a delayed reaction to the vial*, I thought. My head ached, and the answers that I sought still weren't jumping out at me.

I blinked several more times, rubbed my eyes, then looked at Scott again. To my relief, only one of him looked back at me. "Is something wrong?"

"Someone's in the house," he said. "I heard something."

I kept my eyes narrowed. The torches were lit once again, presumably having activated when Scott entered. Hopping out of bed, I crossed to the door and looked out. The hole in the ceiling looked dull blue rather than black. *Not sunrise yet, but close.* "Caleb's probably just getting a snack or something. Did you check his room?"

Scott shook his head. "Not yet, but I don't think it was him."

"Why not?"

"Lots of things. Whoever it was is thicker in the shoulders, and he didn't move the same."

"Move the same?"

"You know." He took a few steps, moving his head and arms

awkwardly. "The kid kind of bobs his head and flounces his arms."

I chuckled. "Oh, yeah. I suppose he does." I swept a hand by my head. "Let's check his room anyway."

"All right," he said, padding after me.

"Could it have been Aceso?" I asked as he drew alongside me.

"No," he said. "This was a dude, and he didn't activate the hall lights. I called out too, but he didn't answer. Aceso would've. And he didn't move like her either."

"What about Olivia?"

His lips pursed. "No chance, man. This was definitely a guy. Anyway, if it was her, she'd have woken us."

"Yeah, probably."

I rapped on Caleb's door. "Slim, you there?" No one answered for a few seconds. I tried the doorknob and flung open the door. "Wake up, dude."

His bed lay empty with the covers tossed to the side.

"See? He's out of bed. It must have been him."

Scott looked doubtful. "Maybe. Like I said, this guy didn't move like the kid, though."

"Maybe he's sleepwalking or looking for a restroom. That'd make him move strangely."

He squinted. "Why would he leave his room, then? There's one in there."

My brow creased. "There is?"

"Yeah," he said. "All the bedrooms have one. I think."

"Even yours?" I asked, thinking of the footsteps I'd heard shuffle by my room earlier in the night.

"Of course," he said. "Once I felt well enough, I checked them all out."

I raised an eyebrow. "Looking for a nicer one?"

"You know it," he replied with a lopsided grin.

"And was there?"

He shrugged. "Nope. At least not any that weren't locked."

"Huh, okay." I stroked my chin. "Were you out of your room tonight? Shortly after we all went to bed?"

"No," he said. "I crashed right away, and I was out." He

touched his abdomen. "Until my stomach started hurting."

Then who was it? The grumbling reply to my call sure hadn't sounded like Caleb. Like Scott said, the voice, even incoherent as it was, just didn't match.

"All right." I sighed. "Let's find him." I waved a finger in a circle. "Once we do, we can check the rest of the house, just to be sure."

"Works for me. Let's check the kitchen first." He smirked. "Knowing the kid, he's stuffing his face."

Scott's guess seemed a good one, but the kitchen sat dark and empty. Turning on the lights, we checked for signs of recent habitation but found none.

"Okay." I scratched my head. "Is there another bathroom he might have used?"

Scott frowned. "I told you, there's one in his bedroom."

"I know," I said, "but maybe he didn't know it was there. I didn't."

Scott nodded. "Good point. There's—"

A patter of footsteps came from the courtyard. Whirling, I raised a hand that smouldered with nascent frost as a figure appeared in the doorway.

"Dude, it's me," Caleb whispered, waving me down with a hand.

I blew out a breath, dropping my arm. "Where were you?"

He put a finger to his lips. "Someone's here, dude."

My eyes flicked to Scott before returning to the teen. "Are you sure?"

Caleb jabbed a thumb over his shoulder. "In the garden."

Okay, this is getting serious.

"Told you, Shivurr," Scott said from behind me.

"All right." I flapped a hand toward the door. "Show me."

Caleb bobbed his head. "Follow me."

He led us along the columned passageway that bordered the peristylium to the back of the house. Stopping at the corner, he pointed to broad double doors that sat near the wall's middle.

"Let's go." Crossing to the portal, I leaned into it. It jiggled but refused to open. *Locked.* The wood vibrated and shook as I tried again, leaning harder this time.

"If he's in there, he must have heard that," Scott said.

I glanced at him over my shoulder and shrugged. "Hello?" I said, rapping on the door. "Is someone in there? Aceso? Olivia?" After a moment with no answer, I turned to my friends, who now stood several feet away, regarding me with wide eyes.

Scott thrust his arms toward me. "Let's break it down."

I grimaced and shook my head. "No one's breaking anything. We're guests here." I snapped my fingers. "Come to think of it, maybe this guy is too."

Caleb studied the door. "Maybe, but I don't think I can sleep again, not without knowing for sure."

Scott retreated into the courtyard, motioning for us to join him.

"What's up?" I asked, moving closer to him.

"One of us can keep watch," he said in a low voice. "We can alternate shifts."

"I don't know," I replied, keeping my voice low as well. "What if this guy's dangerous?"

He pointed to a bench a few feet away. "We can watch from a distance. If the door opens, whoever is on watch can run and warn the others. That way we won't be taken by surprise at least. Besides, we don't know that this intruder, or guest, wants to hurt us. He's ignored us so far, right?"

I nodded. "Yeah, true." *And if he's a thief, I can follow him.* My hands glowed. "And just to be sure, I've got an idea on how to slow him down."

Moving toward the doors, I wondered a moment whether this could be one of the escapees that Olivia had mentioned, but it didn't seem likely. Whoever this guy was, he couldn't be as large as the trolls we'd encountered. Scott and Caleb would've surely noticed if the intruder had been anywhere near that big.

Standing a few feet from the doors, I raised my hands and channelled frost and snow, sculpting it against the threshold with sweeps of my arms. The wood groaned and crystals of frost spread over its surface, and snow welled from the stones of the passageway. Sucking in a lungful of air, I stepped back to survey my work and nodded at the six-foot-high slope of ice-hardened snow that now blocked the way.

"Cool," Scott said, "but . . ."

"Yeah?"

He coughed and cleared his throat. "The doors open inward."

"Oh, that." I studied the doors a moment before waving a hand as if shooing a fly. "Don't sweat it. The snow's just as high on the other side."

He raised an eyebrow. "How can you be sure?"

"Trust me," I said, tapping a finger to my temple. "And I iced up the locking mechanism, too."

"Mechanism?" Scott said. "Big word, man."

I smiled. "I'm buddies with a computer guy. One acquires a certain level of erudition in such company, good sir."

"Oh, indeed, sir," Scott replied. "Quite so." He glanced at Caleb, then at me. "So, who takes first watch?"

"I'll do it," Caleb said.

"You sure, kid?" Scott rubbed his face. "I'm knackered—as the Brits like to say—but it doesn't seem right, leaving a kid to stand watch."

Caleb scowled. "I'm not a kid, dude. I'll be sixteen in a couple days."

"Sixteen?" Scott peered over the tops of his eyeglasses. "Well, we'll have to get you a cake, Grandpa." He grinned and shook his head. "I've got T-shirts older than you."

Caleb shrugged. "Sure, but you're old." He looked Scott up and down. "You've got to be in your thirties, right?"

Scott winced. "I changed my mind. Stay here."

I nudged Caleb's shoulder. "It's really your birthday in a few days?"

"Uh-huh."

"We should celebrate," I said. "We can get a cake from the kitchen. If that box makes pizza, why not cake?"

He nodded. "That'd be excellent, dude."

"Cool, and who knows? Olivia might even get you home before then, and you can celebrate with your family."

"I'm in no rush," he replied, shrugging. "I mean, it'd be nice to see the gang again, but hanging with you guys is pretty cool."

I rubbed my temples. "Thanks, Slim."

My head ached faintly, and I felt sleepier than normal too; usually I'd go days without sleep. *The vials must be wiping me out.*

I looked at the brightening sky overhead. "Come and get me in a few hours. Earlier if the snow melts too much before then. If it does, I'll come and redo it and take the next watch. By that time, hopefully Olivia will be back and we can get some answers."

"Sounds good," Caleb said, sitting on a stone bench and looking at the sealed doors. "Night, dudes."

"Don't fall asleep, Gramps," Scott said, patting Caleb on the shoulder. "All right?"

Caleb shook his head. "No chance of that, dude."

"You want a Coke or something, Slim?"

"How about an Ambrola?" he replied.

"Coming right up."

"I'll come with you," Scott said as we reached the kitchen door. "I could use an Ambrola for later."

"Sounds good." Entering the room, I looked at him over my shoulder. "Do you mind grabbing them? I've got something to do first."

"Sure, man."

While Scott grabbed the drinks, I made my way to the recycle bin, determined to rid myself of the accumulated garbage in my hat. As I sorted through my stash, he came and sat next to me. Leaning back against the kitchen table, he pointed to the soda cans, vials, and water bottles arrayed before me. "What are you doing?"

"Organizing my stuff." I turned and dropped an empty into the stone recycling container behind me. "Half of these are empty."

"It pays to be organized," he said, rubbing his eyes. "Man, I'm bushed."

"You should get some sleep," I said, reaching back into my hat. My fingers wrapped about a hard rectangular object. Recognizing it as the Walkman given to me by Olivia, I pushed it away and kept feeling around inside the void.

"Hey, cool." Scott lifted a plastic water bottle from the table. "You still have them."

"Of course," I said, grabbing another bottle just like it. "They saved my life." I tugged the nipple open and took a swig of water. "And I like the spout. It makes it easy to squeeze out a mouthful and not spill any."

"Yeah," he said, "they're for bicycling."

"Oh, really?"

"Yeah, they fit into a special holder, mostly for long trips." He put the bottle back down on the table. "I had to visit a few different sporting goods stores to get this many. I got some confused looks too. 'How many bikes do you got, son?' one guy asked."

"What did you tell him?"

"Nothing," Scott said. "It was none of his business."

Returning the plastic bottle to the table, I dug my hand into my hat up to my elbow, pulled out another vial and examined it. Seeing that it was full, I placed it next to its brethren.

Oh, shit. I'd better keep these cool, I thought, remembering that the contents of the vials would vanish if they got too warm for too long. I touched the tabletop and laid down a thick layer of frost. *That ought to—*

Pop cans and glass vials shook as the floor shimmied.

What the frost? Wobbling, I flung out my arms for balance as kitchen furnishings warped and wavered and changed colour all around us. *Is that vial still hitting me?*

Scott sprang to his feet and rushed toward me, eyes wide. "Earthquake!"

I grabbed him by the biceps as he bumped into me, and a vial next to me tipped over and rolled toward the table's edge. Snatching it from the air as it fell, I gazed around in wonder.

The air darkened, taking on shades of brown and blue, and the walls, appliances, and cabinets began to fade, becoming translucent. Beyond them, a treeless plain of sand rose toward a starry sky.

Scott grabbed my hand and pulled. "Get under the table."

Before I could react, the walls around us disappeared, replaced by a desert vista, illuminated by the stars of the night sky, this one much darker than the brightening sky we'd left behind in the peristylium.

I'd seen my share of deserts over the past week, but this wasn't one that I recognized. To my front, rolling dunes of sand stretched to the horizon, windswept and devoid of vegetation. I turned, sighting dark, rugged mountains in another direction and flat-topped cliffs behind me.

A shadowy figure, his back to me, scurried toward the kitchen door, both visible as a ghostly image overlaying the desert scene. He wore black boots and light brown pants and a long-sleeved shirt with black epaulettes on the shoulders. The light brown visorless cap on his head looked like a napkin folded into the shape of an inverted canoe.

"Hey," I shouted as the desert solidified and the walls, appliances, and most of the kitchen furnishings vanished. Only the long table, with my cans and bottles atop it, remained.

"What the hell just happened?" Scott asked, still grasping my hand like he was trying to crack walnuts.

"You see it too?" For a moment, I'd thought I was having some sort of psychotic episode or waking dream triggered by the vial I'd taken earlier. If Scott saw it too, it meant it was really happening.

"Yeah, I see it," he said, looking around. "Where are we?"

"I don't know." My eyes flicked skyward, catching sight of an oblong blob of light tracing a line through the sky. "Oh, crap."

Chapter 13

Unexpected Journey

The light came closer, rumbling like thunder, blinding in the night sky. Judging by the trajectory, the mini sun would pass over us, but my palms glowed with frost anyway.

We stood transfixed, watching until it touched down somewhere just over the top of a nearby dune. As it did, a cloud of sand flew into the air, and the ground shook, and my hands flew to my ears.

Moments later, a shock wave of sand and warm air punched against my face and chest, and I stumbled back, using a forearm to shield myself and grunting as the kitchen table pressed against my back.

"You all right, Scott?" I spit out sand. "You okay, man?"

"What the fuck?" Grabbing the table, he hauled himself to his feet, coughing. He lifted his shirt and swiped the cloth across his face. "Was that a missile strike?"

"A meteor, I think."

"Jesus," he said, lowering his shirt. "This is far out, man. How do you suppose we got here? Are we even on Earth anymore?"

"No idea, dude." I looked at the kitchen table. Cans and bottles lay on their sides on the tabletop, while others had been knocked into the sand on the far side. "Shit! The vials." I tore the hat from my head, snatched up the nearest bottle, and plunged it back inside.

"Oh, man." Scott leaned over the table, extending his long arms to grab the cans and bottles that teetered at the far edge. "Do you know how many you have?"

"Yeah, of the vials at least."

"Good," he said. "You'd better keep count. Make sure you get them all."

I scowled. "Damn it. I shouldn't have taken them out."

"You didn't know," Scott said. "How could you? We were safe, man."

I made no reply, too intent on getting my treasures back where they belonged. Once all those visible were safe again, I skirted the table's edge to recover any that had fallen off the other side.

"Want me to look too?" Scott asked.

"No," I said, sticking my palm out toward him. "You might step on one by accident. If that happens, I'd rather just have myself to blame."

I'm blaming myself already, so why not a bit more?

I spotted the first three easily enough, along with half a dozen cans of soda pop. With each one recovered, I felt the tightness between my snowy eyebrows loosen.

"I think we're on Earth, Shivurr."

"Huh, why's that?" I asked, my eyes still fixed on the ground. I smiled, spotting another vial, half buried in sand, and scuttled toward it.

"The constellations."

"Constellations?" I made a face. "How would you know?" I raised my head above the table's edge to regard him. "Did they teach astronomy in programming class?"

Scott sniffed. "Maybe not, but I can still recognize the Big Dipper." He pointed a finger skyward. "And the moon."

"Sorry, Scott." *Calm down, Shivurr,* I thought. *No sense snapping at him because you messed up.* I tilted my head to the side, glancing down. "I'm kind of freaking out over here."

"You think I'm not?" He took a deep breath and let it out. "No sweat, man. I guess we both are. I mean, how do we get back to Aceso's, or even civilization?" He looked around. "This isn't even a desert I recognize. It sure isn't Nevada."

"One thing at a time," I said, returning my attention to the sand.

Scott huffed and nodded. "Just hurry."

With a bob of my head, I resumed my search. I soon recovered two more soda cans, but the last two sample vials remained lost.

Come on. Lighting my palms, I swept them over the sand. *Nothing.* I stood taller again and scratched a temple. *Okay, I've got to be systematic.*

I walked back to the table's end, then began shuffling forward, making arcs in the sand with my feet.

"Uh, Shivurr?"

I felt something hard and smooth bump against the front of my foot. Leaning down, I brushed away sand and pulled forth another bottle. *Yes!*

"What's up?" I said at last.

"Something's coming this way."

I glanced at Scott, then followed the line of his arm to the horizon. A swarm of reddish-orange glows streaked down a sand dune a mile or more away.

My eyes bulged. "Oh, crap."

Scott regarded me over his shoulder. "What?"

"Elementals." I narrowed my eyes. "Lots of them."

His head spun back toward the dunes. After a pause, he clamped his hands to the sides of his head. "Holy shit." He looked around. "We've got to get out of here." Facing me, he pointed at something over my shoulder. "Let's run for those cliffs over there. Maybe there's someplace to hide."

"You go ahead." I kept sweeping the sand with my feet. "I've got to find the last vial first."

"Forget about it." Scott raised a knee onto the tabletop and climbed onto it. "We can come back for it after they've left."

"Just give me a sec." I couldn't leave until I'd found the last vial. Without it, I'd never regain all my memories, and I might not remember the catastrophe that had led to their loss.

He dangled a leg, then stepped lightly to the ground. "I'm helping you look." He crouched low and began sifting through the sand. "Have you searched here already?"

"Yeah," I said, glancing his way. "Forget about it and run for the cliffs. I'm faster than you. I'll catch up."

"No. I'm not leaving you."

"I appreciate it, but . . ." I trailed off as reddish-orange light flickered into view from behind a rocky outcropping at the bottom of the cliffside. "On second thought, maybe it's better you stay here after all."

"Why's that?"

I stuck out a hand. "Because they're coming from that direction too."

Pulling himself to his feet, he peered at the rock face. "Oh, man." He looked at me with wide eyes. "What do we do?"

"Get under the—" I broke off as the air rippled and the earth shook.

Scott grabbed my arm. "It's happening again, isn't it?"

"No!" I stooped low as the walls and appliances of Aceso's kitchen wavered into view. "I can't go back yet. I can't leave it behind."

The sand hardened beneath my hands, softened, then hardened again.

"I don't think we've got a choice, Shivurr."

Then the kitchen and all its contents solidified at last, and the desert sands were no more.

When the realization took hold, I hammered the floor of Aceso's kitchen with a fist. A film of frost formed on the stones, radiating outward from my position, growing with each blow. The vial was gone. An irreplaceable part of myself now lay lost in the sands of some unknown desert, seemingly beyond any hope of recovery.

I felt a tug on my shoulders. "Easy, Shivurr. Take a breath."

Nodding, I pushed myself to my feet.

"I can't believe it." I rubbed my fingertips against my temples. "It's gone."

We stood in silence for several moments, listening to the quiet disturbed only by the hum of appliances and drip of tap water into the sink.

"Hey," Scott said at last. "It's not all bad." The corners of his mouth twitched, then lifted toward his ears. "At least we're still alive, right?"

"Yeah." I heaved in a breath, then let it out in a rush. "That was pretty close."

"I figured we were goners for sure." He slapped my shoulder. "Well, at least me."

"Me too, most likely," I said.

"You think?"

"Sure."

"How do you even know you can die, Shivurr? I mean, given what Olivia and Hanale said, and you heal really fast."

I shrugged. "The same way you do, I suppose." I snorted. "How does either of us know until it happens?"

"Yeah, but I'm human. There are about a hundred billion precedents." He scratched his head and glanced around. "So, what the heck happened? How did we end up here? For that matter, how did we end up there?"

"Beats me." I sighed and studied the floor. "I'm more worried about losing that vial right now." *What if that was the one with the answers that I most need?*

"Let's look around. Maybe it came back too."

I nodded. "Yeah, it couldn't hurt, I suppose."

I ducked my head beneath the table and scanned the floor. *Nothing. Damn it. Not even a grain of sand.*

Straightening, I flopped into a chair, totally defeated.

"Hold up," Scott said from across the table.

"What?" I asked, looking his way.

Chair legs screeched as he drew them across the floor. Smiling broadly, he stooped and raised the missing vial. "Look what I found."

"Yes!" Springing to my feet, I leaned across the table toward him. "Where was it?"

He held it high, and his face coloured slightly with a psychedelic glow. "Just sitting here, on a chair."

"Awesome." I held out my hand, palm up.

Scott smirked and clutched the bottle to his chest. "Hold on. How do I know this is yours?"

My eyes narrowed. "Quit screwing around, Scott. Give it here, before it gets too warm."

He snickered. "Ease up, man." He dropped the vial into my waiting palm. "I'm just kidding."

"Sorry, Scott." Swiping my hat from my head, I plunged the vial inside. "I'm just a bit frazzled." I settled my cap back into place. "Thanks for finding it."

"No sweat." He pursed his lips and looked down. "That'd have been a real bummer, for sure. Weird, though, right?" He grabbed the back of the chair where he'd found the vial. "The chairs didn't travel with us, so how'd the vial end up sitting on one?"

My forehead creased. "I don't follow."

He aimed a finger downward. "It should've been on the floor."

"Oh, yeah. Good question." I crossed my arms and propped my chin between thumb and forefinger. "Maybe it didn't make the trip in the first place."

"Huh?" His brow furrowed a moment before he nodded. "Yeah, maybe. I guess you might have knocked it off the table before . . . the event . . . completed. It's as good a theory as any, I suppose."

I cocked an eyebrow and grinned. "It was probably when you pushed me."

He gave me a puzzled look. "What?"

"Earthquake," I said in a high-pitched, quavering voice, waggling my hands by my head.

Scott laughed. "I was freaked, man. I guess I spazzed a little. What do you want from me?"

I chuckled. "Yeah, you did." I glanced toward the door. "Come on. Let's check on Caleb."

"Okay, sure." He looked around. "Where are the Ambrolas?"

"Uh." I touched the visor of my hat. "I think they're up here."

"Oh," he said. "In that case, keep them. I'll grab a few more."

We found the teen where we'd left him, watching the still-sealed snow-blocked doors. He stood, back to us, on a stone bench, knees bent into a half-crouch, arms extended to his sides.

"Catching some waves, Caleb?" I asked as we neared.

"Whoa." He leaped from the bench, twirling in mid-air to face us. As his sneakers tapped the pavement, he balled a hand by his ear. "Oh, hey, dudes." He lowered his hands. "You startled me."

"Catch," Scott said, lobbing a can of Ambrola toward the teen.

Trapping it against his chest, Caleb gripped it with a hand. "Thanks," he said, reaching for the tab.

"No sweat," Scott replied.

Taking a slug of the Ambrola, Caleb checked his watch. "What took you so long?"

I motioned to the bench. "You'd better have a seat."

"That's wild, dudes," he said after we'd filled him in on our unexpected journey. "I wish I'd seen it. The desert and meteor, I mean." He shuddered, and his eyes were wide in the growing light. "I hope I never see one of those fire elementals again."

"Anything happen while we were gone?" I asked.

"No," he replied, "it's been quiet. Boring, even. I was starting to fall asleep, so I figured I'd work on my stance to stay awake." He glanced at the snow piled by the double doors. "Are you still going to bed?"

"No, I don't think I can sleep now." I sat next to him on the bench. "I'll hang out with you instead."

"Yeah, me too," Scott said, sitting next to me.

"What do you think happened, Shivurr?" Caleb asked. "Was it like how we got here? You know, with the basement."

"You mean, spatial transposition?" I asked.

"Yeah."

"I'm not sure." I glanced toward the kitchen. "This seemed a bit different. More selective."

"What do you mean?" Caleb asked.

"Not everything moved," I said. "Just me and Scott, the kitchen table, and whatever was on it."

"Still," Scott said, "I think it must have been the same technology, even if just modified a bit. The big question is what triggered it and why."

I jabbed a finger at him. "Right. I can't see why Aceso would have something like that in her kitchen, and it's not like we did anything to set it off."

Caleb leaned forward. "Maybe something you said."

"Oh, good thinking, kid." Scott looked at me. "Remember? Olivia said their tech is declarative. You ask their tech for what you want, and it makes it happen, if it can."

"Oh, yeah," I said. "What were we talking about when it happened?"

Scott made a face. "Nothing. Just water bottles."

"Right." I scratched my temple. "I was dumping empties."

"And then?" Caleb said.

"It happened."

Scott snapped his fingers. "Maybe that's it."

"What do you mean?" I asked.

"That you'd laid out everything in your cap." He regained his feet. "Think about it. You said Harland planted a tracker in one of the vials, right?"

"Yeah," I said, drawing out the word. "That's how he found me at Dublin Gulch. He said as much at the time."

Scott's eyebrows jumped. "Why didn't he find you sooner, then?"

"The tracker wasn't any good." I ran a hand across my cap. "Not as long as it was up here."

"Then how'd he find you?"

I shrugged. "I was bored—waiting for nightfall—so I took the vials out to count them." My jaw dropped. "You think he planted more than one?"

Scott's face scrunched. "I don't know. Maybe, but a tracker wouldn't transport us to a desert. And I'm pretty sure even the Bodhi Group doesn't have that sort of tech at their disposal." He pushed his eyeglasses up the bridge of his nose. "Even if they did, why send us to some remote desert and not the Institute or some other Group facility?"

"Right, it's got to be something else." I swept the hat from my head and looked inside. "It can't be hidden in the soda cans, though. They're sealed at the factory. It's got to be in one of the vials."

"Yeah," Scott said with a nod. "Harland figured you'd come for them. Someone else might have too."

"Right, and if they did, it'd just be a matter of time before I'd pull the wrong one." I bobbed my head slightly, biting my cheek. "Well, that figures." I scowled. "I can't risk taking them out again."

"At least," Scott said, "not until we talk to Olivia or Wilhelm about it. Maybe they've got a solution."

I took a deep breath and blew it out in a rush. "They'd better get back soon." *I sure hope the apocalypse can wait a few days.*

Scott stroked his chin. "It's weird, though."

"What is?" I asked.

"If it's the vials," he said, "why didn't you go anywhere when you took them out the first time at Dublin Gulch?"

"Oh, yeah." I stared at the ground. "Maybe the conditions weren't right, somehow, or someone needs to trigger it."

Scott frowned. "What do you mean?"

I told them about the man I'd seen leave the kitchen when we'd first transported.

"Huh, he sounds military," Scott said. "The hat especially. I think they're called garrison caps. So, you think this guy might have, what, initiated the transport from the desert?"

"Yeah, maybe," I said. "I don't know."

He looked at Caleb. "Does it sound like the same guy you saw?"

Caleb shook his head. "I didn't get a good look, but not really."

"Okay." Scott pointed at the snowbank. "I guess your guy is still locked up anyway, so it couldn't have been him."

"Oh, great." Caleb scowled. "You mean, we might have two strange dudes wandering the house?"

I put a hand on the teen's shoulder. "Don't worry, Slim. Maybe I imagined it, or it could be a side effect of the transposition, you know?"

"Shivurr's right," Scott said. "The kitchen and desert seemed to intersect for a moment while things got tuned in. If this guy was in the desert—whether initiating the transport or not—it makes sense that he would've been part of the overlap too. At least, that's my guess. We don't know enough about this technology to say for sure, but I'm betting he's back where he belongs either way." His mouth gaped wide and, clapping a hand to his face, he moaned. "Well, maybe I'd better get to bed after all. Do you guys mind?"

"No," I said, "but we should stay together, don't you think? In case there is a second person here."

"I can't sleep out here," he said. "Not well, at least. I need a proper bed. You heard Olivia. I need to rest to heal."

"I don't know."

"It'll be okay," he said. "I'll lock my door or push something up against it, just in case."

"All right," I said. "I suppose that'll have to do." I nudged Caleb's arm. "I've got this covered, if you want to sleep too."

"I'll stay with you," he replied. "In case there is another dude around here."

Scott stood. "All right. Wake me if something happens. Night, guys."

"Night, dude."

"Sleep well, buddy."

Chapter 14

Automatons

We sat in silence after Scott's departure, watching the frozen door for signs of life and listening to the calls of wildlife that rose with the sun. When the shadows had retreated a third of the way across the garden, I stood and padded across to the blocked doors.

The snow now stood half its original height and continued to sink as meltwater pooled at its base and ran in streams along crevices between paving stones.

Should I raise it again? I looked to the blue-and-white sky. *No,* I decided. Olivia would be back soon. *Besides, it'll be hard to sneak up on us in daylight when we're all awake.*

I turned on a heel. "Hey, Slim."

Caleb lay on his side, knees bent, using his bicep as a pillow. I gave the teen's shoulder a gentle shake. "Hey."

His eyelids twitched but remained closed. "M-mup."

Sure you are. I shook him again. "Time for bed."

"Okay, dude," he mumbled, getting to his feet.

He shambled toward me, head down, eyes still shut. Grabbing his arm, I steered him in a circle and walked him toward the front of the house. Seeing him to his bed, I left, closing the door to keep out the daylight that now brightened the atrium.

On my way back to Aceso's bedroom, I peered through doorways, checking for signs of the man I'd glimpsed in the kitchen, or the—possibly same—individual that Caleb had seen. Finding no sign of trespassers—at least in the unlocked rooms—I circled the garden, staying within the shade of the covered passageway, avoiding the sun that had risen high enough now to shine directly on much of the courtyard.

When I reached the far side, I sat in the shade and pulled Lilith's book from my hat. The teenager had given it to me as a parting gift at Dublin Gulch a few days ago, and I hadn't had a chance to read more than a few pages. *Now's as good a time as any.*

A few chapters later, a slosh of ice lifted my eyes from the page in time to see the snowdrift that I'd raised sink a few inches. The doors through which Caleb's trespasser had vanished still sat closed. The makeshift barricade stood just a foot high now, but there were no footprints, snow shoved to the side, or other signs of disturbance. Which meant whoever Caleb had seen either was still in there or had exited by other means.

A bang from my left drew my eyes to the peristylium's far corner, where a flight of stairs climbed upward and disappeared around a turn.

There's another floor. The house was bigger than I had thought. I put away my book and stood. *I should—*

The distant boom of the front door knocker interrupted the thought, freezing me mid-step.

Olivia? Turning, I dashed toward the sound.

As I crossed the atrium, I pulled up short, catching a glimmer of water at the room's centre. My arms windmilled, and my feet slid across the polished marble until I toed the edge of the pool that lay below the windowless skylight.

Scott's door opened as I did so, and he regarded me with one eye shut tight and the other open a sliver. His hair stood straight up in the back and drool gathered at one corner of his mouth. He mumbled something that I didn't quite catch as I turned to face him.

"I've got it," I said. "Go back to bed."

With a weary nod, he retreated back into his room.

Turning on a heel, I skated down the front hallway and pulled open the door, not bothering to use the peephole in my excitement.

A young woman, wearing tan shorts and a loose-fitting lace-trimmed navy-blue top, stood on the far side with her half-curled fingers raised toward me.

I cocked an eye, looking her up and down. "Hello."

"Are you Mr. Shivurr?" she asked with a lilting Irish accent. Lowering her hand, she shook her head. "What am I saying? Of course you are."

I smiled. "Yeah, it's just Shivurr, though." *Mr. Shivurr is my father's name.* I extended an arm. "What's your name?"

"Maya," she replied, giving my hand a shake.

"Pleased to meet you." I cupped my palms and huffed a blast of cold air into them. "What can I do for you?"

"Orithyia bade me deliver a message."

"She did?" Crossing my arms, I leaned a shoulder against the door frame. "What is it?"

She looked down, traced a finger through the air, and cleared her throat. "Shivurr. I'm afraid that something has come up that requires my attention, and I'll not be able to return to you as soon as I had planned. Please remain at the domus for now. I'll return as soon as possible."

"Is that it?" I asked.

Maya nodded and began to turn away.

"Wait," I said. "Is she okay?"

She shrugged. "As far as I know."

"Does this have something to do with the escaped trolls?"

She shook her head. "I don't know."

"Then what? Please, if you tell me where I can find her, maybe I can help."

She glanced left and right, then leaned in. "Orithyia has left Caelumtor. I do not know to where."

"Oh, nuts."

"Well, don't worry about it. I'm sure she'll be back soon, just as she said."

"Yeah, I'm sure you're right. It's just that . . ." I trailed off, thinking of the potential intruders. I'd hoped with Olivia's return to have finally gotten to the bottom of it.

"Is there something wrong?" Maya asked with a frown.

I looked over my shoulder.

"Yeah," I said with a sigh. "I think we might have burglars in the house."

"Burglars?"

I quickly told her about the strange happenings my friends and I had witnessed the night before, but I left out the trip Scott and I had taken to the desert.

I'd share that with Olivia or Wilhelm, but I'd only just met Maya.

"Well," she said, "would you like me to take a look?"

"The door's locked," I said.

"No matter." She held up a hand, displaying a gold ring on one of her fingers. "I should be able to enter."

My brows rose. "You're authorized?"

She nodded. "I do things for the gods, sometimes, which requires elevated access."

"Aren't you a god too?"

Her pale skin flushed. "Gods, no. You're a sweet one. No, I'm not. I'm just a plain old mortal."

"Really? You're kidding. What are you doing here on Caelumtor, then? I thought it was mostly gods here."

"Oh, there are a few regular folks hereabouts as well."

"Huh." I thought a moment. "People who've washed ashore, right?"

"Among others." She pushed past me. "Come on, then. Let's take a look at this room."

The ice blocking the entrance to Aceso's bedroom had melted even further but looked otherwise undisturbed.

"Well," she said, "I gather the snow is your doing."

"Uh, yeah."

"Can you remove it?"

"Sure, one sec." Stooping, I swept the snow to the side with my hands. Straightening, I tried the handle, but the door didn't budge. "Still locked."

"Let me try." She stepped forward, the doors opening at her touch.

Before she could enter, I put a hand on her shoulder. "Wait. I'll go first."

She shrugged and stepped back. "As you wish. I don't think there's anything to worry about, though."

I pushed the doors inward and peered inside. "Why's that?"

Within, a vaulted and frescoed ceiling hung two storeys above, supported by thick crenellated pillars. Wardrobes and chests lined the walls, and paintings decorated the spaces between. An unmade king-sized bed lay off to the right with a low sofa at its foot. At the room's far side, floor-to-ceiling windows looked out over a lake where waterfowl swam upon its mirror-calm surface.

Seeing no signs of movement, I stepped inside.

"Because," Maya said, "I'm fairly certain it was just one of the automatons wandering about."

"Automatons?"

"You know, androids . . . robots, you might say. Surely you've heard of such things?"

"Are you kidding me?"

"No, not at all." She pointed. "There's one. Hello, robot. Come here, please."

I reared back as a figure stepped from the shadows next to a wardrobe. It resembled a human being, walking upright on two legs, and had the requisite two arms, but that was where the similarity ended. Its shiny onyx head lacked a face or features. No eyes, no nose, and silver muscles and sinews—that looked like steel but flexed and deformed like cloth—took the place of skin.

"They're quite useful," Maya said as the android came closer. "Especially for menial tasks."

Coming closer, the machine man stopped. "Yes, mistress," it said with a voice that seemed to emanate from a rectangular opening in the onyx mask where a mouth should be.

"Have you seen any intruders recently?" she asked. "Anyone that shouldn't be here?"

"No," it replied. "Only authorized persons such as yourself and your companion."

She looked at me. "You see?"

"How does he know I'm authorized to be here?"

"Your ring," she said, glancing at my hand.

"Oh, yeah," I said. "I forgot about it."

"Do you require anything else, mistress?"

"I do indeed," Maya said. "Resume your full duties, please."

"But the mistress is away," said the android.

"Guests are in residence, however," Maya said. "They must be treated according to the customs of xenia."

"Understood," it said, turning away. "It shall be done."

"Well," she said, smiling at me, "there you go. It must have been returning here after finishing one of its chores."

"Chores?"

"They keep the domus clean, the garden healthy, and so on."

As if to demonstrate, the android began pulling covers from the bed.

"Why haven't we seen them before?"

"With Aceso away, they will have gone into low-maintenance mode, doing only the most essential tasks. And they do most of their work at night, when they're less likely to disturb anyone."

I blew out a sigh of relief and laughed. "I guess we were worried about nothing."

"I believe so." She gestured to the door. "Shall we?"

"Sure." I followed her out and closed the door behind myself.

"Well," she said, "now that the mystery is solved, I should be on my way."

"Of course," I said. "Thanks a lot for your help."

"You're very welcome."

After seeing her out, I returned to the atrium.

"Hey, Shivurr," Caleb stood in his bedroom doorway, squinting against the morning light.

"Morning, Slim."

"Were you talking to someone?"

"Maya."

His chin dipped. "Who's that?"

I put a hand on his shoulder. "I'll fill you in over breakfast. Come on. Let's wake Scott."

A while later, Scott plunked plates—piled high with food—down on the kitchen table and slid them across to Caleb and me. "Enjoy."

"Cool." Caleb smushed his palms together. "I thought you said you couldn't cook, dude."

"Just breakfast, mostly." Scott returned to the stove and

glanced over his shoulder at me. "So, tell us about Maya."

"Yeah," Caleb said, drenching his pancakes in syrup.

I puffed my cheeks and huffed cold air around a mouthful of scrambled eggs. "Just a sec," I mumbled, holding up a finger. Swallowing at last, I brought my friends up to speed, telling them of Maya's message from Olivia and about the robot in Aceso's bedroom. "So, it must have been a robot Caleb saw walking around."

"Yeah." Scott cracked an egg. "I suppose that makes sense." The egg sizzled as it hit the hot pan. "Androids. Awesome."

"Yeah," I said. "Wait until you see them. They're pretty cool looking."

"I wonder why I haven't seen them doing housework before, though."

"Oh, that," I said. "According to Maya, they were in low-maintenance mode."

"Oh, yeah." He waved a spatula at me. "That explains it. I suppose I slept a lot those first few days, so even if they were walking around, I probably wouldn't have noticed." He glanced toward the cabinet where pizza had appeared the previous night. "One of you guys want to check that? I ordered some coffee earlier. It's got to be in there by now."

I slid over to the stainless-steel cabinet and pulled it open. Two steaming mugs of coffee sat inside. I fingered the handles, testing the temperature, then grasped them both and brought them over to the table.

Scott put down another plate and sat. "Well, with Olivia gone, it's just the three of us today. I'm not sure what we'll do if we're not supposed to leave the house, though. I guess we could maybe play a bit of chess. I saw a board somewhere."

Caleb frowned. "I don't know how to play."

"No sweat. I'll teach you." Scott snatched up the mug, sniffed the contents, then took a sip. "Primo." He looked at me. "So, this Maya chick . . ."

"Yeah?"

He knit his brow. "You don't suppose she's a slave or something?"

I scowled. "Hell no. Why would you say that?"

Scott shrugged. "They had them in ancient Rome."

Old memories rose up. "Yeah, I know."

He nodded. "They did some horrible shit back then."

"Not just them." I shook my head. "Still, I don't think she's a slave. She just lives here and helps them with stuff. Besides, why would they need them? They've got robots and golems and stuff."

Scott raised his hands. "Sorry, man. I shouldn't have said anything." He looked thoughtful. "Maybe I shouldn't mention this either, but I took some Classics courses in college. Greek and Roman mythology. That sort of thing."

"Okay," I said.

He sighed. "Well, the story of Boreas and Orithyia . . . it isn't a good one."

"What do you mean?"

"Well," he said, "in the stories, Boreas supposedly kidnapped Orithyia. He took her from her father, the king of Athens."

My chin dipped. "That can't be true. They're happy, in love."

Caleb raised his eyes from his plate to regard me. "Maybe she's got Stockholm Syndrome."

"Nah. I don't believe it," I said, recalling Olivia's words at the cottage, just a few nights ago. "Remember, Caleb? The other night, she said history is mostly fiction, especially the stuff about them. About the gods."

"I guess so." Caleb licked his fingers. "I sure hope it's not true. Olivia's super nice. She's like another Teresa."

I blinked. "Who's Teresa?"

Scott chuckled. "He means Mother Teresa. The Catholic nun."

The teen smiled. "Yeah, she's like another one."

Chapter 15

Here for You

Androids—standing just beyond the kitchen door—sprang into motion as we exited. With surprising agility, they slipped past us into the kitchen, presumably to clean up the mess we'd left behind, now that Maya had told the one in Aceso's bedroom that they should resume their full duties. We stood outside awhile and watched them work.

"Damn," Scott said. "I could use one of them at my house."

"Are they like that golem, do you think?" Caleb asked. "I mean, they look totally different, but they're still robots, right?"

"Yeah," I said. "I suppose these are just a different form of golem, or a golem is just a different form of a robot. These sure seem more suited to domestic work, though."

"You could be right," Scott said. "Like a sports car versus a tractor."

"Thanks for breakfast, Scott." Caleb touched his stomach. "It was good."

Scott nodded. "No sweat."

The teen smacked his lips together. "I could really use a toothbrush."

Scott pointed. "Check the lavatory in your room. Mine had a few unopened ones."

"Lavatory?" Caleb snickered. "Okay, guv'nor, dude."

Scott shot him a look. "It's called a vocabulary, kid."

I looked around. "Where to now?"

Scott shrugged. "I wouldn't mind a nap." He looked out at the courtyard. "Maybe we can haul a few couches out there, so we can chill awhile."

I craned my neck. "It doesn't look chill out there to me."

He spread his hands. "We'll put yours in the shade."

"All right." I tugged the zipper of my jacket higher. "I can take it for a while."

Scott's face lit up. "Cool, let's—"

His eyes swung to my shoulder and narrowed.

"Something wrong?" I turned, following his gaze.

Across the courtyard, the entrance to Aceso's bedroom stood ajar and a dark-haired man, his back to us, strode inside. A moment later, his face became visible as he turned and closed the doors behind himself.

"Holy shit." I looked at Scott. "Is that who I think it is?"

"Yeah," he replied with a nod. "If you think it's Wilhelm."

"Cool," Caleb said. "I guess he's back."

Scott frowned. "Yeah. So it would seem."

"Let's go say hello," I said, slapping his arm. Springing into motion, I raced across the courtyard, dodging shafts of sunlight, with my friends on my heels. Reaching the double doors, I grasped the handle and pushed.

The doors shook but didn't open.

"Hello?" I shouted. "Wilhelm? It's me, Shivurr." I tried the handle again. "Open up."

A metallic click followed, and the doors cracked inward.

Casting glances at my friends, I pressed an icy hand to the wood and stepped inside.

I scanned the bedroom, still half blinded by the courtyard sunlight.

"Wilhelm?" I called, entering the room.

Footsteps scuffled behind me.

"Any sign of him?" Scott said.

To the left, stairs, wide enough for two people to walk side by side, spiralled down into the earth.

"Nope." I slunk toward the stairs. "Come on."

At the stairway's edge, I glanced at my friends and held a finger to my lips. Cupping a hand beside my head, I aimed it at the stairwell and listened. A faint patter of footsteps welled up from below, echoing off the stone walls of the shaft. By their tempo, whoever was making them was moving fast.

"Do you hear that?" I said, looking at my friends. "That's got to be him."

Caleb eyed the steps. "What do we do?"

I whirled and began to descend. "Let's catch him."

The ceiling fluoresced as I touched the first step and grew brighter with each footfall. I bounded downward, ignoring the banister along the outer wall, chased by the stomps of my friends. Taking the wide steps two at a time, I traced the wall with a hand, shoving against it when necessary to redirect myself along the curve of the passageway.

Just when I thought the stairs might go on forever, they ended at a wide hallway. Torches flickered every twenty feet into the distance, revealing dark lava rock walls of dressed stone, and statues standing in alcoves opposite each torch.

Movement far down the corridor caught my eye, and I cupped my hands to my mouth. "Wilhelm!"

The figure kept moving, slipping through an archway at the corridor's far end.

"Why isn't he stopping?" Caleb asked.

"I don't know. He must have heard me."

"Even if it's not him"—Scott sucked in a lungful of air and coughed—"he should've reacted, right? Someone shouting at you in a lonely tunnel in the ground, you should at least be curious."

"Yeah." I surged into motion, and the walls blurred. "Come on."

Scott was right. Wilhelm must have heard me call, so why wasn't he stopping? Was it Wilhelm? The figure had sure looked like him, but I'd only seen him from a distance, and maybe I'd been wrong. If it wasn't Wilhelm, then who was it? Could this be the intruder that Caleb had seen, or the one I'd spotted before ending up in the desert? Whatever the answers might be, this wasn't one of the faceless androids. Of that, I was now sure.

Reaching the archway, I burst through. *There*, I thought, spotting him across the floor of the large chamber into which I'd entered. I windmilled my arms, redirecting toward the retreating figure as he opened a door on the far side.

"Wilhelm," I called again as the man turned, regarding me with a blank expression. *It is him.* "It's me, Wilhelm." The door thumped closed. "Shivurr."

Something's not right, I thought, staring at the door. Ignoring or failing to recognize me would have been strange enough, but the vacant expression he'd given me seemed worse somehow. He'd looked right through me. Like I wasn't even there.

"Come on." My balled hand rang against the door's green metallic surface. "Open up, Wilhelm."

The door didn't open.

What the hell is going on?

I kicked it.

Ouch. I spun away, snarling. Bending over, I waggled my injured foot. Peeking just above the horizon of my round bottom half like a snowy moon, it appeared undamaged. *It hurts, though.*

"Is he in there?" Caleb said, jogging closer.

Pulling up behind him, Scott stopped and bent over, hands on knees, huffing air. "Jesus." He stood tall and put his hands on his hips. "I'm out of shape."

"Yep," I said, limping in a circle as the pain in my foot faded. "It's him all right."

Caleb's brow creased. "Why didn't he stop?"

"That's what I'd like to know." I spread my hands. "He looked right at me."

Scott wiped the hem of his shirt across his face. "Let's go back, then."

I scowled. "I'd like a freaking explanation first."

"Easy, man." Scott pressed a hand to his side. "Take a chill pill." He waved his other hand at the closed door. "Obviously he doesn't want to talk to us right now."

I thrust my hands into the air. "Don't you want to know why?"

Scott shrugged. "Does it really matter? At least we know it's him and not some killer or burglar or whatever."

A hum came from beyond the closed door.

I frowned and glanced at my friends. "Did you hear that?"

They nodded.

I tried the door again, but it still wouldn't open.

Motioning for quiet, I put a cheek to the metal and listened to the hum. A moment later, a faint red glow seeped between the door and its frame, and I narrowed my eyes. Then the high-pitched hum and scarlet glow both faded, and I heard a click.

My hand pressed against the door again, and this time it swung inward. The room was an unfurnished rectangular box of stone, twenty feet deep and ten wide, that glowed with a bluish light emanating from the stones themselves.

There was no one inside.

"Where is he?" Caleb muttered.

I pointed to a door on the far side. "He must have gone through there." I crossed the room and tried the door, and it opened at my touch. A dark hallway lay beyond, but I saw no sign of Wilhelm. Closing the door, I rejoined my friends, who huddled by the entrance, looking in. "He's gone. Let's go back."

Scott nodded, slapping a hand to my back. "Finally." He pressed a hand to his stomach. "Let's walk back, though."

I glanced at his waist. "Shit. Your stomach. I totally forgot, man. Are you okay?"

"I'll live." He smiled and began to walk. "Probably."

With a snort, I trailed after him, admiring the chamber's stonework, columns, and statuary, lit by globes of amorphous light high overhead.

Caleb broke into a jog. "I've got to go, dudes. I'll meet you guys back at the domus."

"What's the rush, Slim?"

"I've got to go, dude."

"Go? Oh, sorry I asked," I mumbled as he disappeared through the archway.

As we walked, Scott pointed a finger left and right. "Where do you suppose these other hallways go?"

I shrugged. "Beats me."

"Do you want to take a look?"

"Nah," I said. "Not right now. Olivia told us to stay at the domus today, and we're kind of already bending that rule. Besides, you're—"

"Shivurr!"

Caleb? My eyes snapped to the archway, and I flew across the marble floor toward the sound.

Entering the adjoining corridor, I stopped and my mouth gaped wide.

Down the hall, a skinless humanoid huddled over Caleb, pinning him to the floor.

What the hell is that thing? Even as I thought it, I realized that I'd seen this nightmare of bones, muscle and sinew before. Long ago. Hundreds of years ago, even. *What did Wilhelm say about it? Something about having made it, for some reason.*

All thought of that vanished from my mind as the creature scraped a three-inch claw gently down the side of Caleb's face.

A thin ruby line welled on his cheek.

"Help, Shivurr," Caleb said, looking at me with wide eyes.

"Get off of him." The creature's exposed neck muscles bunched, and its head swivelled toward me. Its fleshless skull had only solid plates of bone where ocular cavities should be. Snuffling air into gaping sinus cavities, it shrieked, displaying a mouth full of two-inch canines. White froth swirled from my wrist to my fingertips, coalescing into a crackling ball of blinding light. I flourished an arm, cutting a crescent of white through the air at my side. "Now."

Slowly, it raised itself from the ground and stood hunched over like an ape, and with jerky, spastic motions it turned toward me.

I nodded. "Good. Now step away from him."

It shrieked again, advancing a step, and my arm blurred. A beam of white—blinding in the dim torchlight—bloomed between us, and frost crashed against the creature's muscled, bony chest. Ice filmed on its bones and tissues, radiating outward from the point of impact. Staggering back a few paces, the thing clamped long hands to its rib cage and tilted its head down to regard itself.

I extended a hand. "Come on, Caleb."

He rolled to his stomach, scrabbled to his feet, and hugged the wall as he slipped past the monster, heading in my direction.

"Hurry, kid," Scott shouted from somewhere behind me.

I dashed forward as Caleb neared, interposing myself between him and the nightmarish miscreation. Even as I did so, it looked up and regarded me with its eyeless face. With a terrible moan, the nightmare shoved its hands outward from its chest, and the hallway blazed as lightning crackled from the thing's fingertips. Pain bloomed in my chest as if I'd been hammered with a baseball bat, and my head rocked back as if I'd been kicked.

After what seemed like a long time, the lightning finally stopped. Fluttering my eyes, I felt for the Underfrost, seeking to shield myself with its energies, as I'd done before, but I couldn't focus.

Damn it. I raised my hands and took a few steps back, expecting to be attacked by claw or lightning at any moment.

"What do you want?" I shouted, hoping to buy some time.

I hadn't expected to be understood, but the creature's throat muscles twitched, making a gasping sound.

"Pardon?" I said as my vision cleared. *Is it trying to speak?* "I didn't catch that."

Exposed jaw and throat muscles bunched and flexed, emitting a garbled moan. "Shh-m-mi-urr-us."

"Say what?" I rubbed my arm through my sleeve and continued to backpedal, and the creature followed. "You'll have to repeat that."

"Shh-iv-urr-us," it said.

My eyes flared wide. *It knows my name*, I thought. *How does it know my name?*

"Um . . . hur . . . fuh . . . you."

I glanced at Scott and Caleb huddled by the side of the archway. "What's that? You're here for me?"

The eyeless skull nodded, pointing a long finger directly at my head.

"Who or what the hell are you?" I met Scott's eyes and tilted my head to the left. *Go, man*, I silently urged.

Instead of running, he scrunched his face and spread his hands, mouthing something in return.

"Ahh-tree-el," the monster gasped.

I cocked an eyebrow. "Atriel? That's your name?"

The nightmare nodded.

"Well, Atriel. I'm not going anywhere with you, so scram."

Atriel hissed and his palms glittered.

Not this time, comrade. I spread my hands. In an instant, a blue-white orb welled out from my middle, surrounding me in a frost shield rippling with the Underfrost's raw power. Atriel's lightning crashed against its translucent blue-white surface but failed to touch me.

I waved a hand at my friends. "Get back, you guys."

Atriel came closer, casting lightning strikes against my shield with each step, giving me no chance to retaliate. He stumbled toward me, lurching in fits and starts as if learning to walk. All I could do was keep reinforcing the shield, and every strike seemed to weaken me. *I can't keep this up forever.*

"Come on." I looked at my friends and pointed a finger at the door through which Wilhelm had fled. "Get inside."

As they began to move, the frost shield flared even brighter, and I looked back to Atriel. Still flinging lightning, he advanced on my position.

No, you don't. Sagging with fatigue, I turned and followed after my friends, bolstering my shield even as lightning continued to pound it. *Just a few more steps.*

"Come on," Scott said from just inside the small room. "Hurry."

I shook my head, unable to comply.

With the frost shield raised, I needed to move slowly to enter the room. If I didn't, I'd bounce off the door frame. While the shield stopped high-velocity kinetic or energy-based attacks cold, it still let slow-moving objects through largely unimpeded. So, I had to move slowly, allowing the energy orb to pass through the walls like they weren't even there. Of course, I could drop the shield, but if I did, I'd surely be struck by lightning before I took a step. I didn't want to go through that again.

"It's getting closer," Scott shouted, looking past my shoulder.

My forward progress slowed as the frost shield came into contact with the wall. Leaning forward as if into a breeze, I pushed past the resistance and crossed to the other side, and the door slammed behind me a moment later. Dropping the shield with a sigh of relief, I turned and joined my companions in holding the door shut.

My friends regarded me with wide eyes and open mouths.

"What do we do now, dudes?" Caleb said in a shrill voice.

The door boomed with an impact.

Okay, that's definitely a dent.

"We need to get out of here and find Wilhelm," I said as the metal rang again. We couldn't leave the door unguarded, though. If we did, Atriel would be through and after us in moments. Yet, even if the door continued to hold up to the assault, we couldn't stay here forever. Looking around the room, I scowled. "We need something to block the door."

"There's nothing," Caleb said. "It's just an empty room. We're screwed."

A sick feeling roiled through my guts. One blast of Atriel's lightning had hindered my ability to access the Underfrost. If he hadn't given me time to get my shield up, he'd have had me. Even now, I still felt the after-effects of his attack. I couldn't give him another chance, at least not with my friends around.

The walls' blue glow took on a pinkish hue.

"Not necessarily," I said, glancing about. *If that glow means what I think it does.* The room cooled as I readied myself for a fight. "I just need to buy us some time."

"Easy, Shivurr." Scott's breath clouded the air. "Remember, the kid and I are warm-blooded."

"No choice." I waved them away. "Get behind me."

All right, time to—

Electric light danced across the door's surface.

I cried out, and my head rocked as if kicked by a mule, and my arms and shoulders quivered. Steam billowed from my palms, which were still pressed against the door's metal. Recoiling, I tore down the zipper of my winter jacket and clapped my scorched hands to my body.

The door banged yet again.

Huh, I thought, struggling to focus. *Why doesn't he just open it?*

"It must have locked itself," Scott said, answering my unspoken question.

Abruptly, the air hummed, and the walls glowed bright red.

"What's with the lights?" Caleb said.

The floor trembled, and the walls wavered and warped.

Scott grasped my shoulder. "Earth—" He broke off as the room stabilized and fell still. The light whitened, then returned to the same hue of blue that it had had when we'd first entered. "Quake?"

Caleb looked around. "What just happened?"

Chapter 16

Astrodome

The dent in the door popped back into place. "I think I might know." I watched the door, waiting for the next blow. None came.

Turning, I leaned against the metal—keeping the fabric of my jacket between it and me—and looked at Scott. "Try the other one."

He bobbed his head, strode to the far side, and pulled it wide. White light from beyond mingled with the blue light of the room.

Ten feet beyond its threshold stood a wall. The last time I'd opened it, a long dark hallway had led straight into the distance, but now the hallway ran left and right. The impossibly abrupt structural change made my theory on what had happened seem all the more likely.

Scott stuck his head out and looked both ways. "It looks clear."

"Good," I said. "You guys go outside, then."

"What are you going to do?"

I jerked my head toward the door through which we'd entered. "I'm going to make sure that thing can't follow us." *At least not quickly.*

"How?"

"You'll see." I shooed them with a hand. "Go on."

Scott shrugged. "Okay. Come on, kid."

Turning, I raised my hands to the door and traced my fingers along its outline, welding it to its frame with ice and frost. Stepping back, I raised a waist-high drift of snow from wall to wall. *I hope that's enough.*

Scott's chin jutted toward my shoulder as I exited the room. "Do you think that'll hold it?"

I waggled my head. "Not for long, but it's just a precaution."

Scott raised a brow. "A precaution?" He paled. "You don't think he's trying to find a way around, do you?"

"I'm pretty sure—"

"I need a bathroom, dudes," Caleb said, holding a hand to his abdomen. He pressed his lips together and grimaced. "Now."

My eyes widened. "Oh, right." I glanced about and pointed down the hall. "Try that way." I wheeled about. "I'll check this way."

I raced along the hallway, trying doors, but none opened.

"Over here," Scott shouted.

I turned, catching sight of Caleb as he pushed past Scott and slipped through a side door.

Leaning against a wall, Scott shook his head. "He's a tough kid. I'd be a gibbering mess if that thing had grabbed me."

"Yeah." I leaned next to him. "He is."

Scott ran a hand through his hair. "I never should've let him come with us. He might have died."

"We were just chasing Wilhelm," I said. "It should have been safe."

"I mean back in Vegas, when we left the Schmidts' house after the fire."

"There's no way you could have known it'd lead here." I looked around. "Wherever here is."

"Yeah, I suppose you're right." He sighed. "So, what now?"

"Now, we need to find Wilhelm. He's got to be around here somewhere. He'll know what to do about Atriel."

"Works for me," he replied. "I just hope Atriel doesn't catch up with us first. What did you mean, about the snow being just a precaution?"

"I don't think we're where we were before."

"Huh?"

"I think we transported when the room turned red."

"You mean like we did in the kitchen?" He grimaced. "You didn't take out the vials, though."

"No, I think the entire room is a transporter."

His brows rose. "You think? To where?"

I shrugged. "I don't know. Somewhere else on Caelumtor, maybe, but there's no way to know, at least not until we find Wilhelm."

Scott blew out a breath. "Well, that's great." He slapped my back and smiled. "We're safe, then." He pressed his palms to his cheeks. "I don't think I've ever been that scared, man."

"Not even when you were shot?"

He shook his head. "Not even then. That abomination was a living nightmare."

A nightmare that had, apparently, come for me, judging by Atriel's tortured words. I couldn't begin to imagine why, though. I searched my memories, hoping for a clue. The creature I'd seen long ago in Wilhelm's castle workshop hadn't been able to speak, as best I could recall, and it certainly hadn't had a name. By Wilhelm's words, he'd made it somehow, but that was hundreds of years ago. It seemed unlikely that it could have been the same creature. Yet, something about the name seemed familiar. Had I known an Atriel before? Something told me that I had, but a face like the creature's didn't seem to fit, and it was a hard one to forget. If I remembered the name, why not that it belonged to this nightmare?

"I guess it happened too fast," I said. "You being shot, I mean."

"Yeah," Scott said. "By the time I realized I had been, I was pretty out of it." He pushed off the wall and made for the door through which Caleb had disappeared. "Shaking the bush, boss."

A while later, Caleb re-emerged. "I feel lighter."

I grimaced. "I don't need to know that, Slim." I knew enough of human biology to make me glad to be a snowman. *Human beings are freaky.*

"No," he said, "I mean I literally feel lighter. Don't you?"

I looked down at myself, considering. "Huh." I bounced in place and waggled my shoulders. "You're right."

"I feel it too," Scott said, emerging from the restroom doorway. He flung his fingers at the floor, sending water droplets flying. "I figured it was just adrenalin at first." He pulled at the neck of his shirt. "Even my clothes feel lighter."

I tugged at my jacket. "Well, that's interesting." I'd been so focused on everything else, I hadn't consciously noticed it. I ran forward and leaped, touching a palm to the middle of the arched ceiling high overhead.

"Whoa." Caleb ran and jumped too. He sailed through the air but fell somewhat short of my altitude. "That's wicked. Weird, but wicked."

"What's causing it?" Scott stomped a foot against the floor stones. "Some sort of antigravity generator in the floor, maybe?"

"Beats me." *To what end?* I thought. I started walking. "Come on. We can ask Wilhelm about it when we find him again."

Recessed crystals the size of baseballs illuminated as we walked three abreast down the broad hallway.

I touched a hand to the walls. Rough and large, the blocks looked much as they had in the halls before we'd entered the transporter room, but these had a reddish rather than blackish hue.

"How do you know this is the way?" Scott asked.

"I don't." I shot him a look. "We'll go this way for a while. If we don't see any signs of him, we'll go back."

"Should we split up? We should find him faster that way."

Caleb shook his head. "Screw that." He touched the red line on his cheek. "Shivurr's our only protection."

"Slim's right," I said. "We need to stay together. We don't know where we are. It could be dangerous here."

Scott held up his hands. "That works for me. It might take longer to find him, though." He glanced over his shoulder. "But I suppose there's no rush now that Atriel's not on our tail anymore."

"It's not?" Caleb said, stopping. "How do you know?"

I told him of my suspicions that the room had transported us somewhere.

"That's great," he said with a smile.

I raised a hand. "We might not have travelled far, though, so we should still keep an eye out."

Scott's eyes popped wide. "Wait. What if Atriel uses the transporter too?"

"That's why I blocked the door. Anyway, I doubt he can."

"Why not?"

"I don't think he's from Caelumtor," I said. "He said he was here for me, which probably means he's from somewhere else. So he wouldn't be authorized to use it." I flashed the ring on my hand. "Not without one of these."

The colour drained from Caleb's face, and he glanced down.

"What's wrong, Caleb?" I asked.

He held up a hand. "I lost my ring."

"Who took it? Atriel?"

"It must have been him." Caleb looked back the way we'd come. "When he had me on the ground, I guess."

"Shit," Scott said. "How? You heard Olivia. They're not supposed to come off."

"Not easily," I said, "but they can still be pulled off."

"Well. That's. Just. Great."

"What do we do, Shivurr?" Caleb asked.

I thought a moment. "We stick to the plan and find Wilhelm. We'll just have to hope the snow I raised will keep Atriel out or that he'll give up. Maybe he can't use the ring to activate it anyway."

Scott's brow creased. "You don't think he's smart enough?"

"Maybe, or maybe the ring isn't usable by just anyone." I broke into a jog. "Come on. Either way, the sooner we find Wilhelm, the better."

I kept my eyes fixed on the passageway ahead, listening for any sound that might confirm that we were going in the right direction. We tried each door that we came to, but none would open. Hearing no sounds beyond any of them, even after knocking, we continued on.

Just a few more minutes, I thought after a while. *There's got to be something this way.*

The tunnel sloped downward. Before long it began to curve and wind back on itself, getting progressively steeper. At last, the walls of the passageway dropped away, and we entered a huge cavern. Floating balls cast pools of blue light onto the floor of the mostly dark space and revealed a domed ceiling high overhead.

Scott whistled. "It's as big as the Houston Astrodome."

Caleb looked around. "No seats for spectators, though."

"What now?" Scott asked.

I hesitated, catching movement near the cavern's centre. Leaning forward, I squinted, focusing in on a person that sat on the floor near the centre of the dome.

"Come on." I broke into a trot. "Maybe that's him."

The figure sat cross-legged, back to us, looking out upon a vast circular hole in the floor, a hundred or more feet in diameter. He didn't move or look our way as we bounded closer in the low gravity.

"Hello," I called to the figure as we neared. If it was Wilhelm, I didn't want to startle him. Some instinct told me it wasn't a good idea to sneak up on gods. "Wilhelm?" I sidled to his right, eyeing the dark chasm. "It is you." Sunglasses covered his eyes, and his shaggy hair drooped down his cheeks. He still wore the blood-spattered T-shirt and shorts that he'd worn when I'd last seen him. I snapped my fingers by his ear. "Boreas?"

He made no reply, just kept staring ahead as if in a trance.

I looked at my friends. "What's wrong with him?"

Scott's lips twisted. "You're asking me? Maybe he's high. He looks like he's at some sort of hippie sit-in."

"Try slapping him," Caleb said. "Maybe he's sleep . . . sitting."

Scott glanced at the teen. "Isn't waking a sleepwalker supposed to be dangerous?"

I cocked an eye. "For whom? Me or him?" I grasped Wilhelm's shoulder and shook him. His head jiggled a bit, but he made no reply. "Wake up, man."

I felt a tap on my shoulder. "Uh, Shivurr."

"Yeah, Caleb?"

He swallowed. "We've got trouble." He pointed a finger back the way we'd come. "Look."

My eyes widened as a dark shape emerged from the same tunnel through which we'd entered the chamber.

Atriel, I thought.

The creature nosed the air like a wolf smelling for prey.

"Oh, shit," I said in a hushed voice. "I guess he could use the ring."

Scott's head swivelled side to side. "We've got to get out of here, man." He jabbed a finger over my shoulder. "There's another passageway on the far side. We can make a run for it."

"Yeah, but we can't leave without—"

I broke off as Wilhelm unfolded his legs and clambered to his feet. Without saying a word or looking our way, he turned and ran.

Scott looked at me. "Where's he going?" he said in a low voice.

I felt a smack on my shoulder. "Dudes. It's coming this way."

Turning, I peered across the cavern floor. Sure enough, Atriel loped toward us, hunched over, pushing himself forward with his overlong arms like a chimpanzee. Instead of his lurching, spastic motions beneath Aceso's domus, he moved more gracefully now.

"Come on." I grabbed Caleb's arm and turned him about. "Follow Wilhelm."

With a nod, he took off, and Scott and I followed.

As we ran along its rim, a rumble rose from the abyss, and its walls shone with crimson light. Warm air wafted from the depths moments later. Wincing, I shied back from the precipice a few steps but kept on Wilhelm's trail. A quarter of the way around, he veered off across the floor toward an opening in the outer wall, and my friends and I chased after him.

Good, I thought. If we made it inside, I could use snow to slow Atriel down. Maybe we could find a room to hole up in. Given time, we could try to snap Wilhelm out of whatever trance he was in, and the two of us could fight Atriel together.

Letting my friends get a few steps ahead, I shot looks over my shoulder at Atriel. The nightmare of flesh and bone moved fast, every step a long jump in the low gravity. He'd already reached the great hole and had begun to circumnavigate it.

Glancing forward, I scowled. *We're not going to make it.* My friends weren't fast enough. I felt pretty sure I could make it myself, moving at top speed, but I'd have to leave them behind. I wasn't going to do that, though.

I pulled to a halt, and my friends ran on, probably unaware that I'd stopped. Turning, I raised a frost shield and waited, watching Atriel round the curve of the pit. He pulled up short, regarding me with his eyeless face.

I scooped a handful of frost from the ether, and snowflakes began to fall.

Atriel pointed a bony claw at my head, and his mouth opened. "C-come with m-me."

"That's not happen—" I gaped as the head of a man—a giant one, half Atriel's six feet—rose from the chasm behind him.

Chapter 17

Titanic Trouble

The giant—a heavily muscled blue-skinned man wearing coveralls—grew taller by the moment. He rose from the pit until he stood twenty feet tall on a circle of stone that plugged the opening in the floor entirely. Fog rising from the platform swirled about the giant's feet.

It's an elevator, I realized.

Atriel turned and screeched, backpedalling away from the newcomer. Stepping from the platform, the big guy flicked long black hair out of his face and regarded the nightmare. Softball-sized eyes narrowed, and the giant stooped. Sweeping a hand through the air, he struck Atriel, sending the nightmare flying. Sailing twenty feet, the creature landed on his back with a crunch and slid across the floor.

I didn't wait to see what happened next.

Whirling, I ran. Sailing over the floor, I dropped my shield and soon blew past Scott and Caleb, who waited for me just inside the tunnel's entrance. I twirled on a foot like a figure skater, a fastball of frost by my ear.

Neither the giant nor Atriel could be seen through the opening, but the noise of their struggles filled the air, and lightning flashes strobed in the cavern's blue light. I resisted the urge to take a peek around the corner; whatever was happening there, I wanted no part of it.

Waving away the frost I'd summoned, I eyeballed the floor and extended both hands toward it. A cloud of snowflakes materialized about me. Even as it fell, drifts of snow and pure Underfrost welled up from the floor to meet it. I swept my hands through the air, shaping the flood of snow, sculpting and tempering it. When I stopped a half minute later, a wall of ice—several feet deep—spanned the corridor from wall to wall and ceiling to floor.

I smacked my palms together. "That ought to hold him for a bit."

"Which one?" Scott asked. "Paul Bunyan or Atriel?"

I stared a moment before answering. "Both, I hope."

"Yeah, me too," he replied. "Where the hell are we, Shivurr?"

Scott kept talking, sounding more agitated, but I'd spotted Wilhelm forty feet down the hall and wasn't really listening. He stood with his back to us, hands at his side. "How did you get him to stop running?"

"We didn't," Scott said.

"Yeah," Caleb said, nodding. "He stopped on his . . ." He trailed off as Wilhelm began to move again, walking down the passageway away from us. "Own."

Scott threw up his hands. "Where's he going now?"

"Come on," I said, striding away. "Let's follow him."

"All right." Scott pulled up beside me. "That sounds better than standing around here, waiting for whoever wins to come and find us."

Caleb drew up by my other shoulder. "You think that Smurf-coloured dude can follow us here?"

I looked at the ceiling. "He'll have to duck a bit."

"More than a bit," Scott said. "He's taller than a Rancor."

"Rancor?"

"From *Jedi*."

Damn, I've got to see that movie, I thought, after he'd described the creature. "This guy looks human, though, and he's real."

"Yeah," Scott said. "He's proportional and everything."

"Whatever he is," I said, "my money's on him winning the fight."

Scott sighed. "In which case, I hope your ice wall holds or that he forgets about us. That was far out, by the way."

"What do we do now, though?" Caleb glanced over his shoulder. "We need to get back to the room, don't we?"

"I haven't thought that far ahead." I fired a glance at Wilhelm, who rambled away thirty feet to our front. "I keep hoping he'll snap out of it and help us out."

Caleb pursed his lips. "What's wrong with him, do you think? He seems too out of it for sleepwalking. He should've woken up by now."

I shrugged. "I don't know. Maybe he's been drugged."

"Or maybe we're the ones sleeping," Scott said. "Maybe we're in Wilhelm's dream, and Atriel's just one of his nightmares."

"You've got that right," Caleb muttered.

Scott snapped his fingers. "Maybe he's been hypnotized."

"Hypnotized?" I snorted. "Can a god be hypnotized?"

"Probably not by any old hypnotist, but Hypnos could do it. He did it to Zeus, supposedly."

I raised an eyebrow. "Hypnos?"

"The god of sleep."

I thought a moment. "I don't recall a god named Hypnos, and I'm remembering more now."

Scott held up a finger. "But not everything, right?"

"True."

"So, maybe Hypnos exists for real."

"All right." I bobbed my head and doodled an imaginary pencil against my palm. "We'll put that on the list. Drugged. Shared dream. Hypnotized." I popped an eyebrow. "Anything else?"

He smiled. "Dick."

"How do you know so much about gods, Scott?" Caleb asked.

"School . . . and Dungeons and Dragons."

Sometime later, we spilled out into another domed room, smaller than the stadium-sized one we'd left behind but still large. Stairs lay before us, leading down. At their base, glowing crystal pillars ringed a circular platform. Directly above it, a crystal the size of a beach ball nestled in the centre of the ceiling, where the dome's curve flattened, looking down like an angry god's eye. As we descended in Wilhelm's wake, jagged lightning flashed and crackled, connecting the eye above with the huddled pillars. With each strike, the rhythmic hum that pervaded the room grew louder.

"Whoa," Caleb said, looking up.

"Quite the light show," Scott said. "What do you suppose it does?"

My shoulders bounced. "No clue. Powers something, I guess."

He chuckled. "You think?"

Wilhelm, still some distance ahead of us, stopped as we reached the foot of the stairs. He waited stooped over, halfway between us and the ring of pillars.

Scott gave me a look. "Here we go again."

"What's he waiting for?" Caleb said, walking closer to him.

"I don't know, Slim." I looked around, spotting another set of steps to my right.

Closer by, four-foot-high boxes of stone sat by the walls. Curious, I wandered over to the nearest one, followed by the footsteps of my companions, and peered within. I reached in and traced a hand over the padding that covered its bottom.

Empty.

Wrinkling my brow, I padded over to the next one, a short distance away. A man wearing dark robes, fingers interlocked across his sternum, lay inside. His eyes were closed, and long brown hair bunched around his head and ears like a halo.

"What are these?" Caleb asked. "Coffins?"

Crouching, I touched a hand to the symbols carved into the side of the casket.

"Yeah, maybe." Scott drew closer. "They remind me of Egyptian sarcophagi, minus the lids." He looked into the next few containers, eyebrows lifting as he did so. "These are occupied too." He craned his neck and rose onto the tips of his toes. "The next one looks empty, though."

Caleb glanced my way. "Are they dead?"

I held a hand over the mouth of the man in the sarcophagus next to me. After a long moment, a puff of moist air warmed my palm. "This one's breathing."

Scott checked the sarcophagus nearest to him. "This one too."

Caleb made a face. "Who are they?"

"I don't know," Scott said. "More of Wilhelm's people, maybe." He looked around. "It's like they're waiting for something."

I grasped the lip of the stone box and studied the face of the man inside. "Yeah." I touched an icy finger against the dude's forehead. *No reaction.* "For what, though?"

"Hey," Caleb said. "Wilhelm's moving again."

My head snapped left, catching sight of Boreas headed for the wall of flashing crystal pillars. "What happened?"

The teen turned up his hands, tilting his head to the side. "I don't know. He just started to move again, same as before."

"Did he say anything?"

"Nope, nothing."

"Come on." Wilhelm slipped between the pillars as I strode after him. "I want a look at this thing anyway." I caught up with him at the circle's centre, forty feet from its periphery. "Are you awake?" Scott and Caleb sidled up beside me a moment later. "Boreas?" A screech filled the air, tugging my eyes to the right. *I know that sound.* My eyes darted about the chamber, seeking the source. "Do you guys see him?"

"There," Caleb said, pointing.

I followed the line of his outstretched finger to the top of the second set of stairs. With another shriek, Atriel stalked into the room. One arm hung limply at his side, and cracks spiderwebbed across his skull as he slunk down the steps toward us. Somehow, he'd found another passageway and followed it to us. I could only guess that he didn't have time to break through the wall of ice that I'd left for him with a giant on his tail.

"Damn." I looked to my friends. "Same plan as before. You guys run. I'll try to—"

Vertical slabs of stone rose out of the floor all along the platform's edge. Separated by mere millimetres and moving fast, they stood higher than me before I even knew what was happening. When they'd risen well above our heads, they stopped, blocking the view of the crystal pillars, the sarcophagi beyond them, and Atriel.

"The ceiling," Scott said, sending my gaze upward.

The giant red crystal above—surrounded by an iris of white stone—seemed to grow larger by the moment.

"Oh, man," he said. "What's happening?"

"It's dropping," I said.

My hands flew outward as something shoved me from behind. As I righted myself, Wilhelm rushed into view from my right, arms and legs blurs of motion. He charged the newly formed walls, not slowing as he closed to five feet. He jumped, springing into the air as if launched from a trampoline. At the high point of his arc, he thrust his hands high, hooking fingertips over the top edge of the wall.

"Holy shit," Scott said. "That's . . . not possible."

Wilhelm hung there like a monkey for a moment before, with a flex of his back muscles and biceps, he hauled himself atop it without so much as a grunt.

The red-and-white stone circle, now just ten feet above him, continued to plummet.

Caleb looked away. "He's going to be crushed."

"Boreas," I shouted, using his older name. Lately, it had been fighting for primacy with his newer one in my mind. "Watch out."

Without looking back, he dropped to the far side. A second later, the stone clunked down, settling into place atop the enclosing walls like the lid of a pot, sealing us inside.

My friends and I stared at each other for a long moment, our faces scarlet in the light of the crystal overhead. To my relief, it no longer emitted the electric arcs that we'd seen upon entering the chamber. The shock of Atriel's attack was still fresh in my mind, and I was in no rush to be electrocuted again.

"He just left us," Caleb said at last.

Scott shook his head. "To protect us."

Caleb raised an eyebrow. "You think?"

I nodded. "He was heading right for Atriel."

Scott glanced toward the wall. "That was a hell of a jump."

"Yeah," Caleb said. "That was awesome."

I looked around. "Don't forget, gravity's a lot weaker here."

Scott's eyes popped wide. "You're right. I totally forgot. I guess I'm getting used to it already." He paused a moment. "It's still an impressive jump, though."

"I need to help him." I winced as the crystal over my head flared brighter, then faded to almost nothing, then flared again.

"What's going on?" Caleb asked as the light continued to strobe.

I looked at the ceiling. "Beats me."

The room shook, and the crystal's light steadied to a constant and comfortable level.

I grabbed my friends' arms. "Hang on."

We held on to each other's forearms, steadying ourselves as best we could as the room continued to shake. A deafening rumble enveloped us, and the air shimmered, elongating and distorting the faces of my friends as if they were reflections in a funhouse mirror.

"I think we're transporting," I said. *But to where?* I wondered.

Scott clamped a hand over his mouth.

"Are you okay?" I asked.

He nodded and clasped my arm again. "Yeah. I thought I was going to hurl, but I'm better now."

After a few minutes, the shakes and rumbling diminished.

"It's settling down," Scott said.

A moment later, the trembling stopped altogether, and the light began to strobe again.

"Ah, dude." Caleb grimaced. "Here comes the light show again."

"No, it's great." Scott let go of me and stepped back. He held his arms out, locking his elbows awkwardly. Bending stiffly at the waist, his torso rotated to the left, then swung right, moving a few inches in the darkness between flashes of light. Smiling, he relaxed his arms. "Not bad, eh?"

Caleb looked at me with raised eyebrows. "Disco's not dead, dude."

I laughed. "Maybe it should be."

"Burn," Caleb said, grinning as the light steadied.

Chapter 18

Colossal Disaster

I slumped as if a bag of bricks had been dropped across my shoulders. *Gravity's back*, I thought as my head sagged forward. My friends stood stooped over as well, hands on their knees. Judging by their faces, they weren't enjoying the extra weight either.

Abruptly, the light overhead flickered, dimmed, then went out entirely, plunging us back into darkness.

"What the hell?" I cupped my hands, and my palms shone, lighting our faces.

Scott's eyes met mine. "Shouldn't the roof be going back up?"

A rumble shook the platform.

"What's going on?" Caleb said.

I looked up, sending light from my palm to the ceiling. In its glimmer, the dead crystal above expanded. "The wall's dropping."

Rock ground against rock as the colossal capstone that lay above us dropped with the walls and canted to the side. My friends squatted, looking upward at the descending ceiling with wide eyes.

"What do we do?" Caleb shouted. "We're going to be flattened."

Scott grabbed my arm. "Can you do something?"

Hunching low, I looked around. The stone disc continued to shift as the wall slabs holding it up continued to drop at different rates.

"Maybe," I said as an idea formed, and the slab sank, now just eight feet from the floor.

I thrust out my arms and willed snow to rise from the air and stone at our feet.

Nothing happened.

What the hell?

I shot a glance at my still-glowing palms, then back at the floor and walls.

With a shift of my attention, I brought the Underfrost's wintry haze to the foreground of my vision. It looked like it always did. Icy blues and whites, varying in intensity as normal, yet for some reason inaccessible to my touch.

I tried to access it again.

Still nothing.

I winced as my head bumped against the ceiling, and I hunched lower.

Come on.

My lips contorted, and my skin tingled, and I muttered curses and ground cold chips from my icy teeth. Finally, the barrier between this world and the Underfrost gave way. Snow erupted, pouring out of every surface and the air itself. With sweeps of my hands, I made two piles against the sinking wall.

"That's not going to be enough," Scott said.

"Make more, dude," Caleb added.

The snow rose to meet the falling rock and began to crystallize, hardening to ice.

"Come on." I put hands to their backs. "Get between them."

The ice pillars creaked as the ceiling's full weight pressed down upon them.

"Will they hold?" Scott said, dropping to his hands and knees.

Caleb looked back from the dubious safety of the makeshift ice pillars. "They'd better."

"They will," I said, flopping to my stomach. Light from my palms danced off Scott's backside as I army-crawled after him. *I hope.* My elbows trundled against the floor until my hand punched against the sole of Scott's shoe. "What's going on?"

"Keep moving," Scott said, and I knew that his words weren't meant for me.

"I can't," Caleb said, his voice muffled and hollow. "It's blocked."

Damn it, I thought. The ice buttresses just weren't large enough to shelter us all.

I looked back. Behind us, the slab continued to drop toward my feet, ready to pinch me between it and the floor.

With no other options, I edged forward, threading my head between Scott's legs.

"Whoa," Scott said. "What are you doing?"

"Sorry, man," I said to his upside-down face. "I'm going to be—"

A sliver of light, coming from beyond Scott, interrupted me.

"The wall's still dropping," Caleb said as the light grew brighter. "It's opening up, dudes."

I hiked my lower half toward my chest, away from the pinch of the falling ceiling. *We're not going to make it.*

A moment later, the wall slab finished retracting into the floor, creating an exit to safety. Moving like a howler monkey, Caleb scurried through with Scott close on his heels. With my back brushing against the sloping stone disc above me, I followed. *Okay, maybe we're going to make it.*

My head rocked as hard rubber bashed against my face. "Ouch." I touched a hand to my nose. "Thanks, man."

Scott muttered something that may have been an apology, but I was too busy rubbing my nose to care. By the time I'd shaken it off and resumed moving, he'd crawled free.

Almost there, I thought as the ice to either side of me groaned. As my head cleared the opening, a crack reverberated to my left. The stone on that side dropped two feet in an instant, squashing my bottom against the floor.

A moan escaped my clenched lips as my friends regained their feet. "I think I'm stuck."

In unison, they turned and reached down for me, and my arms creaked as they pulled, hauling on each one with both of theirs.

"Suck it in," Scott said with gritted teeth.

I nodded, trying to make myself smaller.

Olivia's words on the way to Caelumtor came to mind. *You know you can change form, don't you?*

I imagined my lower half elongating. *Come on.*

My bottom sphere softened and spread outward. As my icy flesh broke contact with the stone above it, I came free, and my friends stumbled as my torso and head lurched toward them.

Catching themselves, they reset their grips and pulled me free at last.

For a long moment, I lay there, watching grey clouds float across a bright blue sky, visible through a large hole in the domed ceiling high above. Sucking in a breath, I rolled to my stomach, pushed myself to my feet, and regarded the platform.

I heaved in a breath as the hum of the crystal columns faded, and their light died. "That . . . was close."

I turned and took in my surroundings. Sunlight peeked between cracks in the walls of fractured stone that enclosed the room in which we now stood. Fallen stone columns littered the floor. Their broken pieces mixed with shattered statuary and other debris to form an amorphous rubble of dust and decay.

Closer at hand, sections of the floor had been cleared of debris. Within these clear-swept areas, three-foot-high red pedestals stood, untouched by whatever calamity had damaged the walls. Verdigrised figures of men and women perched atop them, looking down on us with expressions that ranged across the spectrum of emotion: amused, adoring, enraged, sad, and more. Twelve in all, they encircled the platform like numerals on a watch face.

"This stronger gravity's kicking my ass," Scott said, his face pale. "It feels like I'm wearing a suit of armour."

"Same here." Caleb touched a hand to his abdomen. "I feel kind of dizzy too."

I stood taller with a concerted effort. "We'll get used to it again." Our time in weaker gravity had been short, so it seemed reasonable to think that we'd soon adjust. "Just give it time."

"Creepy, dude." Tilting his head back, Caleb took a step toward the nearest statue. "It's like the eyes are watching me."

Straightening, Scott walked right up to it and whistled.

"That's a lot of bronze." He stretched an arm to touch the figure's contorted hand. "They remind me of the Statue of Liberty." He glanced over his shoulder at me as a wink of sunlight gleamed off a small patch of still-polished metal. "Not nearly as big, of course."

Caleb's head swivelled left and right. "Where are we?"

"Beats me." I looked back at the platform from which we'd just escaped. The red-eyed ceiling disc continued to sink into the melting snow—an upended dinner plate melting into a pile of vanilla ice cream. "Hopefully close to Caelumburg. It doesn't look like we're getting back the way we came."

Scott faced us and thrust a hand at the platform. "What the hell happened to it?" He waved his hands by his ears. "What happened here? Did we cause this, do you think?"

I pursed my lips. "Nah, no way."

"What makes you so sure?"

"There's not nearly enough dust in the air, for one. If this had just happened, the air would be thick with dust and smoke." I thrust a hand at the base of a nearby statue. "Plus, there's none here. Someone cleared the floor at some point after . . . whatever happened."

Scott nodded. "Good point. Have you been reading Sherlock Holmes again?"

I grinned before shrugging. "Their pedestals wouldn't be still standing either, my dear Watson. They must have been moved in after, or maybe they fell too, but someone stood them back up." I held a hand above my eyes, scrutinizing the pedestals and the statues atop them. "They don't look damaged or repaired, though, so my guess is they're new."

"Now you're just showing off," Scott said, slapping my shoulder. "Okay, it happened long before we got here, but what was it that happened?" He glanced at the collapsed transporter. "And why hasn't anyone fixed it?"

My shoulders bounced. "Yeah, not exactly godlike, leaving broken walls and malfunctioning machinery around. Someone could get hurt."

"Or killed," Scott said. "I thought we were done for." He

pushed his eyeglasses back into place. "What took so long? With the snow, I mean. It seemed like you were struggling."

I stared at my palms, rotating my head an inch left and right a few times. "I couldn't touch it . . . the Underfrost." I met my friend's eyes. "It was as if something stood . . . stands . . . in the way. I can see the Underfrost all around us, but trying to touch it is like pushing through—"

"Hey." Caleb crouched next to a pile of rubble just beyond the ring of statues. "What's this?"

"What's what, kid?" Scott asked.

"Just a sec." The teen's torso twisted and writhed, accompanied by a rumbling of broken stone, bent metal, and splintered wood. "Got it." He straightened with a grunt, holding aloft a red stop sign. "Check it out, dudes."

My eyes flicked to Scott, then back to Caleb. "Huh."

Scott strode toward him. "What's a stop sign doing here?"

"I know, right?" Caleb glanced at the floor, then back to us. "Where's the road?"

Scott touched a hand to the metal. "There's no way to know, kid." He looked to me. "At least not until we take a look around."

"Let's do it." I strode toward a twenty-foot-high arched doorway that stood at the far side of the hall. "That's got to be the way out."

The hallway appeared undamaged. Either it had escaped whatever calamity had damaged the arrival chamber or it had since been repaired. White statues of armed warriors stood in alcoves along the walls, and between them, two-foot-high flames burned atop podiums of stone, lighting our way toward the daylight shining in the distance.

I led my friends toward it, ignoring side passages, staircases, and doors. We needed to know where we were, and we could only do that by getting outside.

The hallway spilled out into a large courtyard, dotted with more statues and enclosed by white stone keeps, buildings and walls. Round towers loomed over it, topped by conical black roofs. Above them, clouds churned, painting away the last vestiges of blue that remained in the sky.

"It's a castle," I said, rotating in a slow circle.

"Wild," Scott said. "Do you think this is still Caelumtor?"

"I don't know, maybe. I didn't see a castle there, but it was pretty dark when we arrived."

He sniffed the air. "It smells different, though. Doesn't it?"

Wind gusted across the courtyard stones, and Caleb hugged himself. "It's colder, too."

I turned to face the breeze, looking for an exit. A moment later, I smiled. An iron portcullis hung above an archway across the bailey, guarding a passageway between twin barbicans.

"There's the gatehouse." I marched toward it. "Come on, guys."

Passing through the curtain wall, we looked out upon a broad valley from atop a steep and rocky precipice. A town lay below. Beyond it, green forest stretched for many miles to rocky cliff-sides that loomed above the adjacent trees. Above this, thick clouds dominated the sky, though small patches of blue peeked between gaps in the grey.

Not just any town, I thought. Many buildings were marble-and-stone edifices comparable to those on Caelumtor. Others, like the castle behind us, were newer in style but still old and grand, reminiscent of the Middle Ages. Nestled among them sat squat modern buildings and asphalt streets appropriate to small-town America. Sprinkled throughout the architectural panoply stood giant statues and sculptures atop towering columns of stone. Some of these were large and grand enough to rival the Great Sphinx of Giza or the Colossus of Rhodes.

Magnificent, I thought. *It's alien, but kind of familiar too somehow.*

Scott stepped toward the brink. "What is this place?"

"Not Caelumtor," Caleb said. "That's for sure."

"At least there's a town here. That's lucky." Seeing their faces, I added, "I mean, Caelumtor would be better, but at least we can talk to someone, find out where we are and maybe call for help."

"It's better than sand dunes," Scott said with a grimace. He pointed a finger above my head. "Though, maybe that vial's our way out of here, if we need one."

My eyes flicked upward. "Maybe."

"You mean the one that took you to that desert?" Caleb touched a finger to his chin. "Even if you could make it happen again, won't those fire dudes still be there?"

Scott winced. "That's a good point. Probably."

A flash of lightning forked down from the clouds, striking one of the many towering four-sided obelisks that stood sentinel throughout the town and surrounding region. Judging by the buildings nearby, they had to be at least a hundred feet tall, maybe more.

"Before resorting to that"—I gestured to the stone-paved road that lay to our left, switchbacking down the hillside to the valley below—"let's look around a bit first. This place looks amazing."

The wind clutched and tore at our clothing and limbs as we descended. I snugged my hat low, keeping one eye on the pavement and another on the town. As the path rounded the hillside, the ratio of buildings visible below changed. Modern buildings came to dominate, though older stone ones could still be seen.

I pulled to a halt and narrowed my eyes. The buildings showed signs of damage. Many sported cracked walls, broken windows and collapsed roofs. Others looked like they'd been smashed together. To the left, a stone tower sprouted from within a glass-fronted one-storey building. The sign over the window identified it as a hardware store. To the right, a half-collapsed brick apartment block leaned against a stone one.

It looks like a war zone.

Scott whistled. "Holy . . ."

"What happened here?"

"I don't know, Slim." I started to walk again. "Let's go ask someone."

Chapter 19

Half Hidden

At the road's bottom, flattened trees, shattered statuary and boulders lay across fractured strips of yellow-lined concrete and asphalt. Tall grass grew from fissures that spiderwebbed across the broken road. The buildings to either side looked no better. Their shattered windows and busted walls gaped wide, exposing their innards to the elements.

With my friends in tow, I strode out onto the road and reared back as a flock of birds erupted into the sky. They came from the crown of a broad-leafed tree, poking from the roof of a single-storey gas station convenience store that sat decaying a short distance away.

"Where are we?" Scott said in a low voice.

"Not sure exactly." I pointed to a rusted street sign lying on the ground to my left. Its worn letters read Main Street. "Somewhere in the States, judging by that."

Scott jabbed a finger at the gas station's sun-weathered sign. "Yeah. I don't think they've got those in Canada."

"Gas stations?" I asked.

He laughed. "No, everyone's got gas stations, but they've got different names up there. Company names, I mean."

"How can this be the States, though?" Caleb asked. "A lot of these buildings and stuff are like the ones on Caelumtor. I don't think we've got any buildings like them back home, do we?" He aimed a finger at a towering figure in the distance. "That thing's got to be as big as the Statue of Liberty, but I've never seen it before."

Scott's brow furrowed. "I don't know. Maybe those are part of a theme park or something."

Caleb's face lit up. "Like Disneyland?"

Scott shrugged. "Maybe. This could be like Main Street, USA. Have you been, kid?"

"Nope."

"Whatever it is," I said, studying the nearby buildings, "it looks like it's been abandoned for years."

Scott turned in a circle. "Maybe it's a leftover from the Great Depression, or an abandoned company town."

I walked up to the rusted-out hulk of an old car. "Did they have these during the Great Depression?"

Scott circled the vehicle, running his hands over the lettering at its back corner. "Thunderbird." He glanced at me. "It's from the fifties, I think." He thrust a hand toward another rusted-out wreck that sat some distance away. "That one too."

"Where are all the people?" Caleb said in a hushed voice. "Are they all inside?"

Scott spread his hands. "They probably left after . . . whatever happened."

I cocked an eye at him, recalling his shouted warning in Aceso's kitchen the other night. "What do you figure? An earthquake?"

He nodded. "Yeah. It seems the most likely explanation."

I suppressed a grin. "Isn't it always?"

Scott chuckled. "Stop making me laugh. I'm trying to freak out over here." Sobering, he added, "Seriously, though. This could be earthquake damage."

I pointed to two huge clock faces on the sides of a tower that loomed above its two- and three-storey neighbours, down the street. "Let's head there. Maybe there's a street sign or office building that'll tell us more."

We walked down the centre of the street in silence.

Halfway to the square, Scott muttered, "Don't look, but I think we're being watched."

"From where?" I asked, rolling my eyes side to side while keeping my head still.

"From the balcony below the clock tower," he replied. "Try not to be obvious when you look."

"Are you sure?" I moved my head left and right as if taking in the scenery. "I don't see anyone."

"He ducked down."

"So what?" Caleb whispered. "That's good, isn't it? Aren't we trying to find someone to talk to?"

"Maybe," I said, "but we need to know if he's hostile first."

Scott looked at me. "Maybe we should get out of the street in case he's got a gun."

I pretended to study one of the storefronts. "You think he's a sniper?"

"Could be." Scott pulled up beside me. "I thought I saw a gun barrel, and it's a good spot for one. If he starts shooting, can you take him out? Are your powers still . . . blocked?"

Turning toward the clock tower, I crossed my hands behind my back and tried to bring a frost ball into being. My palm tingled and cooled, but the comforting weight of a frost-charged sphere failed to materialize.

"Yeah, something's still cutting me off from it." I focused again. *Almost.* I grunted, then swore under my breath. "If I give it everything I have, I might be able to push through again, like I did earlier. But if he's got a gun, I won't be fast enough."

"Damn it." Scott looked at Caleb. "If you hear gunshots, run for cover. We should all take off in different directions. It'll make it harder for him to get us all."

I shook my head, almost imperceptibly. "Let's not wait for him to make the first move." If the guy was a good shot, he might kill one of my friends before we even heard the bullet. "On the count of three, you guys run. Take cover in a building. I'll run straight for the tower and try to draw his fire."

"Are you sure, man?"

I bobbed my head. "I can take a few bullets, if I have to." *Not that it doesn't hurt like hell.* I met his eyes, then glanced down, pointing a finger at his waist. "Unlike you guys." Scott swallowed but said nothing. "Plus, I'm fast. He'll have a tough time hitting me."

"All right." Scott sighed. "Let's do it."

"You ready, Caleb?" I asked.

The teen looked ready to puke, but he nodded stiffly.

I counted to three, then yelled, "Go!"

Surging forward, I tilted my head to regard the clock tower. The head of a man appeared above the edge as I did so before ducking back down. I dodged left and right, in case other shooters hid among the ruins. To my relief, I made it to the doors at the tower's base without hearing any shots fired.

Maybe he doesn't have a gun after all, I thought, looking back over my shoulder.

The street lay clear, and my friends were nowhere to be seen.

Tugging the door open, I slipped down the hallway to the base of a staircase, and footsteps pounded down the stairs from high above, growing louder with each thump.

I turned up my hands, furrowing my brow, and a moment later, my palm cooled, and flickers of frost flared within them.

Come on, I thought as the footfalls grew louder. *Yes!*

I smiled as a swirling froth of crackling white blossomed in my hand, and a forty-something man with a salt-and-pepper beard, wearing the clothes of a woodsman, appeared on the stairs above. He froze and stared down at me, both hands grasping the railing. His eyes darted up before returning to me.

"Wait." Not seeing a weapon, I dismissed the frost and held up my hands. "I just want to talk."

He glanced upward again. "What are you?"

"I'm Shivurr. Who are you?"

"Name's Virgil. Virgil Half."

"Nice to meet you." He tensed as I took a step closer. "Whoa, easy now. We just want to ask you a few questions, then we'll get out of your hair." I winced, eyeing the horseshoe of fuzz hugging the back of the dude's otherwise smooth head. "Okay?"

He frowned but nodded. "What do you want to know?"

"What state is this?"

"State?" His eyes narrowed. "As in the United States?"

"Uh-huh."

He grunted. "America's a long way off."

The door rattled, and Scott and Caleb entered.

"It's okay." I pumped my hands toward the floor. "It's just my friends." I turned to my companions. "Guys, meet Virgil Half." I looked back to Virgil. "Like I said, we just have a few questions. We don't want any trouble."

Virgil descended a few steps. "Why are you asking about the States?"

"Uh, we're from Nevada," I said, glancing at my friends. "Right, guys?" New Olympus wasn't our secret to share. "We took a wrong turn, and we're trying to get home."

He cocked his head. "Really?"

I nodded.

He snorted and jabbed a thumb over his shoulder. "Are you with the others?"

"The others?"

He scowled. "The ones that have been going up to the castle. I saw you come down from there."

"Uh, no." I looked at my friends. "We didn't see anyone inside. When was this?"

His eyebrows shot up. "You were inside?"

"Sure," I said.

"Huh."

"What?"

"It's forbidden to enter. Those that go there, they don't come back." His eyes narrowed. "At least not until you and the others showed up."

"Who were the others?" Scott asked, coming up beside me.

Virgil shrugged. "I didn't get a good look. It surprised the heck out of me to see anyone in town. Most folks avoid the area, even ordinary ones like me, but especially their kind."

"Their kind?" I prompted.

"The ones that are more than people," he said.

"You mean people like me?"

He shook his head. "Not quite. These ones look like regular people—but they're not."

"The gods?"

"Um-hmm," he said. "Some people call them that."

"And the castle belongs to them?"

"That's right. They're the ones that forbade entry."

"Why don't they come here?" I asked.

"Something to do with what happened here. It messes with their . . . abilities." He shrugged. "I can't tell you more. The whole thing's way beyond me." He looked me up and down. "What about you?"

"What do you mean?"

"Are you a god?"

I glanced at my friends. "No."

"Hmm . . . looking like you do, I wasn't sure what to think." He looked at Scott and Caleb. "You two look pretty normal, though. I don't suppose you're gods either, are you?"

Caleb guffawed. "I wish."

"Okay, you're not gods," Virgil said. "Then how did you manage to leave the castle alive?"

I spread my hands. "I don't know what to tell you." I thought fast. "We found a tunnel back on Earth, which led to this weird chamber." I told him about the crystal pillars and transporter platform, but I left out the events leading up to our finding it. "When the lights came back on, the thing started to collapse, nearly killing us. We just managed to get out from under it and found ourselves in the castle. With no way to return, we left to try to find our way home."

"Yeah," Scott added. "The gate was wide open and—aside from the transporter nearly killing us—nothing bothered us."

"That's interesting." Virgil stroked his beard between his thumb and forefinger. "Maybe something's changed."

"Anyway," I said, "if people avoid the town, what are you doing here?"

He sat on the stairs and waved a hand at the steps below him. "I used to live here."

"Where do you live now?"

"Lolokly."

Never heard of it, I thought. "Can you take us there?"

His eyes roved to my friends before returning to me. Finally, he nodded. "All right. As it happens, I'm heading back anyway."

"We'd appreciate it," Scott said.

Virgil stood. "I'll just grab my kit, and we can be on our way." He turned and grabbed the railing. "I'm getting a workout today."

As Virgil's footfalls faded, I motioned my friends toward the door, wanting a moment to talk with them beyond the stranger's hearing.

The sun glared as we exited, far stronger than it had been when I'd first entered the building just minutes ago. The clouds had broken up, changing the once-grey heavens to a vibrant blue. I tented a hand against the visor of my cap, and my jaw slackened.

"Holy shit," Scott muttered from behind me.

"Gnarly," Caleb said with a breathless voice.

The sky looked wrong.

The same merciless sun that had dogged my steps in the deserts of Nevada had been joined by parallel streaks of white light that drew thick arcs across the entire azure sky before disappearing into distant clouds.

"This isn't Earth," I said. "Is it?"

"No, it can't be." Scott blew out a breath, flapping his lips. "This is heavy. I think those are rings that go all the way around the planet, like on Saturn."

Caleb slapped my shoulder and pointed. "Check those out, dudes."

In the distance, two huge moons rose from the horizon, visible through a break in the clouds.

"That's wild," Scott said.

Definitely not Earth, I thought, staring a moment. "Can we really be on another planet?"

Caleb shook his head. "How's that possible?"

"I don't know," Scott said. "It's crazy. What's really nuts is, I don't think we're even in the solar system anymore."

I glanced at him with a furrowed brow. "What makes you say that?"

He shrugged. "There are no other planets around Sol—our sun—that can sustain life. Earth's the only one."

"What about Mars?"

"Nah," he said, "it's the next best choice, but it can't sustain life either. Without protection, we'd have been dead in minutes. Even sooner on Saturn." He looked around. "Yet this is like Earth. I've seen trees like this before. The buildings. The street signs. Even the gravity is familiar."

I shook my head. Spatial transposition was awesome, but I had never imagined it could be used to traverse such a distance. Not as far as another planet. Even less so to travel beyond the solar system.

My returning memories didn't tell me much about how transpositions worked, other than that they somehow bent and twisted space-time, temporarily swapping the coordinates of two different volumes of space. According to Olivia, the greater the distance or volume, the more energy required and the harder the calculations necessary to make it work. I whistled softly, imagining what it might have taken to send us so far.

Let's see Harland find me here, I thought with a smirk. A moment later, I groaned, realizing that I couldn't stop the catastrophe that had landed me in his hands from here either. *Once I remember it.*

The door behind us popped open, and Virgil reappeared. He had a cloak draped over an arm, a sword strapped to his waist, and a large pack and quiver of arrows strapped to his shoulders. He held a bow in one hand and walking staff in the other.

"Oh, sun's out, eh?" He looked at me. "You okay to travel in this? Not for nothing, but you look like you might be more sensitive to the sun than most."

"Yeah, I'll be fine. I've been through worse."

"Good." His eyes flicked to the horizon. "It should be darker in a few hours anyway."

Scott raised an eyebrow. "Are you sure about that? The sun's low, but it seems to be rising."

Virgil looked at his watch, then back to us. "Yep, it shouldn't be long now."

"Where is this, dude?" Caleb asked. "This isn't Earth, is it?"

"Dude?" Virgil snorted, glancing down at his grey long-sleeved tunic, brown pants, and boots. "Are you kidding me, son?"

"You'll have to excuse Caleb," Scott said. "He means it like bro, guy, pal, you know?"

"Oh." He cocked an eye. "All right, then."

"Where's here, Virgil?" I asked, reminding him of Caleb's question.

"The planet is called Zarechus." His eyes flicked to the hill. "The castle and the town are known as Abadom."

"And where's that?" Scott asked. "In relation to Earth, I mean."

Virgil tossed his shoulders. "I don't know. All I know is, it ain't Earth."

Scott's eyebrows bunched. "How's this possible?"

Virgil looked at him, sidelong. "You're asking me?" A moment later, he shrugged and gestured at our surroundings. "Probably the same way all this got here." He waved a hand. "Come on. Let's walk. We can talk on the way."

I held up a finger. "Can you give us a minute? My friends and I need to talk first."

He bobbed his head. "All right."

"What do you guys think?" I asked, after we'd moved out of Virgil's earshot. "Do we go with him? With the transporter busted, we need to find another way back, somehow."

"I suppose so," Scott replied. "What choice do we have? We don't know anything about this place. This planet. If we're really on another planet."

Caleb frowned. "Maybe we should just go back and wait for Wilhelm. He's got to know that we're here, right?"

I sighed. "Maybe, but I don't know. He didn't seem to be . . . all there."

"It doesn't matter," Scott said. "Even if he snaps out of it and realizes where we are, the transporter is broken. He's got no way to follow us."

Caleb leaned in. "What if this Virgil guy is a bad dude?"

"All the more reason to follow him, Slim." I lowered my voice further. "But let's not mention New Olympus or our god friends."

"Why not?" Scott said, matching my volume. "If the folks

Virgil mentioned are gods, they might be the only ones that can help us get home."

I shook my head. "Not all gods are good. Don't forget about the Faction."

Scott scowled. "Do you really think they might be here too? We came here from New Olympus, following Wilhelm. It seems more likely this place is theirs, doesn't it?"

I shrugged. "I don't know what to think, except that we should be cautious for now. Let's just avoid mentioning Wilhelm or Olivia or where we came from. I mean, aside from Earth, obviously. If Zarechus is a Faction planet, we don't want people to know that we're friends with their sworn enemies."

I hoped that it wasn't the case, though. If Faction members were here, it'd be dangerous for me either way, once they heard about me. That possibility made going with Virgil and keeping an eye on him all the more important.

Scott rubbed his face. Dropping them, he nodded. "Fair point."

"Okay, Slim?" I said, looking at the teen.

"Sure," Caleb replied. "No problem, dude."

"Okay, Virgil," I said with a raised voice, turning to face him. "We'll come with you."

"All right, then," he said with a nod. "Let's be on our way."

We fell into step beside him, stepping between abandoned cars and over broken concrete as we exited the town square.

"Keep alert," Virgil said as we walked. "Dangerous things sometimes pass through these parts."

Scott grimaced. "Bandits?"

Virgil turned his head and spit. "Worse things than bandits. There's no one for that sort to prey on around here."

"What about as a hideout, though?" Scott asked.

Virgil looked around. "They probably tried at one time or another. Like I said, though, it can be dangerous hereabouts—the storms alone are bad enough—but without people to share the workload, it's a hard place to live for long."

"Yeah," I said, "but not even to scavenge?"

Virgil shook his head. "Pretty much everything of value that could be carried away was taken long ago." He looked back. "Except for whatever's up at the castle. Until you and the others came, no one's tried to enter it, far as I know, for years."

I looked at him sidelong. "Then why do you come here?"

His shoulders bounced. "It's home. At least, it was, and I like to visit now and again and remind myself of where I came from and who I left behind." He looked at me. "Not everyone survived the event that brought us here."

"Oh," I said. "Sorry to hear that."

He shrugged but said nothing.

We walked in silence for a while after that, passing more fractured and fused buildings and abandoned cars. Some of the former were stained green with moss and the decay of time but looked to have been untouched by whatever calamity had struck the region. Whatever had happened, the damage hadn't been complete or followed any discernible pattern.

Eventually, the ruins of the town fell away, replaced by thick forest and craggy pale upthrusts of rock, topped with still more trees, and the broken concrete merged with strangely well-kept roads of paved stone. As we entered a pass between rocky cliffs, the wind abated, and the drone of innumerable insects seemed to rise in volume.

Chapter 20

The Immerwald

With keen interest, I studied the steep bluffs of white and green that towered at the sides of the road. They were stained black in places, with natural alcoves eroded into their sides, and patches of green dotted the rock face from top to bottom, gathering in crevices and upon narrow ledges.

Beautiful, I thought, and my eyes drifted up to the alien sky. "Hey, Virgil." I pointed to the streaks of white that swept across the firmament. "What are those?"

"Pardon?" He glanced at me over his shoulder. Seeing my hand, he looked upward. "Oh, those are the rings of Zarechus." He shielded his eyes to look. "Impressive, aren't they? I nearly flipped my wig when I first saw them."

"What causes them?" I asked.

"I don't know," he replied.

"If they're like the rings of Saturn," Scott said, "they're made up of billions of small particles of rock and ice orbiting the planet."

Virgil shrugged. "If you say so."

Scott looked to the roadside. "It's weird, though. This planet is so Earth-like. The trees, the birds. I'm not a botanist or a zoologist, but I recognize some of them. How could the same species have evolved on different planets?"

Virgil shot a glance at Scott. "I should think that's obvious. Use your head, son."

Scott's face flushed red, and he grimaced. "They were brought here. Probably the same way you and the town were."

"That's my guess," Virgil said, "except they were already here when we arrived. I suppose they must have been brought here a long time before and grown wild since then."

"Are there others like me here?" I asked. "Have you seen anyone like me?"

"No." He smirked. "I can't say that I have."

"Oh." My shoulders sagged as a rising hope of finding my people here receded. "You didn't seem all that freaked out by me. I thought maybe I wasn't the first of my kind that you'd seen."

"Yeah," Scott said. "Most people freak when they first meet Shivurr."

Caleb snickered. "I know I did."

I smiled, remembering when the teen and I had first met, scarcely a week ago now.

Virgil nodded. "Before I came here—to Zarechus—I would have." He pointed at the rising moons. "And I certainly lost it, the first time I saw the sky and realized I wasn't on Earth any longer, but that's among the least of the surprises I've seen since."

"What do you mean?" Caleb asked.

"I've seen life in many forms." He stopped and stared into the distance, apparently remembering. "Monstrous, alien life. Supernatural even. After a while, you come to expect anything." He held up a hand. "I'll admit to a fair bit of surprise when I first saw you coming down the street, but I thought, why the hell not? By the time we met on the stairs, I'd had time to adjust. My main worry was that you were an enemy, though you looked friendly enough, and your companions seemed . . . friendly too."

"You're sure you haven't seen others like me?" I asked.

"Pretty sure, son," Virgil replied. I must have looked deflated because he added, "I haven't been everywhere, though." He pointed to the roadside. "If any like you are on Zarechus, my guess is they live quite a distance that way, where it's always winter."

"Is it far?"

He whistled. "Too far to walk. I've never been there myself. Few people have. Folks say the sun never shines there and snow and ice stretch as far as the eye can see. The only light comes from sunlight reflecting off the moons and the planet's rings."

"It sounds like the Arctic," Scott said. "This planet's version of it anyway, and not a place I'd want to visit."

"Nor would I," Virgil said. "I've heard it gets so cold that if you spit it'll freeze before it even touches the ground." He looked at me. "That sounds right up your alley, though, doesn't it?"

"It does." I looked around, searching my memories. "But I've been to places like that before. They're beautiful in their way, but warm places are more interesting. They're so alive and diverse."

"As an outdoorsman," Virgil said, "I couldn't agree more. Still, it must be rough to be so far out of your element."

I shrugged. "I'm getting used to it."

"How far is it to Lolokly?" Scott asked. "Will we get there soon?"

Virgil shook his head. "We've got about a hundred miles ahead of us."

Scott's jaw dropped. "Excuse me?"

Virgil winked. "Don't worry, fella. We're not walking the entire way."

"What do you mean?" I asked. "We're not riding horses, are we? I don't ride."

"Nope," he said. "Something better."

"A vehicle?"

He smiled. "Uh-huh."

"I hope it's close." Scott held a hand to his stomach. "I'm getting a stitch in my side."

"It's not too far now," Virgil said, eyeing the sky. "It doesn't look like we'll make it before the eclipse, but don't worry, we'll still be able to see all right, as long as the clouds aren't too thick."

Scott looked up at the moons. "There's going to be a solar eclipse? How do you know?"

"They happen every night," Virgil said. "If not for them, the sun would always shine here."

I furrowed my brow. "Are you saying the sun never sets here?"

"That's right," Virgil replied.

Scott's eyes narrowed. "Huh, then we must be at or near one of the poles. That makes sense, given the sun's position, low on the horizon."

Caleb snorted. "It's kind of warm for the North Pole, dude."

"It is," Scott replied, "but it's an alien world . . ." He trailed off, looking thoughtful. "Anyway, it should be interesting to see."

We continued our trek, keeping an eye on the moons as they chased each other across the sky to our left, heading for the sun. Beneath them, a cloud bank—extending to either side as far as the eye could see—roiled and climbed higher, dark as night.

Sometime later, the first of the moons began to overlap the sun.

"Don't look right at it," Virgil said. "Unless you want to go blind."

Heeding his words, I kept my gaze to the right of the first moon until it had fully occluded the light.

"Amazing," I said. The moon was now a gold-ringed marble of black onyx in a sea of orange. "How long does it last?"

"It'll be over soon," Scott said as the rising clouds touched the circle's bottom edge. "Eclipses last only minutes."

The halo flared brighter a moment later, and I raised a hand to shield my face. I lowered it as the light faded in a swirl of thick cloud.

"Let's go," Virgil said, turning back to the road.

We followed after him and walked four abreast. The clouds continued to bleed across the sky and the darkness deepened, colouring the road and woods in twilight and long shadows. In the distance ahead, an obelisk stuck above the treeline, rising even above the cliffs to either side of us.

Scott eyed the blackened sky. "It looks like it might rain soon."

Virgil grunted. "Not necessarily. It's always cloudy at night here. They come with the eclipse. Regular, like clockwork. They bring the night, but not always the rain."

"The clouds come—"

A click and crackle cut Scott off.

"Virgil?" said a muffled, tinny voice.

"What's that?" I asked as our guide unshouldered his backpack.

"One sec." Digging inside, he pulled out a walkie-talkie. "What's up?"

A blast of static followed. "Good, you're outside the distortion field. What's your twenty?"

He sounds a bit like Emmett, I thought. This guy sounded younger, but I detected traces of the psychiatrist's German accent in the stranger's voice.

Virgil glanced around. "Not quite, but I read you anyway. We're almost to the rendezvous point."

A blast of static came from the radio. "We?"

"I've got a few travellers with me."

After a long pause, the radio squawked again. "Travellers? What travellers?"

"I'll explain when we get there, Dieter."

"I do not like this, Virgil."

"Don't worry, they're friendly."

"Very well," Dieter said, his voice half-garbled with static.

Virgil fiddled with the radio's dials. "Are you at the rendezvous?"

"Not yet, but we are almost clear of *der Immerwald*."

"Any trouble?"

"*Nein*, but, as you know, that can change fast."

"Got it," Virgil said. "We'll be there soon."

"Who was that?" I asked as Virgil returned the walkie-talkie to his backpack.

"Dieter," he replied, shouldering his pack. "Our ride through the Immerwald."

"What's the Immerwald?" I asked, following as he began to walk again.

"The forest between us and Lolokly," he replied. "A dark and dangerous place. You remember that monstrous alien life I mentioned?" Glancing at my friends, I nodded. "Well, the Immerwald's got more than its fair share. Plants and trees and creatures that you won't want to meet." He studied the forest a moment. "The woods on this world are wilder than on Earth, and it's easy to get lost in them. The trees have a habit of moving. Mostly, they turn in place, but sometimes they uproot themselves and move elsewhere. It makes it easy to get lost."

"They turn?" Scott asked. "Why do they do that?"

Virgil shrugged. "I suppose because the sun always shines from the same direction. They must want to catch the light on every side."

"O brave new world," Scott said under his breath.

"Why didn't you mention Dieter before?" I asked after a while, not liking the apparent deception.

He shot me a look. "I wanted to feel you out a bit. Make sure you were trustworthy."

I cocked an eye. "And are we?"

His lips quirked. "Well, you haven't tried to rob or kill me yet."

I made a face. "That's not exactly a ringing endorsement."

"Do you trust me?" Virgil said, glancing my way.

I laughed. "All right." I didn't trust him fully yet, but everything he'd told us seemed to be true, at least so far. "Point taken."

Virgil jabbed his chin toward the obelisk. "That's the rendezvous." Symbols could now be seen decorating its surface, even in the dim light. He tented a hand over his eyes. "It doesn't look like Dieter's there yet, but if he's left the Immerwald, he'll be here soon."

As he said so, a low drone came from ahead of us, audible just above the wind and flutter of leaves. The throaty whine changed perpetually as it drew closer, rising and falling in pitch and occasionally subsumed by a rapid staccato rattle.

"That'll be Dieter." Virgil strode faster. "Let's pick up the pace."

A long cylinder thrust from the obelisk's side—nine feet above and horizontal to the ground. An armoured vehicle crawled into view a moment later, rolling atop tightly spaced wheels wreathed in muddy metal treads. Rounding the obelisk, the tank rumbled to a stop, engines coughing, and its main gun and headlights swung in our direction.

"Is that our ride?" Scott asked. "A tank?"

"No way," Caleb said.

As we neared, the sound of the wind and leaves returned as the tank's engine stopped.

Virgil turned to face us. "Stay back a bit, fellas, while I talk to Dieter." He looked at me. "Maybe pull up your hood until I can tell him about you. He's seen as much weirdness as I have, but still it's better to warn him." With a nod, I tugged the hood of my jacket forward. "Good man."

A clunk of metal and gleam of light came from the top of the turret. The face of a man wearing a dark beret and white tank top rose into view a moment later, visible behind a roof-mounted machine gun. Laying the hatch door to his rear with a clank, he hoisted himself from within, climbed down the side, and strode to the front to meet us. By the lines on his face and hints of grey in his short brown hair and three-day beard, he looked to be in his forties. My palm twitched, spotting a pistol in a shoulder holster beneath his arm.

Virgil spread his arms wide and stepped forward. "Dieter!" He clapped a hand to the shorter man's shoulder and drew him away. "*Wie geht's?*"

Dieter grumbled something inaudible in reply.

As they spoke, I stayed behind Scott, and my eyes roamed over Dieter's mud-spattered ride. Metal cans sat above the tank's treads, atop thick fenders that by their thickness probably housed storage compartments. White letters painted across the side of the tank's turret identified it as the Hermes.

I didn't know a lot about tanks and couldn't identify the type, but it didn't look like any I'd seen during my time in Nevada. Still, I felt sure that it had to have come from Earth at some point, probably by spatial transposition. How Dieter had come to possess it was a mystery, but given what Virgil had told us of the Immerwald, I was glad for its protection on our journey to Lolokly. Especially given the trouble I'd been having accessing the Underfrost since our arrival.

Virgil threw his hands out to his sides. "Be reasonable."

Dieter glanced our way and shook his head. "We are not

running a charity," he said, loud enough to be heard. "Everyone pays for passage. It is as simple as that."

Scott pulled out his wallet. "I've got cash." He pulled out a few bills. "How much is it?"

Virgil held up a hand. "Greenbacks aren't any good here, fellas."

"Do you have coin?" Dieter asked. "Drachmas, maybe?"

Scott looked down. "A few quarters."

Dieter shook his head. "Do you have anything with which to barter?"

"How about a soda?" I said, stepping from behind Scott.

The tanker's eyes widened. "*Mein Gott.*" He shot Virgil a look. "*Der Schneemann spricht.*"

Virgil smirked. "Better than I do."

Dieter's head moved back and forth, almost imperceptibly. "Coca-Cola?"

I thought a moment. "I've got a couple of those."

"How many?"

"Four or five."

He made a noise deep in his throat. "Not enough." His eyes flicked to my hand. "The ring would be."

I drew my hand back. "No way."

He lifted his shoulders. "It would be sufficient payment for all of you."

"Sorry."

He looked at Scott. "What about yours?"

Scott shook his head, and Dieter looked back to me. "Your hat and the drinks, then, for you alone."

"I can't do that," I said, frowning. *I'm not leaving my friends behind either*, I thought. "How about the jacket?"

Dieter scoffed. "It looks as if it has been rescued from a fire." He glanced at Virgil. "If they have nothing to offer, you will have to pay for them or leave them behind."

"Come on." Virgil rubbed his hairless scalp and threw up his hands. "I told you. I don't have it with me. I can pay you when we get to Lolokly."

"No," Dieter said. "Your terms are not acceptable." He took

a few steps and thumped a hand against the tank's side. A woman's head popped up through the hatch immediately, as if she'd been waiting there. My eyes flicked to the mounted machine gun next to her. "Figure it out or say your goodbyes while we refuel."

About Dieter's height and age, she wore black pants and a white tank top and, like Dieter, sported a pistol under an armpit. Her hair had been buzzed short, and she wore a hat that looked similar to mine. After she'd climbed down, the two tankers spoke in hushed tones, glancing our way periodically.

"What do we do?" Caleb asked.

I shrugged. "I guess we'll have to walk."

Virgil sighed. "Are you fellas sure you won't give up one of those fancy rings? It'll be better than dying in the Immerwald."

I shook my head. "These are . . . we just can't. A friend gave them to us." *And we've lost one already*, I thought. "They're important."

"Wouldn't this friend rather see you all make it safe to Lolokly?"

He was right. Olivia probably wouldn't mind, but the rings were more than just pretty baubles. As she'd told us, they were passports of a sort, granting us the right to move about Caelumtor freely. Even on this alien world, they'd be the only way to prove our story to any of the gods or their servants that might live here. Besides, we couldn't risk letting them fall into the wrong hands. Caleb's lost ring had apparently allowed Atriel to use a transporter. Mine and Scott's might be similarly abused.

"I'm sorry. We can't." I frowned. "I'm sure she'd be more than happy to pay triple the normal price for us."

"Really?" Virgil said. "You don't even know how much the normal price is."

"Whatever it is, it won't be a problem." I didn't know for sure, but I thought it was probably true. With millennia to acquire and invest money, the Schmidt's had to be rich.

Virgil's eyes widened. "Is that so?" My friends and I nodded, and he stroked his beard a moment. "Let me see what I can work out."

He strode over to Dieter and the woman, who were busy lugging jerry cans toward the rear of their armoured vehicle.

Virgil returned a few minutes later and looked at me. "You got those Cokes?"

I dipped my chin. "Uh-huh."

"Give them to me."

"What for?" I asked.

"I've worked out a deal. I've given him the few coins I have with me. For that and the Cokes, they've agreed to wait here until morning while we head back to Abadom to get the rest of their payment for the crossing."

"You've got money stashed there?" Scott asked.

"Uh-huh," Virgil said. "Not a lot, but enough."

"That's super generous of you, dude," Caleb said.

Virgil held up his index finger. "It's just a loan." His eyes met mine. "One that I trust your friend will pay back to me with a whole lot of interest."

"All right." I looked around and, spotting a boulder, I strode toward it. "One second."

"Where are you going?" Virgil asked.

"He's getting the Cokes," Scott replied.

Slipping into cover behind the giant rock, I swept off my cap and hunted around inside. While Virgil seemed okay, I still wasn't ready to reveal all my secrets to him.

A short time later, I returned, pockets bulging, and began handing cans to Virgil.

"Where have you been keeping them?" He trapped two cylinders between his chest and forearm and took the last two in each hand. "Never mind," he said, walking away. "I probably don't want to know."

He stacked the cans atop one of the tank's fenders as Dieter approached from the vehicle's rear. They spoke a moment, then shook hands, and the two walked over.

"All right." Virgil turned to the smaller man as they reached us. "We'll be back as soon as we can."

"Do not be late," Dieter said. "We will not wait beyond the agreed-upon time."

Virgil's lips straightened into a tight line. "Not even for me?"

"Sorry, my friend," the tanker said. "Not even for you. Time is money. If you are not back by cloud fall, you will have to walk to Lolokly."

Chapter 21

The Nameless

Virgil set a fast pace, and we soon left the cliffs behind. As we returned to the edge of the ruined town, the sky whitened, and the air shattered with thunder. Bolts of lightning struck obelisks throughout the valley repeatedly. The runes on their sides glowed in the aftermath, and a faint hum filled the air between thunderclaps.

A moment later, rain began to fall.

"Holy shit," Caleb said, holding his hands over his ears. "Do you guys see that?"

"It's pretty hard to miss, Slim," I said, shouting over a rumble of thunder.

"I mean the obelisks," he said. "The lightning keeps hitting them. Why not anything else?"

"Yeah," Scott said. "They seem to act like lightning rods."

Caleb pointed at the nearest one. "They're glowing, too. Why do you suppose that is?"

"They harvest the power of the storm," Virgil said. "At least, that's what I've heard."

"For what?" I asked.

He shrugged. "I'm not sure." He pointed to the distant hill of Abadom. A few windows of the castle were lit. "Probably for the castle."

Scott frowned. "Is it much farther?" His eyes darted up. "If not, we should find shelter."

"Not far now," Virgil said. "Let's run. We'll get there faster."

We ran, jostled and shoved by gusts of wind at our backs. I tugged my cap down by the visor, keeping to the rear to ensure no one got left behind.

"Does it matter?" Caleb said as we moved. "We're already soaked."

"Yeah, it does." Scott looked up at the storm. "I don't want to be struck by lightning."

Caleb waved a hand. "Hardly anyone gets hit, dude. I heard it's like twenty people a year at most."

Not counting those that can call it down, I thought, remembering Olivia catching lightning with upraised hands back on Caelumtor.

"That's out of everyone," Scott said, holding a hand to his stomach. "Including those that stay inside during storms . . ." He trailed off, huffing air. "If you limit it to only people that choose to wander around in thunderstorms, the odds are much higher."

"Point taken, dude." Caleb pointed to the roadside. "What about in there?"

Virgil glanced back and shook his head. "It'll take too long to secure."

My brow furrowed. "Why would—"

"Save your breath for running, fellas," he shouted, pumping his arms faster. "It's not just rain that's coming."

Led by Virgil, we raced to the square where we'd first encountered him, then dashed down a side street. A turn or two later, the rain stopped as we passed under an awning projecting from the side of a brick-and-mortar building. A ticket booth sat near the middle of two broad hallways leading to wood-framed double doors with glass windows. Torn fragments of movie posters covered the walls, and fallen display easels littered the theatre's entryway.

The doors creaked open at Virgil's touch, revealing a marble floor, red walls, squat sofas, chairs, low-slung tables, silver ashtray stands, and other furniture. Dropping his pack from his shoulders, he dug around inside. Moments later, he pulled out a small plush purple velvet bag. He unfastened the string holding it shut, then reached inside. Drawing forth what looked like a handful of marbles, he turned back to the dark interior. He muttered something unintelligible into his clenched fist, then made a throwing motion.

The balls lit as they sailed through the air, arcing toward the ground before rising higher, glowing brighter with each moment. They distributed themselves evenly throughout the area, just a foot below the ceiling, where they hovered in place. Their combined light illuminated all but the farthest corners of the lobby.

"Come on," Virgil said, stepping inside.

Stretches of marble floor bridged gaps between red carpeting. Plush sofas, bookended by ashtray stands, lined the walls to our right. Opposite them sat a concession stand. The hands of a white-faced clock hanging on the wall behind it read just after eight o'clock. Judging by its unmoving second hand, it no longer functioned.

"Nice," Scott said. "It looks art deco."

"What does?" I asked.

He waved his hands at the walls and ceiling. "The decor."

Caleb padded over to the concession stand. "Bogus. There's nothing left."

I pointed to the empty glass box sitting on the counter. "Not even popcorn."

He frowned and looked at me. "That would've been choice. I'm getting hungry."

"Scavengers ate it all," Virgil said. "Years ago." He smirked. "I don't think you'd enjoy it now, even if there was some left."

The teen's shoulders slumped. "That sucks, dude."

"Might as well take a load off, fellas." Virgil pointed to the sofas. "Take off those wet clothes first, though. You don't want to get sick." He looked at me. "Give me a hand, son."

"With what?" I asked.

"Securing the entrance," he said, heading for the door.

"Are you expecting trouble?" I said, following him.

Virgil grunted. "I've only seen them a few times before, during storms like this."

"Who?" I said in a hushed voice.

"People. Dead people, covered in moss and vines."

I cocked an eye. "If they were walking around, what makes you think they were dead?"

Virgil crouched. Sweeping a steel chain from the floor with a metallic jingle, he began threading it through the door handles. "The vines growing out of their eye sockets, and their flesh . . . it's like tree bark, mottled and lifeless." He dug into his pack, pulled out a brass padlock, and fastened it to the chain. "Their clothing's all dirty and tattered like they just climbed out of the ground." He turned to face me. "They move all twitchy too, as if they're getting the chair."

"The chair?"

"The electric chair." He moved to the next set of doors. "You know?"

I grimaced. "Yeah." Other, older methods to achieve the same end jumped to the forefront of my mind, and I regretted the return of those particular memories. "That's heavy. What happened when you saw them?"

"The first time, I approached them. In the storm, I thought they were just ordinary people. I soon realized otherwise. They chased me through town. They're fast, but I knew the area and gave them the slip. It's a good thing too. If I hadn't, I don't think I'd be here today. Since then, I don't take any chances when it storms."

"Where do they come from?" I asked.

He shrugged. "All I know is they come with the lightning, just like the clouds come with solar eclipses, and that they're scary as hell." He waved a hand. "Come on. Give me a hand with this sofa." As the thunder crashed louder, we piled sofas, display stands, and whatever else we could find against the doors. A short while later, Virgil grunted and smacked his hands together. "All right, that'll have to do. Why don't you check on the others?"

"Where are you going?" I asked.

"To get some towels."

While we waited, I filled in Scott and Caleb on my conversation with Virgil. They'd arranged four sofas into a square. Stripped to their undergarments, they lay stretched out on opposite sofas. Scott's long legs extended past the edge of his, but Caleb's shorter ones, bent toward his chest, fit easily within the armrests.

Soon after, Virgil returned. "Good thinking, fellas," he said, tossing towels to my friends.

Scott rubbed the cloth against his head. "How long do you suppose the storm will last, Virgil?"

"Not long, I hope," he replied. "We've got that rendezvous to make."

"Will that Dieter dude really leave us behind?" Caleb asked.

Virgil nodded. "If we're not back in time, I'm sure he will. We've got plenty of time, though. If it comes to it, we'll have to chance the storm, but they usually don't last that long."

"I sure hope not," Scott said with wide eyes. "Not with those things out there."

Virgil grunted. "Shivurr told you about them?"

"Uh-huh," Scott said. "Do you really not know who they are? They must have been people once."

"Maybe they're the dudes that used to live here," Caleb said.

Scott aimed a finger at Caleb. "Good thinking, kid."

Virgil frowned. "I hope that's not true. I'd know some of them then, not that I'd be likely to recognize anyone. Not the way they look now."

I considered a moment. "Maybe they're the people that lived here before. Not those from your town, but from the one that was already here. You know? The one you got jumbled up with."

"Maybe, but I've got another idea. It's just a theory, mind you."

"What's that?" I asked.

"The Banished," he replied. "At least, that's what I figure they are."

"Who are they?"

"Criminals," he replied. "Those that have been exiled to the Immerwald. I think they're the ones that never made it back."

"What do you mean? If they're banished, why would they come back?"

"They're allowed to return, if they can survive until their sentence is up and find their way back from wherever they were dropped. The worse the crimes, the deeper inside they get released."

Caleb blew out a breath. "That's harsh, dude."

"It saves on the need for prisons, and at least they're given a chance at returning. Of course, those that commit the worst crimes—the Nameless—are never allowed to return, even if they can make it back. If they do, they're returned to another random spot deep within the Immerwald. That doesn't happen often, though. From what I've heard, the forest takes most of them, quickly." He shrugged. "That's how I've heard it described. The forest taking them. I'd always thought it meant the forest killed them, but I've come to believe that these creatures used to be the Nameless. That the forest took them over, making them puppets that are cursed to wander forever for their crimes."

I glanced at my friends. "Why are they called the Nameless?"

"Because they have none. Their names were taken from them as part of their punishment."

"Taken away?" Scott said in a hushed voice.

Virgil fired him a look. "They do things differently here on Zarechus. Murderers don't get to be famous or even infamous here. If the crime is serious enough, all record of a convict's name, every picture of them, and who they were gets expunged wherever it might be found and replaced with a random identifier. Using their birth names thereafter in any future publication or broadcast is forbidden. Not even family members are permitted to speak their name. At least in public. Soon enough, the Nameless are forgotten as if they'd never been."

Scott frowned. "But what about their crimes? They can't be forgotten. Their victims wouldn't want that, would they?"

Virgil shrugged. "The crimes and victims are not forgotten. Just the perpetrator."

"But why?" Caleb asked.

"So that sickos aren't made famous for their atrocities. Some of them get off on that."

"Brutal," the teen said.

"I get it." Scott looked at me. "Like Jack the Ripper."

Virgil inclined his head. "A monster that's still remembered, almost a hundred years after his crimes." He glanced toward the theatre's entrance. "Anyway, I figure, instead of dying in the Immerwald, these villains became a part of it."

"Are we safe here, though?" Caleb asked.

Virgil nodded. "As long as they don't know we're here."

The teen sat taller. "What if they saw us come inside?"

Virgil shrugged. "If they had, they'd already be at the doors."

"Which are chained up," I added.

"That'll buy us time." Virgil looked toward the entrance. "It won't stop them, though. Those doors are mostly glass, so stay away from them." He sat on an empty sofa and lay back. "There's no telling how long this storm's going to go on, so we all might as well rest. We might need our strength if we have to go out into the storm again."

"Really?" Scott said. "Shouldn't someone stay awake and keep watch?"

"No need," Virgil said. "With the doors secured, no one's sneaking up on us here."

"Works for me." I collapsed onto the remaining sofa, reshaping myself to fit between the armrests. "Can you do something about the lights, Virgil?"

"Sure can."

He shouted a word that I didn't understand at the ceiling, and they dimmed to nothing a moment later. Only the faint light shining through the theatre's glass doors—punctuated by flashes of lightning—remained to illuminate the lobby.

I lay there with my eyes closed, thinking about the Immerwald—a forest so dangerous that those banished there often didn't survive and that might have spawned the creatures that Virgil had described. If half of it was true, it wasn't one I wanted to cross on foot, especially with my ability to touch the Underfrost compromised. Least of all when it meant my friends would be subject to the same perils.

We'd better make it back to the tank in time, I thought.

Before long, a whistling sound came from Virgil's direction, then from Scott's.

Sometime after, I fell asleep too.

Chapter 22

Double Feature

Cracks of thunder shook the building, and I woke with a start. Glancing toward the main entrance, I sighed with relief. Furniture still sealed the doors, and the glass was unbroken.

"That was a loud one." Caleb stretched his arms above his head with a moan. "What time is it?"

I shrugged. "I don't know."

"I'm not sure it matters here," Scott said from the adjoining sofa. His mouth gaped wide. Rubbing his eyes, he continued, "I mean, this isn't Earth, so whatever time it is back on Caelumtor doesn't apply here."

"I think my brain begs to differ, dude," Caleb said. "It feels like morning to me."

Scott checked his watch. "Nah, it's the middle of the evening back home." A gurgle came from his middle. "Which means we missed supper." He rubbed his stomach. "And breakfast seems days ago. We should've packed lunches."

I looked at the empty couch. "Maybe Virgil can help us out with that. Where is he anyway?"

"He went for a walk, I think." Caleb sat taller. "Oh, hey. Do you have one of those Ambrolas?"

"Sure do." I pulled off my hat and rummaged inside. The Ambrolas were much smaller than the other cans, and my fingers soon located one. "Here you go, Caleb."

"Cool." He took the proffered can. "I don't suppose you've got a burger and fries in there."

I wagged my head and turned to Scott, who had closed his eyes again. With a grin, I grabbed another can and placed it on his chest, above his crossed arms. He flinched and sat up, dropping the can into his lap.

"Whoa, that's cold." He looked at me. "Thanks."

"Hey, fellas," Virgil said, approaching from down the hall. "Did you sleep well?"

"Not bad." I glanced at the wall. "It sounds like the storm's still going out there, though."

"Yep." Virgil edged between the furniture and took a seat. "It settled down for a spell a few times but started up again before long."

Returning my cap to my head, I held out another tiny can. "You want one, Virgil?"

"What's that?" He squinted at my outstretched hand. "Soda pop?"

"Yeah," I said. "Sort of."

Caleb sniffed his drink. "Better."

"I haven't tried it myself," I said.

Virgil eyed the can. "I think I'll stick to coffee."

Scott looked up. "You have some?"

"Not yet." Virgil pulled his pack closer and delved inside. "But give me a few minutes."

"Too hot for my blood." With a flick of my finger, the Ambrola cracked open with a short hiss. As before—on the drive to Caelumtor with Olivia—a puff of mist and a brief rainbow of light surfaced from within. I thrust it toward Caleb. "*Prost*, Slim."

The teen smiled, then tapped his can against mine. "What's *prost*, dude?"

"Huh?" I sniffed the open can. "Oh, uh. It's cheers. In German."

"You speak German?"

I thought a moment. "Yeah, I think maybe I do. Again."

"What do you mean?"

"Yesterday, I didn't know it. Now I do." I shrugged. "It must be the vials."

Virgil looked up. "You got vials that teach you languages? Are you a potion maker?"

Nuts. I shouldn't have said anything in front of Virgil. While he had proven trustworthy so far, I still didn't feel comfortable sharing all of our secrets with him. Least of all my amnesia.

"Nah, we're just kidding around." I raised the can. "Time to see what all the fuss is about."

"Go easy," Caleb said. "It's got some kick."

I took a slug, then swished the bubbling liquid from cheek to cheek. *Pretty good.* I swallowed, enjoying the tickle of the Ambrola as it plunged down my throat.

"Hey, not—" I stood taller as energy rushed outward from my middle in every direction. My feet and cheeks warmed as my vision sharpened. "Whoa!" I held my arm out straight and regarded the Ambrola. "This is good stuff."

"I know, right?" Caleb tilted his can against his lips. "It's weird. I'm not even hungry anymore."

"Really?" Scott cracked his can and drank. "I never noticed that before." He smacked his lips. "Wicked. It tastes like the best coffee I've ever had, even if it is ice cold."

Caleb grimaced. "What are you talking about, dude? It tastes like a chocolate milkshake."

I ran my tongue over my icy teeth. "Mine's more like all the best soda pops combined."

"Yuck," Caleb said. "That sounds like swamp water."

"What's that?"

"You know, when you mix all the flavours together."

I shook my head. "No, I've never heard of that."

"It's something kids do. Usually tastes like . . . shit."

I smirked. "How do you know what that tastes like?"

Caleb's brow wrinkled. "Swamp water?"

I shook my head. "The other thing."

Scott chortled. "Yeah."

The teen reddened. "It's just an expression, dudes." He held up his can. "Funny. All these look the same, but I guess they must have different flavours anyway."

Olivia's words from the road trip came back to me. "They're supposed to provide what the drinker needs, so maybe the flavour changes, too."

Scott's brow creased. "You mean changing its taste to match our desires?"

I pointed a finger at him. "Yeah, something like that."

He whistled. "Wow, we could make a fortune with that." He smacked his lips again. "That's so weird. My teeth . . . my whole mouth feels clean, like I just brushed them."

"Are you sure you want to mess around with that stuff, fellas?" Virgil leaned in and looked at each of us in turn. "That sounds like something the gods supposedly drink."

I looked at the can. "Sure, why not?" I grinned. "Its other name isn't Soylent Green, is it?"

Scott winced. "I hope not."

"I don't know what that is," Virgil said, "but if this is like the stuff I've heard about, it might be dangerous for regular folks." He looked me up and down. "I suppose maybe you can take it, but . . ." He trailed off, staring at my friends. "Wait. You're not gods after all, are you?"

"No, man." Scott glanced at Caleb. "Me and the kid, we're nothing like that. We're like you, just a couple of ordinary guys. Hanging out with a snowman. On an alien world."

"Borealan," I said.

"Right," he said. "Borealan. Sorry, Cool Hand."

"No sweat," I said with a smile, feeling a bit giddy for some reason. My hand tingled as I reached for the Underfrost. *Hey, I think I can access it again.* With a thought, I plucked a crackling ball of white from thin air and smiled. *Nice.*

Virgil raised his hands. "Easy now. That's quite a trick, but it looks dangerous."

"Sorry." I lowered my hand, returning the frost to its source. "I was just checking."

He frowned. "Checking what?"

"That I could still do that." It still wasn't as easy as it should have been, but it felt easier than the last time. Something still sat in the way, but I felt better able to force my way through it.

Virgil grunted. "Your abilities must be affected by whatever happened here too. Just like the gods."

Scott cleared his throat. "Is there a restroom around here?"

"There is." Virgil jabbed a thumb by his shoulder. "Past the concession stand and to your right." He stood. "The water doesn't run anymore, so I'd better show you how to work things."

"Thanks, man," Scott said.

"Wait." Caleb sprang to his feet. "I'll come with you."

Virgil returned alone a short while later and took a seat on the couch opposite me.

"You've been here before," I said.

"Yeah, it's been a haven for me." He looked around. "Somehow this building survived the transition with little to no damage."

"Just luck, do you think?"

"I don't know," he said, looking thoughtful. "Whatever the reason, I'm glad it did. When I was younger, movie theatres were a safe place, a refuge. And it's still a sanctuary for me, even now."

"Did you grow up around here?"

"Yep, I saw movies here, back on Earth, but as for here, well, this building's far from the place where it started now."

I thrust a hand at a nearby poster. "It's too bad we can't watch a flick while we're waiting. I've never watched one in an actual theatre." *At least*, I thought, *I don't remember doing so.*

Virgil smiled. "Well, as it happens, we can."

"Are you serious?" I looked about. "What about electricity?"

"That was a problem for a long time." Virgil leaned toward me. "It took me a while to locate a power supply, but that was the easy part. Getting an adapter specially made to interface with the projector . . . well, that took longer."

"Cool! Can we watch one now?"

"Sure," Virgil said. "Why not?"

"Awesome."

He stood. "I'll go and get it set up. When the other fellas return, go through those doors and find some seats. I'll come and join you after I've started the movie."

The auditorium lay dark as we entered, illuminated by only the lights of the lobby behind us. We stood in the open doorway, looking out over the rows of seats that lay before a massive white screen, two or three storeys high and as wide as the entire far wall. Before we could take a step, a jaunty melody filled the air, and the movie screen sprang to life, displaying Earth, spinning on its axis.

"I recognize that tune," Scott said.

"Come on, dudes." Caleb hustled ahead. "Let's grab seats."

Still giddy from the Ambrola, I danced down the aisle after him.

Scott chuckled. "And you guys thought my dancing was bad."

As we filed to our seats, *The Blob* blazed across the screen, black letters in a swirl of red, and a kissing couple appeared.

Taking a seat next to me, Scott gave me a nudge and smiled. "I haven't seen this in years."

"Is that dude supposed to be a teenager?" Caleb said from my other side. "He looks as old as Scott."

"Thanks, kid," Scott said. "I think he was about five years younger than me when this was filmed."

Caleb's brow furrowed. "That's still way too old to be a teenager."

"Why do they do that?" I asked. "Have adults play teenagers, I mean."

Scott smirked. "They're probably easier to deal with than smartass punks."

A creak drew my eyes toward the lobby doors, and Virgil entered. He paused a moment and peered about.

"Over here," I said, waving a hand in greeting.

He nodded and came down the aisle toward us, stooped over awkwardly, with his hands behind his back.

"Do you want some, fellas?" Virgil asked, producing two paper bags heaped with popcorn from behind his back.

"Where did you get that?" Scott asked. "I thought it was all gone."

Virgil shrugged, passing him a bag. "I brought it with me."

"Cool surprise, dude," Caleb said, taking the other bag.

"I'll pop a few more." Turning, Virgil headed back up the aisle. "Keep watching the show."

He soon returned with a few more bags, and we sank back in

our seats, munched popcorn, and sipped sodas that I distributed from my hat. I held back an Ambrola, though, knowing I might yet need its restorative properties here on this alien world. I smiled to myself, revelling in the shared experience—one where we weren't the ones being chased for a change.

Too soon, the words *The End* materialized on screen, replaced by a large question mark a moment later.

"What did you think, fellas?" Virgil asked as the credits rolled.

"I liked the old cars," Caleb said.

"Was there ever a sequel?" I asked, wondering what might have happened to the creature after it had been frozen and sent to the Arctic. "*The Blob Strikes Back*, maybe?"

"I don't know," Virgil said. "Could be."

Scott nudged my arm. "Not as long as the Arctic doesn't melt."

Caleb snickered. "Yeah, right. Like that'd ever happen."

I chuckled without enthusiasm. "You never know."

Caleb leaned closer. "Can we watch another one?"

"Why not?" Virgil said. "I can still hear thunder outside." He pulled on the seatback in front of him and regained his feet. "Give me a few minutes. I'll go start it."

"Cool." Caleb wiggled in his seat. "Which one?"

"*I Married a Monster from Outer Space*," Virgil said with a nod.

Caleb grinned. "It must have been love, dude."

Virgil snorted and looked at me. "The kid's a wisenheimer." He strode up the aisle for the exit. "Be back in a bit."

"This is awesome," Caleb said. "Watching movies. I wonder what else Virgil's got."

"*I Was a Teenage Werewolf*?" Scott held up a finger, flicking eyes between Caleb and me. "Don't say it."

"That'd be wicked," Caleb said with a grin. "Being able to transform, I mean."

Scott touched his cheek. "I don't see how that could even work for a human being." He looked at me. "I bet you could do it, though."

"Yeah," I said. "Olivia told me the same thing."

"It makes sense, right? You're a lot more fluid than Caleb and me."

"Give it a try," Caleb said.

"Turn into a werewolf? I don't think so."

"No, dude," he replied. "Try something smaller. Like legs."

"All right." I stood and thrust my pop can at Caleb. "Hold my drink."

I looked down at myself, picturing my round bottom sphere splitting into two halves.

My brow creased and my eyes closed.

"Come on, dude."

After several moments, my body crunched and crackled, and a cry escaped my lips.

"Holy shit." Scott's eyes lit. "It's working."

I shuddered and grabbed the seatback in front of me, feeling my insides shift.

"Come on," Caleb said. "You're doing it."

I stood a few inches taller now. The ball of snow forming my lower end had elongated, forming into an egg shape with a crease down its centre.

As I watched and focused, the crease split into a seam just above my feet and began to climb. I huffed air through my nose and pressed my lips together. Split into two halves, the ovals of snow now began to take on cylindrical shapes, and a wave of nausea welled through me, and the room spun.

I collapsed back into my seat with water running down the sides of my face and steam wafting from beneath my coat. "Ugh, I think I'm going to be sick."

"You'll get there," Caleb said.

Scott nodded. "You did great for a first try."

"Thanks." I looked down again. My body had reshaped itself back to its familiar form. "I almost hurled."

Without warning, thunder boomed louder than ever and the theatre shook, sending plaster dust cascading down from the ceiling above and rocking us in our seats.

"Holy." Scott glanced toward the ceiling. "The storm's getting worse."

As the booms faded, a thumping could be heard, coming from somewhere beyond the lobby doors, behind us.

Caleb twisted in his seat. "What's that?"

"Come on." I hopped over the seat in front of me and edged my way toward the aisle. "Let's take a look."

With my friends on my heels, I soon pushed through the doors and entered the lobby.

"Hey, fellas," Virgil said, approaching from my left, trailed by one of his floating orbs of light. "You heard that too?"

"And felt it," I said, ducking as another thunderclap shook the walls.

"Don't worry. There are lightning rods on the roof."

Another series of thumps came from my right, even louder this time. Visible in the dim light, a hand withdrew from the glass of the barricaded entrance, and the doors rattled a moment later as if shaken furiously.

"Someone's trying to get in," I said.

A face pressed against the glass. "Hello? Virgil?"

"I know that voice." Virgil's brow wrinkled. "What the hell's he doing here?"

"Who's that?" I asked.

"One of Dieter's crew," he replied, marching toward the glass. "His driver. What are you doing here, Timothy?"

"Let me in," Timothy sobbed. "Please. They're almost here."

Behind him, a woman emerged from the darkness and rain. Stooped over, she tottered closer, twitching spasmodically with each step.

Chapter 23

It's People

No, not a woman. An abomination. A fusion of person and plant, lashed together by vines and vegetation that erupted from eye sockets, skin, and tattered clothing to wrap about her head, limbs, and torso. With each writhe of the wriggling mass of plant matter, she jerked forward, legs moving like a twisted marionette. Sparks of electricity glimmered over her bark-like, yet apparently living, flesh.

Virgil reeled back a step, staring through the glass.

"What?" Timothy shot a glance over his shoulder. "Sweet Jesus." He rattled the doors. "Let me in. Please."

Virgil shook his head. "There's no time. You've got to run, fella." Two other monstrous figures, apparently once men, came into view. "Now."

Vine-covered arms stretched toward Timothy. Letting out a moan and slapping the glass, he turned and ran. Dodging his nearest assailant, he shoved the next one, convulsed as if electrified, and fell to the ground.

Virgil pounded the glass. "No."

"Leave him alone," I shouted, also banging the glass, and the trio paused as if they'd heard and looked toward the door. "That's it! Get over here."

Apparently drawn by my words, the female one stumbled nearer with a drunken lurch, and the others followed after her a moment later. In a burst of unexpected speed, they rushed at the glass, crossing the distance in moments. Surprised, I drew back from the door, raising my hands to protect myself as the creatures collided with it, arms slapping against the barrier like wet meat.

Visible between gaps in the throng, Timothy scrabbled to his feet and looked our way before staggering off. Paying him no heed, the creatures battered against the doors, striking the tough glass with open hands. Beyond them, a half dozen or so more vine-covered goons appeared from both sides of the street.

I glanced at Virgil, who had retreated along with me. "Will it hold?"

He shrugged. "I don't—"

One of the attackers pulled its head back and drove it against the door. The glass made a sound like an egg cracking as more figures bled into view.

I grabbed Virgil's arm. "Is there another way out of here?"

He nodded. "Come on." Moving briskly, he led us into the auditorium, down the centre aisle to the far-left corner, and down a short hallway to a metal door with a push-bar handle. With a glance at me, he gave the door a shove, revealing a rain-pounded alley lit by flashes of lightning.

"Damn it," Scott said as thunder shook the building. "It's a mess out there. Is there another place we can stay nearby?"

Virgil scowled. "Not close." He looked back down the hall-way. "Not one that's defensible."

"Let's head for the castle," I said.

"The castle?" Virgil frowned. "I'm not sure that's a good idea."

I met his eyes. "I know you're nervous about the place, but it'll be okay. We didn't see anything dangerous when we were there, and what could be more defensible than a castle?"

Shrieks and footsteps came from the auditorium behind us, just audible above the raging storm.

"Fine," Virgil said, plunging out the door. "Let's go."

Stepping to the side, I motioned my friends to follow him. After they'd slipped past me, I pulled the hood of my jacket over my head and stepped into the rain. Letting the door slam shut behind me, I leaned my back against it and reached for the Underfrost. Once again, nothing happened.

Before I could try again, the door banged, knocking me forward a step. Turning about, I threw all my weight against it, swinging it back on its hinges but not enough for it to latch. With my momentum spent, my feet slid across the wet pavement, and the door inched wider. As I prepared to run, a patter of footsteps came from my right and hands appeared above mine. Other hands pressed into my back a moment later, and at last the door closed with a click.

"Can you freeze it shut?" Scott said by my ear.

I shook my head. "That's what I was trying to do."

"Try again."

I nodded, closed my eyes, and took a deep breath. As I let it out slowly, a tingle of energy tickled my fingertips. The Underfrost still lay there, I realized, but a wall or field of some kind now lay between me and it. The more forcefully I reached for it, the greater the resistance, but by lightening my touch, I found I could work my way through it.

Time to use it, I thought, pouring frost into the metal, spreading rime across its surface.

A moment later, Scott snatched his hands from the door as ice welled from its frame.

"Give me some room." The hands pressed against my shoulders and back pulled away. Retreating a few steps, I nodded my thanks to Virgil and Caleb. Facing the door again, I swept my hands up and down in short, quick motions as if urging a crowd to its feet. Snow bubbled from the earth and asphalt until the door disappeared behind a drift of white.

Scott slapped my back. "Good enough, man."

Lowering my hands, I nodded. "Let's go."

Turning, I chased after Virgil with my friends by my side. After dodging back-alley dumpsters, we spilled out onto a side street and took a right. Hopping a tipped shopping cart, we pulled up short at a ruined car, its front end two feet from a brick wall.

Gesturing for my friends to go first, I looked back. Seeing no signs of pursuit, I squeezed through the gap last, sidestepped a crumpled baby carriage that sat on the far side, and sprinted to catch up with them.

Virgil turned at the next corner. Halfway down the block, he crossed to the street's far side, skirting a vehicle, its front end crunched against a utility pole, with my friends in tow.

Weaving between two cars, I followed after them. Halfway across, a gust of wind tore at my clothes, sending my hand to the bill of my hat. A moment later, a loud crack and a moan pulled my eyes upward as a utility pole tipped toward me.

"Shit." A veil of frost glimmered before my upraised hands an instant before I knew no more.

Sometime later, something warm pressed against my cheeks, and I opened my eyes. Scott knelt over me, clothes and hair dripping, holding my face in his hands.

He smiled. "Hey, man."

Caleb crouched on my other side, eyes locked on mine. He seemed about to say something but remained silent.

I sat up, wincing. "Anyone get the license plate of the truck?"

"Hey, easy." Scott placed a hand gently against my chest. "You're injured." He glanced over his shoulder. "Can you give us some light, man?"

Virgil, looking similarly waterlogged, stepped closer, holding one of his orbs of light high.

Caleb grimaced and his eyes shone. "Your cheek, dude."

I raised a hand to my face, and ice and snow dropped into my palm. I scooped it into my mouth and swallowed.

"Gnarly," Caleb said, looking away.

"Waste not, want not," I muttered. "Help me up, would you?"

Hands grabbed my upper arms. With a grunt, my friends eased me into a sitting position and dragged me against the nearby wall.

"Where are we?" I asked.

"An apartment building," Virgil replied.

Caleb squeezed my shoulder. "We had to carry you here."

"After we got that telephone pole off of you," Virgil said.

"I got hit over the head with a telephone pole?"

"Uh-huh," Virgil said. "It must have been damaged during the event. Probably by the busted-up car at its base. Since then, time and all the rain around here must have weakened it further."

"Yeah," Scott said, "and that blast of wind finished the job."

"It almost finished me too," I said, feeling a stab of pain between my eyes.

Virgil grunted. "The wires slowed it down a little, and the car behind you took the worst of it, but you still took quite a hit." He glanced at my friends. "If it'd been one of us, we'd be dead."

I pulled off my cap, rubbing my forehead. "Are they still after us?"

"The Nameless?" Scott asked.

"Yeah." I studied the hat in my hands. The left side had collapsed like a stomped-on cake. I snapped my wrist, fluffing it out.

"I expect so," Virgil said, "but as long as they didn't see us come in here, we should be okay for a minute."

Tentatively, I reached up to my head and felt around. Rather than the smooth roundness I had expected, my fingers traversed a concave crater of ice.

Oh, shit. I flipped my cap and rummaged around inside. *Come on.* After a few moments, I pulled a fresh can of Ambrola free, cracked the tab, and drank.

"It's people," Scott said in a hushed and quavering voice. "People."

My cheeks ballooned as I stifled a snort. "Not the time for jokes, dude," I said, smiling and wiping a dribble of Ambrola from my lips.

"I told you, they're not people," Virgil said. "Not anymore."

"Not the Nameless, man. The movie. *Soylent Green.*"

"Oh, never heard of it. It must have been after my time."

A rush of energy surged through me. "If it's people . . ." I crushed the can, wiped a finger along the edge of my mouth, and licked my fingertips. "They're delicious."

I envisioned myself whole and undamaged, and my flesh roiled, pulling meltwater inward to be recooled, while pushing cold fresh snow and ice to the surface. Sounds of crackling ice and rustling fabric filled the air. My rain-soaked jacket stiffened and crusted white as my body cooled. My lower half narrowed as my body redistributed itself, repairing the damage the utility pole had done, and Scott and Caleb withdrew, shivering.

"Whoa," Scott said with a smile, "there's the Shivurr I know."

I wiggled my feet, checking that they both still worked. A memory of them at the end of long human-like legs drifted into my thoughts. A moment later, I snarled and blinked as the sphere forming my lower half elongated, separating into two halves, and my feet retreated. *What the hell?*

"Cool," Caleb said. "You're getting better at making legs, dude."

I shook my head. "Except I wasn't trying to." Clapping my budding legs together, I willed them to rejoin. A moment later, snow and ice merged, forming a whole. Ice continued to crackle a few seconds more, then quieted. "Okay, that's better."

Rolling to my side, I pushed against the wall and clambered to my feet. Hands grabbed my elbows as I slumped a moment later.

"Are you all right?" Scott asked.

I nodded. "I think so." Snugging my hat into place, I turned and leaned my back against the wall. "I just need a minute."

"Do you need another Ambrola?"

I stooped slowly and lifted the can from the floor. "I think this is the last one." Upending it above my mouth, I patted the bottom, nudging out a few final drops.

"A regular soda, then?"

"No, it's fine." I gave the rim a lick, crushed the voided can, then pocketed the empty. "I think I just need time now." A wave of nausea ran through me. "Just give me a minute."

"Sure, man."

"Thanks for getting me out of there," I said, taking in our surroundings.

A dark hallway lay to my left and right. To my front, behind my gathered companions, windowed double doors looked out onto a street. Heavy snow now fell, already forming thin layers atop car hoods, hydrants and postal drop boxes, though lightning still flashed, and thunder continued to crash against the outer walls.

"Of course." Scott gestured at Virgil. "It's a good thing he had a key to the building, or we'd have had to bust down the door."

Virgil jabbed a thumb toward the stairwell, opposite the en-tryway. "I found them in the super's unit, a few years back."

I took a few steps, grabbed the wrought-iron banister, and looked back at Virgil. "Maybe we can hole up in an apartment."

He gave his head a shake, grimacing. "The building's back corner's fallen in, and there may be other openings I don't know about. It's probably none too healthy in here either. There's a lot of mould from past rainfalls." He looked me up and down. "You might be okay, given your unique constitution, but that stuff ain't healthy for most folks."

"Got it," I said, releasing the banister. "We need to keep go-ing, then."

He grunted. "I'm afraid so."

I bobbed my head. "Let's do it." *While the Ambrola is still work-ing its magic*, I thought. I waved everyone back. "Give me some space."

Closing my eyes, I reached for the Underfrost. The barrier hindering my access continued to resist me, giving slightly but hardening under pressure.

My mind returned to the beach on New Olympus, watching Caleb work his feet into the sand until it reached halfway up his calves. From what I could tell about sand, you didn't get deeper into it by pounding on the same spot. That just packed it. You needed to wiggle and push and slide your way through.

With that in mind, I altered my approach, pushing slowly un-til the resistance grew too great, then altering the direction of my touch, always moving deeper without giving up the ground I'd gained, until, at last, I broke through.

My companions edged away as the air swirled white beneath my outstretched hands, and a frost disc settled lightly to the floor, waiting.

"Well, I'll be . . . ," Virgil said in a hushed voice.

"Hop on," I said. "It'll be crowded, but it'll take our weight." *I think.*

Snow breezed past my shoulders and cap as we pushed through the double doors into the street, riding atop the frost disc, inches above the ground. Jagged lightning flashed in the swirling sky to our left, revealing four Nameless standing beneath traffic lights a few hundred feet away. Holding a finger to my lips, I steered us down the sidewalk in the other direction.

"Are they following?" I asked in a low voice.

The fabric of my jacket loosened. "Nope," Caleb whispered, blowing hot breath against my cheek. "I guess they didn't hear the doors open."

"We can thank the thunder for that," Scott murmured.

The sky boomed again a moment later as if to prove his point.

"Good thing we're downwind, too," Virgil said.

"Why's that?" I asked.

"To mask our scent," he replied. "Without eyes, they must rely on other senses, don't you think?"

"Yeah," I said, "I hadn't thought of that, but it makes sense."

Taking us into the street, I looked for signs of danger ahead. Seeing no one, I urged the platform to move faster, and my jacket drew tighter across my chest. I sighed, loving the caress of snow and cool wind on my face.

"Is this snowstorm your doing, Shivurr?" Virgil said into my ear.

"It happens sometimes when I access the Underfrost."

"The Under-what?"

The snow fell harder now, piling in drifts against abandoned automobiles and buildings and reducing visibility to a few hundred feet.

Exultant, I conjured frost balls in each hand before dismissing them. Between the Ambrola and the blizzard, accessing the Underfrost came more easily now, despite whatever damage had been done here.

"Which way, Virgil?"

"Make a left at the next intersection," he yelled over the wind.

After a few more straightaways and turns, the snow eased for a moment, and our destination materialized atop the hill in the distance.

Scott's finger stabbed into view. "There it is."

"I see it." A glimmer of light tugged my eyes down. *What*

the—? I slowed us to a stop. In the road ahead, a ball of light floated a few feet above the snow. Below it, a curved line of raised stone peeked from beneath fresh powder. Floating us closer, I hopped from the frost disc and swiped snow from the stone with a hand. Symbols carved into the surface of a familiar-looking dais glowed weakly. *What's an Allfrost power node doing here?*

"You must flee, Sentinel," said a familiar-sounding voice in my head. "They are coming."

Straightening, I glanced around with wide eyes, seeing no one but my friends.

"Hue?" I said, rejoining my companions.

"Who are you talking to, Shivurr?" Caleb asked.

"An Allfrost—"

A shriek from a side street interrupted me.

Hopping aboard the frost disc, I spun us to face the sound, sending the platform sideways toward the castle at the same time. One of the Nameless shuddered and twitched a few steps our way, still shrieking. Behind it, others emerged from the veil of driving snow.

Shit.

The lead one pumped a fist in the air, and I shielded my eyes as lightning flashed. The Nameless spasmed as electricity arced over its body, and its bark-like flesh began to glow an eerie blue. An instant later, a second bolt struck the road between us. A metallic smell tickled my nose as lightning flashed again. Some bolts arced off the upraised fists of the Nameless mob, lighting them with the same blue glow as the first one. Others struck the ground and buildings to either side of the road, growing ever nearer.

Slowly enough to avoid shoving my friends off the platform, I raised a frost shield, clouding the air blue. A moment later, the blue turned white as lightning struck it, and I felt suddenly drained.

Shaking off the fatigue, I reinforced the shield and scanned the street ahead.

A department store display window lay to our right, and I steered us toward it at breakneck speed.

"What are you doing, Shivurr?" Scott bellowed.

"Hang on!"

The window broke as the frost shield rammed into it, shattering into countless pieces, sending shards of glass and naked mannequins flying.

"Is everyone okay?" I shouted. I felt confident the bubble of frost had protected us, but I figured I should check anyway.

Before anyone could answer, thunder boomed and the single-storey building's ceiling shook.

Clothing racks, long ago stripped of their wares, fell and clattered, bashed aside by the frost shield as I took us through the building and out a hole in the wall on the far side.

Emerging into an alley, I drew us to a halt and scanned the area.

"There," Scott said, pointing a finger past my head. "The gas station."

I smiled, recognizing the weathered sign and tree sprouting from the roof of the dilapidated building.

"Good eye," I said, piloting us toward it. Floating past the rusty pumps, I took us into the street. "There's the road up."

"C-cool," Caleb stammered.

"Are you okay, Slim?"

"Uh-huh," he replied. "J-just a little c-cold is all."

Scott patted my shoulder. "Nameless!" he cried, pointing to a mob of them coming from the clock tower to our right, moving fast.

With a weary sigh, I took us the other way, and the street flared bright as lightning struck the street signs, utility poles, cars, and buildings, seeming nearer with each strike.

Gulping air, I urged the frost disc faster and our surroundings blurred. Then the shield thrummed and whitened, struck by an unlucky bolt that cascaded across its surface. As the arcs died, the frosty veil shimmered and faded to nothingness, and my head and arms drooped low.

"Shivurr," Scott said. "The shield."

"I know." The air around us sparkled faintly. "I need a minute."

"I don't think we have one," he said.

As he said so, the frost disc tilted, matching the slope of the road beneath us on its way up to the castle. Too weary to raise another shield, I deked us left and right, hoping to avoid the next strike but none came.

"They've stopped chasing us," Virgil said.

"What?" I asked. "Really?"

"Yeah," he replied. "It looks like they're giving up."

I blew out a breath. "Good."

"Quit pushing, dude," Caleb muttered.

"Sorry, fella," Virgil replied. "I'm about to fall off here."

"The disc's getting smaller," Scott said.

I looked down and saw that he was right. The circle had shrunk to nearly half its original diameter.

"Huddle up," I said, willing the disc faster. The outer walls of the citadel lay just ahead. "We're almost inside."

Chapter 24

Sword and Sorcery

A long moment later, we passed through the castle gate, and I brought the frost disc to a halt in the courtyard. "We'd better get off before it vanishes altogether."

"That was too close," Scott said, stepping off.

I nodded wearily. "I hope they don't follow us here."

Virgil shook his head and wiped snow from his bare scalp. "I doubt it. They seemed to lose interest as soon as we started to climb the road."

Scott rubbed his hands together. "I wonder why."

"I'm not sure," Virgil replied, looking around. "The castle's protected somehow, I think. By more than just the walls. Have you noticed it hasn't even rained or snowed here?" He blew into his hands. "It's warmer too."

I studied the ground. "You're right. The ground's dry."

"I still hear thunder, though," Scott said. "Like it's still raining everywhere but here."

I glanced up. "It's cloudy here, though."

Caleb hugged his arms to his chest and trembled. "Let's get inside, dudes."

"The kid's right." Scott touched his cheeks. "I think I might have a bit of frostbite."

I cracked a grin and trudged toward the keep. "Come on. Now you know how I feel."

For the next while, we walked the flame-lit corridors, keeping close together, sticking our heads through doorways in hopes of finding a comfortable room to wait out the storm. Eventually, along a second-floor hallway, up a set of stairs to the right of the domed chamber where we'd arrived, we found what we were seeking: a furnished room untouched by the cataclysm that had damaged other parts of the keep. With a few muttered words, Virgil sent his spheres of light up to the ceiling, revealing tapestry-covered walls, a red-carpeted floor, long couches, ornate tables, and plush chairs.

"Nice," Caleb said. "It's a throne room or something."

Scott wagged his head. "It's a sitting room."

"A what?"

"It's like a living room." Scott swiped a finger across a table and held it up. "No one's been here in a while. Judging by the dust, it looks like it hasn't been cleaned since Roosevelt was president."

"Whatever it is," I said, flopping onto one of the sofas, "I'm glad it's here." I swiped the cap from my head and dug inside. "Time for a drink."

Scott turned to regard me. "Got one for me?"

I sighed. "Yeah, sure. I don't have many left, though, so drink it slowly. You want one too, Slim?" The teen nodded. "Virgil?"

"I'm good," he replied, holding up a metal flask.

"Is there somewhere in Lolokly where we can buy supplies?" Scott asked. "I've got bread—money, I mean—if there's a store or something."

"There is," Virgil said, "but your money's no good here, remember?"

"Oh, right."

"Don't worry, though. You fellas can stay with me and the missus until your friends come for you."

"Thanks, Virgil," Scott said. "That's kind of you."

"Think nothing of it." Virgil looked at me. "The wife will be excited to meet you, I'm sure."

"That'll be great." I smiled. "I'd love to see how the other Half lives."

"Good one, dude."

Virgil cracked a grin. "I've never heard that one before."

"Speaking of money," I said, "did you get the extra coin to pay Dieter?"

He nodded. "We're all set there."

"You kept it at the theatre?"

"Yep."

I sat taller. "What about that Timothy guy? What was he doing there?"

Virgil grunted. "I'm not sure." He took a sip from his flask, grimaced, and smacked his lips. "Spying on us . . . on me, is my guess."

"But why?"

"Dieter must have sent him." His eyebrows bunched. "To find out where I stash my coin, maybe."

My forehead creased. "Isn't he your friend?"

"Sort of," he replied, stroking his beard, "but friendship means different things to different people."

"You don't seem all that mad about it."

His shoulders gave a slight roll. "He's paid for it, with his driver's life, unless Timothy managed to escape the Nameless, which I doubt."

Scott frowned. "And we're supposed to trust this guy to take us to Lolokly? What if he tries something else?"

"He won't," Virgil said, pursing his lips. "Not against the four of us. Not when he's down a man."

"I don't know, dudes," Caleb said as he wandered the room. "That Timothy dude might have been acting on his own. Innocent until proven guilty, right?"

"Good point, kid," Scott said with a nod as the thunder outside boomed louder. "It may be academic anyway. If the storm doesn't end before morning, we won't make the rendezvous in time. Not unless we want to run the gauntlet with those Nameless freaks at least."

I looked at Virgil. "How long is this storm going to last, do you think?"

"I don't know," he replied. "It's already lasted longer than I've seen before. Storms this intense tend to burn themselves out quickly. I guess that's why there were so many of the Nameless out there."

"What do we do if we're stuck here?" Caleb asked, shooting me a glance. "We'll starve, dude. Maybe we should've tried to get to the tank instead."

"No," Virgil said. "That would've been a longer journey, and the tank might not be there. With Timothy showing up at the theatre, I'm not sure what to expect."

"Don't worry, Slim. Our friends should find us, eventually."

After saying it, I wondered if it was true. I thought about what Wilhelm might be doing now. Was he looking for us? Had he fought Atriel and survived? I had to hope so. His stupor had seemed to be lifting when he'd left us, and if he'd recovered his senses, I felt sure he'd be working to find us. Locating us on another planet was a tall order, but if anyone could do it, I believed that he could.

I looked around. "We can survive here until then, if we need to. I think I saw a well in the courtyard, so we should have water to drink, at least."

Caleb's lip curled. "Are you sure it's drinkable?"

"I'll try it first and let you know."

"If it's not potable," Scott said, "we can set up something to catch rainwater. I'm more worried about other supplies. Food, in particular." He glanced at his wristwatch. "The Ambrolas we had at the theatre really helped, but we're going to be hungry again before long."

Virgil held up a hand. "You fellas stay here if you like, but I'll be going either way once the storm ends. I need to get home, even if I have to walk."

I cocked my head. "I thought you said it's too dangerous."

"Oh, it's very dangerous, but I've done it before. If you keep near the road and don't attract any attention, it can be done. I don't want to do it again, mind you, but I can't stay here forever."

"Well," I said, "in that case, we'll come with you."

Scott's face scrunched. "But we don't have food or water, and you're almost out of soda pop. Not that we can survive on that."

"There are streams and lakes along the way." Virgil patted the quiver of arrows that rested at his feet. "I can hunt game, and I've got some jerky in my pack too that we can share. Besides, if it comes to it, people can go weeks without food."

"Weeks," Scott hissed.

Virgil snorted. "You make it sound like you've never missed a meal. A thin fella like you must not eat much."

"Not true, man," Scott said, giving his head a shake. "I eat a lot. I've got a high metabolism, I guess. I never seem to gain much weight."

Virgil patted his stomach. "That must be nice." He grimaced. "Fasting's good for you, now and then. It clears the mind and makes food taste better. Don't worry, you and your boy will be fine."

Scott blinked. "My boy?" He chortled. "Caleb's not my son, man."

"Oh," Virgil said. "Your much younger brother, then?"

Scott thrust a finger at Caleb. "Don't even say it."

Caleb didn't seem to be listening, though. "Hey, dudes. There's a big chest here." His head sank low behind a sofa, and a click and creak followed. "It's unlocked." He stood and raised a rounded piece of metal, polished to a shine. "What is this, dudes?"

Scott sprang to his feet. "A pauldron, or maybe a spaulder."

"What's that?"

"It's a shoulder pad," Scott replied, joining him behind the sofa. "It looks like there's a whole suit of armour here." He ducked low and stood, holding a chain shirt in his hands.

"That's a nice hauberk," Virgil said, still reclined on a sofa.

Scott held the mail shirt against his chest. "Do you think it'll fit me?"

I eyed him a moment. "Yeah. Maybe. Try it on."

Scott smiled. "All right." He nudged Caleb. "Give me a hand. You can be my squire."

Caleb frowned. "What's a squire?"

"It's like a golf caddy for knights."

"Oh," Caleb said. "Like in *Caddyshack*?"

"Yep."

"Good movie, dude."

Standing, I wandered the room, curious if there might be other things to find. After a few minutes of fruitless searching, a glint of metal caught my eye.

What do we have here? Stooping, I dragged a scabbard and shield from beneath Virgil's sofa. Sliding an arm through the straps of the shield, I drew the three-foot blade free and held it high.

"Check it out, dudes." Stepping back, I waved the blade through a few arcs.

Scott, half clothed in armour, smiled. "You can't win, Shivurr." Squatting, he clasped gauntleted hands by a shoulder. "If you strike me down—"

A powerful hum and buzz filled the air, cutting off his words.

"What was that?" I asked, glancing toward the hallway.

Virgil sat tall. "It sounds like a power transformer. A really loud one."

"No." Scott's hands dropped. "It's the pillars in the arrival chamber."

The hum ended abruptly, followed by a rumble and thud.

"Yeah," I said. "I guess they're still working, even if the platform isn't."

"Should we be worried?" Virgil asked.

I considered a moment. "No, I don't think so."

"Yeah," Scott said. "It's fine. If they were going to explode, they would've done it already." His gaze dropped. "Let's see that shield."

"It looks like a huge hubcap," Caleb said. "Is that a ruby in the centre?"

Slipping it off, I flipped it over and held it up like a painting. Two concentric rings enclosing a circle decorated the convex side. The ebony outer ring gleamed as if polished; the one inside that shone bright silver.

A circle of red a third the diameter of the shield lay in the centre, inset into the thick metal. "Do they come that big? That'd be a huge ruby."

Scott drew closer. "Maybe it's composed of more than one." He smirked. "Or they used Dorothy's slippers."

Virgil's brows rose. "People on Earth still watch *The Wizard of Oz* these days?"

Scott shrugged. "It's a classic."

"Here." I held the hilt of the sword out to Scott. "It must go with the armour."

"Thanks." He gripped it in both hands. "An elegant weapon . . ."

Chuckling, I handed him the scabbard. "Nice." I held the shield out to Caleb. "Here, Slim."

"Are you sure?" Caleb asked, taking it.

"Yeah." I waggled my fingers. "I can make my own."

"Can you, though?"

"Sure," I said. *I think.*

Virgil looked at Scott. "Do you know how to use that sword?"

Scott nodded. "I've taken a few kendo classes."

"No kidding?" Virgil said with raised brows. "Japanese sword fighting?"

"That's cool," Caleb said. "Why, though?"

Scott shrugged. "My character's a paladin."

Virgil squinted. "Your character?"

"In Dungeons and Dragons," Scott replied.

"Say what?"

"It's a role—"

I held up a hand. "I'm going to go check out that sound."

"Want us to come with you?" Scott asked.

"Nah, stay. I won't be long."

The cage of crystal pillars glowed as I reached the arrival chamber, lighting the faces of the gathered statues like campers at a fire. Standing atop the red pedestals, they cast long shadows in which enemies might hide, and I raised a palm and shone a beam of light into the room's dark corners. Satisfied that Nameless—or worse—weren't lying in wait, I entered and made my way to the room's centre.

As expected, the thick platter of stone that had nearly crushed me and my friends now lay flat against the floor, no longer held up by my hastily summoned drift of snow. Light glimmered above me, and I looked up. Visible through the ceiling hole, black clouds lit by intermittent flashes raced across the sky.

Just lightning and thunder, I thought, dropping my gaze, *but no rain.*

Bending at the waist, I gripped the slab and pulled upward. My limbs creaked, crackled, and popped, but the stone didn't budge, at all.

All right, I thought. *So, super strength is not one of my forgotten powers.* I shrugged. *It was worth a shot.*

I turned, sat on the stone's edge, and eyed the nearest statue: a figure of a long-haired woman standing in mid-stride, holding a bouquet of flowers in one hand. "I don't suppose you know how to fix this, do you?"

She didn't reply, but her eyes seemed to watch me.

Creepy, I thought, standing and walking closer.

I tapped my knuckles to the bronze, and it echoed hollowly. It reminded me of Olivia—lean and athletic.

Had she returned to the domus to find us gone? Was she even now working with Wilhelm to recover us? I had no way to know, but with the transporter down and no way to fix it, they'd have to get to us another way. If none existed, my friends and I would be stuck here on Zarechus permanently.

I walked the circle, studying the faces of the statues. None were familiar to me, but they seemed to alternate between male and female, each in wildly varying poses. I stopped before an unclothed muscular figure with curly hair and a beard that fell to his chest.

That beard's crazy, I thought as a barrage of lightning lit the statue's face and thunder crackled.

I stroked my chin.

I had no hair, of course. Hair was as strange and alien to me as I must have been to my friends.

I chuckled, thinking of Harland Dixon's preoccupation with his hair, and Scott's fear of his falling out. Despite that, for some reason, they shaved what grew on their faces. They wanted it in all the spots that it refused to stay and hated it anywhere else.

Stretching an arm, I ran a hand across the beard. *Huh? It's warm.*

Narrowing my eyes, I focused on the Underfrost.

My surroundings became varying shades of blues and white, darker where things were warmer and brighter where they were colder. A thrown frost ball is a blaze of light in the Underfrost— a roaring campfire flickering black. Those in between, like people, are varying shades of light blue, moving like ghosts through a fog of shifting bluish white.

Bodhi Group scientists thought my ability to see the world in this way to be similar to infrared or thermal vision. To me it wasn't something separate but just an aspect of my eyesight that I could choose to focus on or not, like focusing on a particular voice in a crowded room to the exclusion of all others.

My mouth fell open. Viewed in this way, the statue glimmered cobalt blue.

The whole thing's warm, I thought.

I glanced around.

The other bronze figures were a whitish blue, scarcely distinguishable from the surrounding air.

I lowered my hand and stepped back.

"Why are you different?" Unlike the others, this statue was giving off heat. *Where's it coming from, though?*

Something rumbled behind me, and I spun to face the sound. The fallen stone disc trembled against the floor.

What the hell? It jiggled a few seconds more, then stopped.

"They're here," I said, drawing out the last word and looking around.

Thunder boomed overhead a moment later, and I jumped.

Well, I should probably get back, I thought, turning toward the exit. *They're probably wondering where I am.*

As I stepped onto the second floor, a clang sounded from down the hall.

Chapter 25

The Best Defense

Metal rang again as I slid to a stop by the sitting room door and looked in upon Scott and Virgil, standing facing each other with swords in hand.

As I entered, Virgil raised his weapon and stepped forward. "Again."

"How long's this been going on?" I asked, joining Caleb by a wall.

He grinned. "Since you left."

"Hold," Virgil said a few minutes later. "That's enough for now."

Scott sheathed his weapon. "Phew. I'm out of shape."

"You'll strengthen, in time," Virgil said. "How does it feel? The blade, I mean."

"Good. It's a lot like a katana, except the blade's not curved."

"You did well. If you keep practising, you'll be a swordsman yet."

"Thanks, Virgil." Scott looked at me. "Did you find anything?"

I gave my head a shake. "Not really, but something weird is going on down there." I gestured to the shield in Caleb's hand. "Shouldn't you use that too?"

"Nah," Scott said. "Not with this sword."

Virgil grunted. "Bastard."

My chin dipped. "Excuse me?"

"The sword," he said. "It's a bastard. You can use it single-handed, but you've more power and options with two hands." He looked toward the door. "Excuse me, fellas. Nature calls."

Scott wiped his face. "I'm getting pretty good, don't you think?"

I smirked. "Good against re—"

A shout and clattering like a rock slide interrupted me and, glancing at my friends, I bolted for the hallway.

"*Subsiste*," boomed a deep voice.

"Get back," Virgil shouted as I entered the shadowy corridor.

He stood some distance to the right with his back to me, holding his sword high. A humanoid figure, all boulders and stones, loomed over him, eyes gleaming red.

Knocking Virgil's sword aside, it rushed forward and grasped his arm. "*Quis vos es?*"

A golem, I thought, remembering Septimius, from the arch outside Caelumburg. *Were you the source of the rumbling we heard earlier?*

"Drop your weapon," the golem said, still speaking Latin. Having no mouth, the golem's voice simply emanated from its head with no apparent source.

"Leave him alone," I shouted in the same language, dashing down the hallway toward them.

As I neared, the creature's great head rotated to regard me, and I reached for frost, but my palm failed to light. *Damn it*, I thought. The Ambrola's fortifying effects had worn off, and the barrier between me and the Underfrost had returned.

"Is this person your guest?" the creature said, still holding Virgil's arm.

My eyes flicked to Virgil, who returned my gaze with wide eyes. "Yes, he's with me. Don't hurt him."

"Guests," the voice said, "must stay close to their sponsors at all times."

"He was just stretching his legs," I said.

After a long moment, the voice replied. "Guest's name?"

"Virgil Half."

"Understood." The golem's head swung away, and a beam of light shone from its eyes, painting Virgil's face bright red.

I took a step forward. "Don't . . ." I trailed off as the golem released its grip.

"Are you okay?" I asked, switching to English.

"Yeah." Virgil patted his chest and abdomen. "I think so."

The golem retreated a step. "Guest Virgil Half has been granted temporary access," it said in English. It pointed a hand toward the room from which we'd come. "Restrooms are two doors down, on the left."

"Thanks . . . uh, what's your name?"

"Abadom," the golem replied, sinking into the shadows at the end of the hall.

Huh, the same name as the castle, I thought. "I'm Shivurr."

"I know," the golem replied.

"Nice to meet you," I said over a clattering of rocks that soon quieted.

I looked at Virgil. "What happened?"

"Damnedest thing." He adjusted his belt. "I was just standing by some rubble over there. At least, I figured it was rubble, but it rose up and became that thing and grabbed me." He shook his head. "It's a good thing you came along and that it listened to you."

"Yeah, that's for sure," I said.

His eyes flicked to my hand. "It's the ring you wear, isn't it?"

I took a deep breath. "Yeah, I think so."

Virgil raised an eyebrow. "You think?"

"We were told they'd grant us access to places when they were given to us." I shrugged. "I wasn't sure that they would work here, so far from where we started."

"We?"

"Scott and Caleb have them too. Well, Caleb lost his. It's a long story."

"Yes," Virgil said, "I can tell there's a lot more to your story than you've shared so far. Maybe you're not gods, but you're obviously connected with them in some way." He held up a hand before I could speak. "You're good fellas, though, so I won't pry. You can tell me more when you're ready."

"Thanks, Virgil."

"In any case," he said, "I'm glad you were here. I don't think a sword would've had much effect against that rock fella."

"It's called a golem," I said.

"What's it doing here?" Virgil asked. "Do you know?"

Scott approached from down the hall, and Caleb trailed a few feet behind him, holding the ruby-covered shield.

"He must be a guardian of some kind. That's what the last one I saw was."

Virgil whistled. "That's a hell of a security guard. I suppose that explains what happened to those who came here and never returned. Looters, I mean."

Scott looked down. "Yeah, maybe they're all locked up in a dungeon here."

"Or dead," Virgil replied. "Either way, I'm glad I've never tried to enter here until I had you fellas with me."

"What now?" Caleb asked.

I stepped toward a long vertical slit in the wall near me. Outside, lightning still flashed. "The storm's still going." I looked at Virgil. "When do we have to leave to make the rendezvous?"

He checked his watch. "We've got about four hours at most. Maybe five, if you can spin up one of those floating ice saucers. Do you think you can do that again?"

I nodded. "Yeah, I think so. With enough time to focus."

"What about the golem?" Scott asked. "Do you think it'll come back?"

"I doubt it," I replied. "But we should set a watch, just in case."

Virgil sighed. "In that case, if you fellas don't mind taking the first one, I'm going to get some sleep." He started to walk back the way we'd come. "Wake me when it's my turn."

I told my friends to sleep, and I spent the first part of my watch sipping soda and thinking.

After a time, Caleb swung his legs from the sofa where he had fallen asleep. "Do you have any earplugs, dude?"

I shook my head. "Sorry, Slim. Can't sleep?"

He scowled. "Not with those two snoring."

"Try putting pillows over your ears."

He nodded and looked at the floor. "I miss my friends, dude. What if we don't make it home?"

"We'll make it." I crushed the empty can and returned it to my hat. "What do you suppose they've been up to?"

"Probably hanging out on the beach, mostly."

"Just chilling," I said. "That sounds nice."

He stared into space. "They're probably working too. Alan teaches surfing. Lilith works at an ice cream place."

"What about Brad and Lucy?" I asked.

Caleb tossed his shoulders. "I don't know what Brad does, but I don't think Lucy works. She's Canadian."

I cocked my head. "Canadians don't work?"

He made a face. "Of course they do, dude. I just mean she's here to go to school. Well, not here. I mean, she comes to California for school, not to work." He paused and appeared to study the wall behind me. "I wish they were here, but I'm glad they're safe at home, too."

"Me too," I said, hoping that it was true, and that Dixon wasn't still looking for them in an effort to find me.

He sighed. "Why don't you sleep, dude, seeing as I can't?"

"Okay, sure." I switched places with him and lay back. "Thanks. Just a few more hours, Slim."

Caleb grinned. "Then we get the hell out of Dodge?"

"Dodge?"

"It's an expression about an Old West town. It's in Kansas, I think."

"Like Tonopah?" I asked.

"I guess."

"Have you been there before?"

"No," he replied, "I don't think it exists anymore."

I pulled my cap low. "Why's that?"

He smirked. "Everyone got the hell out."

I chuckled. "Night, Slim."

"Night, Shivurr."

My sleep was fitful, haunted by nightmares and wild dreams. For the first while, monstrous blob creatures, towering golems, and electrified human-plant hybrids dominated. These soon mixed with half-remembered events and acquaintances from my distant past. They all merged in fantastical and nonsensical ways before returning, by dream logic, to Abadom, where I found my-self standing at the edge of the transport platform in the arrival chamber. The inexplicably warm thunderbolt-wielding bearded statue stood before me.

Lifeless and unmoving at first, its verdigrised exterior began to glow, suffusing the figure in an emerald nimbus. The statue's head bent to regard me with green irises ringed in white. Human eyes, I realized, taking a step back as, impossibly, its lips pursed as if to speak.

"Shivurr."

I woke with a start.

The light had changed; Scott and Virgil still slept, and Caleb teetered in a low stance atop the ruby shield's concave side. The shallow bowl rocked back and forth with every shift of his feet.

His head turned as I stood. "Hey, dude. You all right? You were tossing and turning like crazy."

I rubbed the sleep from my eyes. "Oof, wild dreams."

"Like what?" he asked.

"Old memories." I reached a hand into my cap. "Mostly."

"They're coming back, eh?"

"More every day." Pulling a soda can from my hat, I cracked it open and took a slug. "Ah, that's better."

Caleb stepped from the shield and scooped it from the floor. "Can I have a sip?"

I held the can out toward him. "Top of the morning to you," I said, using my best Irish accent.

He snickered, taking the can. "Did you dream you were a leprechaun or something?"

"Or something." My eyes dipped to the shield. "Were you trying to break it?"

"No." Caleb took a sip and handed the drink back to me. "I was land surfing, dude." He rapped the ruby-red veneer with a knuckle. "And I don't think I could hurt it, even if I was trying to. It's super tough." He placed the shield face down again and stepped inside. "I mean, it's supposed to protect you from swords, right? So, it should be able to take quite a hit." He hooked his toes under the leather strap. "Watch."

"Wait." I'd guessed what he had planned to do, but he'd already leaped into the air, taking the shield with him. "Don't."

A moment later, it struck the floor with a thrum like a revved car engine.

"Whoa." His arms windmilled, but he soon regained his balance. "Did you hear that? It sounded like the Doppelgänger effect."

I suppressed a grin. "Uh, I think it's Doppler effect."

"Huh? Are you sure?"

"Pretty sure." I moved closer. "Whatever you call it, it's weird."

"I know, right?" He looked at me. "Should I try it again?"

"I don't know." My eyes flicked to our sleeping companions. "You're going to wake them."

He blew a puff of air through pressed lips. "I doubt it, dude. They slept through worse already."

"You mean the thunderstorm?"

"The snoring, dude."

I snorted. "You've got a point." I glanced again at our slumbering friends. Neither appeared to have been disturbed by Caleb's antics, so far. *It's like they're egging each other on.* "Okay, give it another try."

"Cool." Grinning, he squatted and hopped again, and the shield thrummed even louder beneath him.

My brow creased. "Huh. That's interesting. Try it again."

He jumped a third time, and the thrumming grew louder still.

A throaty rattle pulled my eyes to the left. Virgil snorted wetly, then flipped over to lie on his other side.

"Better cool it, Slim."

Nodding, Caleb stepped out of the bowl and stomped on the shield's upturned edge, flipping the opposite side into his waiting hand.

"Slick move," I said. "Where'd you learn that trick?"

His shoulders jumped. "Skateboarding." He held the shield by its edges with its front side facing him. Light reflecting off the ruby epicentre tinged his features red. "Why do you suppose it makes that sound?"

"Beats me." I thought a moment. "Maybe to intimidate your opponent. It'd be kind of freaky to hear that when you give it a whack with a mace or something."

"Yeah, I suppose." Caleb returned the shield to his forearm. Its scarlet eye seemed a shade brighter in the dim light. "This thing's awesome. Should we take it with us when we leave?"

"I don't see why not. This place seems to be abandoned, and it would be good for you to have some protection besides me." *Especially when I'm having trouble accessing the Underfrost.*

The shield rose, hiding Caleb's face. "Check this out. There's writing here. Etched into the metal."

"Oh, yeah?" Our shoulders bumped as I sidled next to him. "Let's see."

"Take a look." He ran a finger along the inside edge. "What's that say?"

"Fire," I said after a moment, reading the stylized characters etched along the inside rim.

"There's more." Slipping the shield from his arm, he held it with both hands, turning it like a wheel. The text continued, written in other languages, along the entire circumference. "Can you read that?"

I grunted. "Not all of it, but everything I can read says fire in different languages."

"Really?" Caleb said. "Why would someone write fire—"

A beam of red light cut through the gloom, connecting the shield's eye with the plush backrest of a distant chair. The chair sailed back, igniting mid-flight, before shattering against a stone wall twenty feet away.

Virgil's arms flailed. "What in the hell?"

Scott sat up, one arm extended to his front, the other propped against his sofa's backrest. "I'm up." He glanced around. "I'm up."

Virgil stood, and his eyes flicked between us and the smouldering chair. "What's going on?"

"Uh, nothing," Caleb said, lowering the shield.

I made a downward motion. "You'd better keep that pointed away from everyone, Slim."

"Okay." He turned and set the shield atop a nearby table, convex side down.

"Sorry, guys." I paused and eyed the chair, relieved to see it had stopped burning. "We didn't mean to wake you."

"Uh-huh." Scott scratched his head. "And how do you suppose whatever you were doing would not wake us?"

"Well." I raised my shoulders. "With the snoring and all."

"You dudes were sawing logs," Caleb added.

Scott bristled. "I have a condition, man."

Caleb chuckled. "Sure, dude."

"It's called a deviated septum, kid."

"Whatever you call it, you were both sleeping like babies until"—I waved a hand toward the wreckage—"that happened."

"And what was that, exactly?" Virgil asked.

"Far out," Scott said after we'd filled both of them in. "It's not just a shield, then."

"I guess not." Stepping closer to where it lay, I ran a hand along the shield's edge. "It must absorb energy when it gets hit."

Scott stroked the stubble on his chin. "That's probably the thrum you heard—some sort of kinetic energy buildup."

It struck me as odd that the shield had worked for Caleb, though. Atriel had taken the ring Olivia had given the teen. Without it, he had no credentials and therefore no authority. *It must not require any to use*, I thought, *or it identified him in another way.* Olivia had said not all their technology had been properly secured. Perhaps the shield predated updates to their security systems.

Virgil raised a brow. "What do you figure? When the boy said the magic word, it released it as some kind of . . . what . . . energy beam?"

"Or a phaser beam," Scott said with wide eyes. He looked at me. "Or was it more like a blaster bolt?"

I thought a moment. "More like a beam. It just appeared between the shield and chair. It must have covered the distance too fast to see."

"Okay," Scott said. "More like a phaser beam, then." He grinned. "I love it. A shield that absorbs attacks and returns them as an energy beam. That's awesome."

"Yeah," Virgil said, "that's quite a find. But, if you fellas are done messing around, I'm going to try to go back to sleep."

"Good idea." Scott lay back on his couch. Yawning, he looked at Caleb. "You should too, kid."

"Yeah." The teen nodded. "All right."

"Night, guys," I said as they drifted off to sleep, leaving me to finish my watch.

With everyone asleep, I slipped into the hallway and looked out over the darkened valley through one of the vertical slits cut into the outer wall. For the next while, I watched lightning strike obelisks and contemplated our impending journey to Lolokly.

I had to hope that the storm would stop soon, and that the Nameless that I could still see walking the streets below us would leave. If they came from the Immerwald as Virgil supposed, we might encounter them there again anyway, but with us safe inside a tank, they'd have a hard time harming us.

If we chose to wait for better conditions, we probably wouldn't have to contend with them on our journey through town. However, we might just end up meeting them in the woods without a tank to protect us. Even if we didn't encounter them, if creatures like them lived in that forest, we might end up facing off with something even worse.

Which meant that in a few hours, storm or not, we had to try to make the rendezvous.

I scowled as another bolt of lightning struck. If anything, the storm had worsened. The snow that had fallen for a time had turned back to rain, and the wind howled louder. *Forget a tank, we'll need a boat if it doesn't stop soon.*

If only the transporter hadn't collapsed, we could have reversed our steps and returned home to Caelumtor right away. It seemed odd that it would've failed when it did or that it had worked in the first place. Whatever damage had been done here at Abadom had occurred a while ago, so if the platform had been compromised then, why wait to fail until after our arrival here, decades later? And if it had broken long ago, who had recently fixed it?

Was it a trap? If it was, for whom? It wasn't for us, I felt certain. I was a wanted snowman for sure, but no one could have expected we would use the transporter when we had.

The emerald statue with human eyes that had startled me from sleep came to mind. It had been about to say something just before I'd woken.

Was my mind trying to tell me something? If so, what?

Chapter 26

Greetings, Program

Shuffling footsteps behind me drew my gaze from the window. Trailed by one of his light orbs, Virgil came closer, blinking sleep from his eyes. "Evening, Shivurr."

"Hey, Virgil. Can't sleep?"

He coughed and cleared his throat. "Call of nature." His eyes flicked to the side. "That rock fella—"

I nodded and pointed a finger. "The bathroom's supposed to be over there."

"Right." His head bobbed as he shuffled away. "I remember the big fella saying that." He looked back at me. "Do you mind keeping close? I'm not sure I trust this guest access I'm supposed to have yet."

I followed him to the door and waited outside until he emerged a few minutes later.

"Storm's still raging, eh?" he said, adjusting his belt.

I sighed. "Yep. It's not letting up."

Virgil drifted over to a window and looked out. With each lightning strike upon a nearby obelisk, the rain-soaked town below us flickered into view.

"That's a hell of a sight." He looked at me. "I never thought I'd see the town from here."

"It's too bad the circumstances weren't better."

He scowled. "Look, Shivurr. I've been thinking. Maybe the other fellas should stay here."

My eyebrows rose. "Why?"

He blew a puff of air through pressed lips. "It's going to be a dangerous journey. We'll be dodging those Nameless through town by the looks of it. If we don't make the rendezvous or

Dieter doesn't hold up his end, we'll be walking through the Immerwald." He glanced toward the sitting room. "You can take care of yourself, but I'm not sure about Scott and the boy. Scott's passable with a sword, but even with the sword, armour, and shield, they'll be in danger."

"I'll protect them. With my—"

Virgil held up a hand. "I don't doubt it, but it's often hard enough keeping yourself alive."

"So you're suggesting that I abandon my friends?"

He shook his head. "No, not at all. What I'm suggesting is that they stay here, safe, while you help me get back to Lolokly. Once we get there, I'll help you try to find someone or something to help you get home. Then you can come back for your friends."

I considered his words. It had been about a week since I'd run from the Institute, driven by an imperative to stop a catastrophe that I could no longer remember. The urgency that I'd felt leading up to it had only increased since then. Whatever the danger was, intuition told me time was running out, and I couldn't stop it trapped here, on another planet. I needed to get home, and I'd probably get there faster alone, guided by Virgil.

"I'll think about it," I said, feeling suddenly lonely.

"Fair enough." He looked at his watch. "I'm going to try to catch a few more winks before we have to decide."

After he'd left, I turned back to the window, thinking of what he'd said.

Virgil was right. My friends would be safer here, protected by stone walls, golems, and whatever other defenses the castle might possess. If not for those protections—and the edict against unauthorized entry that Virgil had mentioned—scavengers probably would have stripped the castle bare long ago. Certainly the sword, shield, and armour that we'd found in the sitting room wouldn't have remained. The shield alone had to be worth a fortune.

Good thing we have these, I thought, splaying my fingers to study the gem-encrusted ring that Olivia had given me. Even the dim glow of my hat reflected off the ring's many gems. Without it, the golem would never have listened to me. With it, all I'd had to do was ask it to stop and it had.

"Just ask for what you want," Olivia had said.

I snorted. "What I want is for that transporter to be fixed so we can go home."

I froze. *Wait.* My eyes widened.

"I think she means," Scott had said, "you state your desires, but you don't need to know, or care, how the system makes it happen."

I shook my friends awake.

"What now?" Scott moaned with his eyes squeezed tight.

Caleb yawned and regarded me through half-closed eyes. "I was having the best dream, dude."

"Sorry, guys," I said. "This is important."

Virgil rubbed his face. "What's up, fella?"

I held up a finger. "I remembered something. Something that may be our ticket home."

Scott sat up and met my eyes. "For real?"

I bobbed my head.

His brow furrowed. "But how?"

"I think we might be able to fix the transporter."

His eyebrows rose. "How long was I asleep? When did you become an expert in god tech?"

"Are your memories coming back, dude?" Caleb mumbled.

"No," I said. "I mean, yes, but, no, I'm not an expert, but that's just it. I don't need to be."

"Huh?" Scott glanced at the others, then back to me.

"Don't you remember? You said it yourself. We just need to ask for what we want and we'll get it. We don't need to specify how."

Scott stood. "It can't be that easy."

"Why not?" I asked. "We've got to try, right?"

We quickly gathered up our things and descended to the transporter chamber, which lay quiet as we entered. With a few words, Virgil sent his globes of light out and across the room. Growing brighter as they flew, they soon illuminated the entire hall.

I led my friends to the platform and stood before the disc that had nearly crushed us upon our arrival.

"Did it look like that when we left here?" Scott asked. "I thought the cover was a few feet off-centre."

I shrugged. "I guess it shifted when the snow melted."

"Yeah," he said. "I suppose it must have."

"So, what's the plan?" Virgil asked.

I stroked my chin. "I guess we just ask it to fix itself." I thrust my ring hand in the air and cleared my throat. "I wish that the transporter platform in front of me were fixed."

Nothing happened.

Caleb snickered. "I don't think it's working, dude."

I tried again, louder, using different phrases. Finally, I looked at Scott. "Got any ideas? You're the computer guy."

He blew out a breath. "I don't know. I need a keyboard or some kind of interface."

I looked around. "Maybe this place has a holographic interface like Hue."

"You mean the AI you told us about?"

I nodded. "It's not an Allfrost chamber, but why not?"

He shrugged. "I suppose, but we haven't seen anything like that."

"Yeah." I thought a moment. "Maybe we just need to activate it somehow."

He jabbed a finger at me. "You might have something there. It could be there's a magic word or phrase we need to say."

I smiled. "Like on *Star Trek*?"

"Huh?"

"You know—when they talk to the Enterprise computer. What does Kirk say?"

Scott touched his temple. "Uh, just computer." He moved his arms stiffly. "Working. Boop, beep, bop. Jack the Ripper—"

"Computer," I said loudly, "are you there? Computer, please respond." Nothing happened. "I guess that's not it."

"No surprise there, dude," Caleb said. "It could be anything."

Scott shook his head. "No, I don't think so. Why keep it a secret? There would be no need." He held up his ring. "If you're not authorized, it wouldn't matter if you knew the word. Hiding it would be like asking for a password before even showing a command prompt. Without which, you can't input your credentials."

"You think?" I asked.

"Sure," he said. "Even for gods, you'd want the system to be easy to use." He pointed at Caleb. "Like the shield. Its single-word command is written all over it, in multiple languages." He stooped and scurried sideways, eyes fixed on the fallen ceiling stone's edge. "Come on. Help me look. Maybe there's something written somewhere that'll help."

"There's nothing on this side," I said after we'd spent a few minutes searching. "Maybe it's on the underside of the slab." I crouched and wedged my fingers under the edge. "Grab this end, guys. Help me lift it."

The four of us worked our fingers beneath the nearest edge and heaved. Despite our groans and imprecations, the slab rose only slightly before collapsing again.

Standing erect, Caleb rubbed his fingers. "It's too heavy."

Scott looked at me. "If we can get it higher, can you put snow under it, so it doesn't fall back down?"

I grimaced. "I'm not sure I can focus and lift at the same time. Not here with the Underfrost being all . . . messed up."

"Ah, well," he said. "I don't think you'd be able to read it anyway. Not with it sitting on a snowdrift."

Virgil grumbled. "I bet that golem fella upstairs could lift it. He looked plenty strong."

I snapped my fingers. "Abadom. Yeah, now you're thinking."

Scott narrowed an eye. "Its name is Abadom?"

"Yeah, that's what it said."

He tilted his head, looking thoughtful. "Huh."

"What?" I asked.

He shrugged and looked at Virgil. "Didn't you say the castle is also called Abadom?"

"That's right," he replied.

"Hmm," Scott said. "That's kind of confusing, don't you think? The castle having the same name. I mean, what if we were all named Shivurr? We'd be constantly asking each other which Shivurr we meant. And, if he's not the only golem, what are the others called? Are they all called Abadom?"

"Yeah, you're right." I studied the floor, thinking. "Unless . . ." My eyebrows rose, and I snapped my fingers. "Unless Abadom isn't the golem itself but is actually the castle talking through it."

Scott waggled a hand. "Not the castle so much as the AI program that manages it."

I grabbed Scott's arms. "Then Abadom may be the word for which we're looking."

He smiled. "Exactly."

I cupped my hands to the sides of my mouth. "Abadom, are you there? We need your help."

A tumbling of rocks followed, turning our heads toward the far reaches of the room. A moment later, a golem slid into view from behind a statue of a man holding a drawn bow.

Its eyes bathed me in a ruby light. "How may I be of assistance?"

Yes. I pumped a fist. *Greetings, program.* "Abadom, we'd like to use the transporter, please. How do we do that?"

A moment passed, and a buzz sounded. "The transposition platform is not functional."

I grimaced. "Yes, we know. Can you fix it for us?"

"Of course," Abadom said.

I waited, but it hadn't moved after several seconds.

"Will you?" I asked.

"If you wish me to," the golem replied, still not moving.

Scott snorted. "I think you have to issue an explicit command, Shivurr."

"Abadom, please initiate repair of the transport platform, immediately." *I guess Abadom's not as sophisticated as Hue.*

The golem's chin dipped. "As you command."

A rumble and clash of stone came from our rear. I whirled, raising an arm. Three collections of boulders of varying size rose from the nearby debris and settled into the form of more humanoid figures. They moved toward us, sending me and my companions reeling for the far side of the circle. Even as we did so, other rock golems assembled from the ruins behind us and closed in on us as well.

Caleb's head swivelled between them. "What do we do?"

"Slip between them." I stepped forward, choosing a path between two of the golems. "Follow me."

My friends trailed after me, and the golems passed us by and made their way to the platform.

Grasping the stone slab by its edge, they raised it from the floor and ducked beneath it. Pressing the weight overhead, they stood still, forming makeshift pillars, and the air thrummed as red light shone down from the ceiling onto the upraised stone.

I raised a hand against the glare.

Visible between my fingers, the beam enclosed the disc, obscuring the chamber walls on the far side. Abruptly, the thick stone plate sprang from the palms of the gathered golems. Moving fast, it reached the dome in seconds, stopping just short of the ceiling hole, leaving a crown of scarlet light seeping from its edges.

I took a step back as the light at its centre went out, expecting the disc to fall, but it stayed in place.

Unconcerned, the rock golems clonked from the platform and made their way past the encircling statues. Reaching their original positions, they collapsed with a rumble, once again just piles of lifeless stones. Only the first golem to arise remained as if awaiting further instructions.

"Is that it, then?" Scott asked. "Is it fixed?"

"Abadom, is the transporter ready to be used?" I asked.

"Repairs are complete," Abadom replied. "Do you require further assistance?"

I shook my head. "No, thank you. I think that's all for now."

"As you wish," Abadom said, lumbering away.

"Wait." The golem kept moving. "Abadom, please wait."

It stopped mid-step and fixed its red eyes on me.

"How do we use the transporter?"

"When you are ready," the golem said, "you have only to ask."

"What do I say, though?" I smirked. "'Beam me up?'"

"That will suffice."

My eyebrows lifted. "Really? I was just kidding."

"'Beam me up' is an accepted activation command."

I glanced at Scott with a smile, then back to the golem. "And this will take us back to where we came from?"

The golem nodded. "Do you require anything else?"

"That's all for now. Thank you."

Taking a few more steps, the golem crouched low, then collapsed into a pile.

Scott slapped my back. "Beam me up." He snickered. "That must be Wilhelm's doing. I love it."

"Well, I guess we're ready to go." I looked at Virgil. "Are you coming with—"

I broke off as a speck of white drifted into view a foot from my face before settling to the floor. Another flake fell into my waiting palm.

"It's snowing," I said, looking up.

High above, snow streamed through the ceiling hole, obscuring the dark clouds and flashes of light beyond.

"What the hell?" Virgil muttered.

Scott shot me a look. "What are you doing?"

"It's not me." *Not that I mind.* "Is this normal, Virgil?" Such a sudden change would've been bizarre on Earth, but we were on another planet. Weather patterns might have been a lot different here.

Virgil frowned. "No, not around here. Until earlier tonight, I doubt snow's ever fallen here. Seasons on Zarechus, they're not like on Earth."

A breeze blew, swirling the flakes, guiding them to settle about the long-bearded statue that I'd studied on my last visit to the chamber.

Scott touched my arm. "Are you sure this isn't you, Shivurr?"

Snow continued to pile at the bearded statue's base.

"Yeah, I'm sure." I reached for the Underfrost and felt the same resistance as before. "I'm still blocked. There's no way I'm doing this without knowing it."

"Then why's it snowing?"

Caleb pointed to the bearded statue. "Most of it's piling up by ZZ Top, dudes." He looked up at its face. "He kind of looks like Wilhelm, don't you think?"

"Oh yeah," Scott said. "Wil's just got a goatee, though. Judging by the lightning bolt this guy's holding, I'd say that's supposed to be Zeus."

"Who or what is a ZZ Top?" Virgil asked.

A distant clip-clop sound came from the doorway before anyone could reply.

Caleb's eyes met mine. "What's that?"

"It sounds like horses," Scott said, frowning. "Someone's coming."

My neck swivelled, looking for cover. "Everyone hide."

"Where?" Caleb asked.

"Over here." I rushed toward the statues farthest from the doors.

"Why are we hiding?" Caleb said, crouching next to me.

"Just a feeling." Some part of my mind feared those coming weren't friendly. I looked left to where Virgil and Scott huddled one statue over. "Virgil." I thrust a finger skyward. "The lights."

He nodded, and with a hushed word at the ceiling, the orbs and chamber darkened.

The darkness was far from absolute, though. Between the glow of the pillars encircling the platform and the light entering from the hallway and through the hole in the ceiling, much of the chamber was still dimly visible, so we needed to stay hidden.

Hunkering lower, I held a finger to my lips, catching the eyes of my friends, who nodded in return.

The doorway darkened as the burble of voices grew louder, and I edged an eye past the column's side to see.

Chapter 27

Anathema

Three figures entered moments later with their faces hidden beneath the hoods of their dark cloaks. The first two, of similar height, led the way, trailed by the third, who towered a foot or more above his companions.

"How is it snowing in here?" said the shortest one as they drew nearer. He pushed back his hood, revealing close-cut, thinning black hair. "It's not even cold enough for it."

The other threw back his hood as well, uncovering long blond hair. "The weather's been unusual here for years. Ever since the event." Blondie shrugged. "It's probably a side effect of the last transposition. That or the system's shedding excess power. The storm's generating a lot of energy. If it's exceeded storage capacity, it has to go somewhere."

"If you say so," replied the dark-haired man. "I'm just the guy with the ring." Pulling up at the edge of the statues, he looked toward the tallest man, whose hood tilted to face the ceiling. "You'll want to stay close, uh, Lord."

"I told you to speak Latin when addressing him," the blond man said with a voice that held faint traces of a Russian or Eastern European accent. "Lord Baduriel does not yet speak English well."

The giant threw back his hood, and I stifled a gasp. *I know that face*, I thought, retreating fully behind the pedestal. I'd seen it swathed in flames, just days ago. The horns poking from his forehead burned no longer, but there could be no doubt. It was the fire demon that—along with its fire elemental minions—had attacked the Bodhi Institute. The one that had tried to kill me and my friends as we'd fled the battle in a stolen car.

"You'd best tell him not to wander," said the short one as I chanced another look, "or rudeness will be the least of his problems."

"You may speak this fool's language, Aspirant Artyom," Baduriel said in Latin with a deep, resonant voice. "I will learn it faster that way."

"Of course, Lord Baduriel," Artyom replied in English. "As you wish." He looked at the other man. "John was just saying you should stay close to us."

The shortest man, John, held up a hand, and a glint of gold came from his ring finger. "If you get too far from me, Abadom—the keeper of this place—will see you as an intruder. That'll make things . . . dangerous."

Baduriel's horns blazed to life, brightening the area around him. He looked toward the statues and waved a hand dismissively. "Proceed, Aspirant Artyom."

"You heard him," Artyom said. "Let's get this done."

With a cough, John turned toward the transport platform. Fumbling under his cloak, he pulled out a pair of goggles—gold-framed with green-tinted lenses—and put them on. He looked like an old-style drag racer preparing to set a speed record in the desert.

"All right," he said, adjusting the thick leather strap. "Let's see what we've got." He walked to the centre of the transporter pad and looked around. As he came to face the Zeus statue, he stopped his turn and leaned toward it. "We've got one. Just like you figured."

Artyom took a step forward. "Are there any others?"

I ducked behind the pillar as John's head turned my way.

"Nope," he said. "Just the one."

"All right," Artyom replied. "Extract it, and let's go."

"Hey," John said, "that's weird, isn't it?"

"What?" Artyom replied.

I lifted my head above the column's top and peered between verdigrised feet at the intruders.

"Well, I was just thinking," John said. "We rigged this thing to collapse, right?"

"Yeah?"

"So why isn't it?" John looked around. "There should be a body crushed beneath the stone that's floating up there, shouldn't there be?"

Artyom shrugged. "So what? The keeper repaired it and cleaned up the body. That or whoever is in there came through disembodied. Either way, it worked."

"Yeah, I suppose."

"Come on." Artyom stepped forward, holding up a gold jar capped with the head of a bird. "Here's the Animavas. Empty the statue and reset the snare."

The intruder called John took the jar, and a determination to stop whatever they were doing overcame me. I had a growing idea about what—who—they meant to take from the Zeus statue. If I was right, I had to intervene. Even if I was wrong, interfering with whatever the demon Baduriel wanted had to be worthwhile.

I smiled grimly. On the plus side, the chamber had cooled a lot since they'd arrived, and a thick layer of snow now lay across the floor, bringing the Underfrost closer to the surface. The disturbance between it and the regular world still existed, but I could already tell that it'd no longer be enough to keep me from touching the other side.

I glanced at Caleb before looking to the other statue where Scott and Virgil hid. I'd be putting my friends at risk if I did, though. Artyom and John looked normal enough, and I didn't see any obvious sign of weapons on them—though they wore long cloaks that might hide them—but the demon Baduriel was another story. He didn't have fire elementals with him, but I still wasn't sure I could take him, even less so that I could do so without my friends being caught in the crossfire.

I need help, I thought, eyeing the ring Olivia had given me.

I grabbed the edge of the shield in Caleb's hands and raised my forearm, miming that he should keep it in front of himself. His brow creased, but he nodded a moment later. Putting a finger to my lips, I crept from cover, hoping that the falling snow, crystal pillars, and statuary would conceal me.

Taking cover behind the next statue over, I let out a breath and looked past its edge.

The intruder John stood, his left side facing me, looking at the Zeus statue, clasping the jar's lid in one hand.

As he began to raise it, I plucked frost from the air and, slipping from cover, hurled it. "Catch frost!"

A fluorescing streak of white bloomed in its wake, connecting my extended hand with John's head. His skull snapped to the side as the ball struck. With a grunt, he staggered and fell, dropping the jar into the snow beside him. On his knees, he clapped a hand to his head and swiped away the icy residue as if it were burning pitch.

Taking no chances, I tore another handful of frost into being as, behind John, Artyom's eyes met mine.

"Oh, shit," he said, reaching beneath his cloak.

Grimacing, I sent fresh frost flying, striking the fallen man a second time, and he crumpled face first into the snow and fog at the Zeus statue's feet.

An ear-splitting pop pulled my eyes to Artyom, and I snarled as pain and warmth blossomed on my cheek.

Slapping a hand to my face, I jumped back into cover, and two more pops followed.

Counting to three and hearing no more shots, I poked my head out. To my relief, instead of trying to flank or rush me, Artyom knelt by his comrade and swept a hand through the snow.

Before he could see me, I drew back behind cover and considered my next move.

"Is that you, Shivurr?" Baduriel said in Latin, his voice deep and resonant.

I shifted my weight to peer past the statue's right side. "Maybe," I replied in the same language.

The demon ambled closer. "I had heard you were free, but how came you here?"

Stepping between crystal pillars, he stood at the far edge of the transporter platform.

My brow furrowed. "Do we know each other?"

He frowned. "Hmm . . . you have not recovered your memories yet, I see. That is a pity."

I scowled, searching my memories. Only fleeing the Bodhi Institute with my friends a few days earlier came to mind. "I remember you trying to kill me."

His eyebrows rose. "Kill you? No, I do not wish you dead."

A groan of metal and flicker of green came from my left.

Holding his gun and the bird's-head lid clumsily in one hand, Artyom held the jar out toward the Zeus statue with his other. A wisp of green light bled from the bronze toward the open container as if the verdigris patina were being vacuumed away.

The groaning grew louder, mixing with a hiss, as the wisp became a tendril.

I pointed a finger. "Hey, stop that." I looked at Baduriel. "Tell him to stop."

The demon wagged his head. "I think not."

"I said stop." My arm blurred, sending frost at the jar in Artyom's hands.

He reeled back and clutched the jar to his chest as the ball sailed past his nose.

Damn. I bit my lip, watching the frost explode against the far wall. *Oh, wait.*

The green vapour reversed its flow and began to stream back into the statue.

Turning his head, Artyom looked back along the fading frost contrail at me, and his gun arm rose.

Oh, shit. Sidestepping, I took cover behind the statue and tucked my elbows to my sides, making myself small, and pops of gunfire and metallic pings filled the air.

"Hold your fire," Baduriel said with a commanding voice. "Shivurr?"

"What?" I replied, leaning a hand against the statue's red columnar base.

"We need not be enemies."

"Don't we?" I replied switching to English. "You're a fire demon, and I'm an Allfrost Sentinel. You're pretty much the anti-me."

"Yet our goals may align," Baduriel replied, still in Latin, "or at least not be entirely opposed. Let us finish our work and come with me. I will help you get your memories back from those who have taken them."

"Uh, no, thanks," I said. "I've got all the help I need."

"Are you certain?" Baduriel asked.

"Yeah."

He sighed theatrically. "Very well. Then simply let us conclude our business here, and we will leave you in peace."

I shook my head. "I can't let you do that."

The demon's horns blazed brighter. "You do not want to fight me," he said, speaking in English now.

My eyes narrowed. "Why's that?"

He glanced toward the statues where my friends hid, then back to me. "Someone could get hurt."

I scowled. "I don't like threats . . . especially against my friends."

Baduriel shrugged. "Then you have a choice to make. Just remember, you are outnumbered." He turned to Artyom. "Resume the extraction."

I stroked the silver band on my finger. "No, I'm not outnumbered."

The demon chuckled. "Those human mayflies don't count."

"Screw you, demon dick," said Caleb from somewhere to my right.

Nice one, Caleb. "I'm not talking about them." I raised my ring to my mouth. "Abadom, we need you. Invaders are in the castle."

I had no idea if speaking directly to the ring was necessary. In fact, I doubted it, but I wasn't taking any chances.

"Intruder alert, Abadom," Scott shouted a moment later. "Condition red. Shields up."

Glancing his way, I nodded. *Good thinking, Scott.* "Security to the bridge," I added for good measure.

A banging of rocks followed a moment later, and golems began to assemble themselves at the room's edges.

I pumped a fist. "Yes!"

"Emergency lockdown enabled," said the voice of Abadom,

coming from multiple directions. "Prepare for identity scan."

The eyes of the nearest golem lit, draping me in red. Wincing, I averted my gaze and looked to my friends' crimson faces. "It's okay, guys." I gave them a thumbs-up. "Keep Virgil close."

"Intruders detected," Abadom said.

Across the room, Baduriel and Artyom shone scarlet, pinned by the eyes of several golems.

"Belay that, Abadom," John groaned, pushing himself to his knees. Gripping Artyom's hand, he climbed to his feet. "They are my guests, Abadom." At his words, the eyes on Artyom swung away and Baduriel glowed brighter.

The demon's horns blazed higher as his cloak began to smoulder.

John shook his head. "No, Abadom. He's with me too."

"Negative," the golems replied in unison. "Subject Baduriel has been anathematized."

"Leave him alone, Abadom," John said, shouting now. "I command you to stand down."

Baduriel, his cloak smouldering, turned in a slow circle, and the stone automatons closed in.

"Negative. Access is denied. Tier one directives require admin-level permissions to override."

A stone fist bashed Baduriel from behind, and he stumbled forward a few steps. Catching himself, he touched a hand to the back of his head and regarded his fingertips, which glistened in the light of his flaming horns.

Licking them, he stood taller and cast his cloak aside, revealing a lean and heavily muscled body. Flames blazed all over his bare skin, even from his dark trousers, which were evidently impervious or at least resistant to his fire.

Dodging another haymaker, he shot forward—moving too fast to follow—and put an arm between a golem's legs. He thrust his forearm up, popped his hips forward, and lifted the golem from the ground. Bending at the waist, he swung his opponent into his other foes, and rocks crunched, and the chamber shook.

"Finish the extraction," Baduriel said calmly, ducking another blow.

"Cover me," John said, grabbing the jar from Artyom. "Just don't shoot a golem, or they'll turn on you, and nothing I say will save you from them."

"What about the others?"

John raised the jar up to the Zeus statue. "They're fair game."

"Good." Artyom smiled, raising his gun.

Chapter 28

Extraction

Ducking back, I tented my hands and pressed my finger-tips together. Taking a deep breath, I focused my mind and vanished into the Underfrost. Bright blues and whites engulfed me, and the throb in my cheek faded, soothed and revitalized by the Underfrost's chilling energies. Other almost-forgotten aches and pains soon followed.

Oh, yeah, I thought, closing my eyes. A long moment later, I shook my head. *Time to move.*

While Frost Walking, I was pretty much a ghost, invisible and intangible. I could even pass through solid objects, though it was harder and slower than moving through air.

As handy as the ability could be, it could also be dangerous. It was why I hadn't done so since the Bodhi Institute—when I'd taken myself, my friends, and a moving car across the threshold long enough to escape swarming fire elementals.

The longer I stayed submerged, the greater the chance that I'd never resurface. It was too enticing, too addictive, and too tiring. Lost in the pleasure of the Underfrost's embrace, I'd grow ever sleepier, and if I sank too far, I'd probably never come back.

With recovered memories of Borealans succumbing to its lure front of mind, I slipped from cover and hurtled across the snow toward Artyom, who stared through me as if I weren't even there. Ignoring him, I closed on his colleague as a last gasp of green mist funnelled into the urn. I clenched my fingers as he plunked the lid atop the container and turned toward me.

Moving at full tilt, I drew back my fist and came out of the Underfrost swinging. John's eyes widened an instant before my frost-charged fist connected with his jaw. His head snapped back, and his eyes rolled in their sockets. Ducking low, I snatched the jar from the air as it fell.

A yowl behind me drew my gaze, and I spun toward it. Artyom's gun dropped to the snow as he staggered my way, raising a hand to an arrow shaft stuck into his shoulder. Behind him, visible across the transport pad, Virgil nocked a fresh projectile.

I nodded to him before a blaze of movement tugged my eyes to the left. Body aflame, the demon blurred, smacking and tugging stony arms, sweeping rocky legs, sending golems crashing to the ground and into each other. With each move, the air grew warmer, radiating outward from a demonic centre. All around him, snow became water and water steam.

Backhanded by a golem, Baduriel stumbled off the transport pad and into a bronze statue, knocking it from its pedestal. As the melee moved toward the exit, I ran out to the transporter pad's centre, trying to get away from the surrounding bronze. If I was right, the glowing green fog in the bottle in my hand could help us, but not if it was ensnared again.

Here goes, I thought, uncapping the bird's-head jar.

Immediately, an amorphous cloud of green luminescence sprang from the bottle like steam from a kettle and rose up above me. Five tendrils extended from its core, forming arms, legs, and head. The mist shifted further, clothing the apparition in semi-translucent armour.

"It took you long enough, Shivurrous," the spectre boomed, swooping past me to the centre of the platform. His voice possessed an unnatural richness, a clarity that cut through the noise around me as if the words had been placed inside my head directly. "I have been trying to get your attention for hours."

"Give me a break, Wilhelm." I tapped my temple with my index finder. "I've still got memory problems, you know."

Wilhelm looked to the left. "Was all this your doing, Baduriel?"

The demon laughed. "How did it feel, Boreas?"

"How did what feel?" Wilhelm boomed.

"To be a prisoner for once." Baduriel tossed another golem to the floor, and the room shook. "To have your freedom taken."

Wilhelm scowled. "You should not have come here."

Lightning crackled by my cheek and struck Baduriel. A roar escaped his throat and his muscles twitched. A moment later, a golem hammered him off his feet and raised a foot to stomp him.

Rolling away from the plunging boulder, he clambered to his feet and glared our way. "Your time nears its end, Boreas."

"Does it? How so?"

The demon ducked a golem's sweeping arm and backed away. "I will see you scattered across the stars."

Wilhelm floated to the platform's edge. "You and what army?"

"You will see, Boreas." All around, scattered rocks slid together and shattered golems re-formed, and the flames engulfing Baduriel blazed higher. "A cleansing fire is coming. All you hold dear will be lost, and we will be redeemed."

"Stand down, Abadom," Wilhelm said, stopping the golems in their tracks. "There is only one route to redemption for you, demon." His ghostly hands sparkled with electric light. "Surrender now, return to your duties immediately, and I will urge leniency at your tribunal."

"No." Baduriel clapped his hands together, then swept his arms wide. Fire rushed outward from him, engulfing the room.

As it roared toward me, my hands shot up reflexively, and a blue-white haze of frost energy enveloped me, flaring bright as flames washed over it. Through the fading flame, Baduriel escaped into the hallway. Arcs of lightning danced across his flesh as he fled, pursued by the surviving rock golems.

As the sounds of flight diminished, Caleb emerged from cover. "That was awesome."

Scott and Virgil trailed behind him, and the stench of burned hair wrinkled my icy nose.

I dropped the frost shield with a sigh. "Everyone okay?"

All around us, stones rolled and slid across the floor as the broken golems reassembled themselves.

"Totally." Caleb thumped the shield on his arm. "The fire never reached me."

"It got to me," Scott said, stroking a hand across his forehead. "Am I missing an eyebrow?"

"It got to me too." Virgil touched his beard. It seemed shorter and less bushy than before. "If the fire had burned much longer—"

"Watch out!" Caleb pushed me aside, raising his shield. An instant later, the air filled with pops of gunfire and loud thrums.

As the sounds faded, Artyom lowered his gun, turned, and ran after his companion, John, who had just reached the exit.

"Fire," Caleb said, his voice grim. A beam of red blazed from the shield and struck the wall a half foot to the left of the fleeing shooter. He vanished through the door a second later, and two restored Abadom golems lumbered up the slope in pursuit. "Take that, dicks."

I regarded Caleb wordlessly, eyes and mouth wide.

"What?" he said. "He shot at us."

"Nice one, kid." Scott slapped the teen's shoulder. "Good thing for you that guy can't shoot for shit."

Floating two feet above the floor, Wilhelm shoved his ethereal arms outward and spun like a top. The air howled and the bronze figures all around us tumbled from their pedestals. When all twelve lay broken and bent against the outer walls of the hall, he stopped.

"He did not miss." Wilhelm extended a hand toward Caleb. "The shield pulled the projectiles to it."

"Should we go after them?" I asked.

"Let them run for now." He looked around and scowled. "There may be other traps yet, and this place . . . it is enervating."

I glanced toward the hallway. "What if they come back? One of them had a ring that let them in."

"I had presumed as much." He stared into the air above my head. After a moment, his gaze returned to me. "Their authorization has been revoked."

"Are they anathema?"

"Not quite," Wilhelm replied, "but they are on our wanted list now. If they return, Abadom will treat them accordingly, ring or no."

I blew out a breath. "Good."

Wilhelm looked around the chamber. "Abadom, remove the statues, please." More rumbling filled the chamber as the remaining golems re-formed. Without a word, they began grabbing the bronze figures from the floor. Smacking his ghostly palms together, Wilhelm looked Scott up and down and smiled. "Well met, paladin. From whence come thee?"

Scott chuckled. "From Las Vegas ... uh, burg ... good spirit."

"Las Vegasburg?" Wilhelm laughed. "A wretched hive if ever I've heard of one."

"Easy, man," Scott said. "That's my town."

"It's not so bad," I said, getting Wilhelm's drift. "I mean, it's got its share of scum, of course."

Scott grinned. "Oh, right. Don't even get me started on all the villainy."

"Jokes aside"—Wilhelm touched an ethereal hand to Scott's shoulder—"it is good to see you back on your feet and well."

"Thanks, man," he replied with a nod. "It's been a hell of a week."

"That it has." Wilhelm turned to Virgil. "Now, who's this?"

By the time we had made introductions and filled Wilhelm in on our adventures, the chamber had been cleared of statuary. Even the red columns upon which they'd stood had been removed.

"Thank you for watching over my friends," Wilhelm said to Virgil as the last column was removed.

"Think nothing of it," Virgil said. "They're good fellas."

"Nonetheless," Wilhelm replied, "I will not forget it. You have made a friend of me this day." Floating closer to the floor, he slapped my shoulder. Somehow, despite his evident intangibility, I felt it, as if I'd been jostled by a strong wind. "It took you long enough to figure out I was trapped. I figured the snow would give you a clue."

I snorted. "Some clue." My brows rose. "Wait, were you trying to get my attention with all that rain and lightning, too?"

He pursed ghostly lips. "No, not really. The storm powers

Abadom's functions, including the transporter. Your transposition here, followed by mine to come after you, drained the castle's reserves." He looked thoughtful for a moment. "I may have amplified the weather, though, in my efforts to escape."

"How did you end up trapped in the first place?"

He looked down at himself. "With the capstone collapsed, I had to come through disembodied. Without an avatar to anchor me, I was vulnerable to the trap they'd set. Even so, I would have resisted it if I had not found myself here, in this place, where my powers are encumbered."

"Yeah," I said. "Me too."

He grimaced. "The effects span dimensions."

"What's caused it, though?"

He shrugged. "A too-ambitious spatial transposition. Years ago. For that reason, the Antara transporter is not supposed to come here anymore."

"Where's it supposed to link to?" I asked.

"A town called Lolokly."

"That's where he's from," I said, glancing Virgil's way.

Wilhelm regarded Virgil. "A dangerous journey for one man alone."

Virgil tossed his shoulders. "I hitched a ride . . . in a tank."

"And how will you return?" Wilhelm asked.

"The same way," Virgil replied. "I hope." He checked his watch. "If I'm going to make the rendezvous, I should leave soon, though."

Wilhelm nodded. "It is long past time that we returned home as well."

"You should come with us," Caleb said, "and get back to Earth."

"Yeah," I said, "you should."

Virgil grunted. "No, thank you." He looked down. "The missus is waiting for me at home."

"I understand," I said. "Maybe we'll come visit again sometime, or you can come see us." I grinned. "You can bring your better Half, too."

Virgil winked an eye. "How about my Half brother?"

"Of course."

He stuck out a hand. "It's been an honour, fella."

"Stay frosty, Virgil," I said, pumping his hand.

He chuckled. "I like that. I will."

After we'd all said our goodbyes, Virgil left the platform, and we gathered at its middle.

"Say," Virgil said, looking at Wilhelm, "am I going to be all right here? Those rock fellas aren't going to attack me as soon as you leave, will they?"

"On the contrary," the spectre replied, "I've told Abadom to see you to your rendezvous safely."

Virgil frowned. "How did you do that? I didn't hear you say anything."

Wilhelm tapped his vaporous temple. "Abadom need not hear my voice to know my will."

"Oh." Virgil bobbed his head. "Okay, then."

Wilhelm saluted. "Fare thee well."

"Shivurr to Abadom." I nudged Scott. "Beam us up, Scotty."

"Aye, Captain," Scott replied. "Abadom, please activate the transporter."

A spotlight of scarlet lit the platform at our feet, and I looked up as the circle above descended, before turning my gaze forward.

"You dudes are weird," Caleb said with a smile.

Stone blocks rose from the floor, and I waved to Virgil just before he disappeared from view.

A moment later, the transporter lid clunked into place.

Chapter 29

Reflection

Before long, the capstone rose to the ceiling again, and the ring of stone receded back into the floor. A dark-robed grey-haired woman—her face lit by red light and electrical flashes—stood at the transporter pad's edge, regarding us.

"Shivurrous," she said, "it is good to see you again."

"Uh, it's good to see you too." A memory sparked, and I knew her suddenly. "Aceso."

Her eyes drifted to the side. "Mr. Scott, I instructed you to rest, not travel to other worlds."

"Uh, it's just Scott," he replied. "Not. You know. Mister." He coughed as Aceso glared. "Well . . . uh . . . I meant to, but things kind of got out of hand."

"Go easy on him," Wilhelm said from behind me. His human self once more, he sat grasping the sides of one of the stone sarcophagi that sat beyond the ring of crystal pillars. With the grace of a gymnast, he hopped out. "Sending them to Zarechus was my doing."

"Was it?" Scott asked. "Why?"

Wilhelm smoothed his dark hair as he walked over. "To keep you safe while I dealt with Atriel."

I snorted. "Safe? The trip almost killed us."

He spread his hands. "Even the best-laid plans of gods and men oft go astray."

Aceso cocked an eye. "And what delayed your return, Boreas?" For the next while, Wilhelm told her of the transporter trap and the fight with Baduriel. When he had finished, she shook her head. "Then they meant to disembody whoever came through and trap their essence in these statues until they could be retrieved."

He stroked his goatee. "Clearly so. Redirecting the transposition to Abadom ensured no help would come for those trapped and made sure even the most powerful—hindered by the area's disruption—would find it near impossible to escape."

"The demons grow bold," Aceso said. "It is a pity Baduriel slipped your grasp, however."

"Regrettable," Wilhelm said, "but he has always been elusive. He would have to be to have escaped Hades."

"What of the other two?" Aceso asked. "Did you recognize them?"

He shrugged. "Human collaborators, I presume."

I held up a finger. "Baduriel called one of them Aspirant Artyom."

"Did he?" Wilhelm looked at Aceso. "Interesting."

Her nostrils flared. "Then the Eurus Faction are involved." Her head bobbed. "I suppose they had to be."

"Why's that?" I asked.

"The transporter sabotage for one," she said. "Our technology is beyond mortal understanding. They had to have had guidance."

Wilhelm grunted. "I don't know about that. Humanity has come far since the days they believed us to be gods."

Aceso blew out a breath. "They are still as savage as ever." Her lip curled. "Their automobiles, glass towers, and televisions have not changed that. If they had, they'd not still be killing each other while overpopulating and despoiling Earth."

He spread his hands. "Evolution takes time."

"A time that they are unlikely to have," she said, "now that they have unlocked the atom. You know it's true. How many times now have we averted catastrophe?"

"Too many," Wilhelm said, "but the risk of an all-out nuclear war is small."

"Really?" Scott said. "You've stopped nuclear wars before?"

He nodded. "And, like us, the Eurus also work to prevent it."

My brow creased. "Wouldn't the Eurus want one?"

"They would happily see the West destroyed, but they know that a nuclear attack by either side would mean an end for both."

"Mutually assured destruction," Scott said. "They'd be hurting themselves as much as us."

"Precisely," Wilhelm replied. "Preventing nuclear war is one area where we and the Eurus are aligned."

"Huh." My forehead wrinkled. "For a second there, I thought maybe that was the catastrophe that I'd forgotten—the one that I went to the Bodhi Group about."

Wilhelm's eyes narrowed. "Have you remembered something that involves nuclear war?"

I pursed my lips. "No, not exactly, but it fits the bill, right?"

Aceso made a noise in the back of her throat. "How much of your memory have you recovered?"

My shoulders bounced. "I'm not sure." I waggled my head. "More returns every day, but the catastrophe is still lost to me."

Her eyes met mine. "At least you remember me."

"I do." She looked older than the last time I'd seen her but still had the same ice-grey eyes and haughty demeanour. "Thanks for saving Scott, by the way. I don't know what I'd have done if he'd died."

Aceso flicked a hand as if shooing a fly. "You need not thank me. Boreas has repaid me for my efforts."

"How did he do that?"

"By helping me here on Antara."

Wilhelm looked at Scott. "As it was, even Aceso nearly failed to save you."

"Really?" Scott said.

"You had lost a great deal of blood." Aceso pinched the skin of her forearm. "Ours is not compatible."

Caleb's eyes widened. "What did you do?"

Aceso shrugged. "I have some skill in making it, when the need arises." She looked around. "Fortunately, healing a single human being is easier than mending an entire world."

"A world?" Scott pointed at the floor. "This is another world?"

Aceso nodded. "Antara. Surely you've noticed the weaker gravity."

"Sure," Scott said, "but I thought it was just some sort of god tech—an antigravity generator, maybe."

Caleb glanced at me. "Far out."

"I had no idea." I looked about. "Underground, there's no way to tell."

"Can we go up and see the surface?" Caleb asked.

Aceso shot him a look. "Not yet, I'm afraid. You would not live more than a few minutes there."

"Bummer."

She looked around. "Terraformation will change that, in time. One day, Antara will teem with life again. Gravity wells are the first step. We cannot have the atmosphere blowing into space even as we manufacture it." She took a step toward the teen and extended a hand. "We have not yet been properly introduced."

"Oh, sorry. I'm Caleb."

"Aceso." Her eyes flicked downward. "You carry one of our shields."

Caleb's face sank. "Oh, is it yours? Do you want it back?"

She shook her head. "It is not mine to take." She ran her fingertips along its surface. "How came you by it?"

"We found it under a sofa in the castle." I pointed to Scott. "The sword too."

Scott tugged at his chain mail. "The armour was in a chest."

Aceso grimaced. "The owner likely died in the transporter accident."

"That seems likely," Wilhelm said. "If he had lived, he surely would have returned to Abadom to recover it long ago."

"Does that mean I can keep it?" Caleb asked.

"Perhaps," Wilhelm said. "I will first verify that the owner is no longer with us. If so, you both may keep the items you've found. Though I'll have to limit the shield's offensive capabilities. At least when you're back home." He cracked a grin. "We can't have you blasting your classmates with it."

"Wicked, dude."

Wilhelm slapped my shoulder. "We should be on our way."

Aceso inclined her head. "Very well, but we must speak more of Zarechus soon."

Parting ways with Aceso, we made our way to the stadium-sized cavern with the huge pit at its centre.

Wilhelm nudged Caleb and pointed at the void as we slipped past it. "I seem to recall you wanted Shivurr to slap me over there."

The teen smiled but said nothing.

I smirked. "You were pretty out of it, Boreas. It was like you were sleepwalking or something."

"You said it yourself," Wilhelm said with a grin. "I was out of it, literally."

My brow creased a moment. "You mean your avatar."

"Correct."

"But you were walking around and doing stuff."

Wilhelm shrugged. "Even unoccupied, avatars are capable of basic functions to nourish and defend themselves. Though usually we stow them in places of safety rather than allowing them to wander around."

"Like the sarcophagi? Those stone boxes, I mean."

"Also correct," he said. "They sustain our avatars while they're not in use. It's especially important here for our human forms, to protect them from the long-term effects of low gravity. It's partly why I left this body behind on Earth."

"But wait," I said. "How can that be? You . . . this body . . . ran from us and came here. If you were outside of it, how is that possible?"

He tapped his temple. "I have some connection to it even at a distance."

"So you summoned it?"

"Correct," he said. "I brought it here in preparation for my return to Caelumburg."

"But why from Aceso's and not your own place?"

He tossed his shoulders. "It's where I was when Aceso and I left for Antara."

"I see. That's why you were sitting there by the pit. You were waiting for the giant. No, wait. You were the giant."

He nodded. "The titan you saw is another of my avatars— one more useful for the work that needs doing here."

My eyes flicked to Wilhelm's chest and back to his face. "You're not possessing someone, are you?"

Wilhelm laughed. "No, not at all. This is a manufactured biological construct, grown, not born."

"You mean," Scott said, "it's a clone?"

"Not quite; even without epigenetic changes, we take measures to ensure each avatar is unique. It keeps things interesting." He looked down at himself. "You wouldn't want to wear the same T-shirt for eternity. The same goes for one's body. More so, really."

I jabbed a finger at a long scabbed-over cut on Wilhelm's forearm. "What happened there?"

"Atriel," he said.

My eyebrows rose. "You know his name."

He tapped his temple. "I heard some of your conversation."

"What happened to him?"

Wilhelm gave a low growl. "I chased him back to Caelumtor, but he fled the body he'd stolen and gave me the slip."

"That nightmare body was stolen?" I snapped my fingers. "He's like you."

Wilhelm nodded. "He's a member of the Eurus Faction. What we can't figure out is how Atriel entered Caelumtor in the first place."

"I'm not sure I follow," I said.

"To have made it to the heart of New Olympus undetected, he would have had to come by spatial transposition. Yet the entire New Olympus archipelago is warded against arbitrary transpositions. The only ways in are through established transposition points, which are locked to remote locations."

"Which means?" Scott asked.

"It means," I said with sudden understanding, "you can only transport between specific locations." An old memory resurfaced. "And . . ." I tapped the ring on my hand. "Those locations are secure, and their use restricted and monitored."

"Right," Wilhelm said. "And there has been no unauthorized usage."

"Hang on." I stopped walking. "That doesn't make sense."

My companions drew up short.

Wilhelm turned, and his eyes searched my face. "Why's that?"

"Oh, yeah." Scott touched his fingertips to his temples. "The desert. I'd totally forgotten about it."

Wilhelm cocked an eyebrow. "What desert?"

For the next few minutes, I filled Wilhelm in on our trip from Aceso's kitchen to the unknown desert where Scott and I had encountered fire elementals.

"That's disturbing," Wilhelm said after I'd finished. "One of the vials in your cap must contain an object used to anchor and enable the transport. Yet it still shouldn't be possible. You say it was just you and a few objects in the kitchen that transported?"

I nodded. "Yeah, it seemed like it."

He stroked his beard. "That's very unusual indeed."

"Why?" I asked.

"Spatial transposition swaps volumes of space," he said. "Typically, it's a box shape. That avoids cutting through existing objects, slicing them in half. Sometimes a cylinder is more appropriate, such as with the Abadom transporter. A sphere works as well, but both locations need to be prepped to avoid overlap, or at least to ensure that overlap doesn't matter."

"Okay," Scott said, "but how's that different from what we experienced?"

"Think about it," Wilhelm said. "Did the entire room go with you?"

I shook my head. "It was just us that transported. The rest of the room stayed behind."

Scott scowled. "What about the table? It came with us."

I scratched the side of my head. "Oh, yeah."

"Were you touching it?" Wilhelm asked.

I thought back. "Yeah, I was." I glanced at Scott. "You'd just grabbed me and pushed me against the table."

Scott shrugged. "I figured it was an earthquake."

"Yeah, but that's not my point. At that moment, we were also touching."

"Um-hmm," Wilhelm said. "Which is probably why Scott made the trip with you. Somehow, whatever device was used extracted only you and that with which you were in direct contact. I'm not sure how whoever made the device managed it."

"Why?" I asked.

Wilhelm ran a hand through his hair. "Spatial transposition requires exacting calculations. The greater the distance involved, the more difficult it is to get right, and the more energy required to do so." He sucked in a breath. "Taking only individual objects rather than everything in a set volume of space means more things to track, and more things that can go wrong." His forehead creased. "On the plus side, by taking only what's strictly required, you'd keep the energy costs down." He shook his head. "But, to do so on the fly is . . . well, it's incredibly dangerous. Things can go wrong."

"Like at Abadom?"

"Exactly."

"So, you figure that's how Atriel got to Caelumtor."

"I do," he said. "Atriel must have a twin device. When you removed the vial containing it from your cap, it must have activated, bringing him to Aceso's kitchen and sending you to that desert." He blew out a breath. "Only one of our opposing brethren would take such a risk."

"The Faction," I said.

Wilhelm inclined his head. "Right—the Eurus Faction."

"The guys that want to be worshipped by humanity again."

He waggled a hand. "That or at least to rule and subjugate them. It's no accident that they've embedded themselves most strongly in the communist east. As a political system, it's perfect for them: a dictatorship with only one political party. The government controls industry and business, information is censored, and the people are surveilled, powerless, and afraid to speak out, allowing the ruling party to act with impunity."

"And what do you guys want?" Scott asked.

"For humans to live free and in peace—to develop and thrive."

Scott snickered. "You are a hippie, man."

"Guilty," Wilhelm said with a shrug before looking at me. "Did you recognize the desert?"

"No," I replied. "It didn't look like Nevada or Death Valley. Could it have been another planet, maybe?"

"I doubt it." He looked thoughtful. "A transport off-planet would require massive amounts of energy. Too much for a portable device, I should think."

"Oh, right," I said. "I suppose that makes sense."

"We can investigate further on Caelumtor. For now, you should keep the vials safe in your cap." He smiled. "Unless you're looking to take another trip."

"Yeah," I said. "I figured that out myself already."

"Good man." He looked at his watch. "We should move."

Once back on Caelumtor, Wilhelm led us past the archway leading to Aceso's—where Atriel had stolen Caleb's ring—and down an unfamiliar hallway.

"Where are we headed?" I asked after a while. "This isn't the way back to Aceso's, is it?"

"No," Wilhelm replied, leading us up a set of broad stone stairs that cut back on themselves a few times as we ascended. "We're going to my domus. I've got a surprise for you there."

At the top, an iron-banded wooden door opened at Wilhelm's touch, and we entered an opulent, expansive room.

"Whoa, nice," I said, looking around.

Painted gods, humans, and fantastic creatures looked down on us from high frescoed ceilings. A broad canopied bed lay off to our left, beyond which floor-to-ceiling windows looked out upon the marble and stone of Caelumtor's buildings, the sides of which blazed with sunlight.

We slipped through double doors to our right into a plant-filled courtyard—a larger twin to the peristylium at Aceso's, though the statuary, furniture, and their arrangement varied from hers.

Taking an immediate left, Wilhelm led us along the pillared walkway that bordered the garden.

A loud woof came from ahead as we took a right at the corner. A black-and-white snout and lolling pink tongue slid into view from ahead and to the left, followed by a furry body and wagging tail. Turning to face us, the dog woofed again before padding toward us.

"Wicked," Caleb said.

I darted forward. "Hey, Bear." I ran a hand over the fur of the Alaskan shepherd that had been with me only days ago when I'd fought monsters at Dublin Gulch. With Olivia's reassurances, I'd had to leave him to find his own way out of Death Valley, and I couldn't stop smiling to see he'd made it through un-scathed. "Hey, buddy." The Schmidts' dog's wet tongue soon fluttered across my cheek. "Okay, easy . . . easy. I'm not ice cream."

Scott patted Bear's flank. "What's he doing here?"

"Oh my god," said a girl's voice, turning my gaze to the right. "Hey, you guys."

A small-framed raven-haired girl of sixteen stood in the pas-sageway ahead.

"Hi, Lilith," I said, glancing at Wilhelm.

She looked to her right. "Come on. They're here."

Caleb straightened, and a goofy smile spread across his face. "Hey, Lil."

The girl came toward us, wide-eyed. "Oh my god. It's so good to see you guys."

"You too, Lil," Caleb said.

She hugged the teen, then pecked his cheek.

"Holy shit," Alan said, emerging from a doorway. "Hey, dudes."

"We were getting worried," Lilith said, wrapping me in an embrace. "Hi, Shivurr."

Alan exchanged a high five with Caleb. "What took so long?"

"There were complications," Wilhelm said from behind me. "Has Olivia returned yet?"

Lilith shook her head. "No, not yet."

Scott took Alan's hand and slapped him on a bicep. "Where did you get the shiner?"

The teen touched a hand to his red and swollen eye and scowled. "Oh, it's nothing."

"What are you dudes doing here?" Caleb asked.

Lilith looked down. "Bear brought us."

"Yeah, but why?"

"Never mind that," Alan said. "What's with the shield?"

Stepping to the centre of our group, Wilhelm held up his hands. "Hang on. Let's sit down before you get into all that. You guys have a lot to catch up on, so you might as well do it over breakfast."

Chapter 30

Brain Freeze

We followed him a few short steps to the room from which Lilith and Alan had emerged. Inside, breakfast foods littered the near end of an ornate wooden table. Large enough to seat sixteen comfortably, it dominated the spacious high-ceilinged dining room. All around, paintings decorated red walls and a half-barrel ceiling above. On the far side, a huge picture window looked out over the green valley of Caelumtor. Next to it, an android like those we'd seen at Aceso's stood in the corner. Its gleaming dark head stared straight ahead and did not react as we took seats around the table.

"Cool view," I said. "I thought we were in the centre of the valley, though."

Lilith looked at me. "Oh, that's not really a window. Wilhelm said it's an illusion. You'll see. It'll change to something else, eventually."

Alan pulled back an ornately carved high-backed dining room chair. "Have a seat, dude."

"What do you guys want to eat?" Wilhelm asked, glancing from Scott to Caleb to me.

Caleb hooked the ruby shield's straps over a chair back and pointed at Alan's half-eaten plate. "That'd be good."

Wilhelm's eyes flicked to me. "Shivurr?"

"Got anything cold?"

"Uh, yeah." He smiled and winked. "I think I've got just the thing in mind. I'll be back in a minute." He turned toward the courtyard exit. "You guys catch up."

As he passed through the doorway, the waiting android burst into motion and followed him out.

After he'd left, I took a long look at the young couple. Like Caleb, I'd first met them in the Nevada desert days ago when I'd rescued the three teens along with Alan's older brother, Brad, and his girlfriend, Lucy, from two gun-wielding thugs.

"Where's Brad and Lucy?" I asked, puzzled by their absence. The two weren't much older than the teens sitting before me, being in their early twenties. I'd grown close to them too in our brief time together, and I hoped they were okay. If not for them driving me from Lunar Crater to Tonopah, I might not have survived.

"Hey, yeah," Caleb said. "Are they still sleeping?"

Alan grimaced. "No."

Lilith patted her boyfriend's back. "They'll be here." Her eyes met mine. "They're with Olivia."

"We got separated," Alan said. "Some guys were after us." He thrust a chin toward Bear, who sat curled up on a sofa set against a nearby wall. "If it wasn't for Bear . . ."

"And Carver," Lilith added, raising a forkload of pancake to her mouth.

I leaned forward. "Who?"

"A friend," Lilith said, still chewing. "He's a PI. He does work for Wilhelm and Olivia."

Alan nodded. "He and Bear saved us."

"I mean, who was after you?"

Alan shrugged. "Carver and Olivia called them the Eurus Faction." His eyes flicked to his girlfriend. "We figured it had to be the Bodhi Group at first, but it turns out it wasn't them after all."

"It might have been both," Lilith said. "Remember what Lucy said about those guys that showed up at their place. The truck had a dent, remember?"

"That's true." Alan swept an elbow through the air. "I put it there when they kidnapped us back in Vegas. Brad said the one they saw at his place had a dent in the same spot. So we figure those dudes must have been with the Bodhi Group."

"Yeah," Lilith said, "but Olivia's sure Greta's with the Faction."

"Greta?"

"Yeah," Alan replied. "Some redheaded chick from East Germany."

Lilith made a face. "If she wasn't lying about that too."

"A redhead," Caleb said. "Is she hot?"

Alan glanced at Lilith. "Uh—yeah, I suppose you could say that."

"Anyway," Lilith said. "She showed up at the beach and told Alan she wanted surfing lessons, but they were really trying to kidnap us or something. If Lucy, Brad, and Bear hadn't shown up when they did, they'd have gotten me and Alan for sure."

Alan's eyes widened. "Yeah, probably."

Lilith paled, glancing at Alan. "They had guns."

He stretched an arm about her shoulders. "It's all good now."

She nodded. "After he chased them away, Bear found us again, and we followed him to my house."

I squinted. "To your house?"

"Yeah," she said. "Bear told Carver to wait for us there. Then we all went to Los Angeles."

I snorted. "Bear told him to?"

She smiled. "Yeah, Bear can talk." She tapped her temple. "Telepathically."

I glanced at the sleeping dog. "Really?"

"It's true, dude," Alan said. "He's amazing."

"Wow." I sat back in my chair. "I guess I shouldn't be surprised."

"Then what happened?" Scott asked.

"Oh," Alan said, "Carver took us to a hideout in Los Angeles to wait for Olivia or Wilhelm to get in touch."

"How was that?" Caleb asked.

"It was all right at first," Alan said, "but it got boring pretty fast." He blew out a breath. "Until it got crazy again."

"How so?" I asked.

Lilith sneered. "That Greta person found us again."

"She must have followed Carver," Alan said.

"Maybe," Lilith said, "but it could've been something else. Like the turkey vulture."

Scott cocked his head. "Turkey vulture?"

"Yeah," Alan said. "The Faction use them to spy on people."

"Like the one at Dublin Gulch," I said, remembering the bird that Bear had chased away a few days ago.

Alan rapped the table. "That was one of them. It followed us home, I guess."

That's how they found me at Dublin Gulch, I thought. "So, you figure it followed you to Los Angeles too?"

Lilith wagged her head. "No, silly. How could it?"

I frowned. "Huh? What do you mean?"

"Carver shot it," she said.

"Uh, yeah," I said. "I don't think you mentioned that."

"Didn't I?"

"Nope." I waved a hand. "Okay, so not that one."

"Whatever it was," Lilith said, "they found us again, so we had to run."

"How did you get separated, though?" Caleb asked.

"We were"—Alan coughed—"alone when those a-holes showed up."

Lilith gripped Alan's hand in hers. "Lots of them. They had guns too, just like the ones that tried to grab us at the beach." She looked at Alan. "They would have taken us, except Olivia came to our rescue."

Alan nodded. "She's awesome. She took them all down like Wonder Woman."

Caleb smirked. "No doubt, dude."

"She's strong," Alan replied with a nod. He touched his shiner. "I mean, I helped a bit, but she kicked their asses."

Lilith rubbed his shoulder. "You totally helped, Alan."

"Anyway," he said with a shrug, "she told us to go with Bear while she looked for the others. He took us to a room. The next thing we know, we're here." He tapped his index finger against the table. "Well, the tunnels under here, at least."

"When was this?" I asked.

"I don't know. It's been hours, though."

"And they still haven't shown up?"

"Nope," he said, looking at Lilith. "Not yet."

"Damn," I said, "I hope they're all right."

"They're supposed to be," he said, "according to Wilhelm. At least they were."

Lilith nodded. "Olivia contacted Wilhelm after we got here."

She probably used her necklace, I thought, recalling the holographic device she'd used to speak to him in their beachside cottage a few days ago.

"What do you suppose is keeping them?" I asked.

Lilith shrugged. "Wilhelm just said they were taking a longer way back."

My brow knit. "They must not be able to get to a transporter. At least not one that the Eurus don't know about."

"Yeah," Scott said. "They're probably still watching the one you guys took to get here."

Caleb slapped the table and rose from his chair. "What if the Faction dudes use it too? They could come here after you."

"Don't sweat it," Wilhelm said, entering the room with a plate of food in each hand. "They won't be able to use it." He thrust a chin toward the dog, who stretched both legs to his front and yawned lazily. "Bear locked it down as soon as you arrived."

"Oh, good," Caleb said, retaking his seat. "That's a relief."

Wilhelm handed the plates of food to Scott and Caleb and turned to me. "Yours will be here soon." He smiled and took the seat at the end of the table nearest the door. "It's coming from much farther away."

"Aren't you eating?" I asked as he leaned back in his chair.

"I'm good." He sat forward as Bear padded over to him. "I had an Ambrola in the kitchen." He patted the Alaskan shepherd's head and looked around. "So, what were you talking about?"

"We just finished telling them how we got here," Lilith said.

"Any word from Olivia?" Alan asked.

Wilhelm shook his head. "Not yet, but I'm sure things are fine." He frowned. "I'll see if I can reach her after breakfast."

"Cool," Alan said. "So, what have you dudes been up to?"

"Yeah," Lilith said. "Tell us everything."

For the next while, we told the young couple the tale of our adventures on Zarechus. They listened with wide eyes, open mouths, and shaking heads, scarcely interrupting as I related the story with Scott, Caleb, and Wilhelm chiming in periodically, adding details that I'd forgotten or hadn't noticed in the excitement.

"That's wild," Alan said as we finished. "You guys visited another freaking planet."

"Two planets." Lilith shuddered. "I'm glad I missed those Nameless, though."

"Ah, here we are," Wilhelm said as the silver-and-white body of an automaton appeared in the doorway. Its extended arms held a tray of cups adorned with psychedelic stripes of garish colour. A plastic straw stuck out of the mountain of brown ice that rose above the rims of each one. He met my eyes and winked. "I figured you deserved a treat."

My jaw dropped, and I leaned forward. "Slurpees?" I'd had them only a few times in the past, courtesy of Scott. He'd snuck a few into the Institute in a cooler once or twice. Even half melted by their long journey—despite the cooler being packed with ice—I'd enjoyed them immensely. "Cool."

"Take one," Wilhelm said. "There's enough for everyone."

Doing as he suggested, I slurped from the straw and sighed. Savouring the chill, I washed the icy soda from cheek to cheek before swallowing.

"Isn't that like cannibalism?" Alan said with a smirk.

Laughing, I closed my eyes as the rush of cold reached my belly. "Awesome. How'd you get them? Do you have a machine or something?"

"No, these are from an actual store." He wagged a finger at me. "That's a good idea, though."

"Wait," I said. "How can that be? The nearest store must be a thousand miles away . . . more."

Wilhelm smirked. "I ordered it."

I held up a finger. "Ah, through one of those metal boxes, right? Like the one Aceso has in her kitchen."

He nodded. "You got it."

"How does that work?" I asked, taking another sip. "Is it like the food thing on *Star Trek*?"

Wilhelm chuckled. "No, not really."

"Then how?"

He smiled. "Spatial transposition, of course." He glanced around at the gathered group. "We have agents that we employ to monitor the boxes on their end for our requests, which they then carry out."

"Oh." I jabbed the ice with my straw. "So they're like your personal shoppers. You send a note asking for something. They go buy it and put it in the box."

"Sometimes it's shopping," he said. "Sometimes cooking. You name it, we've probably got a box for it."

"That's so amazing," Lilith said. "Talk about convenience."

"For sure," Wilhelm said. "Not that we're not self-sufficient here on New Olympus, but there are things from the mainland that we'd rather not do without." He stood. "All right. I'm going to see if I can contact Olivia." He looked around the table. "You kids stay and hang out. I'm sure you still have catching up to do."

After breakfast, Alan, Lilith, and Caleb went off to shower, and Scott and I went to the peristylium. After ordering fresh Slurpees from an android, we dragged lounge chairs into the shade and sat, enjoying the fresh air and birdsong in the idyllic garden.

"This is cool," I said, stirring the frozen ice with my straw. "I could do this for days."

"It's pretty sweet all right," Scott replied. "Some music would be nice, though. I wonder if Wil's got a boom box around here."

I shrugged. "Beats me."

"Can I listen to your Walkman?" Scott said. "The one Olivia gave you, I mean."

"Oh, right." I pulled my cap from my head. "I think there's a cassette in it. I'm not sure what's on it, though."

Scott held out a hand. "Let's see."

"Here you go," I said after a few moments of searching.

He pressed a button on the side and placed the headphones over his ears. "Creedence. Nice."

"What's that?"

"You haven't heard of them?"

I shook my head. "How could I, unless you introduced me to them?"

"Oh, yeah. It's long past time to fix that oversight." He held the headphones out to me. "Put these on."

As I settled the orange foam pads into place, Scott pressed play. My head bobbed as rhythmic bluesy rock music played in my ears.

"I like it," I said after a moment.

Scott grinned and said something that I couldn't quite make out.

"What?" I tapped the side of one of the headphones. "Sorry, I can't hear you. The music's too loud."

Nodding, he fiddled with the Walkman, and the music grew fainter. "How's that? Can you hear me now?"

"Yeah, that's good. What were you saying?"

He snickered. "I said that I'm not deaf. You were . . . never mind." He leaned my way, holding out the music player. "Here, man."

"Are you sure? I thought you wanted to listen to it."

"That was before you told me you hadn't heard Creedence before."

Taking the Walkman, I set it on my chest and reclined. "This is wicked."

"Let me listen after you, though."

"Sure." I held up the cassette player. "This technology is freaking amazing. Music at your fingertips in a box small enough to fit in your hand."

Scott snorted. "We've seen a lot more amazing stuff than that."

"Like what?"

"Androids and rock golems." He whistled. "The hardware and software to make autonomous, artificially intelligent agents of near-human intelligence, it blows my mind."

I nodded. "And don't forget about the ookmir. And the demons. Oh, and the Nameless."

Scott waggled a hand. "Yeah, but I think they're biological."

"So?"

He shrugged. "I'm not sure about the Nameless, but the ookmir and demons probably evolved through natural selection. The androids and rock golems were designed from scratch. Which means someone had to think of everything."

I glanced at him and cocked an eyebrow. "You think demons evolved?"

"Sure, man. Why not? Maybe not on Earth, or at least not the one we know today, but couldn't they just be aliens or something? Aliens like Wilhelm and his people. They could be from another dimension, even."

"Yeah, true." I picked up my half-empty Slurpee, patted the bottom, and stabbed the straw into the slush. "What about Wilhelm's avatars, though?"

"What about them?"

"They didn't evolve. Wilhelm said they were constructed."

"Yeah," Scott said. "I'm kind of freaked out by them."

"Why?"

"You said it yourself," he said. "What if these avatars are real people being possessed? You've got to admit, it's like *Invasion of the Body Snatchers* or something. What if Wilhelm—the human guy—has been taken over by the green ghost? Against his will."

"You heard him on Zarechus," I said. "Even in his ghost form, he sounded and acted like Wilhelm, more or less."

"Sure," he replied. "I agree that the ghost is the Wilhelm we both know, but what if there's another guy in there that's been suppressed or something?"

I shook my head. "Wilhelm explained that. Avatars are made. Biological, sure, but they don't have minds of their own."

"If you say so, Shivurr."

"Come on, Scott. This is Wilhelm we're talking about. Do you really think he's capable of something like that?"

Scott studied the stones of the courtyard, head bobbing. "You're right. It's just a lot to take in."

"Anyway," I said, "let's talk about something else."

"Sure," he said. "Like what?"

"I don't know." I thought a moment. "Are you going to go back to the Bodhi Institute? If there's anything left to go back to, I mean."

"Maybe." He sucked in a breath and exhaled sharply. "If not, I guess I'll be looking for a new job."

"Are you okay with that?"

"Yeah, I am. I've been thinking about quitting for a while anyway." He glanced around. "Maybe I'll stay here. If Wilhelm will let me."

"What about your cat, though?"

"Shit." He clasped his hands to the sides of his face. "Jane's been alone at my place all this time." He looked thoughtful for a moment, then seemed to relax. "Ah, my sister, Odile, will take care of her."

"I thought you liked your job."

He scowled. "Yeah, but it would be nice not to have to put up with dicks anymore."

"But you don't work for Dixon, do you? Not directly at least."

He squinted at me. "Huh?" Before I could answer, his eyes lit, and he laughed. "No, not Dixon. Dicks. Anymore."

I snorted. "Oh, right. Where's this coming from?"

His eyes met mine. "I'm a failure, Shivurr. I'm in my thirties now, but I'm still taking orders, still a peon."

"A failure? With your skills? Can the Institute even function without you for long?"

He shrugged. "Not as well, but I doubt they'll realize why. They don't value what I do, man. Not really. They don't understand it, so they try to diminish it and make it seem like a commodity—like everyone's interchangeable. Which is bullshit. I play the guitar, but no one's going to pay a hundred bucks to hear me play. With more practice, I might have gotten decent, but you've got to have talent too." He tapped a finger against his temple. "Computers, programming, it's no different, but these assholes . . . they don't get that."

"Sorry, dude. It must suck to not feel appreciated."

He removed his eyeglasses and pinched the bridge of his nose. "Maybe it's just that people suck, man."

"I don't know. I kind of like them."

"Sure," he said. "Some of them are great, but too many of them aren't. Whenever I've been happy in my life, and it changed for the worse, it's been when new people came along."

"I hear you." I bobbed my head, thinking this might be about more than just being appreciated for his skills. "It sure was the case with the Bodhi Group." I thought a moment before continuing. "But, you know, the opposite is also true."

"What do you mean?"

"Well," I said, "when things were at their worst for me, you showed up, and things got a whole lot better, and if not for meeting you, I'd still be in that shitty place."

"Yeah, I suppose you've got a point there." Scott rubbed a hand across his face and flipped his hair from his eyes. "Whatever." He patted his abdomen. "I'm alive at least." He looked thoughtful. "And if I go back home, maybe I'll start my own company. Computers are the future, man."

"And become an asshole?"

He laughed. "Either you're the asshole or you work for one."

I looked at him sidelong. "Really? All bosses can't be bad."

He sighed. "They're not—and someone's got to be in charge—but no one likes having a boss, even a good one."

"And you're okay not being liked?"

"I'd rather be giving orders than taking them. Besides, I'd be a good boss, and it wouldn't hurt to improve the ratio of good ones to bad ones." He yawned. "I've got to get some shut-eye." He leaned back, crossed his arms, and closed his eyes. When I thought he'd fallen asleep, he spoke again. "Shivurr?"

"Yeah, Scott?"

"Don't get me wrong. I like people. I just wish some of them didn't suck so much."

"Yeah," I said, thinking about the Faction. "Maybe we just need to get rid of the bad ones, like they do on Zarechus."

He sat taller. "You mean, banish them to the Immerwald?"

"Sure," I said. "Or any place where they can't make good people miserable."

Scott whistled. "That'd be a lonely world." The corners of his mouth lifted. "I wouldn't mind, though."

"Anyway," I said, "who cares if the Bodhi Group doesn't appreciate you? You're still awesome, no matter what they think."

"I suppose." He smirked and shook his head. "You're right. Sorry, man. I get a bit cranky when I'm tired."

I waved a hand. "Don't sweat it."

"How about you, Shivurr?" he asked. "What do you want to do after you get your memories back and things settle down?"

"I want to find out what happened to the other Sentinels and Borealans."

"And after that?"

"Travel," I said. "I'd like to see New York City, maybe tour Europe, meet people, you know."

"Maybe you already have," he said. "If there's anything good about your memory loss, it's that you get to experience the good stuff again as if for the first time."

"I know, right?"

A few minutes later, his breathing deepened.

Pressing the stop button on the Walkman, I swept off the headphones, returned the music player to the safety of my hat, and rose from the lounge. With a stretch of my arms above my head, I made my way to where I judged—based on Aceso's domus—the kitchen should be.

A hum as I entered drew my eyes to the left, and I smiled.

Doffing my cap, I hustled along a row of drink machines, tapping buttons like a Las Vegas slot player on a winning streak. The colourful cylinders scarcely had time to tumble down to waiting receptacles before I swept them up and stuffed them into my upturned hat.

"Hey, man." Wilhelm regarded me from the doorway with a crooked smile on his face. Instead of his bloody T-shirt and shorts, he now wore a dark navy business suit. "Leave some for the rest of us."

I coughed. "Sorry, Boreas. I got—"

"I'm kidding," he said, waving a hand as if shooing a fly. "Take as many as you like. Seriously. It'll give the automatons something to do."

"Thanks, man." I stuffed another Ambrola into my hat. "I think that'll do it."

"Are you sure?" he asked. "Take more if you like."

I grinned. "Okay, maybe I'll drink one now." I pressed another button, sending a last can tumbling. Snatching it from the receptacle, I cracked it open. "You're looking sharp. Something up?"

"Come on." He jerked his head toward the courtyard. "We should talk."

Chapter 31

Speak of the Devil

Taking a sip, I followed him into the garden and down the shaded walkway to a room floored in marble and carpet. An ornately carved wooden desk as long and wide as a flatbed truck sat near the room's centre, surrounded by plush leather chairs. At the room's edges, floor-to-ceiling shelving lined the walls, crowded with books and sculptures, expensive-looking vases, and other works of art. The tomes formed a wall of brown, green, and red, and their spines glimmered gold, reflecting shafts of sunlight that entered from strategically placed openings in the ceiling above.

Wilhelm gestured toward a collection of comfy chairs to our left that sat facing each other next to a bookcase and a statue of a woman in a dancer's pose. A stone chessboard with intricately carved pieces sat on a pedestal between the two chairs.

"Take a load off," he said, taking a seat.

I smiled to myself, noting that his manner of speaking had—since returning to his avatar—gradually become casual again, different from how he had spoken in his spectre form. He was now more like the Wilhelm he had been days ago when I'd met him at his house in Las Vegas. I wasn't sure if the difference came from a conscious affectation on his part or if his personality and style of speech was actually different for some reason when embodied in his avatar versus his ethereal form. Whatever the reason, I felt comforted by it.

"Thanks." Settling into the other seat, I reshaped my snowy bottom to better fit and stroked the leather armrest. "Nice."

"Music?" he asked.

"Sure."

His face took on a distant expression as if he were trying to remember where he'd left his house keys. A moment later, classical music filled the air, coming from nowhere in particular and everywhere at once.

He sat back and closed his eyes a moment. "I love a little night music in the morning."

Haunting and yet uplifting, the melody seemed familiar. "Is this . . . Bach?" I asked, closing my eyes as well.

"Mozart."

"I like it," I said, opening my eyes. "I thought you were a hippie, though. Shouldn't you be listening to Donovan and stuff?"

"No reason I can't like both, is there?" He cocked an eyebrow. "Don't you like *Star Trek* and *Star Wars*?"

"Of course," I said. "So, what did you want to talk about? Is this about Olivia? Is she all right? What about Lucy and Brad?"

He nodded. "Yeah. She's okay. So are the kids."

I blew out a breath. "Cool, when will they be here?"

"Not for a while yet." He held up a hand. "Don't worry. They're just taking a longer way back. If they don't run into any more trouble, they should arrive tomorrow."

"What are the odds they won't? Run into trouble, I mean."

He grunted. "As good as can be."

"At least Olivia is with them."

"For now."

"What?"

"Easy now, Shivurr. They may be safer without her. Of the three, the Eurus will want Olivia most. She's a formidable protector, but also an attractive target. Whereas they want Brad and Lucy only in the hopes that they can lead them to you and the rest of us. Even if she has to leave them, our friend Carver is quite capable as well. For a mortal."

"Yeah, but Olivia's a god."

He looked at his hands.

"What's up? You look worried."

"Olivia's powerful," he said, "but she's not entirely like me, yet. She's more vulnerable."

"Right, she said that she's still human."

He shrugged. "Not entirely human, but not fully a god yet either."

"She's not yet fully ascended," I said as old memories surfaced.

His eyes lit. "You remember ascension?"

"Yeah," I said. "Some. I don't remember all the details, but it's how a human becomes a god, right?" Wilhelm's face scrunched. "Wait. That's not quite it. It's more about immortality, isn't it?"

He pointed a finger at me. "Now you've got it. What else do you remember?"

"Lots of stuff, but it's all jumbled up. Mostly it comes back in dreams or when someone says something, or I see something that triggers a memory."

"Cool. That's great news." His eyes drifted to my shoulder, then back to me. "Have you remembered why you went to the Bodhi Institute?"

I shook my head. "It's the same as before. It's something big, something catastrophic, involving the Allfrost."

He grunted. "The answer must be in one of the other vials in your hat."

"If we're lucky," I said. "Dixon said they sent some to other facilities."

He frowned. "How many of this batch do you have left?"

"I'm not sure." I tugged the bill of my cap. "A dozen or so."

"Minus the one that sent you and Scott to the desert."

"Right," I replied. "I forgot about that one."

"I'm surprised you haven't chugged them all by now."

"I've been taking them slowly," I said. "They tend to hit me hard. Dizziness, nausea, and sometimes I pass out. It varies."

"Well, if they don't contain the answers we need, we'll have to get the rest from the other facilities."

I scowled. "Except I've no idea where they are."

"I know of one. It's where we thought the Bodhi Group had you at first. It's a major lab. That's most likely where they are."

I leaned forward in my chair. "That's fantastic. I can go in like I did at the Institute."

Wilhelm grimaced. "If you use the Allfrost to transport your-self there, you'll get in easily enough. The trouble is getting out again."

"It can't be harder than the Institute," I said.

"Unfortunately," Wilhelm said, "this one's located in New York City. Even once you've escaped the facility, you'll have to make your way through a city crowded with people. Even New Yorkers will freak out if they see you. That'll alert the Group, Eurus, and possibly other factions that you're in the vicinity. As a major cosmopolitan city, they've all got a presence there as well. Which means it won't take long for them to be on your trail."

I growled and looked down at myself. "Being unique is not without its drawbacks." I rubbed the roundness of my bottom sphere. "It'd be easier if I could pass for a human being sometimes."

"You have before," Wilhelm said with a nod. "Do you remember?"

"Olivia said the same thing," I replied, "and I've tried. I sort of formed legs, but it didn't last long." I sighed. "Maybe in time I can learn how again, or one of the memory vials will restore the ability." I shrugged. "Even if I do, I'll still need clothing or something to disguise myself." I pinched one of my snowy cheeks. "Anyone seeing this is going to know I'm different."

Wilhelm looked thoughtful. "The Miraculeum could help. Do you remember it?"

"No." My brow wrinkled. "Olivia mentioned it the other day. She said she'd give me a tour, but I don't remember anything about it."

"It's a building near here, housing technology capable—with guidance—of miraculous things."

"Like what?"

He glanced down at himself before looking at me. "Manu-facturing life."

I thought back to the troll I'd fought less than a week ago. "Like ookmir?"

He nodded. "And more."

I snapped my fingers. "That's how your avatars are made."

"That's right."

I thought back to my time at the Institute. "So, how does that work? Is it genetic engineering?"

"That plays into it, certainly. Sometimes, those of us, like myself, who specialize in the area—those with skill and desire—develop genetic patterns entirely from scratch. We set the starting point, then allow evolution and natural selection to run its course, allowing our work to emerge into something that surprises even us. Other times, we take inspiration from established life forms like ookmir and tweak them into something new, something better. The latter is much easier, typically allowing for more complex life forms, evolution having already done much of the work."

"Oh, that's how it works." I smirked. "Scott's still worried you're possessing people against their will."

He pursed his lips. "He needn't worry. There's no apparatus for integration in a human being: We could, perhaps, force our way into a body and influence a mind telepathically, I suppose, but it wouldn't be the same. This body is designed to accommodate me. Once inside it, I become it." He tapped his temple. "Without me, it's just an empty organic machine. The lights are on, but no one is home."

"You mean, it has no soul?"

"If you like," he said. "In here, I'm as much a part of it as you are a part of your own body. Which is why, these days, I dislike leaving my avatar. Exiting it, even for another avatar, is unpleasant after living as a human being for so long."

"That's amazing." His words bridged islands of memory into larger ones, and I knew in that moment that what he had said was true. "It's coming back to me now. We talked about this before, right? A long time ago."

Wilhelm smiled. "Do you remember now?"

"Some of it, yeah." *Enough to know it's true*, I thought. I scratched a temple. "But how does it help me pass for a human being? It's not like I can hop inside an avatar."

He nodded. "I suppose not. A human body is far too warm for you for one."

I laughed. "Uh, yeah. That's the problem."

"Perhaps one day." Wilhelm paused a moment, then said, "I had something else in mind in the short term anyway." He stroked his chin. "The Miraculeum may be able to help you re-learn how to alter your form, even if imperfectly." He seemed to be talking more to himself than me. "Upon close inspection people will know something's very off about you since, as you said, your icy complexion will give you away, but with the right clothing, you won't stand out so readily. Even if they do notice something is off—unable to believe their eyes—the average person will likely work very hard to explain away your extraordinary appearance."

I expelled a blast of air. "I don't know, man. Is it dangerous?"

His shoulders bounced. "Less dangerous than trying to escape an urban jungle with the Eurus Faction and Bodhi Group after you."

I thumped an armrest. "What the hell was I thinking asking the Bodhi Group to remove my memories in the first place? What could I have wanted to forget so badly?"

"That's the million-dollar question." He sighed. "As for removing memories, you got that idea from us."

My brow furrowed. "You and Olivia? You've removed memories before?"

"You have too, long before the Institute, after we showed you how. That's how you forgot how to speak English."

"Really?" My forehead scrunched. "Why would I want to forget that?"

"Forgetting English was just an unintended consequence. Much as your more recent and extensive memory loss has been."

"Huh. Maybe that's why I learned to speak it again so quickly at the Institute." Now that I thought about it, words and phrases had seemed to spring to mind almost intuitively, once I'd learned . . . relearned . . . the basics of the language. "What do you think?"

"It's a definite possibility."

"But why would you do that, though? Remove memories, I mean. What could you have wanted to forget so badly?"

"Eternity is long," he said. "If you live any significant length of time, you inevitably end up with things that you would prefer to forget."

"Like what?"

"Emotional hurts and humiliations," he said. "Lost loved ones and friendships. Things you regret doing to others or things others have done to you. After a few centuries, the detritus of history begins to take its toll. When the baggage becomes over-whelming, we sometimes choose to forget. Often when we take a new avatar."

"But those who forget the past are doomed to repeat it, aren't they?"

He smirked. "Often it's an inability to forget the past that causes events to be repeated. Many wars are fought to return things to the way people remember or to right wrongs that they can't forget."

I stared at the wall behind Wilhelm a moment. "So, at the Institute, I might just have wanted to forget some past hurt or something." *Like whatever happened to my people, perhaps.*

"I think it was more than that," he said. "Given the timing, I suspect it's related to whatever danger led you to the Bodhi Group in the first place."

"What, you think I wanted to forget the danger? That I stuck my head in the sand like an ostrich?"

"No," he said. "I think you possessed knowledge so danger-ous, you felt you had to forget it."

"What could that be?"

His shoulders twitched. "There's no way to know without knowing the threat and who is behind it." He met my eyes. "But let's speculate a bit. Perhaps it will jog your memory."

"Okay."

"Who do we know that might be behind a world-ending catastrophe involving the Allfrost?"

"The Eurus," I said.

"And?" he asked.

"Baduriel and whatever other pals he might have. He showed up at the Institute, and his fire elementals attacked your house."

"Yeah, I remember." He sat back. "The Bodhi Group could also be involved. Yet you apparently sought them out for help, so they are less likely. That is, unless they're conducting some sort of scientific experiment that threatens the planet. However, since they've had plenty of time to destroy the world since capturing you, that seems unlikely."

"What about the Soviets?" I asked, thinking of everything Dixon had told me about the Cold War. "Maybe they're planning something too."

"It's possible," he said, "but anything they're up to will almost certainly involve the Eurus, so we can consider them as one and the same for our purposes."

I thought a moment. "It's got to be the Eurus, then."

"What makes you so sure?"

I shrugged. "They seem the most interested in the Allfrost. Olivia said the Faction—Eurus—have been searching for its chambers and leaving their monsters behind, for reasons unknown." I counted on a hand. "Plus, Hue says all the other Allfrost Sentinels have vanished, so maybe the Eurus have been capturing them."

"Who's Hue?"

"The Allfrost AI. The one that manages the chamber on my island, Smaragnisos." My eyes narrowed. "You know about him, right?"

Wilhelm's eyes widened. "He's given himself a name?"

"Yeah," I said. "Sure."

"Huh."

"What?" I asked.

"Oh, nothing," Wilhelm said. "It's just ... unusual." He waved a hand. "Anyway, the Sentinels vanished a long time ago. They and all your people." He stroked his chin. "I'm sure the Eurus are capable of it, but I've my doubts that they're behind their disappearances."

"Maybe not," I said, "but I think they sent those monsters after me at Dublin Gulch. The Bodhi Group sure didn't."

"You may be right," he said.

"Atriel's with the Eurus Faction, right?"

"Yes," Wilhelm said with a grimace.

I rubbed my temples, remembering Atriel's words in the tunnels below. "He said that he was here for me. That proves it. Doesn't it? He came to Caelumtor to get me because I'm needed for their plan."

Wilhelm nodded. "That's logical, if not definitive."

I bobbed my head. "That must be it. They're doing something with the Allfrost, and I'm the last Sentinel. Who else is likely—at least before my memory loss—to know more about the Allfrost?" I snapped my fingers. "That's why I wanted to remove memories, so that even if they caught me, I couldn't help them with whatever they're planning, no matter what they did to me."

He inclined his head. "That's a reasonable supposition."

"The question is, what do they want to do with the Allfrost that's so dangerous?"

"That's a good question," he said. "Once you've consumed the other vials, perhaps we'll know."

"No argument here." My eyes flicked upward. "I'll swallow the rest right now." *No matter what it does to me.*

"Hang on." Wilhelm raised a hand. "Don't forget, if you take out the wrong one, you'll be taking another trip back to the desert."

"Right." In the heat of the moment, I had forgotten. "But you said it yourself. We're in a hurry. Is there something you can do to help?"

"I should think so," he said, "but it'll have to wait until I get back."

"Where are you going?"

"Zarechus," he said. "Something's amiss there. The soul traps, Baduriel, the Antara transporter being redirected to Abadom. It all points to a plot of some kind, and I need to investigate and deal with whatever is going on before it gets worse."

"Oh, yeah." Something that I'd been wondering about came to mind at his mention of the planet. "I meant to ask you about something."

"What's that?"

"I came across an Allfrost power node in the town below Abadom." I quickly told him of the snow-covered power node, and the voice that had warned me of the approaching Nameless. "Do you know why it's there?"

He scowled. "It's a remnant of a failed experimental spatial transposition. You'll find them all over the area, in greater concentration than here on Earth. I suppose the snow that had fallen brought it over from the Underfrost into this reality."

My eyes widened. "You mean the transposition that did all the damage?"

"Um-hmm." He sighed. "We were experimenting with using the Underfrost to enable longer-range spatial transpositions."

I blinked rapidly. "I didn't know that was possible. Could that have been Hue I heard in the streets of Abadom?"

"The one that warned you about those creatures? What did you call them?"

"The Nameless." I repeated Virgil's theory about them. "What are they, Wilhelm?"

"I've only theories," he said, "but Virgil may be on to something. It merits investigation when time permits. As for the hologram, it must have been another one."

"Okay, but if it was a hologram, why didn't I see him? I just heard a voice."

He shrugged. "I expect it lacked the resources to appear visually."

I thought of the dim glow of the symbols on the dais as I'd leaned over it. "Right, that makes sense. Well, anyway, will you be long?"

He shook his head. "A day or two, I should think."

"But what if that's too late to stop this thing?"

He spread his hands. "We're fighting our enemies on multiple fronts, so we've got to prioritize, I'm afraid, which means dealing with concrete threats first."

"But—"

He held up a hand. "I tell you what, Olivia should arrive with Brad and Lucy tomorrow. When she returns, I'm sure she'll help you with the vials. Who knows, I may even be back myself by then. Either way, you shouldn't have to wait longer than a day."

I frowned. "Maybe I should come with you. With my help you might get back sooner."

Wilhelm pursed his lips and gave his head a shake. "No, stay here. Even with your help, Zarechus may take longer than expected."

A realization came to mind. "But that far away, maybe the bad vial won't even work, and I'll be able to take it out safely. You said it would probably take too much energy to reach another planet."

"Probably," he said, "but we don't know that for sure, and it is important that you consume them soon. Ideally here, where you'll be comfortable and safe."

"All right," I said with a grimace.

"Good man." He winked. "In the meantime, have fun with Scott and the kids and give yourself time to reintegrate the vials you've already taken."

"This transporter device," I said after a moment.

"Yeah?"

"How do you think it got in there? Into a vial, I mean." My brow knit. "I don't think Dixon would have put it there. He put a tracker in one of them, but if he had something like this transportation device . . ."

"No, this is our technology." Wilhelm squinted. "The Eurus must have infiltrated the Institute and planted the device."

"But why?"

"The same reason that Harland Dixon did."

"To find me?"

"Right," he said. "Like him, they must have been gambling that you would come for the vials, giving them the chance to grab you."

"It didn't work, though," I said.

"No," he replied. "Atriel must not have been ready for it. If he had been, you'd probably have transported directly to a cell somewhere instead of the open desert."

"Okay," I said, "but if we swapped positions the first time, why didn't Atriel go back to the desert when Scott and I reverted back here?"

Wilhelm grunted. "He must have moved out of range of the object he carried—the one linked to the one in your hat."

"You think he dropped it at Aceso's?"

"Perhaps."

"Then it could still be there," I said.

"No," Wilhelm said. "Wherever he left it—deliberately or otherwise—it'll have gone back to wherever you were in the desert when you came back to Caelumtor."

My eyes narrowed. "How's that?"

"That's how spatial transposition works; each location swaps positions for a brief time, then switches back. These objects might be more selective in what they bring along for the ride, but they'll still work the same way in that regard."

"Okay," I said, "but what if the objects move between switches? Like if the holder of one gets in a car and races down the road. When they switch back, will the returning object revert to the original swap position or to wherever the twin object is at that moment?"

"It would be the current position. To use your example, wherever the car is at that moment."

"Huh. But Scott and I returned to the kitchen when we came back."

"Which means Atriel must have dropped it as soon as he arrived and moved away from it. That ensured that he would remain behind, so he could surprise you and take you back by force."

"Using the object in my hat."

"Right."

I grimaced. "Then why didn't he attack as soon as Scott and I returned to Aceso's kitchen?"

"When he realized where he was, he probably decided to look around first. The Eurus have a great interest in New Olympus, as you might imagine."

"That makes sense," I said. "It also explains why he tried so hard to catch me."

He nodded. "Aside from wanting you for your own sake, you were also his way back."

"And now he's stuck here." I looked around as if he might appear from thin air. "Have you caught him yet?"

His nostrils flared. "Not as yet, but we will."

"Shouldn't we be looking for him now?"

"Hanale is handling it."

"But what if he shows up here?"

"If Atriel hasn't fled the archipelago entirely, he'll likely be staying far away from Caelumburg itself now, where our monitoring and defenses are greatest."

"Likely?"

"Even if he were foolish enough to double back to Caelumburg, you and the others will be safest here. Besides, they've got you and Bear to protect them." His eyes darted to the side. "Speak of the devil. Hello, Bear."

Chapter 32

The Ha'ole

The Alaskan shepherd padded over, coming from the atrium-side doorway. Lying down next to Wilhelm's chair, the dog yawned, displaying a long pink tongue. Snuffling, he rested his snout between his furry paws and looked up at us.

"I wonder where the kids are," I said, looking over my shoulder.

Bear's head rose, and he gave a low woof.

"They're fine," Wilhelm said, stroking the dog's back. "They're just looking around the house."

I cocked my head. "Did Bear just tell you that?"

"Naturally."

I snorted. "You speak dog?"

He tapped a finger to his temple. "Telepathy."

I tucked my chin toward my neck. "Nice. Lilith wasn't kidding." I thought a moment. "How come I didn't hear anything?"

"It doesn't work that way. Besides, my friend, you're not the best telepath."

"Yeah, but neither is Lilith or Alan, right?"

"That's true. Of them, and most humans."

"Then how did he communicate with them telepathically?"

He glanced at Bear a moment. "He licked them."

"Licked them?"

Wilhelm nodded. "His saliva facilitates the mental link, for a time."

"So he's got to lick me too?"

"You? Not necessarily, but it would help. As would closer proximity. Actual physical contact would be ideal."

A rapping of knuckles drew my gaze to the left.

"Hey, dudes," Alan said from the atrium doorway as Lilith and Caleb leaned in behind him.

Wilhelm waved them over. "Come on in, you guys."

"How was the tour?" I asked.

"It's cool," Caleb said. "A lot like Aceso's but bigger."

Alan looked at Wilhelm. "Nice suit."

"Thanks," he replied. "It's bespoke."

"Whoa," Caleb said. "It can talk? That's so cool."

Wilhelm chuckled. "Not unless I'm wearing it."

Alan cleared his throat. "Is there someplace to surf around here?"

Lilith nodded. "A beach, maybe?"

"Caleb says the waves are choice," Alan added.

Wilhelm shook his head. "It's best you stay close to the domus for now."

Alan's brow furrowed. "Why's that?"

Caleb paled. "It's because that freaky dude, Atriel, is still out there, right?"

Among other things, I thought, remembering the troll escapees.

"He is, yes. However, that doesn't mean you can't surf." Wilhelm thumped Bear's side. "Care to take our friends down to the lake, Bear?"

The dog rumbled a reply.

"That's settled, then." Wilhelm pushed himself to his feet. "Surfboards are in storage. Bear will show you to them." He glanced at his wrist. "You've got about three hours until the next rain, so you should be able to get in some good waves before then."

Caleb frowned. "Nuts. More rain?"

Wilhelm slapped a hand on the teen's shoulder. "The trees must drink." He looked around. "I have to take off. I'll be away for a day or two. While I'm gone, make yourselves comfortable. Ask the automatons if you need anything. They can assist with most requests."

"Where should Scott, Caleb, and I sleep?" I asked.

"There are free rooms off the atrium. Lilith and Alan can show you, I'm sure."

After the teens had changed into android-provided swim-wear, Bear led us through the domus to a stone-walled room packed with surfboards, other sport paraphernalia, and a large chariot of gold. After a long time spent browsing the surfboard selection, we exited the room's far side through stone doors that split open at our approach.

Beyond them, a pathway led down past lush trees and other plant life to the waters of a lake. Sunlight glared off the water's mirror-calm surface, holding back a wall of fog that hovered a half mile offshore. Behind us, Caelumburg's domes, spires, and blocks of marble and rock loomed, backed by the green slopes of the enclosing valley.

Lilith crossed the fine white sand lining the shore with Bear at her side and toed the glassy water, sending ripples outward. "How are we going to surf that?"

Sitting on his haunches, the dog barked three times.

Stooping, Lilith ruffled the dark fur on his back. "What are you barking at, Bear?"

"Maybe don't stand so close to the water, Lil." Caleb glanced at me. "You don't suppose something like Ken's in there, do you?"

"Who's Ken?" Alan asked.

"A kra—" Caleb began.

"Whoa." Lilith straightened and tottered back toward us, keeping her eyes fixed on the lake. Backpedalling into Alan, she pointed. "Look."

A swell of water, foaming white at its crest, rolled out of the fog. Curling at the top, it drew closer.

"Woo-hoo," Caleb hooted, flapping his arms.

"Sweet," Alan said as the ten-foot-high wave curled and broke.

"Let's go." Lilith's feet splashed in the surf, kicking up clods of wet sand as she bounded toward the retreating water.

The boys ran after her, shouting and laughing. Climbing atop their surfboards, the trio paddled out from shore, not stopping until they had reached the edge of the distant fog bank.

Alan cupped his hands to his mouth. "Do it again, Bear."

Dancing on his legs, the dog barked again.

Lilith waved the boys back with a hand. "Me first, you guys."

She lay prone and began to paddle as the water swelled once more.

"Go, Lil," Alan cried as the wave lifted him.

Within seconds, the girl leaped to her feet, stretched out her arms, and rode the wave to shore. Trotting out of the froth, she smiled and ran over to stand beside me. The boys out on the water cheered and waved their arms and waited while the water calmed again.

After thrusting her board into the sand, Lilith squeezed my shoulders before dancing away. "This is so amazing, Shivurr."

"No argument here, Lil," I said with a smile.

"I wanted to thank you again . . . for saving us." She embraced me a moment. "I don't think I ever properly did after Lunar Crater."

"No, you did, and you're totally welcome."

"I was upset." She bit her lip and studied my chest. "Why'd you do it? Risk exposing yourself like that, I mean."

I shrugged. "You guys were in trouble."

"But you didn't even know us then."

"Didn't matter. Besides, those guys were dicks."

Lilith grinned through tear-filled eyes. "Yeah, they were."

I tugged the bill of my cap. "I've still got your book, by the way."

"What did you think of the trolls?" she asked.

"Trolls? I don't think I've gotten that far yet. Things have been kind of crazy since Dublin Gulch."

She chuckled. "I know. I just figured you'd be interested, you know, having met one yourself. The ones in the book turn to stone in the sun."

"Really?" An old memory of fighting trolls in broad daylight bubbled to mind. "I'm pretty sure that wouldn't happen to the one I tangled with the other day."

We turned back to the water as Caleb rode in to shore. As the teen came over to us, Bear barked again and Alan caught the next wave.

"Come on, Shivurr," Caleb said as the three teens prepared to return to the water. "Give it a go."

Alan's eyebrows rose. "You surf, dude?"

Caleb clapped a hand to my shoulder. "Yeah, he does."

"Cool," Alan said. He tilted his surfboard toward me. "Go for it, dude."

"No need." I stepped a few feet from the group, held my hand palm down, and touched the Underfrost. *This is so much easier here than at Abadom.* A swirling pinprick of white winked into being a half foot from the sand. I swept my hand in a circle as the tornado of frost expanded, forming into a floating disc of ice.

The platform dipped as I hopped aboard.

"That's wicked," Alan said.

At my command, the disc accelerated and shot out over the water. Floating inches above the rippling surface, it rolled and rocked over the shrinking waves to the fog's edge. I spun it about to face my friends, now small figures on the sand. Bear barked thrice more, and the frost disc tilted forward forty-five degrees, propelled forward by the wall of water behind me.

The wave barrelled, and I touched a finger to the water and hooted. Glancing at the water curling a foot overhead, I steered the disc at a tangent to the wave, then whirled it a hundred and eighty degrees, then again until I reached the shore. Back on the sand, my friends surrounded me, giving me nods and words of approval before paddling out to do it all again.

We took turns surfing until thick clouds rolled in overhead, darkening the sky. Leaves rustled and trees swayed as the wind gusted off the lake, and I snugged my cap lower as Lilith rode into shore.

"Looks like it's going to rain," Alan said.

I nodded. "Just like Wilhelm figured."

"That dude should be a weatherman."

I snorted, remembering. "He is. Literally." I glanced toward the domus. "We should probably get inside."

"Why?" Alan said. "We're already wet." The approaching clouds flashed, and booms of thunder followed moments later. "Maybe you've got a point. It'd suck to be electrocuted."

Caleb looked at me as rain began to fall. "Too bad Olivia's not here. She'd be our lightning rod."

While the teens showered, Bear and I hung out in the atrium, watching rain cascade into the impluvium—the pool's name returning, abruptly—from the ceiling hole above. Sighing, I stroked Bear's fur as rolling thunder shook the domus walls.

"There you are," Scott said, closing the door of a bedroom to my right. "How was the surfing?"

"Wicked," I said. "Sorry, man. I should have asked if you wanted to come, but I figured you were probably still sleeping. I know you need to rest."

He held up a hand. "Don't sweat it. I don't know how to surf anyway." He thrust a thumb over his shoulder. "Besides, it gave me a choice of bedrooms."

"Are they that different?"

He wagged his chin, smiling. "Not really, but now I don't have to wonder."

"Do you need to get your stuff from Aceso's place?"

"What stuff?" Scott said with a smirk. "My bloody clothes?"

"Oh, yeah." I glanced around. "Is Wilhelm still here?"

"Nah, he left a while ago. He said he had to go to—" A rapping from the front of the house interrupted him. "Who the hell's that?"

"Dunno," I said. "Let's go see."

A short hallway led to a wooden door akin to the one at Aceso's. The peephole's cover creaked as I pulled it open and looked through. Recognizing the face on the other side, I tugged the door inward.

"Hey, Hanale," I said with a smile.

The burly god's grim expression clashed with his cheerful floral shirt and neon shorts. "Haukea Kane," he said, using his Hawaiian nickname for me: snow-white man. Slapping my shoulder with a wet hand, he stepped inside. He thrust a dripping chin at Scott. "Hey, brother Scott," he said, pronouncing brother more like bruddah.

"Hey, Hanale," Scott replied.

Hanale patted his prodigious stomach. "Howzit? Better?"

"Pretty much," Scott replied. "It only hurts when I laugh these days."

I looked at Scott with a raised brow. "You two know each other?"

"Sure," Scott replied. "Hanale's stopped by Aceso's a few times."

"What brings you by?" I asked the god as we strode down the short entrance hallway to the atrium.

"I must speak with Huhu Makani." Bear woofed a reply. "He's not here?"

"No," I replied, "Wilhelm's gone to Zarechus."

"What for?" he asked.

My shoulders bounced. "To deal with a crisis there."

Hanale grunted and exhaled. "Lots of them today."

"What happened?" I asked. "Can you tell us?"

"The *ha'ole*, Atriel, is gone," he said. "You know 'bout him?"

"*Ha'ole*? That means foreigner, right?"

He nodded.

"Yeah, I know about him." *It's my fault he got in.* "You're sure?"

"Buggah doubled back. Got to a transporter."

A meaty hand tugged at my shoulder as Hanale stumbled. Grunting, I wrapped a long arm around his thick waist.

"Here, have a seat," I said, steering him over to a sofa that sat next to the impluvium.

"*Mahalo*," he said.

"You're welcome."

The wood of the couch creaked as Hanale sank onto it. "I almost had him, but he put up a fight." He twirled a finger next to his head. "*Lolo*, that buggah."

"Are you all right?" I remained standing as Scott drew up a chair to sit nearby. "You look a bit pale."

The big man shrugged. "Just drained, brother. It's been a crazy few days."

"Yeah," I said, "I can imagine. What about the fugitives? The ookmir that ambushed us on the road in, I mean."

"Recaptured," he replied, "but there were more."

"You're kidding."

He held up a hand. "Don't worry. We've found most of them, and they've been stripped of their avatars and returned to their prisons. In fact, I just caught another one, Caelus, with Atriel before he escaped."

"Were they working together?" I asked.

"It looks that way," he said. "May be how Atriel found the way out." He looked me in the eyes. "He after you, brother?"

"That's what he said." I repeated the speculations that I'd already discussed with Wilhelm.

"No need to worry about him now."

"Too bad you didn't catch him; I'd have liked to talk to that guy."

"He got lucky." Hanale smacked a fist into his palm. "With Caelus's help." He stood. "You want to speak to him?"

"Uh, sure," I said. "You coming, Scott?"

He shook his head. "Nah, you go, man. Someone should stay here with the kids."

"Good idea." I stooped and rustled Bear's fur. "Keep an eye on everyone, okay, buddy?"

Bear gave a short yap and flicked a tongue across my hand.

"Good dog."

Chapter 33

There Is Another

Hanale strode the stone-paved streets unbowed by the deluge that stuck his shirt to his back and hair to his scalp. Surrounded by a protective bubble of frost energy, I trailed a few feet behind, enjoying the stunning daytime beauty of Caelumburg's trees, gardens, imposing buildings, and statuary.

The gods love beautiful things, I thought, following Hanale up broad steps toward the white columns of a large marble building. Crossing the building's portico, we entered a vast hall. Balls of light floating high above lit the room, and thick pillars held up the ceiling.

No longer exposed to the rain, I dropped my frost shield and sighed, glad to be relieved of the strain of maintaining it. I could have kept it up much longer, but it wasn't exactly comfortable to do so.

I paused at the foot of a line of red carpet that ran toward the far wall, giving my eyes time to adjust to the change in lighting.

Five-foot-high stone pedestals crowded the area. Upon each rested either a figurine, bottle, urn, vase, or other container. The statuettes reminded me of their larger cousins that had ringed the transporter platform on Zarechus. However, these were far smaller, distributed in a grid rather than a circle, and there were many more than a mere dozen.

With a glance over his shoulder, Hanale led me down the ribbon of carpet to the hall's far side, where a troll—Caelus, I presumed—stood, arms crossed, awaiting us.

"Shouldn't he be in a cage or cell or something?" I whispered.

"He is in a cage, brother," Hanale replied in his usual booming voice. "You don't need to whisper, either. He can't hear or see us, yet."

"Really? How's that?"

"He's surrounded by a force field," he said. "It blocks sight and sound beyond its edges and shows him what we want him to see or hear, if anything."

"Oh, yeah," I said, noticing a shimmer in the air between us and the troll.

Abruptly, Caelus held out his arms and sidestepped. He looked like a fearsome mime, outlining the limits of an invisible box. Judging by his movements, red stones bordered by black defined the area of his confinement. True to Hanale's words, he appeared to have no clue as to our presence, neither looking our way nor pausing in his efforts as we neared.

"Is this the prison that he escaped from?"

Hanale shook his head. "This is just a temporary holding area." He gestured to other red squares stretching into the distance to the left and right. "As are those." He turned and swept a hand to our rear. "When we're done, he'll be wrested from his stolen avatar and returned to his prison."

I looked out over the field of pedestals. "There are prisoners in all these things?"

"Not all." Hanale took a few steps and grabbed one. "This one's empty."

"How can you tell?"

"It's cold to the touch," he replied, setting the Hydra-like figure back down. "Those that are occupied are usually warm."

"Because of what they contain?"

Hanale inclined his head. "The greater the power, the harder to contain it."

I shuddered. "That sounds awful. At least being trapped at the Bodhi Institute wasn't boring. It'd suck to be stuck in one of these things with nothing to do."

He shrugged. "Eventually—for some after months, others millennia—they will be released and given a lower life form to occupy until they prove they're worthy of more."

"That's a pretty harsh punishment," I said, studying Caelus.

Hanale cocked an eyebrow. "You might not think so if you knew their crimes."

"Yeah, maybe."

"Let's see what Caelus has to tell us."

"If he can't see or hear us, how do we talk to him?"

"Let me open a window." He drew up next to a crystal-topped black post at the corner of Caelus's red square. As he placed his hand upon the white crystal, it shone green.

My eyes flicked left and right, noting a line of identical posts in both directions. *Those must be some sort of control interface*, I thought.

"Aloha, Caelus," Hanale said a moment later.

The troll froze and looked toward us. "Hanale." He walked over, eyes flicking to me. "And this must be the Borealan that Atriel was so interested in."

The big man gave a pleasant smile. "That is what—"

The troll lunged, swinging a massive fist.

"Look out," I said, reeling back a step.

The blur of motion slowed to a stop just a few feet from Hanale's head.

Hanale cleared his throat. "Why bother trying, Caelus?" He looked back to me and waved me forward. "You can't even hurt yourself in there, let alone us."

The troll sat and studied the claws on one of his hands. "Well, it doesn't hurt to try." His eyes flicked to me before returning to Hanale. "So, what is this about, then?"

"Atriel, for now. Then we'll get to how you escaped in the first place. If you're helpful, you may spend fewer centuries confined."

Caelus looked at me with a curled lip, then back to Hanale. "What do you want to know?"

The troll's musty scent permeated the air. *I guess the force field doesn't block everything.*

"Why was Atriel here?" I asked. "What does he want with me?"

"Answer him," Hanale said with crossed arms.

The troll's lips spread wide in a toothy grin. "He didn't tell me much. Only that you're a potential key to the Eurus's plan."

"How, though? What could I offer a bunch of gods that they couldn't do themselves?"

"What indeed?" Caelus sneered.

"No games," Hanale said. "Unless you want a dung beetle for your first avatar when you're finally freed again."

"You've got a nasty streak in you, Hanale." Caelus held up his hands as if in surrender. "Fine. I will speak plainly. Though we were allies for a time, both desiring to escape, it is no matter to me whether the Eurus succeed in whatever it is they are planning. I doubt I can tell you much you don't already know, however, for Atriel told me little." He looked back to me. "You're an Allfrost Sentinel, are you not?"

I inclined my head, feeling a surge of pity for Caelus that I willed aside. After my incarceration at the Bodhi Institute, it was hard not to feel sympathy for anyone else held against their will. Being trapped in a figurine or vase or whatever must have been pretty boring. Who knew how long he'd been in there before his failed escape? A year, a decade, maybe a lot longer. Whatever he'd done, I felt certain he'd earned it, so great was my faith in my godly friends.

"Their plan involves the Allfrost," Caelus said, "and they need one like you to help with it."

"I had an inkling of that, sure," I said, "but what is it they want to do with it?"

The troll shrugged his massive shoulders. "I don't know the specifics. All I know is that they intend to alter it somehow."

"What's their connection to Baduriel?"

Caelus furrowed his brow. "The demon lord?" His eyes darted to Hanale and back to me. "He and his brethren seek to return to Earth, to be redeemed from bondage and rejoin the Eurus."

"What do you mean? He's a demon, not a god."

"You speak of his avatar, not Baduriel himself." Caelus swept a hand from his neck to his waist. "I was once a man. Today, ookmir. In another age, a demon. These are mere vessels, replicas of lesser life forms that we inhabit. Our essence remains the same."

I glanced at Hanale before returning my gaze to Caelus. "Are all demons gods, then?"

Caelus's brow furrowed. Leaning forward, he stared into my eyes. "Ah, of course. You've lost your memories, haven't you?" I glared silently, and the god in a troll body chuckled. "Atriel's words make a lot more sense now."

"What words?"

He smirked. "He said that you might not be able to help them anymore and that they had captured another who could. It is why he felt content to leave without you—once I showed him the way." He looked to the side. "Alas, I was—"

I stepped forward. "Captured another? Like me? Another Sentinel?"

"Presumably so," he replied. "Given their plans for the Allfrost."

My eyelids fluttered.

Another Sentinel? If it was true, it meant that I wasn't alone. *He could tell me so much.*

Not only where the other Sentinels were, but where the other Borealans had gone to or if any still existed.

"Where are they holding him?" I took another step closer to the troll, and the air seemed to thicken, holding me back.

"I do not know," Caelus replied.

My shoulders slumped.

"But," he continued after a moment, "I might have an idea, if you'll give me something for it."

"Yes?"

Hanale glowered. "Don't test me, Caelus."

"Come now, Hanale. I have been cooperative, have I not? All I ask is you not add more time to my incarceration."

"Tell us what you know," Hanale said. "If it's helpful . . ." He shrugged without finishing.

Caelus frowned. "Very well. I suppose I can expect no more." He sighed. "I believe he came from a desert. I do not know which one."

At his words, a vision of the desert to which Scott and I had travelled sprang to mind.

Of course, I thought, recalling my discussion with Wilhelm. We had swapped positions with Atriel, which meant he'd been in that desert when the devices had activated. A desert where moments later a meteor had struck, and fire elementals had appeared. *Baduriel's got to be working with the Eurus.*

"Did he say anything else?" I asked.

Caelus harrumphed. "Only that the foes of the Eurus would perish in flame. The usual bluster."

"Do you think he told the truth?" I asked Hanale as we left the building.

Not knowing Caelus, I wasn't sure I could trust anything he'd said, but what he'd told us seemed to fit the facts.

The rain had abated, leaving a faint mist behind. Shafts of light, breaking through thinning cloud cover, gleamed off rapidly disappearing puddles in the streets below, and the song of birds and buzz of insects already filled the air.

"Probably," Hanale said as we descended the stairs, still wet with precipitation. "Lying just means a longer sentence for him now."

Movement in the street drew my eye. A dark-haired woman, head down, dressed in flowing ivory-white robes strode toward us, sandalled feet slapping the wet marble. As her face rose, I recognized her.

"Hey, Cleo," I said, raising a hand.

"Good day, Shivurr," she replied with a faint smile. "I'm glad to see you've returned from your travels intact."

Hanale chuckled. "Haukea Kane has a knack for finding trouble."

"It finds me." I jabbed a thumb over my shoulder. "You've had your share of it here too."

"That is true," Cleo said. "Regarding that . . ." She turned to Hanale. "We've found another fugitive."

Hanale's brow creased. "Where?"

"Near Caelumtor's rim," she replied. "Leonidas is bringing her in."

"Good," Hanale said. "Any sign of the others?"

"Yes," she said. "That's why I came to find you. The Arborati have found another."

"Who are the Arborati?" I asked.

Hanale glanced my way. "Sentient trees."

That's wild, I thought, picturing the tree that Olivia had shooed from the road on our way up to Caelumtor and the oak in the pool at the Schmidts' Las Vegas home. *And they can walk too, apparently.*

He looked back at Cleo. "Strange that the Arborati should not have seen them until now."

Cleo nodded. "Allowing themselves to be seen now may be a trap. That's why I thought it best to fetch you before pursuing them. If our quarry bands together, I may not be able to defeat them by myself. At least, not without destroying their stolen avatars."

Hanale grimaced. "Then they're getting away."

Cleo pursed her lips and gave a slight shake of her head. "Golems are trailing them."

The big man grunted. "Those rock brains?"

"There were no other guardians available nearby," Cleo said. "We're stretched thin, across all New Olympus, not just Caelumtor."

He looked at me. "I must leave. Do you remember the way back?"

I nodded. "Sure, no problem."

I thought about offering to help with the escapees but held my tongue. After chatting with Caelus, I had other plans, and I figured Hanale would decline my offer anyway.

He slapped my shoulder. "Then I will see you there when we've finished, Haukea Kane."

Chapter 34

Altered States

Keeping to the shadows, I traversed empty streets on my way back to the Schmidts' domus. I could only guess that few people lived in Caelumburg, or they were busy elsewhere. Then again, they might just have been keeping a low profile until all the fugitives were caught.

Scott and the gang reclined on the sofas in the atrium as I entered.

"There he is," Scott said, jabbing a chin in my direction. "How'd it go?"

For the next while, I brought my friends up to speed.

"Holy," Alan said. "Another Allfrost Sentinel? You really think there's another guy like you out there?"

"Well," I said. "Not exactly like me."

"No way," Caleb said. "Shivurr's one of a kind."

"What are your people like, Shivurr?" Lilith asked, absently stroking Bear's head, which lay in her lap.

"I don't remember much." I shrugged. "Just vague shapes and impressions. If Hue hadn't told me about the Sentinels and that I was one, I wouldn't even be sure they existed. Anyway, from what I do remember, I think our forms vary a lot."

Scott nodded. "Yeah, some of the Group's scientists figured you could change shape, within limits. Apparently, the crystals inside you just need to alter their arrangement; the snow and ice follow."

"That jibes with what little I remember," I said. "I think some Sentinels even look, or looked, a bit like you guys. If you were made of snow and ice."

"They could look like people?" Alan said. "That's wild."

"Shivurr's people," Lilith said with a frown.

"Yeah," Caleb said. "That's what we're talking about: Shivurr's people."

She scowled. "I mean that Shivurr is a person."

"Well, sure." Alan's face reddened. "Of course he is. I just meant, like us. You know, a human being."

I held up a hand. "It's okay, Alan. I know what you meant and, yeah, they looked human. At least, they had arms and legs and heads that looked like you guys."

"Humanoid," Scott said. "Homo sapiens sapiens."

"Right." I grinned. "If you want to get all technical."

Scott spread his hands. "I work with scientists."

Caleb bobbed his head. "Yeah, you looked almost human at the apartment building."

"You mean when the Nameless were after us?" I asked.

"Yeah." He pointed at my feet. "You almost had legs. Remember?"

"Of course," I said.

"Maybe that's because you could do it before. Look human, I mean."

"I suppose so, but I can't do it now."

Scott put a hand on my shoulder. "Maybe you'll remember how once you've swallowed the rest of those vials."

"Maybe," I said, "but I'm not sure changing form to look truly human is something I could ever do. Olivia said I could only sort of resemble one at a distance." I pulled the cap from my head and looked inside. "Though I guess I'll find out soon."

Scott's eyes widened. "You're not going to take them out now, are you?"

I snickered. "You don't want to take another trip to the desert?"

He shook his head. "I'm good. What are you going to do about it?"

"The bad vial?"

"Yeah."

"Wilhelm said he'd help me with it when he gets back, but if Olivia gets here first, I'll ask her."

"Cool," Scott said, "then we've got time to hang out."

Lilith rubbed a hand over Bear's upturned belly. "You guys want to go for a walk or something?"

"It's better if we stay inside, for now," I said, thinking of the escapees still out in the wilds of Caelumtor somewhere. "At least until we get the all-clear from Hanale."

"Do they have a TV around here?" Caleb asked. "It'd be nice to watch a show or something."

Scott stood. "If I know Wilhelm, there's got to be one around here." He cast me a glance. "Not like Aceso's place."

Bear raised his head, barked, and scrambled from the sofa.

"He says there's a room at the back," Lilith said, hopping to her feet.

"He says?" Scott said with a raised brow. "You understood him?"

Alan touched a finger to his temple. "You hear him in your head, dude."

"Not always," Lilith said. "Just when he's close to you, sometimes. I don't know how it works exactly. He did it with Lucy first."

"Right," Scott said. "I remember you saying something about that at breakfast. That's amazing. A telepathic dog."

Bear padded over to a nearby hallway and barked again.

I smiled wryly. "I guess we'd better go with him."

We followed the dog through the house, up a flight of stairs and down a hallway to a large windowless room where a collection of full-sized arcade games lined a wall. As with the rest of the house, comfortable seating abounded, most of which sat focused around a large TV placed against a wall. Like their Las Vegas home, a wide assortment of videotapes, books, music albums, and the means to play them were stacked neatly on shelves nearby.

We played arcade games for a while, joking and laughing and enjoying each other's company. When our fingers tired, we popped in a movie. Unasked, as far as we knew, a group of androids appeared, bearing pizza, popcorn, and cold drinks. My guess was Bear had somehow made the request on our behalf, seeing as he'd left and returned along with the androids.

Halfway through a second movie, Lilith fell asleep, resting her head on Alan's chest. Sometime later, he joined her, tilting his head back to face the ceiling. Watching them with a smile, my mind drifted. I'd had bad luck in recent times, but I'd been fortunate in finding friends such as these.

Knowing what I planned to do, I felt a surge of melancholy, and I shrugged it off. Like a desert snowflake, this moment would melt and vanish all too soon, and there would never be another exactly like it. I refused to ruin the moment with thoughts of the past or the future. The plan that had been forming in my mind since I'd learned of the other Sentinel would just have to wait a few hours more.

When the credits rolled on a third movie, Scott pulled himself to his feet and rubbed his eyes. "I'm going to turn in. I'm bushed."

"Me too." Caleb looked at Alan and Lilith as the couple stirred. "Are you guys coming?"

They nodded and got to their feet, bleary-eyed. Together, we made our way to the atrium, said our good nights, and retired to our chosen bedrooms.

Closing the door to mine, I swept the cap from my head, laid it on the bed, and gave it the stink eye.

I peeled a cloth bag from a nearby pillow and placed it to the side. *Here goes.* With a nod to myself, I raised my hat and reached inside. After some fumbling, my fingers gripped the cool smooth glass of a vial of my stolen essence.

Pulling in a breath, I drew the bottle clear, raised it to eye level, and shook it gently. The contents swirled and shimmered like the others I'd drunk in recent days.

I exhaled. *Not the one.*

Popping the stopper, I chugged the contents. Before the liquid could take effect, I reached for another vial and, verifying it too contained only my essence, consumed it as well.

A moment later, the room tilted, and the walls began to blur. I clapped a hand over my mouth. *All right, a couple more and that's it, for now.* After a moment of searching, I pulled out a third vial. I could tell something was different about it as I pulled it into the light. The weight felt off, and the contents sloshed about more readily. Holding it up, I could see that something hard and cylindrical lay within, suspended in a fluid that didn't fluoresce like the other vials.

I snatched up the pillowcase with shaky hands as the room began to waver. *Just like Aceso's kitchen*, I thought. I dropped the booby-trapped vial into the cloth sack, balled it up, and shoved the package back into my hat. As the bundle crossed into the null space beyond my cap's inner crown, the room settled as if a switch had been flipped.

Phew. I swept up the cap and returned it to my head. *Just in time.*

The room spun. At first I thought the transport had resumed, but I realized a moment later that it was just me. My hand shot out, catching the edge of the bed as I sank to the floor.

The room was dark when I woke sometime later, stretched out on the carpet. With a groan, I slapped an arm across the edge of the bed and raised myself upright. I rubbed my temples, willing away the dull ache that pulsed behind my eyes.

Blowing out a breath, I removed my cap and dug inside, searching for a can of Ambrola. Gripping one of the small cylinders, I pulled it free, cracked the tab, and drank.

"Oh, yeah," I said aloud.

As my mind cleared, lost memories hit me in a rush. I snarled and rubbed my temples, riding out a flood of random faces and events. Lacking context and time to adjust, they were like skimming a library's worth of books with half the pages missing and the other half shuffled into a random order.

I sucked in a breath and let it out slowly. Reintegration would take time and might require other vials to bridge gaps between memories before I could fully make sense of them. Fortunately, I didn't need to comprehend everything right away. I just needed to remember one thing, if I could: what threat had led me to the Bodhi Group?

To guide the recall process, I thought about when I'd first met the Bodhi Group scientists at the Nevada Allfrost chamber. It worked, sort of. New details about those early days sprang to mind, but nothing that explained the exact nature of the danger. They just told me with greater certainty that which I already knew. The Allfrost was central to the Eurus Faction's plan, and I played some important role in stopping it, or bringing it to fruition.

For that reason, as my reclaimed memories now confirmed, I'd asked the Bodhi Group to help me forget something integral to the Eurus's plan. The Group had taken things way, way too far, much further than I'd intended, but that was how it had all started.

Just like Dixon said. I scowled. *The bastards.* I looked down at myself. "Was it okay because I look like this?" I said aloud. "If I looked human, would you have done it?"

A spark of realization snapped my eyes wide.

I sprang from the bed and made my way to the en suite bathroom.

"Uh, lights, please," I said as I entered. The ceiling glowed a moment later, allowing me to see myself in the mirror set above the sink.

I looked into it and visualized my round face elongating. A moment later, a moan escaped my lips as the ice of my face crunched and crackled, reshaping itself into a more human-like configuration. The change didn't hurt exactly, but it was an unsettling feeling.

I ran a palm down each cheek and nodded. "Not bad."

My features lacked much of the definition of a true human face, but it was a start. My long nose had shortened and spread to the side, forming a mound. It wouldn't have been mistaken for a human nose, even if it had been made of flesh, but it was at least more suggestive of one than my regular nose.

Taking a step back from the sink, I turned my eyes down, unzipped my jacket, and concentrated anew. The snow and ice of my body shuddered and swelled, blending into a single oblong mass. My arms shortened, and the excess snow redistributed itself, tightening my jacket about my shoulders and chest. Next, the bones of my legs, buried in the snow of my lower sphere, lengthened. Snow just above and between my feet split in two, forming a vertical chasm. At my urging it grew higher as the retreating snow collected around the shafts of leg-ice beneath.

At last, the sounds of shifting ice abated.

I stepped back to see more of myself in the mirror, still holding an image of my desired form in my mind. I looked like a sculptor's unfinished statue of a human male. I now had two legs that loosely approximated those of a human being, and my torso was more elongated, more cylindrical than spherical.

I wouldn't fool anyone up close, but at least now I wouldn't stand out quite so obviously as before. People see what they expect to see, and looking like this, I'd have a better shot at moving around in the regular world without raising alarms. Even if humans saw me in this form, I'd stand a chance of not being recognized. However they described me, they wouldn't say snowman, unless they got close enough to feel the chill radiating off me or see the stark white of my complexion. With the right clothes, in the dark of night, I'd probably be okay moving around in populated areas—while keeping my distance from others—if I should ever need to do so.

With a nod to the mirror, I returned to the bedroom. With each step, I felt the snow around my legs losing solidity, collapsing back to their former configuration. My eyes narrowed and the process stopped, then reversed, and I had visible legs again. Touching my hands to my face, I could tell it had reverted to its rounder original form too, and with another exertion of thought, I felt its surface re-form back to its more human one.

For the next while, I practised walking and maintaining my desired new shape. It took a while, but eventually, I managed to keep my new form while walking across the room with little change in my appearance. The only problem was it took all my concentration. Carrying on a conversation while maintaining my altered form was probably going to be difficult. Touching the Underfrost at the same time? Forget about it. Which meant my newly rediscovered ability's usefulness was going to be limited to stealth.

After a moment's thought, I shrugged. *I'll take it.* Using the

Underfrost would give me away as much as my regular appearance would anyway.

Satisfied that I could summon the form and keep it, I relaxed, and my body reverted to its default form.

When the process had finished, I sighed with relief, a bit drained from my exertions.

My limbs and outer shell of snow tingled and ached in the aftermath, like they did after heavy or prolonged use of the Underfrost. Experience told me that the sensations would soon pass, so I ignored them as best I could.

With a sigh, I left the bedroom and made my way to the kitchen to grab another Ambrola. Though plenty remained in my hat, I didn't want to dig into my stash until I had to. For what I had planned next, they might be the difference between life and death.

Chapter 35

Trading Places

Popping the can open, I made my way back to the atrium, gulping it down on the way. By the time I got there, I felt restored. I tossed the empty into a nearby trash can and made my way to Scott's door.

Turning the knob, I peered inside. "Psst, Scott," I whispered. "You awake?"

The snoring that filled the room faded, then stopped. "Huh?"

"It's me, Shivurr."

A groan and rustling of fabric followed. "What's going on, man?" I opened the door wider, allowing in the light from the atrium behind me. Scott swung his legs over the side of the bed and sat up, rubbing his face. "Something wrong?"

"No," I said, motioning him down with a hand. "Everything's cool."

He checked his watch, then regarded me with a cocked eye, keeping the other scrunched shut. "The fuck, man? It's the middle of the night."

"Sorry, dude," I said. "I need your help with something. It's important."

"Can't this wait?" he asked, smoothing his hair.

I shook my head. "No." *Not with an Allfrost Sentinel in the enemy's clutches.*

Scott sighed and stood, nodding his head in apparent resignation. "Fine. Let's get this over with."

"Follow me." I left the room with Scott in tow.

I made for the hallway that led to the front door. As we crossed the atrium, Bear padded into view, sat on his hind legs, and regarded me silently. Kneeling, I ruffled the fur on his head, and he swiped a rough tongue across one of my cheeks.

"Hey, buddy," I said, looking him in his golden eyes. "We're going for a walk. You okay to stay here and protect the kids?" Bear gave a low woof. "Good boy." I stood taller and looked at Scott. "Let's book."

Scott tousled Bear's fur and followed, muttering to himself.

"What's that?" I said, pulling open the front door.

The rain had stopped, and the moon shone, and the stars sparkled. In the distance, dark clouds and lightning loomed just beyond Caelumtor's rim. The stones of the street were still damp, either from the night's dew or as a leftover from the recent rainfall.

"I said, it's a hell of a time for a walk," Scott replied as he fell into step beside me. "What's so important that it couldn't wait until morning?"

"Getting that captured Allfrost Sentinel back. Maybe saving the world." I shrugged. "No big whoop."

"Okay. When you put it that way, I'm on board. How, though?"

"I'll tell you when we get there." What I had planned was going to be pretty dangerous, and I didn't want to give Scott time to balk or try to talk me out of it. *He might succeed.* "We should probably be quiet. There might be escaped trolls or something around."

Scott glanced left and right. "You think?"

"Probably not," I said, recalling Hanale's words, "but why take the chance?"

"At least the moon is out," he said, "so I can see some of the architecture."

"It's pretty cool," I said, glad to change the subject, even if we were still talking.

Scott smiled. "I haven't seen anything like it since my last trip to Europe."

"When were you there?"

"I did a tour years ago, after college."

"Huh," I said. "I didn't know that."

He shrugged. "We usually just talk about movies and stuff, I guess."

"So, where did you go?"

"All over." He gestured at the facade of a nearby building. "It's kind of weird to see all this looking so new. Most of the stuff in Greece and Rome is just fragments. Whereas this all could have been built in the last twenty or thirty years. I mean, there's algae and weathering, but not as much as you'd expect, especially with all the rain that falls around here."

"They have ways of preserving and restoring the stone," I said absently, focused on what I planned to do. "Automatons do some of it."

"How do you know that?" Scott asked.

I blinked. "I remember it."

"That's wicked, man," he said. "You drank another vial?"

"A couple."

"Sweet." He looked around. "Man, the variety of architecture here is wild. I'm no expert, but some of these look medieval. Don't they?"

"Oh, yeah?" I said. "I hadn't really thought about it."

"It makes sense, though."

"How's that?"

"They—the Olympians—have lived through it all."

"Yeah," I said. "Olivia said they keep the best of each era, and they've a deep appreciation for aesthetics." The latter thought was as much a returning memory as a realization. "I suppose, unlike Europe, these ones haven't been destroyed or damaged by war either, so they've got a mix of them now."

"Of course, there's Abadom," Scott said. "That place has seen better days."

I nodded. "Nothing like getting smushed together with other buildings to mess up a place. Even one made by the gods. Though, to be fair, half of the damaged buildings looked like they came from somewhere else. Look, man. Can we smell the roses later? Things are about to get real."

"Okay. Sure thing."

We walked in silence for a while after that, through the dark and foggy streets. Me, lost in thoughts of what was to come. Scott, I presumed, still thinking of the wonders of Caelumtor.

"So, where are we headed?" Scott said a short while later.

"It's just up ahead." I pointed a finger to the stairs leading up to the building where Hanale and I had interviewed Caelus.

I hopped up the marble stairs two at a time, and Scott jogged to keep up.

"What is this place?" he asked as we passed through the pillars leading in. "Some sort of temple?"

"A prison," I said.

Balls of light flared to life overhead as we entered the vast hall, illuminating the field of pedestals scattered about the floor.

"Wait," Scott said in a low voice, tugging at my shoulder.

"Why?" I asked. "What's the problem?"

He pointed a finger toward the far side of the room where Caelus lay on his side, facing us, with closed eyes, apparently fast asleep—a massive lump of green flesh swelling and deflating. "Is that a troll?"

"They're called ookmir."

"Whatever, man. Let's get the hell out of here."

I waved a hand, dismissively. "It's okay. He can't see us."

"No duh," Scott said. "What if he wakes up, though?"

"He won't be able to see us even if he does."

Scott's eyes flashed. "Are you sure?"

"Yeah, it's cool." I moved toward Caelus's slumbering form. "He's contained in a force field or something."

"Huh," Scott said after I'd told him what Hanale had told me. He looked around as we came to a stop before Caelus. "It's weird to think he's going to end up in one of these things for who knows how long. What do you suppose he did to deserve it?"

I shrugged. "Dunno, but that's not why we're here."

"What's up, then?"

"Patience, Grasshopper," I said, leading him away from Caelus and off to the right. "All will be revealed."

Scott snorted and followed.

I stood before the square of red flooring next to Caelus's and gestured to the black post. "Come on. Put your hand on the crystal."

"Why?"

"Just trust me."

"All right." Scott reached out a hand toward the crystal as if the air were thick molasses.

"Come on. It won't bite."

With a nod, he placed a palm on the ball, and it lit green at his touch. "Now what?"

I walked to the centre of the square and turned to face him. "Now, lock me in."

Scott raised an eyebrow. "Say what?"

"Raise the force field or whatever."

"How do I that?"

When I'd come here with Hanale earlier, I couldn't have answered the question. Fortunately I'd recalled more about the control interfaces since taking the most recent vials of my essence. I tapped my temple. "Think about raising the shield or something. Issue a command. It's a telepathic interface. Come on, you're the computer programmer."

I just hoped that the access Olivia had granted us would be enough.

"So what? What do you—" His lips froze in mid-sentence and his gaze seemed to see through me. "Oh, wow."

"What?" I asked.

"I see now," he said. "This is far out, man." His eyes danced left and right. "Here we go."

A faint thrum reverberated a moment, and the room went black. I could see nothing at all. It was as if I'd been put in a windowless metal box that had been buried a thousand feet beneath the ground. I couldn't hear anything either, except for the sound of my own breathing.

With a thought, my body illuminated, allowing me to see myself and the floor beneath my feet but nothing beyond.

"Scott? Are you there?"

No response. I walked forward and extended an arm toward

the circle's edge, which ended at a wall of pure darkness. The surface, if it could be called that, felt spongy, giving slightly beneath my fingertips. I pushed harder, feeling more resistance as I did so, then punched it with a fist.

My hand sank in an inch before flying back. I smashed a fist against the darkness again and again, and each time my hand flew back—undamaged—as if I were battling a trampoline tipped on its side.

I stepped back and studied my uninjured knuckles a moment before a flash of light to my front pulled my eyes upward.

"Hey, Shivurr," Scott said. "You all right?"

"Yeah, I'm fine."

"Sorry, man. I saw you punching, but I wasn't sure what you wanted me to do."

"Don't sweat it," I said. "I was just testing things out."

"It seemed like you couldn't even see me," he said.

"I couldn't," I replied.

"Huh," Scott said. "Weird. I could see you."

"That's how it works," I said. "Do it again. Keep it in place until I give you the thumbs-up, all right?"

"Sure. Why, though?"

I sighed. "I need to be sure it'll hold."

Scott's brow wrinkled. "H-okay. Here's goes."

The room darkened again. In the light still cast by my luminescing form, I unleashed a torrent of fist and frost against the abyss. A few minutes later, panting, I leaned over a moment to catch my breath before facing where I judged Scott to be and raising both thumbs. The darkness vanished a moment later.

Scott whistled. "That was some light show, man. You scared the shit out of me."

I chuckled. "Sorry, dude. I think it'll hold."

I wondered for a moment whether I could escape by phasing over to the Underfrost—Frost Walking—but decided it didn't matter. The creature this prison might soon contain could no more Frost Walk than I could fly. *Besides*, I thought, *it probably wouldn't work either*. I had to figure that a prison built to contain ephemeral gods would have that covered too.

"Hold what?" Scott smirked. "You're not going to turn into a werewolf, are you?"

"Nope," I said, sweeping the hat from my head.

"Then what?"

"I told you. I'm going after the captured Allfrost Sentinel."

Scott furrowed his brow. "How does me locking you in this thing do that? You don't even know where he's being held. If he even exists."

"The booby-trapped vial."

"The what?" Scott looked thoughtful. "Oh, I see. You're going to take it out."

"Exactly," I said with a nod. "If it activates—and I think it will—I'll end up back there again."

"So what? It's just a big desert."

"I think there's got to be a Eurus base nearby."

"In the middle of a desert?"

"Sure," I said. "What else would Atriel have been doing there? And don't forget about the fire elementals. It's a perfect place for them to hide. It's got to be where they're keeping the Sentinel."

"All right," Scott said. "But how do you know Atriel will be where you want to go? You said he escaped from Caelumtor using a transporter, and those things are fixed to particular locations, right?"

"Yeah."

"Which means he didn't have a direct route back, and you're as likely to end up transporting somewhere else, nowhere near the desert."

I shook my head. "I don't think so, man. I don't think Atriel has the other piece with him anymore. He can't have it, really. If he did, he would've transported back to the desert as soon as we came back to Caelumtor. I think he knew that and dropped it exactly where he came across, in Aceso's kitchen."

Scott's eyes widened. "You're right." He pointed a finger at me. "If he had taken it with him and walked somewhere else, then we would've returned to a different location."

"Exactly, but we returned to the same spot we left. I think he did that to reduce the chance we'd realize what had happened."

"Yeah, right. Like we knew enough about this tech back then to figure that out."

I shrugged. "Yeah, but he couldn't have been sure of that. For all he knew, I might have already gotten most of my memories back, and I might have figured it out. Besides, he wouldn't have wanted to return anyway. Not right away. Not before he captured me. So, he had to get rid of the device."

"Which means?" Scott asked.

"It means that the other device must be lying in the desert sand. Right where I need to go."

"Okay," Scott said. "That makes sense. Supposing you're right, how do you get back from another planet?"

"I don't think it is another planet," I said. "Wilhelm told me it requires a lot of power. You saw those obelisks on Zarechus."

"What about them?"

"I think they're there to absorb and store the power needed for interplanetary travel. All that power can't be contained in a device small enough to fit in one of the memory vials."

Scott frowned. "What about to the moon? That's pretty close."

I cocked an eye and looked at him sidelong. "Really?"

He coughed. "Never mind. Obviously it wasn't the moon."

"Like you said, there are no planets in the solar system that can support life, so the desert's got to be on Earth."

"Fair point."

"Besides," I said, "the Eurus are interested in the Allfrost, and it's here, on Earth."

"Okay." Scott held up a hand. "Okay. You've convinced me." He looked thoughtful. "Why not wait, though? You can get some help from Wilhelm, Hanale or Olivia."

"There's no time. They're busy with their own crises. By the time they're available, who knows what may have happened? The Sentinel might be gone or dead or forced to help the Eurus in their plan, whatever it is." *Besides,* I thought, *I have to go after Atriel alone.* Scott and Caleb could've died on Zarechus, and I couldn't risk their or any of my friends' lives again.

"Okay, but if Atriel doesn't have the other piece, he won't swap places with you, so why bother with me locking you in this thing?"

"It's just a precaution. In case I'm wrong or someone else has found the device on the other end. I can't risk bringing another intruder here, at least not unless he can be contained."

Scott's eyebrows shot up. "Yeah, that'd be bad." He pursed his lips. "But how are you going to get back? Once you've found the guy, I mean. You're going to have to drop the device, just like Atriel, or you'll revert here too, so you'll be stuck just like he was."

I shook my head. "I won't need to drop it. I'll put it back in my hat. That should stop the reversion. It has so far. I'll keep it there until I need it, then pull it out and come back."

"That's brilliant," Scott said with a nod. "But we'll lose Atriel or whoever gets trapped inside this circle. If someone gets trapped."

"That's okay," I said. "We'll still be better off."

"Maybe one of the Olympians can help," Scott said. "If they get back before you do."

"How's that?" I asked.

"They can subdue whoever comes through and take the device. Then he won't revert when you come back."

I shrugged, nodding my head. "Sure, that'd be ideal, but it's a secondary concern. If it works out, great, but don't sweat it if it doesn't."

"So, how long should I wait here?"

I thought a moment. "Wait thirty minutes. That should give me enough time to assess whether it makes sense to stay there. If I'm not back by then, you can go back to the domus and come back here in the morning. If I stay longer than thirty minutes, there's no telling how long I'll be, so there's no point you waiting here. Plus, you can tell the others what's going on. That way they can tell Wilhelm or Olivia if they show up back at the domus while you return here."

"But you may end up being stuck inside this thing all that time. Are you okay with that?"

"Sure," I said. "In the worst case, it'll be seven or eight hours. I can handle that." I smiled. "Just don't sleep in."

"Why not set a maximum of an hour? Then you can look around, then come back and go again later."

"No," I said. "If I switch with Atriel or someone else, they'll probably realize what's happened and be waiting for me the next time." I sighed. "It could go either way. We just don't know, so this is the best we can do. If the worst that happens is I spend the night here after I get back, I'm fine with that."

Scott bobbed his head. "Okay, man. You ready, then?"

I pressed my lips together and nodded. "Do it."

Scott's eyes met mine. "Good luck."

"Thanks," I said.

When darkness fell once more, I illuminated my body, removed the pillowcase with the tainted vial from my hat, and waited.

Chapter 36

The Mechanic

Before long, stars flickered into view overhead, revealing rolling dunes of desert sand and the hulking forms of rugged mountains. I knew it immediately as the desert to which Scott and I had transported from Aceso's kitchen. Returning the pillowcase and vial to the safety of my hat, I blew out a breath and studied the cliffsides that I'd seen on my last visit.

"All right, let's—" I stopped speaking, interrupted by a jangling rumble from behind me. As I turned, the bulky rectangle of a tank appeared atop a nearby sand dune and rolled down its slope straight toward me. Glancing down, I realized that my body still shone like a firefly.

Nuts.

I snuffed the light and fired a look back at the horizon, catching sight of the tank's turret swinging toward me.

Oh, shit.

I raised my hands and concentrated, and a bubble of blue-white energy enveloped me as the tank's main gun puffed smoke. The air boomed and roiled white a foot from my face, and I stumbled back. With scrunched eyes, I averted my gaze as my body shuddered and my head rang. A cloud of dust and fog roiled about me, thickest at the front, lit by faint flickers of my fading energy shield.

Seriously, not even a warning shot?

Before the dust could settle, I lumbered to the left, letting the last remnants of my protection fall. Though the shield had safeguarded me, I didn't think I could make another one strong enough to withstand a second strike, and its bright glow painted a target on my back.

I sucked in a cloud of sand and chemicals and coughed, waving my hands before me as I zigzagged away with my head hung low and shoulders drooping.

Twenty feet from the point of impact, I cracked an eye. Able to see sand beneath my feet, I heaved in gulps of fresh air. My head still rang from the roar of impact, and my shoulders sagged as I plodded another few steps and looked back.

The tank continued its crawl toward my last position. Just a hundred feet away, the high-pitched whine of its engine and squeal of its treads grew louder by the moment.

Hoping the dim light concealed me, I skirted left. Belatedly remembering my hat's ability to glow, I tore it from my head.

Phew. The fabric emitted no light. Reacting to my low energy level or stressed-out mind or both, it had lost all its shimmer.

"It's like that mood ring Lilith wears," Wilhelm had said when he'd returned the upgraded cap to me back in Nevada. "It reacts to your physiology and changes colour based on it."

My polar ice cap, he had called it. Grabbing its peak, I flipped the hat back onto my head, satisfied that it'd be safe to keep wearing it, at least for the moment. Either way, I had to keep it with me. Not only did it contain my emergency provisions and vials of my stolen essence, but it also held the device that was my ticket back.

The tank squealed to a halt as I continued to circle it. Moments later, a clank, just audible above the rumbling engine, came from atop it, and a hatch swung open.

As I approached the vehicle's rear, a head poked from the turret. With a grunt, a man clambered out, jumped down to the sand, and looked my way. He wore a hat, combat fatigues, and black boots that looked just like those worn by the figure I'd seen scurrying away from me in Aceso's kitchen.

I froze, hoping he couldn't see me.

A long moment later, he turned away and strode to the front of the tank, and I let out the breath I'd been unconsciously holding.

Head down, he wandered over my arrival point, looking side to side. A minute later, he looked around again, then scratched behind an ear. With a shrug, he returned to the tank and climbed up the side and back into the open hatch.

That's right, comrade. Nothing to see here.

As the hatch closed, shouted words—unintelligible over the vehicle's running engine—drifted toward me on the wind before ending with a clank.

I burst into motion, running on tiptoe for the tank's rear.

Ten feet from the metal beast's backside, its engine revved, and it lurched into motion. Abandoning stealth, I sprinted the last few steps and leaped. I landed on the vehicle's back ledge, and the ice of my hands and belly watered beneath the hot metal.

A moan escaped my lips, and I crawled to the turret, pulled myself to a standing position, and hunkered next to it. Away from the engine, the metal felt somewhat cooler, but I sent frost to my feet anyway.

Well, that sucked. I'd been here only minutes and had already been attacked. *Maybe I should go back.* It would be easy enough to do, even here atop the tank. All I had to do was take out the pillowcase with the vial, and I'd be back home in moments.

I shook away the thought. *It was just bad luck.* They had no way of knowing I was coming. The tank, I reasoned, must have been passing by and happened on me by pure chance. My body had been fully alight when I'd arrived, signalling my presence as surely as if I'd lit a signal fire. *I guess they figured they'd shoot first and ask questions later.* I nodded to myself. *Yeah, they probably didn't even know what they were shooting at.*

On the plus side, the tank's crew now probably figured what-ever they'd shot at had been destroyed with their first volley. Es-pecially when no counterattack by me had been forthcoming. Which meant they wouldn't be looking for me or giving their superiors a reason to do so.

As the cliffs that I'd observed upon arrival loomed larger, I smiled. *It may have worked out for the best anyway.* I'd intended to explore the cliffs, before I'd been attacked, and now I was getting a free ride right to them. Even better, if I was right, the tank was connected to the Eurus base that I'd hypothesized lay nearby. Why else would it be here in the desert, where fire elementals had been seen? And, if so, they were probably heading back to base, taking me exactly where I wanted to go.

I nodded to myself. Its presence here was just too big a co-incidence otherwise, so I kept still, channelling the Underfrost to protect my melting feet, watching and waiting.

Before long, the tank entered the deeper gloom of the towering cliffsides.

I hope you're right, Shivurr, I thought to myself.

Sometime after, shadows and light danced upon the canyon walls, and the tank rounded a bend. Ahead, a stone wall, topped by floodlights, slid into view. A squeal of metal cut the air and the engine groaned, and I pressed a hand to the gun turret as my weight pressed against it.

A moment later, the tank swung right, heading toward the palisade's middle.

A gate rolled aside at our approach, and I crouched low, doing my best to keep the tank's turret between me and the sixty-foot watchtower next to the entrance.

Twenty feet from the wall, the engine pitched higher as the driver accelerated inside. Past the gate, the tank's headlights bounced off darkened tents and buildings of concrete and corrugated steel as we drove deeper into the military encampment.

Before long, the tank decelerated and turned a corner, making for a group of soldiers standing next to a collection of parked vehicles. Beyond them, a huge opening in the canyon wall shone with artificial light.

Crap. My eyes scanned the sides of the roadway, finding nowhere to hide as we rolled closer to the gathered soldiers. *Time to ghost.*

Focusing my mind, I vanished into the Underfrost before jumping from the vehicle's rear. Through a cloud of exhaust, I scurried toward a narrow alley between two squat windowless corrugated steel buildings. Behind me, the tank's brakes squealed again and its engine wound down before stopping completely.

The raucous voices of men followed, shouting greetings.

Russians, I thought, recognizing some of their words. *This must be the place.*

Wilhelm had told me the Eurus were based mostly in the East, while the New Olympians held the West against them. It made sense that they might have Soviet soldiers working for them. This camp might even be a Soviet base, commanded by the Eurus.

I nodded to myself. The Eurus likely weren't as hesitant to involve themselves directly in mortal affairs as my god friends. With the resources and capabilities of a god, a person could rise to great power within the Soviet hierarchy, I felt sure. The things they could offer others as bribes would no doubt convince many to do whatever they wanted. And where bribery failed, a threat from a god would surely succeed.

The only reason they might choose not to rise too high would be to avoid drawing attention to themselves and becoming a target of their enemies. For that reason, my guess was that they'd operate from the shadows when they could, using their secret influence to move mountains—or establish military bases—only when they needed to do so.

Pushing aside those thoughts, I resurfaced from the Underfrost with an exertion of will before making my way down the alley.

Now that I'd found the place, I needed to get out of sight and figure out where in the sprawling encampment the Allfrost Sentinel was being held captive. Searching the entire camp would take too long, and the longer I searched, the greater the chance that I'd be spotted. While I could retreat to the Underfrost, I couldn't remain there for long without running the risk of never returning. Indeed, each time I went there, it seemed harder to bring myself back. Which meant I needed another way to find him without being spotted, and my best bet was getting help from someone that knew where they were keeping him.

Whether they want to help or not.

Halfway down the passageway, I pulled up at a door leading into the building to my left. The knob twisted in my hand, and I pushed the door inward and stepped inside.

Fluorescent lights, spread wide apart, dimly lit the interior in stark, unpleasant light, and a smell of spilled oil and radiator fluid wrinkled my nose a moment later. Workbenches cluttered with tools and machinery lined the walls. Military vehicles, some jacked up and missing tires, others with hoods raised, sat scattered across the oil-stained concrete floor. Spotting a window on the building's far side, I closed the door behind myself and strode toward the rectangle of light. Halfway there, a clang of metal against concrete and a harsh shout froze me in my tracks.

A long, rattling squeak followed.

I lunged behind a nearby truck and peered out. Thirty feet away, booted feet slid into view from beneath a jeep. The grey-clothed legs, hips, and torso of a person came next. A man, judging by the shape of the body and sound of the voice. He lay flat on his back, a few inches above the floor, on a padded, wheeled rectangular plank. Grunting, he scraped his heels against the dirty floor and crept clear of the front bumper.

The man—a mechanic, I presumed—regained his feet and looked my way. I drew back behind the truck and held my breath, listening.

"*Kto tam?*" he said.

The tap of footsteps followed and grew louder.

I pressed my lips together and shook my head. *I'm busted*, I thought, padding along the side of the truck, away from the footsteps.

As I shuffled along the truck's rear bumper, the noise of the camp grew abruptly louder, and I craned my neck in the direction of the sound.

A man, his head tilted down, entered through a door at the far end of the garage.

"*Privet*," said the new arrival, a soldier, judging by his garb. He closed the door behind himself, turning to face the mechanic, who came into view from the left with a hand raised in greeting.

While the two talked, I doubled back to the front of the truck to better see.

Well, this sucks. I doubted that I could subdue both men without making enough noise to wake the whole camp.

"Good day, comrade," the mechanic said in English, his accent heavy. "I am Russian."

What the hell?

The soldier chuckled. "*Khorosho.*"

"Where is train station?" the mechanic said with a toothy grin. "My name is Yuri. What is your name?"

Huh, I thought. The simple, common phrases reminded me of my days learning English at the Institute. *He's showing off.*

The soldier laughed again and slapped the mechanic on the shoulder. "You are improving, Yuri."

The two practised their English awhile longer until the mechanic, Yuri, waved a wrench at the vehicle next to him. "I must fix."

The soldier walked toward the door through which he'd entered. "*Do svidaniya.*"

Finally, I thought as the door closed behind him. *Time to get some answers.*

The mechanic's back wriggled as he leaned over the jeep's engine and reached in with both hands. Slipping from my hiding place, I crossed the floor in a wide arc, padding on tiptoe.

This is going to be a piece of cake.

My foot struck something, and I winced and stumbled as something metal tinkled across the floor.

Shit, I thought, and the mechanic whirled to face me.

I rushed forward, grabbed the fabric of his coveralls, and raised a clawed finger to my lips. "Shh." Yuri's eyes flared wide. "Not a word." He nodded slowly but made no reply. "I'm looking for someone. Someone like me. Where are they keeping him?"

"What are you talk about?" Yuri asked in a low voice. "Are you demon?"

"N-no." My eyes widened. "Don't bullshit me, man." I opened my hand and—with a moment's concentration—reshaped my fingers, and my already sharp fingertips extended, becoming three-inch daggers. "I don't want to hurt you, but I will if I have to." *I think.*

Yuri's eyes drifted to my dagger-like fingertips. "You mean prisoner?"

I nodded. "Yeah, the prisoner. Where is he?"

"In tunnel," Yuri replied, jutting a chin over my shoulder.

"What does he look like?" I asked, studying the mechanic's eyes, searching for signs of deception. "Does he look like me?"

He made a face. "I fix truck, jeep. Prisoner, they bring him in box. No one see him. No one but guards . . . and demon."

"All right, Yuri." I released my grip on his coveralls. "I'm going to need you to tell me everything that you know."

A few minutes later, it turned out he didn't know much more than he'd already revealed. With some cajoling, he drew a map on a pad of paper taken from a nearby workbench. I took it from him and studied it. The crude drawing showed a circuitous path through a warren of tunnels cut into the cliffside.

"This is kind of a roundabout route." I held out the map and stabbed a finger at it. "Are you sure there isn't a more direct way?"

"No. Short way no good; locked."

"Hmm." I folded the paper and slipped it into an inner pocket of my jacket. "All right, then."

Now what do I do with you? Something told me knocking a person unconscious without killing them wasn't as easy as it looked in the movies. Besides, even if I managed it, there would be no way to be sure he wouldn't just wake up a few minutes later. If the map he'd drawn was accurate, I just needed to keep him from raising the alarm for ten minutes, maybe twenty, to give myself some wiggle room. Judging by the mechanic's expression, he had guessed the thoughts racing through my mind.

"You got any rope around here, Yuri?" I asked before he could bolt.

"Tow rope," he replied. "This way."

I watched him dig around in the back of a truck, my fingers tingling with frost, until he pulled out ropes with big metal hooks affixed to each end. I gripped one in my hands and twisted a section into a U shape. I scowled, realizing they were too thick and unyielding. I'd never be able to tie it tightly enough to hold him. *They must be for towing tanks.*

I opened my hands, and the hooks clanked against the floor. "This won't do. What else you got?"

Yuri shrugged. "That all I have."

"Bullshit," I said, still trying to play the tough guy. "You've got to have some better rope around here."

"*Nyet.*"

I sighed. "You're making me frosty, Yuri." I held out my hand and summoned a frost ball. "You wouldn't like me when I'm—"

He raised his hands. "I take you."

My eyes narrowed. "Take me?"

"*Da.*" He waved a finger, first at me, then himself. "We go. You, me. I take you see prisoner."

I dismissed the frost and looked down at myself, considering. It was an idea. If he came with me, I could keep an eye on him and make sure that he didn't raise an alarm. It would also help to have someone that knew the layout lead the way. I'd have to keep a close eye on him, but it could work. As I reached that conclusion, an idea came to mind, one that might slant the odds a little more in my favour.

"Okay." I formed my fingers into daggers as I'd done earlier, then raised them, and Yuri shrank back. "But if you call for help . . . just don't, all right?"

Though we'd originally been of similar height, I towered over Yuri now. Looking down, I realized that my body now stretched itself out over a length of seven feet. In my desire to appear menacing, I'd apparently shape-shifted, making myself appear larger and more imposing.

By the look on the Russian's face, it had had the desired effect.

For a moment, I felt bad to be threatening him. The guy hadn't done anything to me, but what choice did I have? Besides, scaring him had to be better than bashing him over the head, and I knew for a fact that it was better than getting caught would be for me. I wasn't going to be captured by anyone ever again if I could help it. Besides, I had a mission. A mission to rescue someone like me. Someone being held against his will.

Maybe Yuri was just a poor slob trying to get by, but he was working for bad dudes. Scott had said, "Either you're the asshole or you work for one." He'd just been venting his frustrations and didn't really believe it himself, I felt sure. But as far as I was concerned, doing an asshole's dirty work made you one too. *Maybe a bigger one.* Without those who carried out their orders, a despot was nothing but an average guy with a limited capacity to cause misery. It was their hierarchy of followers that allowed them to subjugate and terrorize and kill. To make a hard world harder.

Yuri nodded. "*Da.*"

"Cool." I plucked the fabric covering his chest. "Now, where do you keep your spare coveralls?"

Chapter 37

Prisoner

We left the building a short while later, exiting through the side door by which I'd first entered. I adjusted my jacket over the clean pair of coveralls that Yuri had pulled from the bottom drawer of a tool cart. I'd donned a pair of scuffed steel-toed worker's boots as well. Neither the coveralls nor the boots had been my size or shape, so some alterations had been required. Without a tailor handy, I'd had to shape-shift to grow a pair of legs, shorten my arms, and suck in my gut.

Yuri had watched wide-eyed and pale as a ghost in the harsh fluorescent light but otherwise handled my transformation pretty well, though he'd muttered "demon" more than once under his breath as I did so. I had to suppose that, as a mechanic working in a stronghold of alien gods and demons, he'd become somewhat accustomed to extraordinary sights. If not, he probably would have needed fresh coveralls himself before I was done.

Before we'd departed, I had checked myself in a dirty rearview mirror lying on a nearby workbench. Anyone getting too close would see through the disguise before long, even though I'd altered my face too. My smaller nose and more structurally complex face seemed likely to be enough in the dark. *As long as no one gets too close.*

Beyond my hat, I couldn't do much about my hairless, too-white scalp. To my relief, the telltale glow still hadn't returned to my military cap. I'd have stuffed it into a pocket, but I preferred to keep it on, if only for the coolness that it radiated down upon my skull. Following a step to the side and behind Yuri, I pulled it lower, channelling the Underfrost to cool my soggy feet. It wasn't just my feet that felt uncomfortable, though. My whole body ached, the way my chest did whenever I held my breath too long.

We hid in the alley at the side of the garage as a twelve-foot-tall hulk of green muscle loped past the opening.

They've got trolls here too, I thought.

When it had disappeared into the shadows to our right, I nudged Yuri, and we took a left toward the cavern.

We soon slipped past the tank that I'd rode into the facility upon, keeping out of the pools of illumination cast by light stands arrayed about the yard. I leaned right, shying from the heat still radiating from the metal behemoth's cooling engine. The tank's crew and the crowd that had been gathered when I had first arrived had dispersed.

My darting eyes spied only two figures moving about the vicinity, aside from Yuri and me. Both walked some distance off, eyes aimed down and ahead, apparently intent on getting wherever they were going. To my relief, neither of their heads turned in our direction, and we made it to the mouth of the cave that delved down and into the rocky cliffside without raising an alarm.

Inside, I squinted at the brightness within spilling from banks of fluorescent lights strung overhead, and I felt relieved to see no one moving about. Occasional cuts and scrapes in the stone to either side and above could only have been made by heavy machinery, indicating that the natural cave that had been here originally had been reshaped and enlarged. Whoever had done the work had been careful to leave pillars of stone behind to support the massive ceiling that loomed sixty feet or more overhead. Shabby-looking office buildings, stacked shipping crates, and mobile homes filled the area. Fortunately, most buildings were either windowless or unlit, suggesting that those who occupied the structures during the day had gone elsewhere for the evening.

"Where to now?" I whispered next to Yuri's ear.

He pointed an arm at a windowless two-storey grey building abutting the far wall with a number of doors leading inside.

"Okay, let's—" My cheeks bulged as a wave of dizziness came over me. Rivulets of meltwater ran down my forehead, and my coveralls tightened as my body swelled and shifted.

No. A ripping sound came from my lower half. *Not now.*

Yuri cast an eye over his shoulder with a raised brow. "What you doing?"

I gripped his bicep with a hand and held up a claw-like finger, stopping him in place.

Closing my eyes, I took a breath and focused, picturing the form that I wanted to keep. In this the coveralls helped, allowing me to focus on the areas of my body where the garment felt most tight.

After a few seconds, I could feel the transformation slow and finally halt.

Yes. My lips spread wide as the process reversed, and my clothing grew looser. *Phew.* I dug a hand inside my winter jacket. My probing fingers brushed across rips in the canvas covering an armpit. *Nearly hulked out there.* Looking down, I saw ice-white snow peeking from rips in the inseam of my coveralls. *Too bad Scott wasn't around to see it.*

With a shake of my head, I used my free hand—the one not holding Yuri—to pull up the zipper on the front of my coveralls, which had been tugged open by my expanding chest.

"Okay," I said at last, giving his arm a push. "Let's move." Without a word, Yuri resumed walking, heading for the far wall, dotted with closed doors. "Are there guards?"

"*Nyet*," he replied. "Not yet."

"Come on." I gave his bicep a squeeze. "There must be guards."

He nodded. "By prisoner hole."

"You've got him in a hole?"

"*Da*," he said with a nod. "In coffin in hole."

"He's dead?" *I'm too late.*

"Not dead," Yuri replied. "Frozen."

"Yeah?" I smiled. "Me too." *He's got to be a Sentinel.*

My hands rose as we reached the far wall, and Yuri pushed open the doors.

Seeing no one on the other side, I lowered them, and we crossed into the air-conditioned interior.

"How do you know about the prisoner?"

"What mean?"

"You're a mechanic," I said. "You fix truck, right? How do you know so much about the prisoner?"

"Base small," Yuri said. "Guards talk."

I followed him through the warren of concrete tunnels, keeping my head down and mouth shut in case—like the Institute—they had cameras. If they did, I had to hope the guards weren't looking too closely. I figured there was a good chance that they wouldn't be until we got to wherever they were holding the Sentinel.

It seemed I was right. Though we had to duck into a few doorways and linger at corners a few times to avoid others, the halls were pretty quiet. All in all, things were going well, and with a bit of luck we'd soon reach our destination.

The thought bothered me for some reason. *Too well, maybe.* Keeping a hand on Yuri, I fumbled in my pocket and pulled forth the rudimentary map that he had drawn. I studied it a moment, then pulled my guide to a stop. "This isn't the way."

"What?"

I cocked an eye at him. "This isn't the way you drew on the map."

"*Da,*" he replied. "This way *luchshe.*"

"You're saying this way is better?"

"*Da.*"

"Bullshit." I tapped the map with a sharp finger. "We're going straight, but the map has us going around this area. You said this way was locked."

Yuri licked his lips and shrugged. "This way better."

"Uh-huh. I told you that." I narrowed my eyes. "What's going on?" I wriggled my fingers in his face. "Are you leading me into a trap?"

"No trap," he replied. "Not this way."

"Oh, I see. The other way was a trap. You didn't think you were coming with me when you drew this thing, did you?" I gave his arm a shake. "What's the other way? A barracks full of soldiers?"

Yuri glared. "Monster."

"Monster? What kind of monster?"

"Fire monster."

"Just one?"

He moved his chin faintly from side to side.

I scowled. "Hmm, I can't say that I blame you." I grabbed the breast of his coveralls and pulled his face close to mine. "But we're in this together, Yuri. Our fates joined." I plucked a frost ball from thin air and held it up, and his face shone in its dangerous light. "Screw with me again, and I'll show you monster. Frost monster. Got it?"

His Adam's apple bobbed. "*Da.*"

I gave him a gentle shove. "Let's go, then."

A while later, faint voices from somewhere ahead sent us through the nearest unlocked door into a small windowless meeting room. Closing the door softly, I met Yuri's eyes and held a finger to my lips as footsteps grew louder. "How much farther?" I asked after the footfalls finally diminished.

"Next corner."

"Show me." I held out the map he'd drawn me. "Show me where we are on the map and where the guards are positioned."

He snatched the map from my hand, studied it, then pointed a meaty, grease-stained finger. "Guard here," he said before moving his finger. "You, me, here."

"How many?"

He shrugged. "One." He held up two fingers. "Most two."

"Can we get by them?" I asked.

Yuri looked me up and down, then shook his head. "Maybe, if guard blind."

"Yeah," I said with a nod. "I kind of figured." *But I've got a plan for that.* I pointed to the far side of the meeting room. "Move over there, please."

He licked his lips and swallowed but did as I bade him. I felt Yuri's eyes on me as I walked over to the table that dominated the room. Leaning against the table's edge, I tore wire from a push-button phone sitting near the table's centre. I fumbled with it a moment and pulled the telephone wire loose. Setting the phone down, I followed the line to the wall plug and pulled it loose as well.

"Now," I said, wrapping the wire around one hand. "Have a seat."

For the next while, I tied Yuri to an office chair. I took care to also wrap some of the wire through the leg of the table to keep him from wheeling the chair into the hallway. I was a total novice at tying people up, but I only needed to buy myself enough time to reach the prisoner and use the device in my hat to escape.

I grunted as I tugged the last knot tight, then stood tall and began to undress. My altered form had taken me as far as it was going to, and there was no way I was going to be able to maintain it doing what I had planned next. Fully disrobed, I groaned with pleasure as my body morphed back to its proper form.

Oh, yeah, I thought, reaching for my winter jacket.

"Sorry about this, Yuri." I tore a strip from the coveralls' already ripped fabric. Wadding the cloth into a neat ball, I held it near his mouth. "Open, please." He scowled but obeyed. "I can't risk you calling out," I said, stuffing it into his maw. Shredding off another piece, I stretched it over his lips and tied it snugly behind his head. "You understand, right?"

Yuri mumbled something unintelligible.

I smiled, slapping him on a shoulder. "Perfect." I couldn't even tell if what he'd said was Russian or English. "Just hang out here until someone finds you, okay?"

His eyes narrowed, but he nodded.

"Good man." Doffing my cap, I rummaged inside. "I just need a drink, then I'll be out of your way." I cracked the seal on a can of Ambrola and drank deeply. The aches and pains of my recent transformation bled away, and I stood taller, feeling a tingle of energy surge from my toes to my scalp. "I'd offer you some, but . . . well, don't worry, it's not vodka or anything."

According to many at the Bodhi Institute—none more so than Dixon—the Soviets drank it like water from an early age. I made a face, remembering the time I'd tried some courtesy of the security director. *Nasty stuff.* A burble of voices came from the hallway, interrupting my reverie. I held a finger to my lips, padded over to the closed door, and listened.

"How long until we can question him again?" asked a deep, resonant male voice in Latin.

"A day," said a woman. "Perhaps more."

"Why not sooner?"

"He nearly died during the last session."

"How can he have resisted so long?"

"He's resilient and endured torture before, I think."

I held my breath as footsteps tapped past the door and stopped.

"Send him to Balbarith," said the man's voice, "and he'll soon break."

The woman snorted. "We need him sane and able to function to be of any use. His task will require finesse. Patience. Everyone breaks in time."

"And if he dies before then?"

"We are pursuing other options in parallel."

"What of Shivurr?"

"Atriel may return with him yet. Fear not. Even without either one of them, we have options. Our plans would be delayed, yes, but not for long. That is, if you can finish your work."

The male voice growled. "The nodes and chambers are well hidden—the nodes in particular, since they've a habit of moving—but we are on schedule."

"How long before all is ready? If we do not act before the enemy knows our plan, then all may be for naught. Which means you and your fellows shall remain as you are, unredeemed, condemned to ten thousand years more subjugation and slavery."

"I am aware," growled the other.

A pounding of boots rose in volume beyond the door, and a conversation ensued between a new male voice and the woman's, this time in Russian. To my surprise, I even understood some of it, making me wonder if Russian was yet another language returning courtesy of the vials.

"Atriel has returned," the woman said in Latin a moment later. "He requests that we join him."

"Where?"

"By the desert arrival point."

"For what reason?"

More Russian words were exchanged.

"It seems he's lost the Alterclavis," the woman said at last.

I let out a breath as the sound of footsteps faded away, and my eyes rose to regard the bill of my hat.

I wasn't sure what an Alterclavis was, but if Atriel was looking for it in the desert, I thought I might be able to guess. It had to be the transposition device he had left behind in Aceso's kitchen. Linked to the twin device, now safe in my hat, his device would now be lying inside the force field on New Olympus, next to which Scott waited for my return. Which meant that they could search as long as they wanted, but they wouldn't find it.

Normally, losing something small in the desert sand wouldn't be a surprise, but I had an idea that these folks had ways of finding this Alterclavis beyond using their eyes. When they didn't find it, they might conclude someone had taken it. Since I'd be suspect number one, they might then decide to search the base. Which meant I had to get to the prisoner and get away soon, or I might be forced to leave without him.

I counted to thirty, giving the trio plenty of time to get away, then opened the door. I half expected to see the three standing there waiting for me, but the hallway lay empty. Creeping into the corridor, I snugged the door shut behind myself.

With a glance in both directions, I moved toward the room where Yuri had told me the prisoner could be found, hoping that he'd told the truth. If he hadn't, I'd have to continue my search without his help. With time running out, going back for him wasn't an option.

Chapter 38

The Judas Hole

Yuri hadn't lied. Around the next corner, two burly Russian guards, holding assault rifles, stood to either side of broad, windowed double doors at the end of the hall.

Taking a deep breath, I closed my eyes. The air soon fogged and frost formed on the wall next to me as my body cooled, crackling and crunching like footsteps on packed snow. I opened my eyes onto a hallway transformed. The dull puke-green walls now shone blue, twinkling with the Underfrost, even as the air roiled with the swirling currents of its energies.

Oh, yeah, I thought. Intuitively, I knew that I'd crossed over fully to the Underfrost, that stark and infinite wellspring of power that gave me life yet promised oblivion if I stayed too long.

With the peril of Frost Walking front of mind, I stepped into the open and called out. The guards remained as they were, one studying his weapon, the other staring straight at me with half-closed eyes as if struggling to stay awake.

Cool. As expected, they couldn't see me because, in a way, I was no longer here, not entirely. I was just a ghost now, a phantom of frost, just the other side of a threshold between the regular world and an alternate one. Both bordered and overlapped the other, yet only I—and I supposed others like me—could perceive the one that I now occupied. The guards could no more see me than they could see the sun's ultraviolet rays or hear frequencies of sound beyond a certain range.

Reassured, I burst into motion, flying over the floor at them. Twenty feet away, they still gave no sign of being aware of my approach. At ten feet, one shuddered and glanced at his comrade. As I passed through them, the one that had shivered said something in Russian. His unintelligible words faded as I passed through the solid double doors as if they were mere air.

The room beyond had all the makings of a laboratory of some kind. Cabinets and counters lined the walls, computer monitors, towers, printers, and other components rested on rolling carts, scattered about the floor. Two gurneys—unoccupied—had been shoved against a wall.

In the room's centre, a mechanical arm stood bolted to the floor. Wires ran from its base to a control panel sitting on a stand next to it. The arm's articulating hand hovered over a bulbous metal plate in the floor—a domed manhole cover—with a handle inset into the centre. Stickers of yellow and orange with Cyrillic lettering and unfamiliar symbols decorated the floor around it.

That's got to be where they're keeping him. I swept across to the control panel and studied it. Incomprehensible characters glowed across the control pad, but I recognized the two joysticks at its centre. I reached out a hand, and my fingers sank through the pad as if it weren't there, or I wasn't.

Oh, right. Closing my eyes, I envisioned myself rising from the Underfrost back to the regular world. A pool of warmth swelled over my extremities, and I gasped as it enveloped my chest. Huffing a few shallow, foggy breaths, I stifled the panic that threatened to overwhelm me as my body and mind strove to adapt to the change. The room was cooler than I'd normally had to endure in recent days, but in comparison to the blissful cool of the Underfrost it felt sweltering.

Still longing to return to its chilling embrace, I reached for the joysticks once more. They moved at my touch, but nothing else happened. I pressed a green button on the right side and tried again. The robotic arm whirred left, then right, as I tugged the leftmost stick side to side.

Okay, this must be down, I thought, pushing the rubber forward with a smile. I grimaced as the metal hand dropped faster than I had expected, striking the manhole cover with a clang before I could pull it out of its dive. *Shit.*

A knock and a faint jangling of keys came from the doorway, and the two guards pushed their way inside a moment later. They raised their weapons and pointed them at me, shouting in Russian.

"Whoa, dudes." I raised my hands. "Easy now."

Blinking my eyes, I vanished into the Underfrost—for the third time in about an hour—and with a moan of pleasure slid left, out of their firing line, just in case. Both soldiers gaped at the spot where I'd just been and raised their weapons higher but didn't fire. Invisible, I skirted the room, coming up behind them as one of them reached for the two-way radio at his hip.

Pushing back across the veil between worlds, I gripped their necks in my hands and channelled the Underfrost into their hot flesh. An instant later, my head rang with the boom of gunfire as one or both tugged the triggers of their assault rifles. Their shoulder blades squeezed together as they snarled and wriggled, trying to face me, but I held my grip tight, locking my fingers into cages of rock-hard ice. Their struggles weakened soon after, and they sank to the floor.

Pushing their weapons aside, I reached for their necks again—only faint tendrils of fog came from my fingertips now that I'd released the Underfrost—and felt for a pulse. Both still lived, but seconds passed between their heartbeats. They were young, though; they'd recover, I had to hope.

A patter of footsteps and raised voices came from the hallway, and I ran toward the still-open doors. Snugging them tight, I turned the bolt to lock it and stepped back. I raised my hands and channelled more of the Underfrost. Immediately, snow welled from the floor and fell from the air, burying the doors' bottom halves in a drift of snow and ice.

Racing for the mechanical arm, I shook off the urge to return to the Underfrost's cool embrace. Others of my kind, I knew, had in the past failed to resist its lure and been lost forever. If you stay too long in the Hotel Underfrost, chances are you'll never leave. Fortunately, I had other desires that helped me resist the temptation today. *Best not do it again for a while, though, if I can help it.*

Easing a joystick back, I raised the robotic hand from the floor, then fiddled with the other stick to open its fingers. Having worked out the basics now, I lowered it down, grasped the manhole cover's handle, and directed the robotic hand to pull. The mechanical arm lifted the metal cover easily, and a frosted cylinder, seven feet long and two feet in diameter, came with it.

When the cylinder had cleared the floor, I strode over to it, touched a palm to the icy film coating it, and rubbed. Beneath the frost, the tube shined a dull silver.

Is that aluminum or stainless steel?

I circled the tube, tracing my fingertips over its surface, searching for a way inside, but I felt none.

A bang drew my eyes to the right. The snow-blocked double doors quivered, and angry shouts sounded from the far side. The unmistakable fumble and scrape of a key against a lock followed a moment later.

Crap. The snow that I'd raised to block the doors wouldn't keep them out for long by itself. The deadbolt clicked to the open position, and I felt inside my cap, pushing soda cans and vials aside. *Come on.*

The doors shuddered and opened a crack, thudding against the snowdrift.

Where is it? My fingers brushed the pillowcase at last, and I smiled. *Yes!*

Shaking my head, I held the vial through the fabric and donned my cap.

"See you, suckers," I said, wrapping my free arm about the hanging man-sized pod.

Chapter 39

Revelations

Visible past the capsule's side, a man's head and shoulders pushed through the widening doorway. Seeing me, he aimed a handgun in my direction and, with a snarl, fired. As the gun's muzzle flashed, I pulled back, and the room went dark.

I glanced around, still hugging the cylinder.

Did the power go out? I hesitated, listening, but heard no sound other than my own movement.

Warm light flared, slamming my eyes shut. Cracking them a sliver, I spotted Scott amid the glare, hand on the crystal that controlled the force field that had surrounded me. To his rear the prison hall lay quiet, still lit by balls of light floating high above.

"Welcome back, man," he said.

I blinked my eyes and smiled. "It's good to be back, dude." I stepped away from the capsule and stuffed the pillowcase and vial back into my cap. "I almost didn't make it."

"And you brought me a present," Scott said with a grin.

"Yeah, I—" The capsule teetered. "Shit." I lunged for it, wrapping it in a bear hug, and looked at Scott. "Give me a hand."

Scott raced to my side, raising his long arms high to steady the capsule. "Let's lay it down."

"Okay," I said. "To the left ... easy ... easy." The tube clanged against the red stone, and I stood erect. "Let's roll it." I patted the metal. "There's a seam on this side. I think it's the opening."

We rolled it into position, and Scott held it steady while I fingered the lid.

"You think he can breathe in there?" Scott asked. "You guys breathe, right?"

"Sure," I said. "He's in stasis, though, I think, so he probably doesn't need to breathe."

"Yeah," Scott said, "or maybe this container has its own air supply."

I scowled. "I can't get it open."

Scott grunted. "There's got to be a latch or something."

After spending a few minutes more pounding and prying, I looked at Scott. "Screw it." I moved to the manhole cover capping one end and waved a hand toward the other end. "Let's carry it back."

Scott grasped his side of the cylinder and lifted. Veins and tendons stood out on his neck, but he got it high enough to rest some of the weight upon his knee. He adjusted his hands and nodded to me with a tight expression.

I raised my end, and my arms creaked. Softer areas of snow throughout my body hardened to ice, adapting to the weight. It had to be close to three hundred pounds—manageable between the two of us, but not for long.

"Quick." I flicked my nose at one of Scott's shoulders. "Let's go."

With a glance over his shoulder, he pulled, and we started to move.

"Anyone back yet?" I asked as we reached the prison hall's exit.

Scott's shoulders twitched. "I'm not sure."

"You didn't go back to the domus yet?"

"Nope," he said. "I know you said thirty minutes, but I figured I'd wait a bit longer, just in case."

"I'm glad you did." *Even if we agreed to thirty.* I looked back over a shoulder. "It's better than sitting back there all night. Did Caelus give you any trouble?"

He huffed before responding. "Magilla Gorilla? Nah. He just lay there the whole time." He glanced down. "So, this is him, eh? The Allfrost Sentinel."

"Yep."

"That was pretty quick," he said as we emerged into the still-dark night. The sky had grown lighter, but the sun had not yet risen. "Any trouble?"

"Some," I said, lowering my end. "Here, let's put it down a minute. You look like you're going to tear something."

We clanged the cylinder against the stone landing and stood erect. I placed a hand atop the capsule, ensuring it didn't roll sideways.

"Yeah," he said, rubbing his back. "My rectum."

"Wrecked him?" The corners of my mouth lifted as I thought of one of our past conversations. "It damn near killed him, is what I heard."

Scott laughed. "It's possible that I'm a bad influence on you, Shivurr." He sat on the edge of the cylinder and gazed down the steps at the shadowy street below.

"You think?" I shook my head. "Nah. If not for you, I wouldn't even know what an asshole is."

Scott turned to me with a raised eyebrow and lopsided grin. "Pardon?"

"Uh, that came out wrong," I said. "I mean, being what I am, not, you know, having one."

Scott chuckled. "No sweat, man. I get it."

"Okay, cool."

"Besides," he said, "now that you can shape-shift, maybe you can have one too."

I winced. "No, thanks. You guys, people, I mean, are so weird, dude."

Scott snorted. "Says the snowman." He paused. "So, what's some?"

"Huh?" I squinted at him, and he patted the capsule. "Oh, the trouble. Right." I quickly told him of my recent adventures. "It got pretty hairy, but fortunately I know a few manoeuvres." I tapped the side of my cap. "Another thirty seconds, though, who knows? I might have been a goner." I rapped my knuckles against the metal container. "Anyway, we should move."

"Holy shit, man." With a grunt he raised his end of the capsule from the stone. "A tank shot you in the face, and you walked away from it."

I pointed to the stairs behind him with my nose. "Do you think you can make it down the steps in one go?"

He glanced back. "Maybe you should go first now."

I nodded, and we wheeled about.

Adjusting my grip, I pushed the capsule away from my body so that I could see the stairs as we descended them. Being lower than Scott, I bore most of the weight, and I lifted my end higher, trying to keep the container as level as possible.

Halfway down, my arms burned, and I stepped faster.

"Almost there," I said, glancing up at Scott.

"Not so fast, Shivurr." His eyes flicked to me, then downward. "My fingers are—fuck."

The metal bashed me in the face as it shifted. My feet slid along the dewy stairs, and I pushed hard against the cylinder, trying to arrest its motion.

What's going on?

The far side of the canister swung to my left, with Scott stumbling behind it. It struck the stairs with a loud clang and tore free of my grasp.

I lunged after it. Grasping the manhole cover that capped my end like a steering wheel, I wrenched my hands counter-clockwise, hoping to halt the canister's momentum.

The lid stayed locked in my grip, but the capsule continued to roll. A moment later, a shriek like tearing metal cut the air, and I stumbled back, falling to the stairs, clutching the manhole cover to my chest. With a glance to Scott, I looked down and watched the tube tumble its way to the bottom and roll into the street.

"What the hell, Scott?"

"Sorry, man," he said, extending a hand toward me. "I tripped."

I scowled and took his hand. "You should've told me you needed to rest."

"It happened too quickly." His eyes flicked to the circle of metal that I still grasped in my other hand. "Is that piece important?"

I grimaced. "I hope not. Come on. Let's take a look. He might be injured."

"Nah. He's an Allfrost Sentinel, right? If he's half as tough as you, he's got to be fine."

I flew down the steps, leaving Scott to trail behind. The tube had spun upon hitting the street, leaving the now-open end pointed away from me. A cloud of thick fog billowed from that side, shaded green by light emanating from within.

Reaching the bottom of the broad staircase, I ran along the cylinder, placing a hand to steady it as it rocked back and forth. As I peered inside the tube, a wave of cold spilled out toward me. I fanned away the fog, but more roiled from within to take its place.

"At least it's open," Scott said, pulling up beside me. "Is he okay?"

"I don't—"

The opening hissed, and I scuttled back, eyes fixed on the hole. A head wreathed in fog slid into view, followed by a torso, carried on a metal plank. Metal supports unfolded beneath the plank, supporting it like the legs of a table. When the man's hips appeared, the ejection stopped.

I illuminated my body and swept away the vapour with a hand.

"That's not an Allfrost Sentinel," Scott said as the vapour cleared.

The nude occupant looked to be a man of about fifty years.

Grey stubble covered the occupant's shaven head and cuts, burns, and fading bruises his face and torso.

Scott pulled off his eyeglasses and squinted. "Who is that?"

The man's eyes were shut, whether because of the two shiners he sported or because he now slept or had died, I wasn't sure.

What I was sure of was that I recognized him. "No way."

"Holy shit." Scott edged closer. "Is that who I think it is?"

"Yeah." I furrowed my brow. "It's Dixon."

I moved closer and brushed the bruises on the security director's face with my fingertips. His skin felt colder than it should, even to my touch, and he looked thinner than he had when I'd last seen him—less than a week ago. He'd been injured then, too, after his helicopter had been knocked out of the sky by a fireball spat by a Drogre—a giant humanoid fire-breather.

"How's this possible?" Scott asked. "You left him at Dublin Gulch with the Bodhi Group incoming."

"Yeah." I glanced at Scott. "Vehicles were heading our way. I figured they had to be the Bodhi Group." I shrugged. "I guess they were actually the Eurus, coming to pick up their monsters."

"Jesus," Scott said. "Is that all from the helicopter crash, do you think?"

I grimaced and shook my head. "I don't think so. I think he's been tortured."

"Damn. They shaved his head, Shivurr. Why would they do that?"

"I don't know, man. To degrade and demoralize him, maybe?"

"That's not right." Scott ran his fingers across his own scalp. "Dixon loves his hair."

"I know, but it'll grow back." *If he's alive.* I touched a hand to Dixon's chest and waited. "He's breathing."

"Yeah?"

"Slowly," I said, "but, yeah. Come on. Let's get him—"

Something grabbed my hand and pulled.

"You were right, Shivurr," Dixon said in a ragged voice as he released my hand. "You were right."

"Shit," Scott said, reeling back. "He's awake."

Dixon raised his head. "They've got to be stopped."

I knelt and looked him in the eyes. "Who does?"

"The Reds . . . the demons . . . they're going to wipe us out."

"How, Harland?" I asked.

Leaning closer, I began removing the straps tying him down.

He coughed, swallowed, then wiped chapped lips. Thick white saliva gathered at the corners of his mouth.

"Give him something to drink," Scott said.

I reached a hand to my cap. "Right."

Dixon shook his head. "The Allfrost . . ."

"What about it?" I said, cracking the seal on a can of Ambrola.

He paused, staring past me. "T-they're corrupting it. They're going to use it to launch a first strike."

"A first strike?" Scott said. "You mean a nuclear strike?"

Dixon nodded and sank back onto the metal. "They're going to use it against us."

"Nuclear?" I looked at Scott. "That makes no sense. It'd be suicide."

"The Allfrost is the trigger," Dixon said, trembling. "Jesus, I'm freezing."

"Here, drink this." Placing the rim of the can by his lips, I poured, and his lips wrinkled and his Adam's apple bobbed. "Better?"

"Give him a minute," Scott said. "Let it work."

I returned his glance and nodded.

A few minutes later, Dixon wrestled himself to an elbow. "That's good stuff." He took the can from me and held it high. "What is it?"

"Soda pop," I said as Scott muttered something.

Dixon eyed Scott. "What's that, Green?" he asked, using Scott's last name.

"People." Scott coughed. "They really like it."

"I can't say I blame them." Taking another gulp, he swallowed, regarding me with one eye squeezed tight. "Got any scotch, though?"

I shook my head. "What's this about a nuclear strike?"

"Help me out of here first," he replied, handing me the can.

"Are you sure?" I asked, crushing the empty between my palms. "You look . . . you don't look well."

"Yeah," he said. "I think I can sit up at least. It's better than lying here like an invalid."

Draping one of Dixon's arms across my shoulders, I pulled him clear of the tube. He swung his legs to the side and sat hunched over with his head down.

"Feel better?" I asked as Scott settled onto a stone bench nearby.

"Like hammered shit." Dixon smiled faintly. "So, yeah, much better. Thanks for asking."

There's the Dixon I know. "Good."

He looked at me, then at Scott. "I don't suppose you've got a spare pair of pants?" Dixon's face brightened as I shrugged out of my thick winter jacket and handed it to him. "I appreciate it," he said, shoving an arm into a sleeve.

"Are you still cold?" I asked, thinking that I should have saved the ripped coveralls I'd worn in the Eurus camp.

Dixon's eyes widened. "Surprisingly, not really, no." He looked at Scott and tilted his head toward me. "So, you were helping him."

"He's my friend," Scott said. "What the Group was doing to him . . . what they did . . . it wasn't right. Shivurr's not the enemy."

Dixon looked thoughtful a moment. "I suppose I should've known. I guess I didn't think you had it in you." He jabbed a thumb at me. "Winterboy got a lot geekier when you came on board. His sudden interest in all that sci-fi movie and video game crap should've tipped me off."

"How'd you get them?" Scott asked. "Some weren't even on VHS yet."

Dixon gave a wry smile. "When necessary, I sent an agent to the movies with a video camera."

"Never mind that," I said. "What does the Allfrost have to do with the attack?"

"They're going to use it to detonate our nukes, somehow. From what they told me during my interrogation, they've been modifying it."

"What do they need me for?"

"Not sure. Best I can figure, they're looking for something. You're the only one that knows or knew where it is, apparently."

"Then as long as I can avoid them, we're safe."

"Maybe. Maybe not. They were really interested in the tissue samples of you. They wanted me to help them obtain the ones we still have. The ones at our other labs."

"Why?" I asked, though I thought I knew.

Dixon tapped his temple. "They want your memories. They must figure they can extract what they need to know from them."

I studied the ground a moment, pursing my lips. "But they can't be sure that those vials have what they're looking for, can they? I've still got a bunch that I took from the Institute. They could contain those memories."

Dixon shrugged. "Yeah. I suppose. I guess they're playing the odds. They get those, maybe they get lucky, and they're probably still trying to find what they're looking for on their own, too." He spread his hands. "I'm not saying that they still wouldn't love to catch you, but they may not need you, is all. Which means keeping you away from them may not be enough to stop them."

"Hiding isn't a solution anyway," Scott said. "You don't want to be on the run forever."

I rubbed my temples and scowled. "Okay," I said after a moment. "It's late. Let's get back to the domus. We can figure things out tomorrow."

Dixon raised a brow. "What dumbass is that?"

"Domus," Scott said with a snort. "It's a house."

"Oh, of course," Dixon said, chuckling. "That makes more sense. I'm going to have to brush up on my Latin if I get the chance." He sighed. "After the week I've had, I'm starting to think it isn't a dead language after all." His eyes flicked to me. "I've always wondered why you could speak Latin but not English."

"I guess I didn't hang around people much." There seemed no point in telling him that—as Wilhelm had told me—there was a time that I could speak English, long ago, before coming to the Institute. "Mortals, at least."

His eyes widened. "Mortals?"

"Come on." I reached out a hand. "We'll fill you in on the way."

After pushing the gurney back inside, Scott and I carried the metal pod, much lighter unoccupied, while the security director shambled beside us.

Chapter 40

The Last Sentinel

Dixon regarded our surroundings with gaping mouth and wide eyes, occasionally muttering to himself, while Scott and I filled him in on New Olympus and Caelumtor, the gods and their factions, and how I'd come to find and rescue him from the clutches of the enemy.

"So, it wasn't me you were rescuing," he said. "You were after one of these Allfrost Sentinels?"

"Yeah," I said. "I had no idea the Eurus had you. I thought your agents were coming for you back at Dublin Gulch."

"Nope," he said. "Those bastards got to me first."

"I'm sorry that happened to you." I thought I meant it, but a darker part of me felt glad that my former jailer had had a taste of imprisonment. "It sucks, doesn't it? Being a prisoner."

He frowned and nodded. "It does." He sighed. "Thanks for getting me out of there. I don't . . ." He trailed off and looked down. "I know you wouldn't have taken the risk if you hadn't thought I was someone else, and I can't say I blame you, but thanks. I owe you."

I shrugged but said nothing.

He looked up. "I'd still like to know how you managed it. Is there a landing strip nearby?"

Scott chuckled. "Nope."

"Come on. You didn't walk here from the Gobi Desert."

"Is that where it was?" I asked.

"You didn't know?" Harland said. "How's that possible?"

"Let's talk about that in the morning," I said as we strode between two marble statues and entered the lush garden fronting the Schmidts' grand home of stone and terracotta. "We're here."

Placing the stasis tube by the door, we strode inside without knocking.

Bear met us as we emerged into the atrium. Spotting Dixon, he gave a low growl and nosed the security director's hands and feet.

"Easy, pooch," Dixon said, placing a hand over his groin and deflecting the dog's snout with his other. He glanced at me. "Hell of a time to have my nuts hanging out."

I pointed to a motionless android on the room's far side. "Scott, see if it can find some spare clothes, would you?"

"No sweat," Scott said, heading for the robot.

I turned to Dixon, who looked quite pale. His shoulders slumped, and the skin of his face sagged, and the wrinkles on his forehead, the corners of his drooping eyes, and his cheeks seemed deeper than they had less than two weeks ago at the Institute.

"Let's find you a bedroom."

He probably hadn't slept much in the days he'd been trying to find me, then he'd nearly been killed in the helicopter crash, then captured and interrogated by the Eurus. *His week's been worse than mine, possibly.* The Ambrola had given him a temporary boost, but clearly his full vitality had not yet been restored.

"That sounds good to me," he said, following. He didn't walk so much as shuffle his feet forward. "I could sleep for a week."

I led him to an open door next to my room and peered inside. The bed lay empty. "You can take this room. There's a bathroom in there, off to the side. Have a shower, get some sleep, and we'll talk more in the morning."

"I appreciate it." Dixon slipped off the winter coat and handed it to me. "Thanks for the loan."

"You bet," I said, shuddering at the warmth as I put it on. "Scott's getting you some clothes, too."

Dixon's eyes drooped. "All right."

"Good night, Harland."

"Night, Shivurr." Dixon took a step across the threshold, then stopped and turned. He met my eyes.

"Something wrong?"

"Thanks again for saving me." He held up a hand. "I know you didn't know it was me, but thanks."

"You're welcome."

"Do you mean that?"

My eyes flicked to his bruises and back to his face. "Yeah, I do. You didn't deserve whatever they did to you."

His lips pursed. "I'm surprised you feel that way."

I snorted. "Me too."

His eyes darted to my shoulder, and I turned to follow his gaze. Scott approached from across the atrium with clothes draped over an arm.

"Good man, Green," Dixon said as he took them. Shoving a T-shirt under an arm, he shook out the legs of a pair of worn and sun-bleached jeans and held them at his side. "A bit short, but they'll do." He jabbed a thumb over his shoulder. "Time to hose off the undercarriage. I'll see you boys in the morning." Shoulders sagging, he shambled into his room and closed the door.

When he'd gone, Scott slapped me on the back. "I'm turning in too, man." He yawned. "I'm bushed. What a night."

"Tell me about it. Sleep well, dude."

He bobbed his head and blinked. "Good night."

Alone, I wandered over to the atrium pool and looked out the ceiling hole at the fading stars in the brightening sky. After a time, I took a seat in a high-backed chair at one end of the pool and studied the reflections on the water. A short while later, Bear padded over and nudged my hand, and I reached out to pet him.

What a night indeed, I thought, recalling Scott's last words.

I leaned an elbow on an arm of the chair and rested my chin between thumb and forefinger. I'd gone to rescue an Allfrost Sentinel from captivity and instead returned with the man that had denied me my own liberty for years.

I couldn't regret rescuing Dixon, though. Instead of worrying about him chasing me, I had him as an ally now. More importantly, the Eurus couldn't use him, and their sinister intentions for the Allfrost were now known. Besides, saving him had been the right thing to do even if it had been unintentional.

He'd been my jailer, but there had been no malice or sadism in his actions. He was, as he had told me in the past, just doing his duty for the country he loved. And if I was being honest, he'd been kinder to me than he had had to be and because of that I couldn't quite hate him.

It didn't make what he'd done right, and I hadn't forgiven him for it—and wasn't sure I ever would—but I didn't wish on him the torture he'd clearly suffered or the death that had no doubt awaited him after it was over.

I snorted and shook my head. *Maybe Caleb's right, and I do have a bit of Stockholm Syndrome.*

Even if I did sympathize with Dixon, I didn't trust him fully yet. We both wanted to stop what the Eurus had planned, but we might have different ideas on how to go about it. Which meant I'd be keeping an eye on him, starting with sitting here outside his room until he woke.

How the Allfrost could be used by the Eurus to launch a nuclear first strike on the West, I didn't know, but maybe that answer lay in one of the vials I had yet to drink. However they planned to do it, they obviously needed a Sentinel's knowledge of the machine to pull it off.

Dixon was no Allfrost Sentinel, though, so if they thought he could help them, it had to be—as he had said—by using him to get the other vials of my essence that the Bodhi Group still possessed.

Did those other vials contain the knowledge they needed? For all I knew, they might, so I'd have to recover them myself before the Eurus could. Even without Dixon's help, they'd still be trying to do so, so I'd have to be quick about it. If I failed, I'd never be whole again, and the Eurus might gain the knowledge that they needed to destroy half, maybe even all, the world.

I scowled, thinking of the non-existent Allfrost Sentinel that I'd hoped to rescue. *It would have been nice to find someone like me, though.*

Extending an arm, I held my palm to the ceiling, summoned frost from thin air, and stared at the swirling energy in the palm of my hand. Waving it away, I looked down at my lower half. A moment later, the snow and ice shifted, morphing into two legs. Pushing against the chair's armrests, I stood, watching ice spread over the surface of the pool at my feet as flakes of snow fell from above.

Maybe I am the last Sentinel. I glanced at the doors where Dixon and my friends lay sleeping, then to Bear, who sat on his haunches, looking up at me. I scratched him between the ears. *But I'm not alone.*

Author's Note

Shivurr's adventures will continue in the next novel in the *Phantom Frost* series. Visit alfredwurr.com for details about and links to other books in the series.

While you're there, take a few seconds to subscribe to my free, no-spam monthly author newsletter and get in on news about my upcoming releases, deals, giveaways, and more.

If you enjoyed the book, please consider reviewing it. Either way, thanks for reading and supporting my work. It means more than you know.

Acknowledgements

Special thanks to my beta readers for taking the time to read the book and provide invaluable feedback.

Lorelei Pierce
David Kuik

Book cover by Damonza.com.
Editing by Clio Editing Services.

About the Author

An avid fan of science fiction and fantasy, be it in movies, books, video games, or RPGs, Alfred has also been, and in many cases continues to be, an Olympic freestyle wrestler (winning national and international championships), a computer scientist (M.Sc.), a software developer and consultant, and a video game developer.

He lives with his wife, Lorelei, in Canada, where staying frosty comes easy half the year.

Subscribe to Alfred's mailing list to get news, updates, and more at: alfredwurr.com/subscribe. You may also contact the author at: alfredwurr.com/contact-page.